SHOOTOUT

A full-powered Hellbore shot explodes across my bow as I hurl myself backwards. The plasma bolt misses by only 6.52 meters, carving a 40-meter crater into the eastern cliff face. Now I withdraw around a bend in the valley and replay my sensor data, and bitter understanding fills me as I see the deep impressions of his tracks far above.

He has the advantage of position and of knowing where I must appear if I wish to engage him. I compute a probability of 68.052% plus or minus 6.119%, that I will get my shot off before he can fire. They are not the odds I would prefer, but my duty is clear.

My suspension screams as I red-line the drive motors, and clouds of pulverized earth and rock spew from my tracks as I erupt into the open, Hellbore trained on LNC's position.

But LNC is not where I thought. He has moved less than eighty meters—just sufficient to put all save his turret behind a solid ridge of rock. His Hellbore is leveled across it, and my own turret traverses with desperate speed.

It is insufficient. His systems damage slows his reactions, but not enough, and we fire in the same split instant. Plasma bolts shriek past one another, and my rushed shot misses. It rips into the crest of his covering ridge. Stone explodes into vapor and screaming splinters, and the kinetic transfer energy blows a huge scab of rock off the back of the ridge. Several hundred tons of rock crash into LNC, but even as it hits him, his own plasma bolt punches through my battle screen and strikes squarely on my empty VLS cells. And agony howls through my pain receptors as the plasma carves deep into my hull....

—from "The Traitor" by David Weber

BOOKS IN THIS SERIES
The Compleat Bolo by Keith Laumer
Created by Keith Laumer:
Bolos, Book 1: Honor of the Regiment
Bolos, Book 2: The Unconquerable
Bolos, Book 3: The Triumphant
Bolos, Book 4: Last Stand

BOLOS
BOOK 4

LAST STAND

CREATED BY
KEITH LAUMER

EDITED BY
BILL FAWCETT

BOLOS: LAST STAND

This is a work of fiction. All the characters and events portrayed in this book are fictional, and any resemblance to real people or incidents is purely coincidental.

A Baen Books Original

Baen Publishing Enterprises
P.O. Box 1403
Riverdale, NY 10471

ISBN: 0-671-87760-7

Cover art by Paul Alexander

First printing, March 1997

Distributed by Simon & Schuster
1230 Avenue of the Americas
New York, NY 10020

Printed in the United States of America

Table of Contents

THE SIXTH SUN

by S.M. Stirling

The American soldiers gathered at the base of the
sacrificial pyramid. Morning sun shone bright on the fresh-
cut limestone, and on the bougainvillaea that was already
beginning to curl up from the base. Two months had
washed away the last lingering traces of the smell of rotten
blood, leaving only the scents of dust and people and
growing things in the plaza. Around them the town of
Cacaxtla was bustling to life, a group of children on their
way to school, farmers heading out to the fields. The
put-put of a methane-fired tractor slapped back from
the walls of the buildings around the plaza.

That was louder than the burbling of the ceramic diesels
in the UTAV's waiting to leave; the little six-wheeled jeeps
were almost hidden under sacks and crates of supplies,
netting bags of squirming live chickens and bunches of
bananas.

"Sure you're not coming?" Captain McNaught asked.
His freckled brow wrinkled. "I've got a feeling we're going
to need every good soldier we can find back home."

Lieutenant Bethany Martins smiled and shook her head.

1

"There's no home back there, at least not for me, Captain," she said.

"Me neither, sir," Company Sergeant Jenkins—Tops— agreed. "Bad's it was in my neighborhood, I think I'm happier rememberin' the way it was than seein' it the way it is."

Behind the big black NCO, privates Michaels, Smith, McAllister and Sanchez nodded solemn agreement. They'd been down in the Republic of San Gabriel for years, and the news out of Reality—the United States— had gotten steadily worse every one of them.

McNaught's eyes narrowed. "Maybe you're right. Maybe there's nothing left to go home to. But I've got to know."

Bethany winced and looked away from the bright sunlight. The Captain had a wife and three kids in New Jersey. Had. Who knew now, with the way things were back in Reality.

But there was no one waiting for her, or the others. "These folks need us too," she said, waving a hand out over the upland valley drowsing in the sun. "We ran out those lunatics who were running the place."

A vivid flash came to her, the feather-decked Jaguar Knights and the rough grit of the altar against her skin as they bent her back and raised the obsidian knife to cut out her heart. Political scientists were bad enough, but an anthropologist run amok on Identity Politics was something else again.

"If we all leave, seven different brands of bandit will be all over them like ugly on an ape—they'll be dead or starving in a month, like everyone else down here."

Like everyone else everywhere, she thought but did not say.

"All right," the Captain said, his eyes distant, as though already seeing the Jersey shore. "I won't force it. You people've got a right to your own lives. You've been good soldiers. It's been an honor serving with you." He drew himself up to attention, his clean but ragged uniform loose on his thin frame, and snapped them a salute straight out of West Point.

Martins, Tops and the rest answered him in the same brisk, professional manner. Then the Captain went down the row shaking hands.

When he got back to Bethany he said softly: "I'll miss you, Lieutenant."

Bethany felt a lump in her throat. She whispered hoarsely, "I'll miss you too, sir." Her throat was tight. "Damn, it would be good to see Santa Fe again."

"Not too late."

"Too late years ago."

She swallowed and the pain seemed worse for it, hot and tight, beginning to rage out of control. She whimpered. *I will not cry,* she told herself. *I will not!* The pain spread, clawing at her vitals, spreading remorselessly until it filled her, left her standing dumbstruck and immobile as the Captain drove away.

She closed her eyes and gasped. When she opened them, her eldest son was smiling down at her, standing awkwardly with his hat clenched in his hands. The big master bedroom of the *jefe*'s house was shuttered and dim, light slashing in as hot bars between the louvers of the blinds. There was a sickbed smell of medicine, and her canes stood in one corner. Her M-35 was neatly racked above it, oiled and immaculate though she hadn't carried it in . . . how long? A decade?

"You slept Mom, almost an hour, I think."

She drank in his face; he looked so much like his father. Her breath rasped in her throat and her mouth was dry. She didn't ask for water. Swallowing was agony.

"Mama?" said a voice from the opposite side of the bed.

She turned, and there was her youngest, James, a wet cloth in his hands. He placed it between her parched lips, and as she sucked the moisture from it she thanked him with her eyes.

She gritted her teeth and swallowed, tried to suppress her moan. When James took the cloth away she was panting as though she'd run a race.

It was time.

"Boys," she smiled briefly. *They were not boys any longer, but married men.* "My sons," Bethany began again, pride in her voice even now. "I want to talk to the Beast. Take me to it."

"Mother," Joseph said, just a hint of asperity in his tone. "We can't move you. You're too sick." He frowned. "I can bring you a helmet . . ." he added reluctantly.

"Mom?" James's lips drew back from his teeth in a parody of a grin as he struggled not to cry, his eyes were awash with tears. "Mom?" he said again.

"Yes," she said gently. "I need to go." She was panting again. "Maybe—in some way—it can help. The autodoc . . ." Her voice faded away.

James nodded helplessly, beyond speech.

"All right," Joseph said at the end of a long, drawn-in breath. "It's worth a try."

They lifted their mother with the featherbed she was lying on. The brothers' eyes snapped up and met in consternation. She was so *light*! They might have been lifting the bedding alone.

"Move it!" Bethany snarled, partly to break the moment, partly to disguise her pain as they shifted her.

The brothers smiled fondly at the tone of command. That was more like the mother they knew.

Silently, the brothers carried their mother into the street. The people of Cacaxtla had been waiting all day, some for days before that; they gave way silently, many kneeling to pray and crossing themselves, many weeping. It had been thirty-five years since the Lieutenant came, a generation of peace and plenty for Cacaxtla, amid a chaos which had eaten whole continents.

Across the plaza the Bolo loomed above their heads like a mountain, its hundred and fifty tons stretching twenty-four feet in height. The late evening light threw the crags and hollows of its surface into high relief, emphasizing the brutal power of the great war-machine; the heavy crusting of hardened lava gave it a primeval look, like the spirit of some god of war. Behind it stretched the marks of its four treads, ground into the paving stones the day the Captain had driven it to rescue the soldiers—and Cacaxtla—from the Jaguar Knights and the First Speaker, the man who'd brought the Old Faith back to bloody life here. It hadn't moved since that day.

The people of Cacaxtla had painted its entire exterior surface with colorful depictions of that rescue, what had led to it and what had come after; it might have been a natural pyramid . . . except for the cannons.

The three of them stared up the rough, bright side of the Bolo.

"How're we going to get you up there, Mom?"

Joseph had known it would be a struggle, but now he was here, he knew it to be plain impossible. He imagined ropes, and pulleys. "Maybe we could get some help." He looked away from his mother's contemptuous stare.

"Don't even think it," she warned. "I don't want this—turned into—a circus." Bethany Martins lay gasping, her breath spent; her hatred of her own helplessness was a tangible force in the gathering night, like hot light on their hands.

Joseph glared off into the darkness.

"Mom," James leaned over her. "If I tie the featherbed around me and carried you up that way . . . would it hurt you too much?"

She shook her head. "At least *one* of you knows how to get things done," she rasped. "Do it, boy."

James climbed as gently as he could, unnerved by the hot, light weight of his mother curled against his back. His heart thudded, fear making his palms wet and slippery against the lava and durachrome. Catching his breath on a sob, James gritted his teeth, unwilling to put his mother through the shaking she'd get if he broke down and cried. He looked up at Joseph, who was just reaching the hatch.

"Mom," Joseph said softly, "it won't open for me."

"Markee," came Bethany's muffled voice. "Open the hatch."

With a sigh of hydraulics the hatch came up, releasing the scent of stale, dry air. A light went on below to guide their way down into the cramped interior.

Joseph knelt on one crash-couch and carefully caught his mother as James untied the ends of the featherbed from around his shoulders and waist. Then he laid her gently on the other seat, propping her up against its straight back, though she winced with pain as he did so.

"Markee," Bethany said hoarsely.

She coughed once, then stopped herself, knowing how easily she could lose control and never stop. The bright smooth surfaces of the interior shone back at her, the flat-screen displays and touch-controls like a breath from the past. *Thirty years*, she thought. Thirty years of adobe and stone, wood and woven cotton . . . the high-tech womb was so strange, now. . . .

"These are my sons. Register Martins, Joseph A., the village Jefe and senior civilian on site. Log and identify. Say hello, Joseph."

"Hello," Joseph said awkwardly. He sensed a flicker of light, touching his eyes too briefly for certainty.

Bethany took a few moments to recover; her face was slicked with sweat, but the pain, for the moment, seemed to be abating. As much as it ever did.

"Register Martins, James Q., he is the senior . . ." She pursed her lips in doubt. James had no official title, for all the village acknowledged his position in practice. "He's captain of the village militia." She grinned briefly to think of a lieutenant appointing her son a captain. "Log and identify."

"Hello, Markee," James said.

Bethany smiled, a rictus of thin lips over teeth. He was quick, her James.

"Acknowledged," the Bolo said in a voice as sweet as warm honey. "Hello Jefe, hello Captain. I'm honored to make your acquaintance."

James blinked. He'd spoken to the Bolo once or twice, to obtain information, or to report in from a distant site, asking the Bolo to relay a report. But this was different. The machine was acknowledging him personally. *An interesting legacy, Mother.*

"It will recognize your authority now," Bethany said. "Leave now, come back for me later."

"We can't leave you alone, Mother," Joseph said, his eyes wary.

She looked at him. "I'm going to take off my shirt—for the sensors," she replied. "Half an hour, come back. I'll let you know if I'm ready." She sat drawing deep breaths, her gaze steady.

Joseph had never been able to outstare his mother and he couldn't now. He turned his head and sighed, then turned and began to climb up the handholds to the hatch above.

James leaned over her and whispered. "I don't want to go." His eyes pleaded to stay, to keep her safe, to help—somehow.

"Go."

He kissed her cheek and stood, his lips pressed into a straight white line.

Bethany waited until the hatch sighed shut before speaking.

"Markee bring up the autodoc, tell me what you see."

"Blood pressure . . ."

"In plain English."

There was a pause. "You are in the last stages of terminal cancer. Six to eight weeks before complete failure of essential functions."

That long! Six to eight weeks of *this*. Bethany remembered her mother describing how grandfather had died, how at the end he would beg for the painkillers even though they couldn't touch his agony. *And we've got nothing that strong*, she thought, her heart giving a little bump of panic. Eight weeks, losing her dignity, crying and screaming . . . and the pain. She swallowed hard and winced. It was already as much as she could bear. She imagined herself mewling and writhing—her sons' horrified, helpless faces.

"Is there any medication left?" she asked.

"Negative, Lieutenant. All that remains in the pharmacy is a single shot of fast acting poison to be used to avoid capture."

Bethany closed her eyes in relief. *Good,* she thought.

"I have instructions for you," she said.

"Waiting."

"I want you to defend the people of Cacaxtla from any outside aggressors. Someone from outside—comes here, kills and steals—you destroy them."

"Understood, Lieutenant. What about aggressors from inside Cacaxtla? My programs indicate that there are often internal pressures in a community that might lead to aggression."

"Let the people work it out for 'emselves. Can't protect people from—stupidity. Just don't let 'em be—victimized by outsiders."

"Yes, Lieutenant."

"I want that shot now." Bethany closed her eyes, breathing hard and waited.

"You are in danger of capture?" the Bolo asked. "I detect

no enemy activity." The machine could not *sound* confused . . . Bethany smiled again through the pain, remembering the computer-geek corporal who'd first programmed in that sultry voice. Vinatelli was thirty years dead, but the Bolo Mark III still bore the mark of his lonely fantasies. "You entered with family members."

"In danger of extreme torture," Bethany said.

"From outside the community?"

"From inside me!" Bethany snapped, knowing the autodoc would confirm that she was telling the truth. "Give me the damn shot. Now!"

There was a slight hiss, but no prick of a needle. Then she felt a warmth begin to flood her veins, followed by cold. It became a little harder to breath, her heart faltered. Bethany gasped and widened her eyes. Breathed out once more and slumped unblinking in the command chair.

The brothers had been pacing for over an hour. The mountain air was becoming distinctly chill, and still the people waited behind them, some wrapped in shawls or blankets, others simply standing.

"Maybe she's fallen asleep," Joseph said. He frowned. "I wouldn't want to wake her."

He and James looked at each other.

"Markee," James said, "is Lieutenant Martins asleep?"

"No, Captain."

It was their mother's voice, younger and stronger than they'd heard it in years. Both men straightened and stared at each other in astonishment, hopeful smiles beginning to curl their lips.

"Mom," Joseph said and began to climb.

"You're all right, Mom?" James said, his heart lifting, trying not to hope too much.

This time it was the sultry sweet voice of the Bolo that answered. "Lieutenant Bethany Martins cannot answer at this time."

Joseph froze on the ladder and James slapped the side of the tank like an angry child.

"What do you mean she can't answer?" he demanded. "If she's not asleep why can't she?" His eyes widened. "Does she need help?"

"No sir," Bethany's voice answered, "no help is required."

Joseph climbed back down and slumped against the side of the Bolo.

"She's dead," he said flatly.

"What are you talking about?" James snapped. "She sounds fine." *She does!* he insisted to himself, ignoring the inner voice that told him she wasn't making sense. He started up the Bolo's craggy side.

"Markee," Joseph said, "please confirm. Is Lieutenant Bethany Martins dead or alive?"

"Lieutenant Bethany Martins is dead, sir," the Bolo murmured in its soft voice.

James's breath exploded out in shock, as if he'd been punched in the gut, up under the breastbone. His body hunched around the pain. He turned to stare down at his brother who stood with his face buried in his hands, shoulders shaking.

He stumbled back down, almost falling off. James started to walk away, numb with shock when Joseph's hand stopped him.

"We've got to bring her out," Joseph said, his voice high and tight.

James flung off his brother's hand.

"She didn't even say goodbye," he snarled, his face red with fury. "She knew she was going to do it and she didn't even say goodbye."

Joseph's face was white and blank.

"You think she committed suicide?" The idea had obviously never occurred to him. "She tricked us into bringing her here for help . . . and then . . . ?"

James continued as though he didn't hear him, "She didn't trust us, dammit! She wanted to come here so bad, let her stay here. Let her rot here! I don't want to see her face again."

"We can't just . . ."

"Yes we can. Let the damn thing be her tomb! Can you think of a better one? And while we're on the subject of the Bolo, why the hell was that thing talking in our mother's voice? Huh? Why would she *do* that to us?" James's eyes were bright with tears and the certainty of betrayal.

"The stories . . . Remember? The guy who first programmed it had it fixed to answer certain questions put to it by superior officers in a way that would make them think he was awake and sober. Apparently when we—superior officers—asked the right questions it supplied pre-programmed answers."

"Yeah?" James growled. He strode to the Bolo and shouted up at it. "You are never to use Bethany Martins' voice again! Is that understood, Markee?"

"Affirmative, Captain."

"And you are never to speak to *anyone* again unless you are directly spoken to and required to answer. Do you understand?"

"Affirmative, Captain."

Then James spun on his heel and stopped at the staring eyes. The crowd were looking at him, and he could see their bewilderment and fear. He drew a deep breath.

"Lieutenant Martins is dead," he said. A murmur went through the crowd like a giant's sigh, louder than a wail might have been. He licked dry lips. *What would Mom have said?* "We'll carry on."

Unit #27A22245 Mk. III
Communications—negative broadband scan.
Systems check. 03/02/2045; 0700 hours.

Power: 99.3% capacity. Nominal.
Mobility: restricted. Tread l2 broken; treads l1, r1, r2 jammed. Drive and suspension, nominal.
Weapons: main gun — nominal.
              infinite repeaters — units 1-7 nominal.
                    —units 7-12 nonoperational.
Sensors: 32.3% capacity.
AI: 97.3% optimum. Nominal.
Query: resume standby yes/no.
:[decision tree]—affirmative.
Unit #27A22245 Mk. III resuming standby status.

"We thought it was the end," Tops said, his voice only slightly cracked with age.

The sun felt good, though. He could feel his bones creak as he stretched and the waiting circle of children leaned forward for the end of the story. Wryly, he flexed his great knobby hands. *Hell, who'd have expected me to live long enough to die of old age?* A few of the youngsters shifted restlessly. He looked up at the bulk of the pyramid, shaggy under its coating of green, and continued:

"The Glorios were all around us and throwing everything they'd been saving up our way. It wasn't enough for them that we were pulling out of San Gabriel; they wanted our heads. When the 'plane came to take us home there was no way that flyboy could land and Captain McNaught told him: 'Get away from here, you can still save some others.' And that was a hard thing to hear . . ."

"Sergeant Jenkins," a boy called. "I have some questions."

Tops sighed in weary irritation. It was Bethany's grandson, Paulo. Who was ten, the age of extreme obnoxiousness.

"What is it?" he asked warily.

"Why do they call the Bolo 'the Mountain That Walks,' when it can't even move?" Paulo paused long enough that Tops had opened his mouth to answer when he asked: "Or why is it called the Beast, when it's not alive and never has been?"

Tops tried to wait him out, but the smaller children who'd been listening to his story began to get restless.

Just as he started to speak Paulo, his young face as innocent as a puppy's, said, "And why, please tell me, is it called the Beautiful One, when, even with the paintings, it's ugly as sin?"

"It's called the Beautiful One for its voice, Paulo," James said from behind him.

Paulo gasped and spun around guiltily.

"Please excuse my son, Tops. He doesn't want answers, he wants to get out of his lessons."

Paulo's face turned red.

"As you don't want to study, Paulo, come with me. I'm going on patrol and you can do the camp chores for me. Perhaps when we get back you'll be more appreciative of the opportunity to study with Sergeant Jenkins, eh?"

Well, that's some punishment, Tops thought. You could see the kid trying not to skip as his father led him away. *Maybe I'm turning into a boring old fart.* Maybe he should tell his war stories less often. He shifted to a sun-warmed bit of the Bolo he was leaning against; the heat soothed the stiffness in his back.

"All right boys and girls, let's get back to work," he said.

Seven-Deer danced. Though he was almost fifty his battle-scarred body was lean and muscular, lithe and graceful in the dance. It was a rare strand of silver that marred the jet black of his gleaming hair and his grimly set face bore few marks of age.

As he danced he sang the sorrows of his people, his voice rough with grief. The children sat enraptured, their dark eyes glowing as he unfolded the history of the people of the Sixth Sun. How the First Speaker had brought them back to truth and the rightful ways of service to the gods, after the Ladinos brought disaster on the world by leading the people astray, making them serve Quetzacoatl-Jesus. How the First Speaker had led them to the upland valley where his command of the volcano kept them safe.

He told of the coming of the evil Yanquis, who invaded their valley, which was like a paradise. And, being greedy and cruel as the four hundred Southern Warriors who had sought to slay their brother Huitzilopochtl—Left-Handed Hummingbird, they fell upon the people of Cacaxtla and slew the First Speaker of the Sun. Cowards, they hid behind the bulk of their war-machine that was like a mountain. Evil, they would not accept the honored place of a Beloved Son sent as messenger to the gods.

The children gasped in horror at this part—always—as though their innocent minds could not accept such wickedness.

Seven-Deer sang on, his voice moving from sadness to the joy of victory as he told of how the exiles descended the mountain and how the Jaguar Knights had fallen upon their enemies like the wrath of the Sun. Thus making a safe place for the people here in the lowland jungles, taking some of their enemies as slaves to serve them, but sending most as messengers to the Sun to plead for aid.

He spun and leapt and the children's small chests swelled with pride to think of the victories of the valiant Jaguar Knights. Every boy among them dreamed of a place in that ferocious company.

Then Seven-Deer danced the promise. All who left the Valley of Cacaxtla, the place like paradise, were exiled princes whose time of vengeance would come. All who remained in the valley were traitors whose blood would nourish the gods, food waiting for the harvest.

It was their duty and privilege to prevent the destruction of the Sixth Sun as the Fifth had been destroyed. For it had been blotted out by indecision and faithlessness as much as by foreign greed.

He finished his performance on this solemn note and stood straight and tall, his breathing only slightly heavier than normal. Servants wiped the sweat from his face and body, naked save for a loincloth; the heat beat down through the steamy lowland air, making water run over his brown skin. One of the priests brought the feathered cloak and another the elaborate headgear that marked him as First Speaker of the Sun People.

"Three-Coyote," he intoned. "Bring forth your beloved son."

A stocky warrior led a bound and naked man to the altar. The prisoner glared defiantly and spit at the people where they knelt around the earth and timber mound. He was an escaped slave, one who had unwisely behaved like a warrior and now would pay the price.

Behind his impassive face Seven-Deer sneered. It was disgraceful that they should be forced to send a mere slave as a messenger. It smacked of impiety.

Four priests grasped the prisoner, who had begun to struggle, and slammed him onto the altar, stretching his limbs so that his chest arched upward drum-tight. The man cursed them and spat in Seven-Deer's face as he raised the knife.

It was with rather more anger than was proper that the First Speaker plunged the knife downward.

Smack!

"Jesus! Will ya look at the size of this thing?"

Gary Sherman thrust the bloody corpse of the insect under Pasqua's nose.

"Oh, for God's sake!" she snarled pushing his hand away. "I'm driving Gary, show some sense."

The road they were on was muddy, slippery, and narrow. In fact it all but vanished in the thick, steaming greenery that slapped the sides and roll-bar of the jeep. The jungle smelled *thick*, like spilled beer on a hot day, or wet rotting bread.

Gary glared at his partner, an attractive woman in her late twenties; straight, shoulder length black hair held back by a yellow scarf, almond shaped green eyes hidden by dark glasses.

This woman is not good for my ego. He doubted she'd look at him twice if he was on fire. Not that he was much to look at, he admitted self-pityingly, with his hair creeping towards the back of his neck and a stomach that made it look like he was smuggling kettle-drums.

He sighed dramatically as he rubbed his hand against his thick khaki covered thigh to scrape off the squashed mosquito.

"Will you tell me what the fuck we're doing out here in the green hell?" He watched her from the corner of his eye as she pursed her—*luscious*, he thought—lips.

"Language, Gary," she admonished. "In answer to your question, *you're* here because you wanted to be. If you'll recall, you insisted on coming along. To help."

"Yeah, to help," he said impatiently.

Actually, he'd been hoping that the jungle at night, the howling of the monkeys, the roar of the jaguar, the creeping of the jeep-sized insects, might loosen her up a bit. God knew, *he* could use some cuddling after four days of this shit.

He should have known better. From what little she'd let drop she'd spent her early years hangin' with the Giacano Family, the Dukes of New Orleans. An old-fashioned bunch whose reputation made the jungle at night seem safer than your own living-room. Pasqua had to have crossed 'em. What else would a beauty like this be doing scraping a living as an arms dealer in darkest

Central America? This place made the East Coast baronies look like civilization.

"*I* am here pursuing a hot lead that might help us get rid of that damned railgun you bought," she continued.

"That gun's a beauty," Gary said defensively.

"That gun's a white elephant," Pasqua sneered.

"It's also the best weapon we've got," he insisted. "XM-17 Railgun, yessir. That baby'll take out a Bolo. You know that?"

"Yeah, and I know how common Bolos are in Central America, too. Every piss-ant town's got one in the plaza. It's amazing we haven't sold it yet."

"Sarcasm doesn't become you, baby."

Pasqua braked hard, put the car in park and turned slowly towards him.

"We've discussed this before, Gary."

He could almost feel those hidden green eyes melting holes in his face. Her right hand twitched slightly, and he remembered the *jefe* of the port town. His successor had been perfectly willing to do business on an impersonal level, after Pasqua shot his predecessor.

"Aw, Pasqua! C'mon, you know I dint mean anything." He looked at her, trying to keep his face innocent. Then he rolled his eyes, looked out his window into the jungle.

While she waited.

"Okay," he turned back to her, "I'm sorry that I called you baby andthere'saguybehindyouwithagun."

"What?"

"Behind you. A-guy-with-a-*gun*."

She turned in slow, graceful stages to look out her side of the jeep. It was hard to see the man at first. He wore a tight-fitting brown uniform dotted with black splotches. His face had broad black stripes around the eyes and mouth, accented by more dots, his black hair was pulled up into a topknot.

Very, very slowly, Pasqua took off her sunglasses so that he could see her eyes.

His own eyes were calm and cold. He stood absolutely still, his M-35 pointed at the center of her chest.

"Hola," she said, and saw him stiffen. She took a closer look and saw that under the war-paint the man was an Indio. *Bingo*, she thought. If the rumors back in Puerto Zacarta were right. She marshalled her few words of Nahuatl and tried again. *"Greeting, warrior. We seek your First Speaker."*

Apparently it was the right move. Now she could see a dozen of the leopard-spotted men as they moved closer.

There was a brief conference, their eyes never leaving Pasqua and Gary; the language had far too many consonants for her taste.

"Weapons," the man grunted.

Not without a pang, Pasqua lifted the PPK from the holster at her belt; it was a Family heirloom. Tradition had it that her great-grandfather had killed a Cajun detective with it, right after the Collapse. The Indios took it, and Gary's antique Glock, and the M-35 from the rack behind the driver's seat, and their machetes. Fortunately they missed the switchblade tucked into the back of her pants; that was an heirloom too. A Giacano without a switchblade was naked.

The . . . soldiers, she supposed . . . arrived at a decision and the others melted into the jungle again, leaving their original captor behind. He motioned them out of their jeep. Pasqua dragged a folder out with her and he raised the gun threateningly.

"First Speaker," she said, holding it up to show that it could never be, or hide, a weapon.

He jerked his M-35 down the trail and Pasqua and Gary started walking.

❖   ❖   ❖

"And why did you not bring this with you," Seven-Deer asked contemptuously, tossing the pictures Pasqua had brought with her into their faces.

Pasqua and Gary were on their knees, their hands tied before them, broad sticks thrust behind their elbows. "You may not even have such a thing." He stalked like a panther to the low dais where his throne, a wide chair covered with deerskins, sat. "It would not be the first time our enemies, the Ladinos, thought us such fools, too weak in the head to know any better."

The situation's a little extreme, Gary thought, *but I know a bargaining ploy when I hear one.* Except for the occasional Nahuatl word they'd been speaking in Spanish.

"Pitch!" he whispered to Pasqua who turned to him with frightened eyes. "He's interested. Or we'd be dead. Pitch!"

"The only reason you are alive," Seven-Deer said as he lounged back, "is that you spoke a few words in a civilized language. Enough to pique my curiosity. And the woman wears the color of the Sun."

Pasqua blinked. *My scarf?* she thought.

This bunch of indigs were crazier than most, but they had a pretty big stretch of territory marked out and a lot of it was farmed. They probably *could* pay a reasonable price for the XM-17, in goods that would be valuable back in the north, in the Duchy of New Orleans, to the Caqique of Florida, to one of the seven kings of Cuba, or any of the Duchies from Charleston north. Timber, grain, rum, coffee, slaves, you name it.

"Speak! Why have you not brought this 'tank-killing' gun with you for me to see with my own eyes?"

"It . . ." Pasqua choked on a dry throat and had to begin again. "It is too big for us to bring, *Uetlatoani*," Pasqua said obsequiously. "It is as big as a mountain and would take a great truck . . ." she realized these people had nothing like that and hurried over what she feared they might see as an insult: ". . . or many men to move it. Surely you can understand that I would not make such an effort if you were not interested?"

Seven-Deer, the First Speaker of the Sun People straightened slowly and rose from his throne, his obsidian eyes gleaming.

"As big as a mountain," he whispered.

A smile spread slowly across his face and leapt like a spark to the faces of the Lords and Generals and Ladies around him. The people murmured the words, ". . . as big as a mountain . . ." over and over again, turning it into a chant, clapping their hands and stamping their feet joyously.

Seven-Deer stabbed a finger at his prisoners like a spear.

"You will take us to this wonder!" he shouted and the room erupted in cheers.

When the Yanqui woman had said the words ". . . as big as a mountain," to him, a fire had been lit below Seven-Deer's heart. Now, in the awesome presence of the giant gun he felt elevated, touched with the Sun's own power, mind and heart and soul blazed together with purpose. And that purpose was *vengeance*!

"It's called the XM-17 Railgun," Pasqua was saying as she escorted-shooed him to the gunner's seat and urged him to take the control yoke in his hands. "This is a computer generated holographic magnifying sight." She flipped a couple of switches and the village down the road from their compound sprang into view, hovering before Seven-Deer's astonished eyes in every known shade of bilious green. "This red dot," she pointed at a dime-sized red dot in the upper corner of the holo, "shows where the gun is pointing. To move the dot, move the control yoke."

Seven-Deer cautiously did so and the dot jiggled its

way down to the center of the scene in the holo. He laughed like a child.

"Isn't that neat?" she said, smiling and nodding like this was a perfectly normal presentation.

"How does it work?" Seven-Deer growled.

"When it's fired two charged bars come together to shoot out a rod of depleted uranium sheathed in steel."

"The rods're only about a foot long," Gary said moving up to his other side. "But when ya press the firing stud it's like, slam! bam! thank you ma'am!" he slapped his hands together and laughed heartily. Until he saw the First Speaker's expression.

"How does it fire?" Seven-Deer asked through gritted teeth.

Pasqua and Gary looked at each other nervously.

"We only have twelve rods, and can't afford to waste any, so I'm afraid we can't allow you to test fire it." The First Speaker stared at her disdainfully and she sighed. "When you have the *right target* in view," she said emphatically, "press the firing studs at the top of the hand grips on the control yoke. Here and here."

"Eexxcellent," Seven-Deer said like a man being told "yes" by a reluctant lover.

He centered the sights on the village church, a small stone building at the center of the Plaza. He powered up the gun, the bars began to charge with a low hum that quickly escalated to a piercing whine.

"What are you doing?" Pasqua asked. But she knew and she was numb with horror.

"Testing your merchandise," Seven-Deer answered. He pressed the firing studs, the bars clanged together with a scream of electronic excitement and the depleted uranium rod emerged with a supersonic *crrraaaaccckkk!* that numbed their ears.

In the holo the village church burst apart into a blizzard of gravel. An instant behind, the sound of the explosion reached them and looking up they saw a grey-brown plume boiling into the sky.

"He fired the bastard," Gary said in disbelief.

"You . . ." Pasqua began and stopped. Around her Seven-Deer and his followers were cheering and dancing in delight. Instinctively she stepped back, flight on her mind, when Seven-Deer's hand flashed out and caught her wrist.

"Oh, stay," he said grinning, "you would not wish to miss the ceremony."

Several of the Indios had grabbed Gary and were dragging him to the front of the gun. Seven-Deer dragged her along behind them and when they had Gary spread-eagled at the base of the railgun he flung her into the arms of a group of his followers. Who twisted her arms up behind her and bound her hands, then pushed her to her knees in the dirt.

"You can't do this," Gary was shouting in panic. The front of his khakis were stained dark. "You want the gun, take it," he said frantically, his eyes bulging as he watched Seven-Deer approach, leisurely drawing a long obsidian knife. "Please don't," Gary said.

Pasqua was so terrified she couldn't even scream. Her traitorous mind filled with all sorts of babble. *I told you not to buy that gun, Gary.* And *Please don't, no, please!*

Gary's last desperate scream began when the knife went up, but it didn't end for a surprisingly long time after the knife came down.

She saw Seven-Deer lift a bloody heart high and thought inanely, *So you did have one after all, Gary.* Then she blacked out.

When she came to, Seven-Deer's blood-smeared face was smiling into hers, his black eyes dancing with a mad glee. He trailed one blood-wet finger down her face and she whimpered with terror.

"And when we retake the valley of Cacaxtla," he said,

"we will send you back to the sun. For surely you are his servant. How he will smile to see you again."

Seven days of chores, James thought. *And not a whimper.*

Either Paulo was becoming a stoic, or he'd learned that pouting and complaints would get him nowhere. Probably the latter; the kid was smart—he knew that this was the best way to make his father feel like a heel. It was even working, sort of.

He snapped the bolt back into the M-35, sipping at a final cup of coffee as he watched his son carefully tamping down the campfire with water and entrenching-tool loads of dirt. The upland forest was chilly in the morning; they were a thousand meters above the valley floor, and it was never really hot here. A clean crisp smell of pine filled the air, and he could see for miles across tumbled blue hills. From what his mother had said, back in the old days—before her time, even—most of these hillsides had been logged off or burnt off and then farmed. He shook his head in wonder, trying to imagine that *many* people in the world.

Paulo was frowning seriously as he policed up the campsite, checking that nothing was left or out of place. It gave his face a look of his mother. Maria used to say that Paulo could wrap James around his little finger. His smile faded. It had been four years since his wife's death, four years of trying to be mother and father both, trying to anticipate what Maria would have said or done. In a way it helped to keep her close to him.

Paulo suddenly looked up and grinned at him. James nodded solemnly and slung his rifle, turning to the UATV.

"You can fix it can't you?" Paulo stood across from him looking serenely confident.

"I think so. This time."

The UATV's were incredibly hardy machines, capable

of running on almost anything combustible, with six spun alloy wheels that never seemed to show wear. Even the engine parts were incredibly durable . . . but when they wore out, you were in trouble. Nobody made things like that any more; there were machine-shops in the valley, but they worked with metal, not fiber-bound ceramics.

"This is the compressor," he began.

Paulo leaned close, and James remembered the same expression on his own face as his mother ran him through the checklist. She'd been a tougher disciplinarian than he ever could be, though. *I suppose because she'd spent so long with her life depending on the equipment,* he thought. Her life and others. James had drifted into command of the valley militia, but there hadn't been anything more than a skirmish with wandering bandits since he was Paulo's age.

I try to remember it's not a game, he thought.

"I don't think she's got much longer though," he concluded.

Paulo's head came up and he looked around, a puzzled frown on his young face.

"What?" James said.

"Listen . . ." After a moment Paulo said, "It sounds like men singing."

"Or mourning," James murmured. And there were a *lot* of them.

He slipped on the helmet, buckled on his equipment belt and the body armor that never quite fit; none of Bethany Martin's original platoon had been quite his size. His M-35 suddenly felt more serious in his hands.

"Stay here," he said to Paulo. "I'll be right back." Powering up the helmet, he trotted off into the trees.

Paulo frowned after his father. *Why do I have to stay behind?* he asked himself. *I'm not a baby. And besides, I heard them first.* Whoever *they* were. Paulo chewed his lip thoughtfully. Fair was fair, he had a right to take a look.

Paulo reached into the UATV, grabbed his slingshot and bag of stones—in case—and padded into the woods after his father.

He moved quickly, but kept some attention on where his feet were going; Dad had taught him that, and he was good at it. And . . . yes, there was a shape in camouflage-mottled fatigues and helmet. *He's* really *quiet,* Paulo thought, impressed. James turned around suddenly and he froze, though his cover was only a screen of thorny bushes. His father had told him that motion in such a circumstance was as bad as being in plain view. After a quick glance down his back-trail, James hurried on. Paulo found it hard to suppress his delighted laughter.

Dad doesn't even know I'm here! he thought in wonder. *It works!*

Paulo ghosted onward, silent—although his grin was the facial equivalent of a shout.

The farther he went, the louder the singing became. James still couldn't make out any words, but thought there must be many, many voices to make that sound. His mouth was dry; he took a quick swig from his canteen and went down on one knee, acutely conscious of the sweat trickling down his flanks under the armor. *What was it Mother said . . .* Ah, yes. He licked a finger and checked the wind direction; very slow, but from the low ground up to him. *In case they have dogs.* He was approaching an overlook on the old road leading out of the valley; he dropped to his belly and leopard-crawled to the lip of the cliff. In response to his whisper the helmet-visor supplied times-four magnification, making everything nearby jerk and quiver disorientingly with each motion of his head.

He grunted in surprise and felt his jaw drop. Below

him, down below the boulder-strewn hillside and the sparse trees, was an *army*.

An army of sweating men, perhaps as many as seven hundred, yoked to an enormous gun with long sisal ropes. Other men in tight, spotted brown uniforms moved up and down the line of chanting pullers striking them ferociously with whips. He could see one stagger and fall; the uniformed men closed in, kicking and striking with the butts of their rifles—good rifles, M-35's like the one across his back, not the single-shot black-powder models the traders brought around these days. One of them stood back and fired a burst into the fallen laborer.

I guess that means they're not volunteers, James thought.

There was . . . he called for more magnification from the crystal-sandwich visor . . . a bound woman spread-eagled at the base of the cannon. Just above her head sat a man in an elaborate feather headdress and very little else, pounding an enormous drum.

They'll never get that thing into the valley, he thought incredulously. The road was completely blocked by the old lava flow. Though thirty years had gentled its contours considerably, *still*, they couldn't possibly . . .

He winced as he watched one of the spotted slave-drivers whip a cut right through one man's shirt. *And skin,* James thought as the blood began to flow. Yes, they did think they could get into the valley on this road. *And with that kind of brutality they may be right.*

"Unit push," he whispered, though he doubted the strangers would hear him over the mournful singing. "Conito, come in." No answer. Someone was *always* supposed to man communications, but over time people grew lax. He'd skin the bastard who'd left the com empty today. "Record," he ordered. "There's something weird here . . . and dangerous . . ."

The world flashed white. There was a moment of dazzling pain, and then blackness.

Paulo knew this place. It was near the cliff that overlooked the ancient road. He watched his father drop to his belly and crawl forward. Looking around he spotted a suitable tree and climbed. When he'd lodged himself comfortably in the crook of the tree Paulo looked out over the old road and lost his breath.

Never had he seen or imagined anything like this. People were dragging a big, *huge* gun up the road. And other people were *hitting* them to make them do it! Paulo's stomach clenched and his mouth watered, he felt like throwing up. He closed his eyes and took deep breaths like his father had told him. And did feel a little better.

He looked out over the road again, a flicker of movement caught his eye, something closer. Something *close*.

A man was standing behind his father, one of the spotted men. A long shape was in his hand, a sort of wooden paddle with edges of shiny black rock. The blade shattered on the durachrome, but the helmet flew off and clattered down the steep hill. James's head dropped to the dirt.

Paulo felt his mouth drop open, and his hands trembled for an instant. Then he fumbled for his slingshot, loaded it with the heaviest stone that came to hand, whirled it around his head and let fly with a snapping twist of his body and arms. The same motion he used to hunt ducks . . .

The club was raised for a killing blow when Paulo's stone struck the man's temple. The *thock* sound was clearly audible even twenty feet away, and he dropped limp across James's unconscious body.

Paulo didn't see him fall, as he half slid, half fell out of the tree, his palms burning from scrapes as he scrabbled to save himself. Then he was racing towards them, his skin icy cold, his heart beating until his throat felt like it was being squeezed shut. Paulo's sight tunneled in on his father's boots where they stuck out from beneath the other man's body.

"Dad!" he said, his voice shrill with alarm. "Dad?" he said again, touching the blood in James's hair warily. His father moaned softly. Paulo sprang up and began trying to move the man who lay across him, thinking he must be smothering his father.

He yanked and pushed frantically, sobbing with frustration as the body refused to budge. The man's dead weight was so *heavy!* Finally Paulo sat down and kicked him off, the limp form rolling heavily against his sandals.

James moaned again. *Good! That must have been the right thing.* Paulo pulled off his shirt and began to wrap it snugly around his fathers head.

"Dad?" he kept calling softly. "Dad?"

James suddenly lifted his head with a gasp.

"What . . . happened?"

"This guy came up behind you and clobbered you with a club, so I beaned him with my slingshot," Paulo babbled. "He's right there."

Paulo's father turned to him, head wobbling, his eyes unfocused and looking odd somehow. Then Paulo realized what it was, one pupil was noticeably larger than the other. *Concussion! Oh no.*

Tops taught everyone about concussion in survival class. This was serious, maybe life-threatening. He held up two fingers.

"How many fingers am I holding up?"

His father looked at him owlishly.

"Two," he said.

Paulo let out his breath in a rush of relief. "Then you're okay. You can see all right."

"No. People always hold up two fingers."

"Daaa-ad."

His father dropped his head and moaned again. This time it was echoed by the man who'd hit him. Paulo froze.

"Dad?" he said, his lips stiff with terror. "Dad? He's alive."

Wake up! James shouted in his own mind. The voice sounded like his mother's.

Get moving, c'mon, on your feet soldier!

He fought the nausea that struck him every time he lifted his head and struggled to coordinate his limbs—which moved slowly and clumsily, however hard he willed them to obey.

"Daaa-ad!" Paulo said, panic creeping into his voice. "He's waking up, Dad. What do I do?"

Paulo pressed his lips firmly together as he looked frantically from his prone father to the stirring enemy beside him. He started looking around for a big rock. *Too small, too small.* Unngghh! *Too big. Rotten stick. I don't believe this!* he thought. *All I want's a damn rock!*

James lifted his head and the world spun, grimly he pushed himself up on his elbows and waited for the dizziness to subside. He took deep breaths and the nausea abated somewhat. His head throbbed, and he tried to ignore the pain. He opened his eyes. The world was doubled, sometimes tripled and blurred. He might as well be blind. He closed his eyes.

"Paulo. Help me up, son."

Paulo was beside him in an instant, heaving like a hero. James laughed, and stopped when that made the world spin.

"Easy, boy. I'll end up in a tree. Slow and easy does it. I can't see real good, so we've got to take things one step at a time."

"Okay, Dad." But Paulo was anxiously watching the man on the ground. He wasn't moving much, he rocked a little, and twitched his hands and feet, but his eyes were still closed, so Paulo didn't know whether he was coming to or dying.

Once on his feet, James swayed for a moment, his balance uncertain. Then he steadied, as much from sheer will as receding trauma. He fumbled at his equipment belt and pulled the bowie knife from its sheath. It was over a foot long and point heavy, and felt good in his hand. His mother had taught him how to use it, though he'd never had to, and had given it to him when he went on his first patrol.

"Son," he said. "Lead me to him." *I don't want to do this in front of you,* he thought. *I don't want to do this at all, but we have to. Better me than you.*

Paulo took his hand and put it on the stricken man's body. James felt his way to the man's throat. He placed the knife carefully, making sure his other hand was out of the way of the more than razor sharp edge of the blade. Pressing his lips together he applied pressure and dragged the knife towards him.

There was a bizarre and ugly sound from the severed windpipe and hot fluid cascaded over his free hand.

James gasped and fell back on his heels.

"C'mon, son," he said, "let's get back to the UATV. We've got to warn the village."

Paulo was staring at the dying man. *There's so much blood,* he thought. He'd seen animals die, he should have expected it, but . . . His mind whirled and for a moment, the man's throat seemed to be the only thing visible at the end of a long tunnel. He'd never missed his mother more, he wanted to feel the safety of her arms around him, lifting this horror out of his mind forever.

"Son!"

Paulo stared at his father's blood-drenched right hand, reaching out for his.

"Here I am," he said and took it.

We might as well be advancing in the damned Bolo!
James thought as he noisily stumbled for perhaps the
fortieth time.

"I'm sorry, Dad!"

"It's all right son, it's not your fault. Let's rest a moment."
He started to squat when Paulo yanked at his arm.

"Not there, Dad." He pulled his father away from the
ant-hill. "Here's okay."

James sank down with gratitude, feeling weak and cold.
Maybe a little shocky, he thought, wishing he could sleep
for a few hours.

"How close are we?" he whispered.

"Not far," Paulo said. "Just down there." He pointed,
then whipped his arm down, blushing. "And through some
trees," he added hastily to cover his error.

James thrust his chin forward and put his hand on
Paulo's shoulder. "Son," he said, "I'm . . . going to send
you on ahead to scout. I'm making too much noise and
that guy back there must have friends. So I want you to
sneak up on the UATV, wait for a few minutes to see if
there's anybody around—do *not* break cover—and report
back to me. Can you do that?"

"Yessir. I'll be careful," he said quickly, anticipating
his father's next words.

"See that you are," James growled.

Paulo looked back from the bend of the trail to where
his father sat waiting, his arms loosely draped over his
knees, eyes closed, his face gray with fatigue. *Should I
go back and hide him?* he wondered. Dad looked so
vulnerable. Paulo wavered, looked down the trail towards
the UATV. *No, he'll say I'm wasting time, or something.
And he'll be embarrassed.* Resolving to hurry, Paulo moved
on.

Paulo knew they were there before he saw them. The
spotted men were talking and laughing like they had no

reason not to. They were speaking pure Nahuatl, he realized, unmixed with English or Spanish as it was in Cacaxtla.

Paulo dropped and began to crawl. Sneaking-through-the-woods was the best part of school, and he'd always done well on the tests. He peered through the bushes, keeping his head low to the ground.

There were five of them, stripping the UATV with surprising efficiency for men who were making so much careless noise. *I wish they were as clumsy as they are stupid,* Paulo thought bitterly. He didn't understand this. Why were they being so obvious? Surely they knew someone would be coming back for the vehicle.

Then realization hit him with a chill like snow down his back. "The answer is implicit in the question," his father was fond of saying. "Your grandmother taught me that." This was a trap. Their noise was intended to draw someone carelessly into the open, too intent on the outrage before them to think about an ambush.

He almost panicked. That meant that somewhere around him were other men in spotted uniforms. Deliberately he squeezed his fear into a small box inside himself. *Later,* he promised himself, *later.* Then, moving with exquisite care, he hurried back to his father.

"Damn!" James smacked his fist into his other hand, and swore more ripely and bitterly inside his mind. "So now our second line of communication is cut off." *There's only one thing left to do,* he thought. *Paulo will have to go alone.* Given a day and a half, cutting directly across the hills and moving as fast as he could go, James figured the boy could reach the village with a warning.

No, that's too optimistic. Two days. Maybe. *At least the gun people won't be able to move too fast. That ought to give us some time to prepare.*

He wondered if the Bolo could still defend itself, let alone the people of Cacaxtla, neglected as it was.

"Son," he said and reached out for Paulo, who grasped his hand. "We've got to warn the village, so they have time to prepare for this." He paused, his face set.

"I know, Dad." Paulo looked at him warily, wondering what was coming.

"You've got to go alone. I'll only hold you back . . ."

"No!" Paulo snatched his hand away in horror. Leave him? Leave his own father out here *blind* and all alone. "I can't."

"You have to. The village is more important than any one person," James said calmly.

"No. I mean I can't. I don't know the way."

James frowned. "The valley's not that big son. I don't think you can get lost."

"Dad, it's huge. And this is only my second time on patrol with you, I've been this far from the village only once before. And I didn't pay that much attention, I mean, I didn't know I'd have to. Honest, Dad, I'll get lost. Don't make me do this, please." He was panting when he finished speaking and shaking with pure terror. He knew that leaving his father alone out here would be like killing him. And he couldn't bear to lose his father, too.

"Son . . ."

"I can't. You know the landmarks, you can guide me. We'll go together."

For a moment there'd been something so like his grandmother in Paulo's voice that James blinked.

"Okay," he said slowly. "Then we'd better get started." James pulled some of his makeshift bandage down over his eyes. It was easier that way, without the blurring, shifting light to confuse him.

"First, look for the peak of the old volcano. Can you see it from here?"

❖   ❖   ❖

Seven-Deer had taken upon himself the task of feeding the servant of the Sun. It pleased him mightily that Tezcatlipoca had chosen a Yanqui, one of those who had brought about the downfall of his people, as an instrument of vengeance. He took it as a sign of favor that the god would make such a joke. Smoking Mirror had a sense of humor; it made Seven-Deer slightly ashamed that he'd never been able to emulate his god in that.

"A full bowl," he said, and the cook-slave dipped his ladle once more.

The First Speaker of the Sun threaded his way through the encampment; it was crowded and noisy, inevitable with so many slaves along. The stink was not as bad as it would have been down in the lowlands. They must have climbed at least five hundred meters already; the air began to remind Seven-Deer of his youth in the cool uplands of Cacaxtla.

"I have brought food," he said, as he gracefully mounted the gun carriage, disdaining to use his hands for climbing. The rungs that led up the side of the wheeled gun's boxy mounting were cool beneath his iron-hard soles, not like metal or stone.

"I'm not hungry," Pasqua said coldly.

"You will like it," he said cheerfully, sinking into a crouch beside her head. "It comes from my own table." He filled the spoon and thrust it at her mouth.

Pasqua turned her head away and the spoon relentlessly followed. She turned to glare at him and he smiled benevolently.

If she'd had appetite the sight of him would have killed it. He still was smeared with Gary's blood, his hair was caked with it and the sweetish smell of rot was thick on his hands.

She opened her mouth to say, "I don't want it," and Seven-Deer thrust the spoon home. Immediately she spat it out. Not on him, though she'd have liked to, but she didn't want to inspire him to anything too creative. The Duke of New Orleans had some *extremely* creative people on his staff, and she'd had to attend those events as a child, like anyone in the Family.

"I'm nauseous," she snapped. "I can't eat, okay? You wouldn't want me to choke on my own vomit before you get to cut my heart out. Now would you, babe?"

Seven-Deer's face stiffened with offense. To be refused thus by this ignorant Yanqui slut was . . . a test perhaps. The Sun sought to determine his worthiness. He placed the bowl down gently near her bound right hand.

"Very well," he said quietly. "Let the insects have it. And may its scent torment you. Perhaps tomorrow you will have a better appetite."

He rose and descended the steep gun carriage as gracefully as he'd come. Pasqua would have paid any price to see him slip and fall flat on his face.

Her lips and the inside of her mouth were burning fiercely from the spoonful of food he'd forced on her. It brought tears to her eyes. She waited; the camp grew quieter, fires died down, only a few sentries moved. Her mouth still burned.

Geeeez, she thought, *that stuff would burn through steel.* She turned her head and looked consideringly at the abandoned bowl. *You don't suppose . . .*

Her numb hand plopped into the bowl and scooped up some of the contents, bending her wrist as far as she could. Pasqua slid the mess onto the vegetable fiber ropes that bound her. "Whoooo!" she yelped as the chili sauce penetrated to burn the chafed and bleeding skin below. Which motivated her to yank her bound hand frantically.

Maybe it was the grease, maybe it was because the rope was thoroughly wet, maybe it was because she was so desperate to get that stuff *off*, but this time her hand and not a little skin, came free.

She rubbed her wrist off on her shirt; it didn't stop

the burning. Frustrated, she turned to getting her other hand free. Bound as she was she could barely reach the knot. It had tightened with her struggles and with bearing her weight all day. A fingernail bent back and she suppressed a yelp of pain. She sucked the finger, then spat as her tongue began to burn again. The need to swear seemed almost as imperative as the need to breathe.

With a sigh, Pasqua scooped up a handful of her supper and dumped it over her other wrist.

After she'd freed her feet, Pasqua snatched the yellow scarf from her hair and rubbed as much sauce as she could from her wrists and hands, though the flames were dying now. Then she tossed it aside, glad that her shirt and slacks were gray and unlikely to call attention to her in the darkening jungle.

She moved carefully and quietly, keeping low, sometimes on hands and knees. The slaves were sleeping all around the gun carriage, so thickly that it was difficult to step between legs and arms and heads. In their exhaustion they slept through her quiet passage, even when she accidentally touched one of them.

Her eyes were on the jungle when a man sat up and looked at her. Pasqua froze, a nasty, almost electrical shock frissoned over her and her breath stopped in her throat. The man's face was blue-grey in the darkness, his eyes black pits. He stared at her unmoving. Then he smiled, and silently, he lay back down.

Thank you, God, Pasqua thought. As she moved into the jungle she made vague, but fervent, promises about being a better person hereafter.

Sometimes, just before turning in, Sergeant Jenkins liked to wander around the village, to settle his mind and his aching bones for sleep. And on nights like this one when he was feeling especially solitary he'd stop to have a few words with the Bolo.

Since Lieutenant Martins' death no one spoke to Markee. And occasionally Tops felt a little guilty about it. He knew that the Bolo wasn't lonely, didn't feel neglected or slighted being ignored by the populace, didn't feel anything at all in fact. It was as empty of self-awareness as a toaster.

But when it spoke it sometimes seemed so like a person that he made a point of visiting from time to time. And if he took solace in knowing that it had seen him young and bore memories of his old comrades, well, so what? Besides, sometimes it picked up a faint radio broadcast from back in Reality and he enjoyed hearing them, weird as they were. The Lord of Philly had declared war on the Jersey Barons? Either that was a sports broadcast, or things had gotten unreal in Reality.

"Good evening, Markee," Tops said, settling himself on a familiar outcropping on the Bolo's lower surface. "Tell me what's new with you?"

"I've received a most disturbing message from Captain Martins, Sergeant. As follows . . ."

James Martins' voice came from the Bolo's speakers, weakly, as though over some distance. "Unit Push. Conito, come in." There was a pause and then an impatient sigh. "Record. There's something weird here . . . and dangerous . . ." There was a sparkle of static and then nothing.

"That's it?" Tops asked.

"Yes. It has been ten hours and thirty-four minutes since I received this message. Nothing at all since. This is unlike Captain Martins, who is punctilious about following up on his recorded messages."

"Hmph. Any other chatter on the unit push?"

"Negative, Sergeant. As far as I can tell Conito has yet to hear this message."

Tops straightened his spine, his eyes blazing with outrage. Lord knew Conito had his problems. His wife had died in childbirth leaving him with twin babies to take care of. But this kind of neglect was unheard of.

"These damn kids," Tops muttered. "They're spoiled, is what. We did our job too good. Think the world's their friend, never going to do 'em any harm." He stood up. "I'll see to it Markee. Keep an ear out for the Captain."

"Yes, Sergeant."

Joseph opened his door to find Tops on the doorstep, standing in the halo of bugs that orbited around the methane lantern above the door.

"Hello, Tops," he said, surprised. "It's late," he said doubtfully. And the old man was in uniform, from boots to helmet.

"I know what time it is, Jefe. I have something to tell you." Tops pushed past Joseph and into the house, then turned to face him.

"James is in trouble," he said shortly. "The Bolo intercepted a partial message from him. He said, 'there's something weird here, and dangerous,' then nothin' but static. That was over ten hours ago. Markee hasn't heard anything since."

"Conito hasn't reported . . ."

"Conito hasn't accessed his messages yet. Anymore than he's been monitoring the unit push. I heard the recording. It was broken off. He's in trouble."

Joseph looked at him doubtfully. He licked his lips and looked away, then back again.

"What do you expect me to do?" he asked.

"I *expect* you to send help." Tops began to do a slow burn as the Jefe's eyes flicked away again.

"Don't be lookin' away like I've done somethin' socially unacceptable. Your brother was cut off in mid-report and hasn't been heard from in hours. You have the power, and the responsibility, to send help." He stood glaring at Joseph. "And that's what I expect you to do."

Joseph rolled his eyes. "Probably the UATV broke down. That one's on its last legs. And the helmet coms aren't much better. What's more," he said, spreading his hands and smiling reasonably, "the Bolo's in even worse shape than the UATV. It might have misheard James."

"I heard the recording myself," Tops said through clenched teeth. "With my own ears. It was very distinct, Joseph. You could access that recording yourself if you wanted to."

Joseph's shoulders slumped and his mouth twisted impatiently.

"*Querida?*" a voice called from the hall stairs above. "*Mi oorazon?*"

"It's late . . ." he began.

"Either you send someone to check this out or I'm going," Tops said fiercely, his breath beginning to come hard.

"Will you relax, old man," Joseph said, putting his hand on Tops's shoulder and guiding him to the door. "There's nothing we can do tonight anyway. It'll have to wait till tomorrow."

Tops's big fist flashed out and caught the *jefe* on the side of the head like a five-pound maul.

Joseph heard the sound through the bones of his skull. It didn't hurt; mostly he was conscious of outrage, and surprise that the old man could still move that fast. He was older than Mother. *But I can't hit him back—*

It was then that he realized he had dropped bonelessly to the floor. He thrashed helplessly in slow motion until the sense returned to his eyes, and the pain began. Then he stared up at the elderly man who'd flattened him.

"That was from the El-tee," Tops said furiously. "Cause she'da given you one those for even *thinkin'* about leaving one of your people hangin' fire after a message like that. Let alone your own brother."

Tops's eyes flashed in the candle light, yellow around smokey black irises.

"You listen to me little boy, it's a bad ol' world out there. And there's always a chance that trouble will find its way to your door. Now, to me it sounds like trouble is knockin', and it's knockin' real loud." He pointed one massive finger in Joseph's face. "Now you send someone out there to help your brother!"

Joseph glared at him, rubbing his jaw and wondering if he should have Tops thrown in jail. Tops glared back with an outraged sincerity that finally penetrated the Jefe's hurt pride.

"You're right," Joseph said grudgingly. "It does bear investigating." He picked himself up and headed for the door. "You needn't worry," he said over his shoulder as Tops started to follow him, "I'll see to it. They'll leave tonight."

The woman's voice called again from upstairs. Tops flexed and shook his right hand as he walked out into the street and closed the door; it was lucky he hadn't popped a knuckle, doing that. Normally he didn't believe in hitting a man with his bare hands, not unless he was naked and had his feet nailed to the floor . . . but you did have to make allowances for the El-Tee's son.

Paulo's whole body burned as his father's weight dragged at him again. It was so dark now he could barely see and he was trembling with exhaustion, as sweat-sodden as his father, sick with listening to the rasping breath of pain above him. He wanted to stop, to eat, to take a sip of the little bit of water in his father's canteen. He wanted to sit down and cry like a little kid. *But I can't. Dad's hurting worse than me. I've got to keep up.*

As it had grown darker Paulo had concentrated on the ground before them, avoiding rocks and roots and vines with considerable efficiency, considering the gloom. Besides, tired as he was his head just naturally tended downward. The noises of the insects and frogs lulled at

him, like he was home and had the window open, looking
out at the moon . . .

BONK!

"Aaauggh!"

James's head had connected solidly with a low-slung
branch. The pain from his forehead telegraphed itself
to the wound on the back of his skull and the agony washed
back and forth like reciprocal tidal waves. He fell to the
ground uttering a shrill, almost silent, scream.

Paulo fell to his knees beside his father. "Dad!" His
hands hovered uncertainly over the writhing form and
tears began to fill his eyes. "Dad?" he said again, his voice
tight with desperation and tears. "I'm sorry, I'm so sorry."
He broke down and began to cry, ashamed and unable
to stop. He pushed his hands against his mouth to stifle
the uncontrollable sobs. If he could stop them his eyes
would quickly dry, he knew.

Suddenly his father rolled to his knees and began to
retch, straining mightily to no effect as his stomach was
utterly empty. At last the spasm passed and he rolled to
his side, groaning.

"Dad?" Paulo's voice was very small.

"S'all right," James said, panting. "C'mere." He lifted
his arm and Paulo collapsed next to him.

James folded his arm around his son. "Not your fault,
kid. You're doin' okay."

The pain was receding to an echoing ache and he was
horribly aware of his own pulse as it beat through his
head. White dots sparked behind his eyelids and the
nausea was definitely back to stay for awhile.

"Gotta rest," he said quietly. Shame brought heat to
his cheeks as he realized he had to place yet another
burden on Paulo's shoulders. "You've got to find us some
shelter, son. Doesn't have to be much. Just good cover,
with maybe a wall at our backs. Don't go far."

He tightened his arm at the thought of losing his son

out here in the dark. "If you don't find something quickly, come back, we'll just spend the night here."

Paulo sat up. "Okay, Dad."

"Here," James said. "Take a drink," and he passed over the canteen.

Paulo took it gratefully and allowed himself two swallows, holding the second in his mouth a moment to saturate his dry tongue.

"I'll be quick," he said and leaned forward to kiss his father's cheek, startling him.

He hasn't done that since his mother died, James thought as the sound of Paulo's footsteps faded away.

It seemed only an instant later that Paulo shook his sleeve. "Dad. I've found it," he said.

James struggled to his feet and Paulo led him, being particularly careful to watch above as well as below this time.

A short distance later Paulo drew them to a halt.

"There's these bushes," he explained, "you have to crouch down and crawl. But it's like a hollow behind 'em and there's a wall with an overhang. It's almost like a cave," he ended eagerly.

"Good job, son," James said. "You go first." He got on his hands and knees and followed his son through the bushes. "This is good," he said once inside the hollow, noting the dryness of the thick bed of leaves and the absence of any musky animal smell. "You rest."

"You need to rest more'n I do," Paulo protested, determined to stay on guard all night if necessary.

"I couldn't son. My head won't let me." James knew that Paulo was at the end of his strength and would soon be asleep whether he wished to be or not. Besides, once they got within sight of an unmistakable landmark, if his eyes were still useless, he intended to send Paulo on alone. The boy would need his strength for that. "Go to sleep."

With a relieved sigh, Paulo surrendered and lay down on his side, curling up as comfortably as he could.

James heard his son's breathing change to the rhythm of sleep and then he knew no more.

Moving quickly, but quietly, Pasqua pressed on. She was half in a dream state, but breathing comfortably and moving efficiently, body wolf-trotting without being told to. A method one of her father's bodyguards had taught her, part of her survival training. She was skirting the trail that led into the valley, approaching only close enough to see it every two hundred paces, then fading back into the jungle. Woods, actually. They were pretty high up here. The weather was nice, not like the steambath down below; that had been as bad as summer back home. This was like October on the Bayou Teche, or over in the piney woods on the Gulf Coast; the Family had hunting lodges there.

If I warn whoever's in the valley about the Knave of Hearts and his laughing boys I'm a hero, she reasoned. *If I try to get back to the coast I run into the very unhappy people he's run that* damned *gun over and I'm toast. Tough choice.*

She shrugged mentally. *The weather's better up here anyway.* Later, she could loop around and back to the coast and pick up her stuff. Nobody would have touched it; not when her name was Giacano. Even if she'd severed formal connection with the Family, nobody had put an open contract on her. And nobody would want one of the Duke's schooners to pay a visit, which they would if news came back that she'd been ripped off. Just on general principles, mind, not out of familial affection.

Pasqua gauged her level of exhaustion and decided to find somewhere to sleep for a couple of hours. She slowed down and almost immediately her limbs felt weighted with sand, her chest aching with the effort of breathing the thin upland air. *Sleep,* she thought, *what a concept.*

AAWwwnkkk!!!!

My God! She froze, but her heart went into overdrive. She could almost feel it on the back of her tongue.

AAWwwnkkk!!!!

Snoring! But was it human?

Creeping forward, though her gut insisted she should run, Pasqua came upon a lush growth of bushes pressed against an overhang.

If I were a bear, she thought, *this is where I'd sleep.* Did they have bears in this country?

AAWwwnkkk!!!!

Human, she thought and straightened, her mouth a grim line. The switchblade went *snick* in her hand, oiled deadliness. *Maybe one of the Lord of Multiculturalism's merry crew.* Cautiously she began to move back. The satisfaction of giving one of them an extra mouth wasn't worth the risk.

"Daaaa-ad," a sleepy child's voice said. "Y'r snorin'.'"

A grin spread slowly across Pasqua's face and her eyes gleamed. *Hunters maybe,* she thought. *Definitely not Jaguar Knights.* Maybe marks.

"Hey," she whispered and could almost feel them come aware. "I need help."

"Hey! Conito!" Tops trotted out into the road and the UATV stopped. He suppressed a smile at the sight of Conito's weary face and the carload of militia around him.

Hey, poetic justice, pal, he thought, pleased at how the punishment fit the crime.

Conito was looking at him dubiously. "You can't come with us, Sergeant Jenkins." His voice was respectful, his attitude courteous.

Tops was surprised at how good the respect felt. *Has*

it been that *long since someone talked to me like I'm a grown man?* Still, he was being brushed off, told to go away like a good little nuisance so the responsible people could get their work done. This from *Conito*! A guy who'd never finished anything except getting his poor wife pregnant. The guy who'd left the unit push unmonitored probably since James had gone out.

"Well, thank you for the invite, son, but I've got some sleep to catch up on." Conito's tired eyes narrowed slightly. "Maybe some other time. What I wanted was to give you this." He held up his own helmet. "I've been workin' on it and it's probably the best one in the village right now. It's also hooked into the Bolo."

Conito had taken the helmet with pleasure and had passed his own, marginally working one to his second. But his head came up at that.

"Why's that?" he asked. "Nobody talks to the Beast."

Tops forced himself not to be sarcastic. It was an honest question, nobody had spoken to the Bolo for years. He set his hands on his hips and looked down at Conito, just a bit longer than was comfortable for the younger man.

"I don't know why we didn't think of it before," Tops said mildly, "the Bolo can monitor the unit push twenty-four hours a day. If something urgent comes through it can set off an alarm. Oh, yeah, the Beast says the last transmission came from the cliff that overlooks the old road out of the valley." He turned and headed back to his house.

"That oughta make it easier to find 'em," he said over his shoulder. He didn't grin at Conito's stupefied expression until he'd turned his head away.

Tops was halfway up the Bolo's craggy side when a child's voice asked severely, "Where are you going, Sergeant Tops?"

Startled he looked down into the big brown eyes of Joseph's youngest daughter. Catherine was frowning fiercely, her arms crossed over her chest, one pudgy bare foot tapping impatiently.

"What are you doing out here so late?" he countered, keeping his voice low.

"You had a fight with my daddy," she accused. "You woke me up and I couldn't sleep anymore."

"Does he know you're out here?" Tops whispered. *Quiet down kid, you'll wake up the whole town.*

She looked disconcerted, but her head went down like a little bull's. "Where are you going?" she repeated.

"Shhhhh! I'm going to visit your grandma," he said.

A look of absolute horror went over the little face.

"Are you going to die?" Her eyes were huge.

He barked a laugh, he couldn't help it. "Naw. Not for a long time. I'm just goin' for a visit."

"You promise?"

Tops smiled, touched. *She's loud, but she's really a nice little kid.*

"I'll not only promise that, I'll promise not to tell anyone I saw you out so late. If," he held up one finger, "you promise not to tell anyone you saw me up here."

"Okay," Catherine said cheerfully, "I promise."

"You go home now," Tops said and nodded.

"Okay." She turned and padded off into the darkness. Halfway down the street she turned and waved, smiling sweetly, then hurried on. He watched her open her door, she looked up and waved one more time, then entered.

Yeah, and I'll bet if I hadn't been watchin' you'd've bopped off into the night on some business of your own, wouldn't cha? The kid was just like the El-Tee, stubborn and fearless. He shook his head and resumed his climb.

He paused at the top and bit his lip, feeling like he was violating a tomb. Then he had to grin as he imagined

Bethany Martins turning to just stare at him if she'd known his thoughts. He shook his head.

"Open the hatch, Markee," he said.

The rush of cool dry air that flowed over him smelled every bit as bad as he'd expected. Like a long dead corpse to be exact. He wrinkled his nose disgustedly. *This ain't going to be no day at the beach*, he thought.

The near-mummified corpse in the command chair looked nothing like his old friend. *Thank God for small favors*, he thought. If anything he was surprised at how small it was. The El-Tee loomed much larger in his mind's eye.

He spread one of the blankets he'd brought over her and very gently began to pry her off the seat. It felt like moving furniture, there was nothing human-feeling about the shape under the blanket at all. Thank God they still had a few of the body bags left; they folded down to handkerchief size, but they sealed air-tight.

A gruesome few minutes later, a clean blanket covering the command seat, he sat down gingerly. "Key in the view from that helmet, Markee," he said. With a nervous glance at the body-bagged form beside him Tops settled in for his vigil.

In the "I need help," Olympics these indigs have got me beat, Pasqua decided. *Why me?* she wondered as her heart sank. *A guy who's effectively blind and a scared kid. Does someone plan these disasters for me? Has Grandfather got the squeeze on God or something?*

The thing to do was cut and run, she could think up a dozen plausible excuses without breaking a sweat. Some of them were even true.

"What did you say his name was?" the man—James—said.

He was lighter than the average around here, and spoke English with a mixture of accents, local and what sounded like old American. Crisper than her own Canal Street dialect. Good-looking guy in his early thirties, broad shoulders and a working-man's hands. Wearing an old United States uniform, of all things; Pasqua recognized the body armor. The Family had . . . inherited . . . a lot of Army equipment during the Collapse, and still had it stockpiled.

"It's got too many notes for me to say, but it comes out as Seven-Deer," she said cautiously.

Something about the man said he wasn't a friend of the Jungle Cardiac Removal League. The way both of them paled at the name confirmed it. The boy looked up at the man, and he put an arm around his son's shoulders.

"Okay, I'll help you get back home," Pasqua said, not believing the words as she heard them coming out of her own mouth.

She looked out at the tumbled mountains, at the tall volcano standing white-topped to the west. Above it a face seemed to loom in her mind's eye. Her father's.

"The last thing a Giacano needs," he'd said the last time she'd seen him, his dead-fish eyes weighing her like so much meat, "is a fuckin' conscience."

She'd flown to Central America the next day, losing herself down here and never expecting to see home again. Not wanting to once she realized she was free.

James's mind went over and over the woman's story. When he'd heard her voice in the night he'd feared for a moment that it was some trick. Then she'd explained her presence.

". . . Seven-Deer . . ."

His head had come up with a jerk that hurt him and he could feel the blood draining from his face. Paulo took his hand and squeezed it tightly and he'd been ashamed of his own fear. To the Valley's children Seven-Deer was the bogeyman.

"You're sure his name was Seven-Deer?"

"Yes." Her voice was cautious, as though she feared they might be allied with him. "Why?"

He'd told her and then insisted that they begin walking. The urgent need to warn the his people burned within him.

Seven-Deer has a very old grudge. Not that he needed the excuse.

Pasqua was so thirsty she didn't think she could even cry. And she was tired enough to want to. They'd been walking, or rather, stumbling all day and the sun was beginning to set. *God, I never imagined a path could be a luxury. Just to be able to walk five paces without tripping,* she thought, suppressing a groan, *I'd pay for the privilege.* How could country with this much rainfall not have springs or rivers?

"Because we're sticking to the ridgelines," James said.

She started, realizing she'd spoken the last thought aloud. *I must be more worn down than I realized.*

"Stop," James said quietly, holding up his hands.

Pasqua looked back at him; from the way he held his head it was apparent he'd heard something. She looked around, straining her ears. All she could see were pine-trees, scrubby on the upper slopes; further down were tropical oak, and a tormenting sound of rushing water. Sweat dried on her face and body, the rest letting her realize that although the sun was fierce the air-temperature wasn't much above seventy. Wind soughed through the trees, cool and fresh-smelling. She pushed away knowledge of aches and sore feet and paper-dry tongue. At last she heard a faint yipping.

"Coy-dogs?" she asked.

His lips pressed thin and he shook his head, then winced. His hand brushed his forehead.

"Voices," he said, very quietly.

Just then a stray breeze brought the sound of laughter and she stiffened. Her eyes flicked to Paulo but his expression was the same he'd worn all day, frightened and determined.

"We'd better keep moving," she said.

James shook his head and winced again.

"Will you just *say* things and quit wagging your head around," she said impatiently. "Why not keep moving?"

"They might be valley people," he said. "In which case we should warn them. They might even be looking for me . . . and Paulo," he added.

"In which case we should avoid them because they're making enough noise to attract Seven-Deer's whole cavalcade of fun. Or it could be a trap."

"Then we'd better find out," James said. "They might have water . . ." He let the thought dangle.

If she weren't so thirsty, Pasqua might have smiled. *The man's a manipulator,* she thought. *A clumsy one, but when you have the right hook you don't have to be an artist.* She licked dry lips and Paulo mirrored her action.

"Okay," she said. "Let's go."

The closer they got, the more obvious it became that there was some sort of sick celebration in progress. Sound echoed off the oaks, through the screens of hanging vines. The yipping and the laughter were interspersed with conversation and screaming; a hummingbird went by her head and hovered over a flower in cruel obliviousness. Pasqua grabbed James's arm.

"These are not your friends," she whispered urgently. "We've got to get out of here!"

"I need to know," James said and started forward.

"No, you don't," she insisted. "If you want to know what's going on I can tell you. They're killing people! Okay? And they'll be happy to kill us too. Now that you know that, can we go?"

She yanked at his arm but he balked.

"We need to know how many there are and how they're armed," he persisted.

"I can tell you that too," Pasqua snapped. "I was their prisoner, remember. There'll be fifteen of them and they carry M-35's just like you do, as well as obsidian swords and knives. Let's *go*."

"No," Paulo said unexpectedly. He took his father's hand. "Those are our friends. Maybe we can help."

"Help!" Pasqua squeaked, but she was talking to their backs. For a moment she stood there, immobilized, half of her wanting to head for the inner valley and the village, half wanting to follow.

"Shit," she muttered and started after them. *If they do happen to make it back to the village I won't win any hearts for having deserted them out here.*

Right now, she needed friends . . . and these two weren't fit to be allowed out alone.

With a shrill, yipping cry the Jaguar Knight plunged the ball down on to a sharpened stake planted in the ground.

That's not a ball! Paulo thought and gagged. It was a head, still encased in its helmet.

The stake was surrounded by the dead bodies of the Cacaxtla militia. The Jaguar Knights, yipping out their victory, did a little impromptu dance around the pile, then leaping and prancing they went to a UATV and one by one got in. One of them stood on the back, waving his M-35 and jigging enthusiastically until the UATV started and he tumbled backwards into the laps of his laughing fellows.

"What's happening?" James ground out, his face grim.

"I'm going to assume the UATV is the valley's," Pasqua began.

"They're dead," Paulo near shouted, tears running down his cheeks. "They're all dead!"

James pulled his son into his arms, and brushed his free hand over the boy's hair.

"Hush, son. There may be listeners."

"They're all dead," Paulo insisted. Then he sniffed and rubbed his nose. "Those men rode off in the UATV. There isn't anybody here but us. Dad," he went on in a small voice, "they cut off somebody's head."

James hung his head. "Who, son?"

"I don't know, it's still got a helmet on."

James stiffened. "We've got to get that helmet," he said. "Then we can warn the others."

"Very noble of you," Pasqua drawled, knowing he wouldn't be the one to retrieve it. "But as you've already suggested they may have left watchers behind."

"Why watch the dead?" Paulo sneered, stung by her tone.

"To see if anyone approaches them," Pasqua answered through clenched teeth. "They know someone will come looking eventually. Why else make such a big deal out of this?"

"To intimidate us," James suggested, then he sighed. "We still need that helmet," he said firmly. "We can't count on our luck, such as it is, holding."

Pasqua made a sour face.

"I'll go," Paulo said, anger and pride in every syllable.

"Don't be ridiculous," Pasqua snapped. "You stay with your father." Then she dropped to her stomach and crawled off into the surrounding bushes.

James listened for a moment, and under the concealing bandages his brows went up in surprise. "She's good," he commented.

Paulo gave a little growl. "Well, I don't like her," he muttered.

James smiled. "Sometimes, son, people I haven't liked at first turned out to be my best friends."

Paulo stayed silent. He was in no mood for a little

homily on understanding. Paulo wasn't going to like her.

He looked out over the field again, to where the bodies were piled and fury rose within him. These were people he knew! Familiar faces that he'd seen every day of his life. How *dare* they hurt them? He balled his hands into fists until the knuckles turned white and ground his teeth, his eyes blazing. If he could, he'd show them, he'd hurt them like they'd hurt the valley people. Worse! He'd . . .

One moment the head on the stake wore a helmet, the next it was just a head on a stake. Paulo turned away, feeling sick again.

James felt the tension in his son's body change.

"What is it?" he asked.

"She's got it," Paulo answered, then he turned his back on the bloody field.

Half an hour later Pasqua stood up and walked towards them, the helmet swinging by one strap.

"I'm *not* putting this on," she said.

"Give it to me," James said. Taking it he pulled off his bandage and wiped the wet inside of the helmet. Then he inverted it and put it very carefully on, wincing when it came into contact with his wounds.

"Unit Push," he said.

"Go ahead, Captain Martins," replied the lush voice of the Bolo.

"Markee?" James was astonished.

"Never mind Markee," Tops said. "Where the hell are you?"

The squad of fifteen knelt before him, heads bowed, one fist and one knee on the ground, radiating shame as the Sun did heat. Seven-Deer stood before them, resplendent in jade nose and lip plugs, gold rings weighing down his ears, arms crossed over his brawny chest. His face was implacable, but a fear from the World Beyond the World tickled the back of his neck like a chill breeze.

The servant of the Sun had vanished. Oh, not vanished really, escaped. But it should not have been possible. Too many things had gone awry to allow that escape. She got free of her ropes, with no one noticing. She climbed down from the gun carriage, with no one noticing. She walked through the crowd of sleeping slaves, with no one noticing. And she slipped through the squad of fifteen kneeling before him . . . with no one noticing. As if she'd had supernatural help. Perhaps the people of the Sun were being led to their destruction?

Tezcatlipoca is a trickster, he thought. *Smoking Mirror does what he does and no man can understand him.* Seven-Deer had thought that he understood the will of Tezcatlipoca. *Perhaps . . . perhaps it was a lesson, intended to punish my pride in thinking so.* After all, the girl was not important now that they had the gun.

The tension within him released slowly. If this was true then he should not punish the men before him. This was also a relief. The people of the Sun were few and every man was needed. Nevertheless, Smoking Mirror's power must be acknowledged.

"Look at me," he said to the kneeling men. "It is not I who must be propitiated. The gods demand their due." He looked into each man's eyes and saw that he was understood. "You shall give blood to Tezcatlipoca, but you may not impair your battle-worthiness. One of your number, a volunteer, or one selected by vote, will be permitted the honor of giving more on behalf of all."

The men looked at one another, then one by one they pointed until all were pointing at the same man, the squad leader, Water-Monster.

He rose with pride and stepped forward to stand at attention before Seven-Deer.

Two priests came forward in their stinking black robes; one bore a thin-bladed knife, the other a basket. The first gave the knife to Water-Monster, who bowed as he accepted the blade. Water-Monster took the blade and sang out a prayer, then he grasped his tongue in one hand and plunged the blade through its center with the other.

Blood ran down his chin and splattered his chest. His eyes filled with water, though he allowed no tears to fall, pupils contracted to pinpoints and his breath came fast.

The other priest came forward and presented the basket. Without taking his eyes from Seven-Deer's, Water-Monster's hand fumbled within it and caught the end of a rope studded with thorns. He fitted it carefully into the slit he'd made and began drawing the rope through. His face and body were slicked with a cold sweat and he trembled from the agony as foot by foot he dragged the lacerating rope through his tender flesh.

He bore the pain well, though to his shame he gagged once or twice. Behind him, his squad took out their knives and slit their ears, singing a song in praise of Tezcatlipoca.

"Tops? What—"

"Where *are* you, James? We've got a search party out looking for you."

"Where we are is too far from Cacaxtla to do any good," he said. "I've got bad news, Tops. The UATV you sent out . . . they won't be coming home."

There was silence for a moment. James could almost feel Tops's mind clicking into gear, long-disused reflexes opening smoothly. Then: "What are we up against, Captain?"

"Seven-Deer," James said succinctly. "And at least two hundred Jaguar Knights. In addition, they've got upwards of six hundred . . . slaves, I guess."

"*Slaves?*"

Why are you surprised? Tops asked himself. *This is Seven-Deer we're talkin' about.*

"They're dragging a weapon, Tops. It's a massive cannon.

The chassis is mounted on eight balloon wheels, about chest height on me. The gun itself is strange," he paused. "It's about twenty feet long with two rectangular bars bracketing its entire length. And it's thin, looks more like a pipe than anything else. There's a seat for a gunner behind it. I'm assuming that the chassis contains some sort of mechanism for positioning the gun. That about wraps it up. I don't know how they expect to get it into the valley, but if they do, I think we're in deep trouble."

A good assessment, Pasqua thought. Even though James couldn't see her she kept her face immobile.

Tops sighed. "I can't even picture it, Captain. Did it look like something they cobbled together from parts?"

"Excuse me, Captain, Sergeant," the Bolo interrupted. "From the description I would say that the enemy have obtained an XM-17 Railgun. It was an experimental model that was undergoing its final testing phase just before this unit was dispatched to San Gabriel. At that time there were no plans for bringing one this far south."

"That's all you can say?" Tops asked.

Then, with an inward curse over the literal-mindedness of the Bolo, he asked: "What capabilities?"

"The XM-17 Railgun is capable of penetrating the armor of any known self-propelled vehicle at a distance of fifteen hundred meters."

After a long moment he asked carefully: "Including yours?"

"Yes, Sergeant," the Bolo said in its cheerfully sexy voice.

"Can you defend yourself against it?" James asked urgently.

Paulo stared at the dark, curved surface of the helmet's face plate and wished he could hear what was being said to his father. James's hands were bunched into fists and his voice was tight with anxiety.

"In my present state of repair, Captain, I would estimate

that I have only a twelve percent chance of successfully defending myself. That estimate is my most optimistic, based on the assumption that the Railgun will be facing me head on, giving my own guns a direct shot at it. I cannot turn, nor can I deploy my infinite repeaters owing to the heavy coating of lava stone on my chassis."

"Tops . . ."

"You don't have to say it, Captain. We'd better get the whole village busy chippin' that stuff off."

Tops was sweating now, though it was still cool and dry inside the Bolo. "We should have done it years ago—"

"—but as my mother always said, if wishes were horses there would be even more horseshit in the world than there is."

"Can you get us more information, sir? Where the main body of 'em are, their direction and speed so I can tell Joseph and the council. And if you can, slow 'em down."

"Tell him your condition," Pasqua said suddenly, prompted by a sick suspicion.

"Will do," James said. "Out."

"Will do what?" she demanded, dread sitting in her stomach like raw dough.

"Find 'em, find out how fast they're moving, slow 'em down if we can."

"*What*?" She exploded. "Are you crazy? Did that knock on the head kill more brain cells than we realized? Why didn't you *tell* him that you're as good as blind and being assisted by a ten-year-old and a civilian? What are you going to do, throw spitballs, tie a rope across the trail and trip all six hundred slaves? What are your plans, generalissimo? I can't wait to hear."

"Lady, you can leave any time you want to," Paulo said, eyes blazing. "My father and I can handle it ourselves."

"Ah, glorious!" she sneered. "I'm in the company of heroes."

"No," James replied with strained patience, "you're in the company of people with family and friends who are in the path of terrible danger. That head down there belonged to a friend of mine. I'm not going to let those spotted thugs kill his children."

Paulo threw Pasqua a look of smug contempt.

She hissed in exasperation. *I hate this!* she thought vehemently. *Playing hero's one thing, actually becoming one is* not *something I want to do!*

More hateful still was the blood-freezing realization that she wasn't going to leave them to it, but was going with them . . . to help them in any way she could. There wasn't even the possibility of profit in it.

Father had been right. She *was* crazy.

Tops leaned back in the command seat and ran his hands nervously over his short white hair. *Seven-Deer! My God! I'd hoped that bastard was dead.* He slid a glance over to the body-bagged form beside him.

"El-Tee, I like your oldest boy, I really do. But Joseph's the kind thinks if you postpone trouble it's bound to solve itself." Tops thought he knew Bethany Martins well enough that she'd agree with his assessment, and that she'd agree with what he planned to do now.

They'd see combat soon. He sighed, and the adrenaline hummed and sparked along his nerve endings. He hadn't missed the feeling at all, hadn't wanted his own children to ever know it.

So much for that blind hope. He smiled; that was something the El-Tee would have said. He gave himself a little shake, being right beside her body wasn't good for him. Next thing he knew he'd think she was talking to him.

"Markee, do you have a view on the plaza?"

"Negative, Sergeant. Those cameras not damaged by the lava were covered by it."

Oh well. "Open up your P.A. system," he ordered. "Good'n loud, but not painful."

"Ready, Sergeant."

"Attention people of Cacaxtla."

He leaned forward as he spoke.

"We are in an emergency situation. There is an invading force on its way into the valley, composed of approximately two hundred hostiles." He'd considered telling them who it was, but didn't want to send the whole town into a blind panic. "Children and noncombatants are to be evacuated. All able-bodied persons are to report to the Bolo immediately to begin clearing it of debris so that it will be combat ready."

He paused. "Can you hear how they're taking it, Markee? I don't want a panic."

There was a moment's silence, then, "The consensus seems to be that you've lost your mind and are reliving the glory days of your youth," the Bolo reported.

Damn! He hadn't expected that.

"The Jefe is approaching and is demanding that you come down," Markee continued. "The Jefe's authority exceeds your own, Sergeant," the Bolo observed. "I must request that you leave now."

"Whose authority exceeds the Jefe's?" Tops asked desperately.

"The Captain's would, as military authority would always exceed civilian in the deployment of this unit."

"Then get on to him. Ask for his orders. This is an emergency, Markee, if I go out there it's over. For all of us."

A moment later James's voice came through, sounding weary but determined.

"Attention, please. This is Captain Martins speaking. The valley is under attack. The UATV that was sent out to assist me and my son has been overwhelmed, the crew killed and the vehicle stolen. An escaped prisoner of the hostiles has informed me that Cacaxtla is their destination . . ." He paused. "And that Seven-Deer is their leader. Follow Sergeant Jenkins' instructions; he is acting with my authority. Jefe, I expect you to offer him your complete cooperation. Markee, you will follow Sergeant Jenkins' orders as though they were my own. Martins out."

"What's happening?" Tops demanded. "Open up a channel to the outside, Markee, I need to know what's goin' on."

Joseph stood outside the door of the *jefe's* house and slowly closed his mouth.

"Oh, I wish he'd really finally gone crazy," he whispered to himself.

People were boiling out of their homes, some with their napkins still tucked into their collars. Children were crying—adults, too—and a babble of voices rose higher and higher. Lanterns came on outside the homes and shops, turning evening into daylight as if for a fiesta, Christmas or Lieutenant Martin's birthday.

This is a hoax. Something they cooked up before James went out.

The thought still echoed in his mind and he stood paralyzed by doubt. The sense of being the butt of some military joke brought a flush to his cheeks, he could feel the warmth of it.

No. James was a careful planner and a considerate man. If he had something like this in mind surely James would have discussed it with him. Suddenly he felt a horror more real than his own embarrassment, more immediate than the terrible knowledge that everyone would be looking to *him* to do something.

Eventually, a panicked corner of his mind screamed. *This is real! Seven-Deer is coming.* Joseph thought of his wife and daughters. *He'll kill us all.*

He looked around.

"Enrique, Hernando, Susan," he said, beckoning to the three. "Gather up all the tools you can find that might be used to chip off this rock. Consuela, Perdita, Joan, put together some teams to organize an evacuation . . ."

Joseph's mind clicked into another level of awareness, wherein he organized and ordered even as another part of his mind made plans. Men and women flew to undertake the tasks he assigned them and there was room for pride in his busy mind.

We'll be all right, he assured himself. *If we can just hang on, like this, we're going to be fine.*

"Unngghh! This, *ungh,* is, *ungh,* ri-dic-ulous." Pasqua continued applying pressure to the lever planted under the boulder James had selected even as she protested.

"This won't, unngghh, slow them down by more than a couple of hours." The huge stone was rocking and she expected it to give momentarily.

"Keep pushing," James said, heaving on the lever beside her.

Slowly, almost with grace, the boulder toppled to the sound of pebbles cracking under its great weight. Then faster and faster it roared down the slope, slapping tons of loose dirt and smaller stones free from the slope to accompany it down to the road. Dust rose in a choking cloud, and bits of vegetation were thrown back at them with the dirt.

Pasqua stood panting, her hands on her knees as she watched it. Then she straightened and wiped the sweat from her face with her sleeve and sneezed. She'd never worked this hard in her life. They'd already cut down two massive trees with James's flex-saw.

When he'd handed her one of the toggles at the end of the durachrome coil of toothed wire she'd been astonished.

"Where'd you get this?" she asked, wondering who her competitor was.

"Part of my mother's kit," he'd answered calmly. "You ready?"

And suddenly she was a lumberjack.

She didn't know how long she could keep this up. There'd been nothing to eat for two days now and she was thirsty beyond belief. Her lips were cracking and her head ached terribly. Pasqua shot a glance at James. He was gray-faced, his jaw slack, he sat with his hands limp beside him, drawing in great gulps of air. If she was hurting, he must be half-dead. She frowned, ashamed of her selfishness and moved to pity by James's condition and to admiration for his uncomplaining strength.

He'll kill himself if I don't stop him. She wondered who the hell his mother had been.

Then she cursed herself mentally. "Heroes live short lives," her father used to say, with a snake cold smile implying the brevity was deserved. And that he'd implemented Fate's sentence himself fairly often.

I should leave them, she scolded herself. *They're going to get themselves killed.*

All she had to do was get across the valley and out again. Seven-Deer hadn't indicated any particular ambitions beyond taking Cacaxtla. Even if he chose to hunt her down he wouldn't be able to until he'd subdued these people.

Which won't be easy, she thought, stealing another glance at James and levering herself painfully back to her feet. Paulo scooted closer to his father, looking worried, and she closed her eyes at the expression on his face.

"We'd better get moving," she said through clenched teeth. "The noise and the dust are going to bring the Nahuatl Strength Through Joy brigade running."

James nodded, exhausted, and heaved himself to his feet, one trembling hand lifted to his forehead. Then he put his arm around Paulo's slim shoulders and let his son lead him away.

Seven-Deer trembled with rage as he stood on the worn surface of the road. Gullies and undergrowth creeping over the ancient pavement were bad enough.

Another road block. And the perpetrators gone like smoke. He drew in a deep breath and held it, while his dark eyes blazed like fire.

"Find them!" he roared and his hand flashed out, pointing to two captains of fifteen. "GO!"

The men turned and vanished into the trees, their squads leaping after them. They disappeared at a steady ground devouring lope, fanning out until they were lost among the trees and brush.

Seven-Deer watched them go, fury bringing a slaver of foam to his lips. And underneath, inching its way to the surface, as a snake works its way up from the underworld, fear crawled. He cast his eyes over the slaves that labored on the road, dragging boulders and baskets of dirt away.

There. That one was taller than the rest, and despite hunger and days of dragging the gun he still looked fit. Seven-Deer motioned to the feather-decked priests behind him.

"We will send a messenger," he told them. "I fear we have offended Tezcatlipoca and I would win his favor again."

He watched the priests move off to gather up the sacrifice, then turned his eyes to the surrounding cliffs. Not wondering at the fact of resistance, but at the curious weakness of it.

James struggled to speak, to report on their most recent delaying tactic, a pile of brush they'd heaped in the center of the road and set on fire. He'd envisioned it much larger, but Pasqua and Paulo hadn't been able to drag the enormous limbs needed into the road. As for himself, he could barely lift a hand. *Hell . . . I can hardly talk.*

Suddenly the helmet was lifted off his head. The cool air and the sense of space around him made his head spin. "Hey!" he snapped.

"Take a break, soldier," Pasqua sneered.

"Dad, I found a spring. Here."

And there was the canteen at his lips. He pawed at it eagerly, too weak to support it himself, sucking down the icy cold liquid. The tissues of his mouth seemed to expand and his throat felt more like flesh than rock once again. It almost hurt to drink, but he kept on.

Paulo held the canteen for his father and looked him over critically. *This is it,* he thought. *Dad can't do any more.* Unformed lay the thought, *I won't sacrifice him.* The village meant nothing if his father didn't survive. He glanced over at Pasqua who was walking off a ways, the helmet in her hand. *I can't believe she's still with us. Y'can tell she'd rather be anywhere else.*

Though he didn't much like her, Paulo was grateful that she'd stayed. He swallowed convulsively at the thought of being alone, nobody to help his father but himself.

Pasqua drifted out of earshot of the man and boy and, with a moue of distaste, put the helmet on. It was a standard model, as expected, and she quickly activated it.

"Listen up," she snarled. "We've bought you all the time we can. Martins is injured and the boy and I are exhausted. Seven-Deer's about two miles from the old lava flow. What they'll do when they get there is anybody's guess. But he *is* coming and we can't stop him."

"Who the hell is this?" Tops demanded.

"Name's Pasqua. I'm that escaped prisoner Martins told you about."

There was a pause, then: "How bad is he?"

"He's concussed and has been for at least three days—I think he hit his head again after the first injury. He can't really see, his vision's doubled, and we haven't been getting enough water. And we haven't eaten for two days." *And then it was rotten fruit.*

"How's Paulo?"

"Spunky, doing a grownup's job, but wiped out. We're coming in." She could feel her face settle into grim determined lines. An expression few people would argue with. *Pity he can't see it,* she thought.

"We're evacuating the village," Tops said. "By the time you get here the noncombatants will be hiding out in the hills. Tell James they're hiding by the thermal pool." Tops paused, then asked: "Is he . . . able to . . . is he coherent?"

"Yes. Or has been. But right now he's dangerously exhausted for a man in his condition."

"Okay," Tops's mind was working overtime. "Listen, there's a cave a half mile from the old lava flow. It's well hidden and there's even a small cache of emergency rations. It's a good place to rest. Can he make it that far?"

Two and a half miles? Pasqua chewed her lower lip. *Not bloody likely.* Part of the problem was they were starving. James especially would need the food before he could make the walk.

"No," she said aloud. "But if I can retrieve those supplies, maybe."

Tops gave her directions, hoping she was the kind of person who could visualize what he was describing. He made her repeat them until he was satisfied and she was obviously annoyed.

"I'll contact you when I've got something to report," she said tartly and broke contact.

"You do that, honey," Tops muttered unhappily. He

sighed deeply, rose and began to climb from the Bolo's innards, reluctantly about to add to Joseph's burdens.

The cave was almost cozy; five feet by ten, a volcanic bubble in the dark basaltic lava of the ridges that surrounded the valley. With the radiant heater and thermal-film blankets in the cache—more Old American stuff—it was even comfortable, compared to what she'd been going through lately.

"You need more rest," she said to James.

"We need more time, but we haven't got it," he said.

Reluctantly she nodded; he was well enough to see that, at least. "Yeah, that was them at the spring." Not while she was there, thank God, but who else would leave a flake of volcanic glass? Even after the Collapse, most people didn't make knives out of obsidian; they hammered them out of old car springs or rebar, like sensible people. Besides, the urge to spy on the gun convoy ate at her like acid, and she knew better than to press her luck that far.

James's sight was working its way back to normal, though his vision was still poor, and the headache was bearable. He felt almost cheerful.

"Let's set up a nice little booby-trap for them," he suggested. "It might make 'em a little slower to follow us."

Pasqua grinned. "Or that much more eager. Remember, we're not dealing with normal people here."

"Well, I think it's a good idea," Paulo said defiantly, tired of the way Pasqua always seemed to disparage his father's notions.

"It is," Pasqua said holding her hands out, still smiling. "I was just making an observation."

"We'll set it up like we're still here," James said. "Son, you can make up dummies and put one of the thermal-film blankets over them. We'll scatter some of the empty packets around and maybe leave a small fire smoldering . . ."

"You're an artist," Pasqua said.

"Thank you, ma'am. Got it from my mom."

"She sounds like an interesting lady," Pasqua said. "Wish I could have met her."

James turned and looked at her for a moment, blinking and squinting. "You know, lady, I think you and she would have gotten along fine . . . or one of you would have gotten killed."

Pasqua chuckled, looking around the cave with a considering eye. *Damn! Why am I feeling so good?* It wasn't as if this was a pleasure cruise up the Mississippi to pay a social call on the Despot of Natchez and get in a little roulette, after all. But she felt more cheerful than she had in years.

James went on: "Um. I can't do the close work on setting up the explosives, Pasqua, but I can talk you through it. There's nothing to be afraid of, we're not going to be doing anything too radical." *Not with the materials we've got anyway.*

"*Pphhh!* Teach your grandmother to suck eggs," she said. "I'll tell you how to set a booby trap."

She plucked one of the grenades from his utility belt and held it up.

"What would really be great is if we had some plastique to wrap around this little darling. There's nothing like a little MDX," she said wistfully. "Gives it a nice explosive bonus. I remember one time, Guido gift-wrapped a grenade that way and planted it under this guy's car seat— he'd been muscling in on Giacano territory over in the Atacha. BLAMMO! That sucker went off like an ejector seat, right through the roof of his car and he didn't have a sun roof until that moment."

She smiled nostalgically. "Anyway, getting down to business. You anchor one end of a wire, thread's no good—

breaks too easy—about two inches above the ground, right in the path of your target. You attach the other end to the pull ring. Then, you tease these little flanges open, juuust enough to loosen the pin, but tight enough so that it won't fall out, then . . ."

Pasqua continued to describe the proper method of setting a man-killing trap wearing the happy, innocent expression of a woman explaining her favorite recipe.

She was about to conclude with one of Guido's favorite expressions, *And den ya watch da pieces fly upward*, when she noticed their faces. Both their jaws had dropped and their eyes stared unblinking at her.

Uh oh. "Y'know," she chirped, "I never noticed before how much alike you guys look. Paulo, you're going to grow up to be just as handsome as your father."

They both blushed, glanced at each other, then looked away, turning their attention to preparing the campsite.

Whew! she thought. *I've got to watch my big mouth.*

The fire in Water-Monster's wounded mouth burned as hot as the fire in his heart each time he thought of his shame at allowing the servant of the Sun to escape. A shame his whole squad shared, but blamed exclusively on him. He could barely speak with his tongue so swollen, and the frown of confusion on his second's face drove him to fury.

"Th tacka! Ya ool. Wa da th tacka ay?"

"Captain," the second's eyes slid rapidly north and south as he desperately tried to decipher Water-Monster's lispings. Inspiration struck before the Captain did.

"The tracker's have found a definite trail leading from a small spring to a cave a half mile away, lord."

Water-Monster's smile of pleasure was like a spurt of venom.

"Ooh ow!" he bellowed.

The second's brows went up and he gritted his teeth,

as behind the Captain's back he frantically signalled the puzzled troops to move out as commanded.

They approached the cave with caution, ghosting through the twilight, moving as silently as the jaguar from whom they took their name despite the steep slope and the loose volcanic scree underfoot. It was quiet. Birds and insects stilled their cries in alarm as the men passed.

Water-Monster frowned. It was possible that cave was deserted; their quarry might have rested and gone. The tracker had stated that the trail he followed was at least a day old. His nose flared. Yes, the unmistakable scent of woodsmoke. Their quarry had grown careless, building a fire that was too large and not made of thoroughly dry wood. His eyes scanned. Yes, a trace of smoke rising dark against the dark stone of the cliff ahead.

Suddenly his second was beside him whispering. "There are three, Captain, sleeping near a small fire." Water-Monster's heart leapt. "A ga?" he asked.

"No, lord, no guard." The second smiled too, pleased at the ease of capture.

Water-Monster moved up to where the foremost of his troops were and looked into the cave. He could see three humped shapes behind a very smokey fire. *How can they stand it?* he wondered. Down in the lowlands, it might have been a smudge fire to drive off mosquitos. But why here, in these cold uplands? He gestured four of his men to move up and into the cave.

They moved forward with exaggerated care, around piles of leaves and other debris, delicately placing their feet on the few spots of bare ground. They entered the cave like shadows, hugging its walls as they moved towards the sleepers.

When they were well inside Water-Monster rose and followed them. Striding arrogantly through brittle leaves and crackling brush he anticipated their quarry's horror when the noise of his passage woke them and they stared up into the implacable faces of his warriors.

This pleasant image accompanied him to the underworld as the grenade beneath his feet went off, shredding his body before he could even cry out. The impact was less on the men farthest from him. They were able to scream again and again as ricocheting fragments of rock and metal tore through them.

Water-Monster's second and two others came running, peering into the smoking interior of the cave just in time to receive the full blast of the second grenade, set to go off five seconds after the first.

"Do you think it worked?" Paulo asked for perhaps the hundredth time, as they lurched down the slope.

James looked wearily down at his son, who was gazing adoringly up at Pasqua. He stifled a spurt of jealousy. Ever since she'd allowed Paulo to help her set the booby trap for Seven-Deer's troops the boy's attitude towards her had changed drastically. *I always thought I'd be the one to teach you the "arts of war" as Mom used to call 'em.* He sighed and Paulo looked up at him. James's eyesight had improved to the point where he could read the worry in his face.

"It's nothing, son. I was just thinking about how you're growing up."

Paulo looked puzzled, and cocked his head dubiously, as though wondering where *that* had come from.

"You have grown, you know," Pasqua said. "An experience like this changes you." She made herself stop talking before she annoyed everybody, including herself.

They turned a corner. She stopped with an involuntary gasp. Both the others looked at her.

"It's *beautiful*," she said.

The valley was like a bowl—a bowl with a broken rim, a rim of forested hills, rising to one tall volcanic peak to

the west. Rivers ran through it, silver in the evening light.
Fields were squares of color, like a quilt ranging from
yellow-gold wheat through infinite shades of green, from
pasture to orchards and patches of woodlot. Tile-roofed,
whitewashed houses stood scattered amid the fields; a
larger clump made the village, around the open plaza
and the vine-grown shape of the pyramid; the gardens
and trees were splashes of color dividing the buildings.
The scene breathed peace to her, like something from
before the Collapse—long before.

A second look revealed things even more unusual than
the undisturbed pastoral scene.

"You've got a power grid!" she said.

"Well, of course," Paulo said. "We're not *savages*."

James smiled. "Geothermal," he said. "Enough for
essentials."

Pasqua nodded soberly, impressed. The Duchy was
wealthy, but there was little electricity there outside the
houses of the Family and the *caporegime* and *consigliere*
class. This *was* something out of the ordinary, and to
find it here, lost in the mountains . . .

"The thermal springs are there," James said, pointing.

"Unca Jamie!" a child shrieked.

Pasqua jumped and her brows went up as a little yellow-
dressed, dark-haired cannonball slammed into James,
nearly knocking him off his feet.

"Pick me up! Pick me up!" the little girl shouted and
James stooped to comply.

"This is my niece, Catherine," he said as the little girl
rained kisses on his cheek. She turned to gaze at Pasqua
with bright eyes.

"Hi," Pasqua said.

"Are you a fairy princess?" Catherine asked seriously.

"Uh, no." *Mafia princess maybe.* Pasqua couldn't help
smiling at the little girl. It was nice to be asked.

"Captain!" A man in a camouflage uniform emerged from the trees, relief writ large on his homely face. "Good to see you sir."

"Good to see you too, Zapota. How's it going?"

"Well, sir. Everyone's bivouacked around the old thermal pool and the work in town is progressing." His eyes flicked to Pasqua and back to the Captain.

Introductions followed; they turned a corner on the well-graveled road, past an old but well-maintained blockhouse, and into a clump of whitewashed houses. The smell of roasting meat drifted by, and Pasqua heard her stomach growl.

"I want to eat, I want to bathe, I want to sleep."

"No problem," Zapota said smiling. "My little helper there can guide you."

"This way!" Catherine shouted, pointing imperiously. James winced slightly as she tugged at his hair, but he was smiling as he followed the chubby finger.

Pasqua wiped the sweat from her forehead and chin with the end of her scarf, then looked wryly at her battered hands. This was far more like honest labor than anything she'd ever done before, and while the experience was interesting she couldn't see making a habit of it. It was a bit of a consolation that so many others were doing exactly the same work, but not much.

Getting this damn pumice off the damn tank is practically a war in itself. The Family had a couple of Mark II's in storage, but they were no preparation for the sheer *size* of this thing. It was difficult to convince your emotions that this was a machine, not part of the landscape.

A familiar voice caught her attention and she looked down. Far below her James conferred with his brother, the Jefe of the village. She smiled slightly. A few days rest and some food had put him back on his feet and she had to admit, he was pretty. Pretty impressive, and just *pretty*. Straight features, olive tan, white teeth when he smiled, level brown eyes. *Nice butt, too,* she decided, then reflected that a couple of days rest and food had done *her* a world of good, too.

"Yes, it's an assumption," James said. "But it's an educated guess. The gun was a prototype, they can't have much in the way of ammunition for it. Which means that we need that wall around the village."

It was a mere palisade, constructed of raw trees and fence posts, but better than the nothing they'd started with. Joseph had fought them over every inch of it.

"If we get the Bolo up and running the wall is irrelevant," Joseph insisted. "That's where we should concentrate our efforts."

James turned and stared at him. "I've said it before, I'll say it again. One lucky shot and we don't *have* a Bolo." The two men glared at each other. "We're building the wall." James stalked off, leaving civilian authority stymied and enraged behind him.

Pasqua's eyes met Tops's where he was engaged in a more delicate bit of chipping around the Bolo's infinite repeater ports. She smiled ruefully, "I'll bet the old girl loves to hear stuff like that," she said.

Tops chuckled. "*It* doesn't mind," he said. "Markee, you don't take that kinda talk personally do you?"

"The Captain has made an accurate evaluation of our situation, Sergeant Jenkins. If I were capable of taking offense I cannot imagine why the truth should cause it."

"Be nice if people were that reasonable," Pasqua said.

"Sergeant," the Bolo interrupted. "I have received a report from our scouts on the valley's perimeter. Seven-Deer is over the barrier. If he continues at this rate he should be here in two days."

Fear rang like a silver bell, shrill and cold along her nerve endings.

"Damn," Tops swore. "How'd they get through the lava so fast? Must be thirty, fifty feet thick."

"Hypervelocity shot, sergeant. They have expended three rounds."

Pasqua redoubled the speed of her chipping.

Seven-Deer gazed down from the pass at the village of Cacaxtla and sneered at the pathetic palisade that now surrounded it.

It was a flimsy thing, backed by earth only in places. The great gun would sweep it aside like an anthill. His eyes lifted to where, in the center of the Plaza, the Mountain That Walks was partially visible behind the buildings that surrounded it. It sat like a spider in its web. He squinted; attendants crawled over the spider's great body, doing things he couldn't discern at this distance.

It is useless anyway, he thought smugly, *whatever you are doing. Soon your blood shall slake Tezcatlipoca and Xipe Totec's thirst.* A huge grin split his face. Tomorrow at dawn they would wheel the great gun into place and destroy the Mountain That Walks. And then . . .

Ah, revenge is so sweet that even anticipating it is pleasure. The evening breeze lifted his hair and he inhaled deeply of its freshness.

He turned back to his campsite; where screams indicated that they had begun to slaughter the slaves, lest their great numbers prove an inconvenience in the morning. Besides, his men were hungry. The gods would take the blood and hearts that were their due, and the Sun People the remainder.

And Seven-Deer had always preferred liver, in any case. Grilled over an open fire, with some chilies and wild onions . . . delicious.

That the attack would come in the morning everyone knew, with an instinct as sure as that which told them the sun would rise.

Pasqua tossed and turned on her pallet in the women's great tent. She'd been put in with the combatants; those with young children were still up by the thermal springs. It was a compliment, in a way. It hadn't even occurred to anyone that she wanted to run. Finally she rose—exasperated and exhausted—but with energy thrumming through her body like a low voltage electrocution.

She slipped from the tent and the camp with no one the wiser, heading for the village and the command center, through the chill night. Sentries were no problem; one of them was smoking as he walked his rounds. Simply freezing in place was enough to send them on their way regardless.

Jeeze, she thought, *if he wanted to, Seven-Deer could cut every throat in camp and nobody'd notice.*

These people were so good, so kind and wholesome. *And so bloody helpless! It's going to be a slaughter in the morning.* Maybe that wasn't fair. James was one tough hombre, if he was more typical than his brother . . .

When did you ever see a place where the Jameses outnumbered the Josephs? she sneered.

She stopped just outside the palisade, her palms sweating, heart beating frantically.

I should run, she told herself. *I should grab some food and a canteen and get the hell out of here.* Staying was suicide. No sensible person would place themselves in danger for the benefit of strangers. She could picture the weary, disgusted look in her father's eyes if he but knew, and blushed with shame.

She frowned. *But he doesn't know. And Paulo and James are hardly strangers. More importantly, their danger is my fault.* She squared her shoulders and stepped forward.

"*Alto!* Who goes there?"

"A friend," she said. "Take me to Captain Martins."

❖			❖			❖

"You *what*?"

James' cry echoed back from the plastered walls of the room; from the looks of it, it had been his living room before the emergency. Maps and documents covered everything now, except a charcoal portrait of a smiling dark-haired woman. *Paulo's mother, I suppose*, Pasqua thought.

She held her hands up placatingly. "We owned the gun, but he stole it from us," she insisted.

"But you were *going* to sell it to him. Isn't that right?"

She put her hands on her hips and bit her lip, closing her eyes to avoid his.

"We were arms dealers. Yes—we would have sold it to him. Just as we would have sold it to you."

"But *he* is an insane mass murderer bent on conquest and bloodshed, while *we* are farmers who only want to live and work in peace." James glared at her.

"Well," she said, still not meeting his eyes. "Arms dealers *are* known for their flexible attitude and lack of curiosity about end-use intentions."

He turned from her with a sound of disgust and Pasqua thanked heaven that she'd asked to see him alone. *If the others were here I'd be dancing at the end of a rope by now.*

He ran his hands through his hair. "Why are you telling me now?" he asked, with his back to her.

She pressed her lips into a tight line, then forced herself to speak calmly. "He fired off a shot to test the gun the day he stole it. I think it's probable that he used it to clear the road when he got to the lava flow—the Bolo thinks so, too. Three shots should have been enough. Which leaves him with eight."

He turned and slumped into his chair, then he glanced at her guilty face. "It would have saved some arguing with my brother if I'd known that," he muttered sardonically. "It's nice to know that his resources are limited, but otherwise . . ." He made a gesture implying the irrelevance of the information.

"Know your enemy," she quoted.

"Yeah," he said narrowing his eyes. "Sometimes it's a little hard to identify 'em at first."

"I'm not your enemy," she said through gritted teeth. "I just wanted to make a clean breast of things."

"I look like a priest to you?"

"Dammit, James! I want to help."

"Oh you will, lady. You're going to be right by my side when Seven-Deer and his men come pouring over the hill. For now," he said rising and taking her arm, "go and get some rest."

"I'm sorry," she said impulsively. "I am so sorry."

He smiled tiredly. "Sometimes you can find absolution under fire. My mother used to say that."

The remaining fifty slaves and even some of the Jaguar Knights heaved on ropes fed through massive pulleys anchored to huge posts they'd driven into the ground. The slaves, though few, were the strongest and their will to live was evident in the way they struggled to pull the great gun to the top of the ridge. The balloon tyres turned slowly, inch by inch, dragging the weight of synthetic and metal forward. The turbogenerator whined, burning the last of their cane-spirit and pumping the capacitor full of energy.

Seven-Deer smiled benignly. He had ordered the slaves whipped, and the Jaguar Knights assisting them, so that their blood might be a gift to Tezcatlipoca, earning his good will. When the gun was in place, the rest of the slaves would be destroyed.

"Pull!" he shouted. "Bring forth the instrument of our vengeance so that our enemies' hearts may rot within them. Know, my people, that this dawn will be our enemies' last!"

The Jaguar Knights cried out in exultation, and smiling at their acclamation, Seven-Deer turned and stood with his arms crossed on his breast, legs apart, his head high and a smile of victory already brightening his face.

The railgun rose over the hill, haloed by the rising sun. The long thin tube, bracketed by the two rails looked unimaginably strange as it seemed to pierce the ball of the sun.

"Does that thing have a body?" one of the men asked.

"Jeeze, Hernando, I thought you said you had the biggest equipment around," a woman commented to general laughter.

James powered up his helmet. "Tops," he said, "can the Bolo tell where that thing is going to hit?"

"You'll have to ask the Beast that," Tops answered. "It knows what it can see."

James scowled, he didn't like talking to the Bolo. "Markee, can you see where they're aiming?"

"Yes, Captain."

"Can you advise us in time for us to move out of the way?"

"Negative, Captain. The XM-17's aiming system is very simple to operate, a target can be obtained in seconds. I believe there would be insufficient time for humans to react to my warnings."

"We needn't stand on the wall while they're shooting," Pasqua said. "I'd stake my life on it that they won't come down here until the Bolo's out of commission."

He turned to look at her. Her eyes slid away from her reflection on his faceplate's opaque surface.

"Good suggestion," he said. "Unit push. Stand down from the wall. They probably won't charge until and unless the Bolo's destroyed. No sense in risking our necks for nothing. Fall back to the first row of houses, take shelter in the basements. Avoid the ones between the gun and the Bolo; I think we can assume they'll be casualties."

James held his position and Pasqua stayed beside him as she'd promised Paulo.

"If I can't be there you have to be," he'd insisted fiercely. He'd met her just outside the women's tent in the blue-grey light just before dawn. "Dad's making me stay here," Paulo muttered resentfully. "He needs someone to watch his back." He'd glared at her then, dark eyes glittering with unshed tears, silently demanding her word.

"I'll do it," she'd said simply and he'd nodded once and walked away.

"It isn't necessary for you to stay," James said quietly.

"I want to see."

They turned and trotted back, through the vegetable gardens and the flowers, into the courtyard of a building and down into the cellar. Above was a distillery; the fruity-sugar smell of rum was strong from the wooden vats behind them. As one, they stepped up to a shelf that gave them a view through the narrow ground-level windows.

After that they were silent. Their bodies tense as drawn wire, the mounting horror of the giant gun being brought into position bearing down on them like a physical weight.

"Tops, how's it going?" James asked suddenly, breaking the long silence.

Tops paused; they could hear a rasping sound as he raised his visor and wiped the sweat from his forehead.

"I've got the infinite repeater ports clear," he reported. "The Bolo says it can use 'em. But," he paused and licked dry lips, "it can't turn and it can't walk. And you'll have noticed, sir, that bastard's comin' up from behind."

"Thanks, Tops. Martins out." James turned back towards the ridge and found himself staring into the barrel of the railgun. "Shit!" he snarled and grabbing Pasqua around the waist, dove from the wall just before it disintegrated.

The impact of the blast knocked the breath from their bodies and carried them for yards, before the giant, invisible fist that had smacked into them allowed them to fall. Dirt and fragments of wood pummeled them where they lay, writhing as their stunned lungs refused to take in air. Beams sagged into the cellar as the endless rumble of falling stone from above avalanched down.

At last, with a painful spasm, James was able to draw breath, only to cough uncontrollably as he inhaled the dust that was still settling around them. Pasqua gasped and began hacking a moment later.

"Tops," James croaked, "what's happening?"

"Oh, thank God," Tops said. "I thought you were dead for sure, sir. They're dancing around and slapping themselves on the head up there, yellin' and singin' from the sound of it."

The buzzing in James's ears was fading and he could indeed hear, very faintly, what sounded like singing.

"It would be really nice if Markee could return the favor," James prompted.

"Workin' on it, Captain."

Yeah, workin' on it, Tops thought as he and his crew hammered desperately at rock that had flowed deeply into the Bolo's crevices, freezing it in its current position. *Why didn't we do something about this before?*

He knew the answer, of course. They didn't want to admit that a day like this would come. *I'm as spoiled as any of the kids who were born here,* he castigated himself. *Only I don't have an excuse, because I knew better than to believe we were safe.*

Somewhere behind him a house rose like a flock of startled birds, broke apart in midair and fell into a pile of rubble. The shockwave smacked his ears painfully and he felt the heat of the blast on his skin, though the explosion was a quarter of a mile behind him.

He hammered, they all hammered and prayed that they'd free the Beast in time.

Seven-Deer's joy was like a swelling sun in his chest. He grinned as the wall blew apart and the first row of houses disintegrated. Fire began to spread from the demolished buildings and he was certain that they had killed at least two of the defenders.

Tezcatlipoca, he prayed, *such sacrifices I shall give you! The ground will flow with a river of blood, all offered for your pleasure.*

Carefully he aligned the red dot on the next row of targets, the last row of buildings between the gun and the Mountain That Walks.

"Soon," he crooned softly. "Soon you will die, monster."

James levered a beam aside. They both stuck their heads through, coughing at the thick smoke that was beginning to spread. He stared up the slope, through the ruins of his town at the gun that was tearing his world apart. He looked at Pasqua, prepared to hate her, only to find a pitifully shaken woman. Her green eyes were wide with shock and horror, pale lips trembling.

"I swear to God," she said, "I will never sell another gun as long as I live."

"Better late than never," he muttered.

The ground quaked as another shot hit home. Anything solid enough to slow the ultradense material of the penetrator caused it to give up every erg of energy it possessed . . . and at those speeds, the kinetic force involved was *huge*. More buildings fell. The dust and smoke made it as hard to see as it was to breathe, but James knew that the Bolo was now fully exposed to Seven-Deer's gun.

There seemed to be a long breathless pause. No sound of triumph came from the ridge. Only the clatter of settling rubble or the sound of flames taking root in the houses around them was to be heard in the town.

Pasqua found James's hands with her own and he clasped them, pressing them to his chest as they watched the distant figures on the hill. They were fanning out, shaking themselves out into combat formations and coming down.

Seven-Deer didn't seem to think there would be much resistance. James wished he didn't agree.

"Sergeant," the Bolo said in its incongruously sweet voice. "You and the rest of the crew should seek shelter now. The enemy is targeting this unit."

Tops glanced behind him and froze. All that stood between him and the tank killer was an impenetrable cloud of dust.

He stood and shouted. "Everybody off the Bolo, get to cover!" Then he leaped himself, wincing at the pain in his ankles and knees as he struck the paving stones. Long time since he'd done that. It didn't stop him running as fast as he could; men and women dropped their tools and scrambled down the sides of the tank, moving with desperate speed around him.

A bolt pierced the drifting cloud of smoke and dirt. Far too fast to see, but the incandescent track it drilled through air and dust was solid as a bar for an instant, burning a streak across his retinas.

A flash like a dozen bolts of lightning burned through his closed eyelids and upraised hand. Heat slapped at his face, as the hypervelocity shot liberated *all* its energy. A plasma bloom of vaporized uranium and durachrome washed halfway across the plaza, burning everything it touched to ash. A hundred and fifty tons of war machine rocked with the blow, surging backward on maglev suspension, wheeling in a three-quarter circle as the off-center impact torqued against the enormous weight of the Bolo. Lava stone fell from her sides like rain and clouds of electric sparks burst from her.

Tops rolled to a halt in the shadow of a house and turned to watch, sick with dread.

But the Bolo was not shattered. A disk twelve feet broad on its surface was *clean*, polished as if by a generation of sandblasters to a mirror finish. The rest of it looked different too; it took a moment for his blast-stunned mind to grasp why.

Pasqua leveled her M-35 and stroked the trigger. *Braaaap*. The 4mm slugs whipped away downrange. A Jaguar Knight tumbled; perhaps her fire, perhaps someone else. She spat aside to clear her mouth of some of the gritty dust and blinked at the rubble and smoke before her.

"It's been good to know you!" she shouted over the noise.

James nodded without looking around. Mortar shells began dropping on the rubble at the edge of Cacaxtla; the Knights had their heavy weapons in operation.

Move, baby, Tops thought. *Move!*

He held his breath and watched the huge machine. Under the impact of the railgun shot the whole surface of the durachrome armor had *flexed*. The lava that had covered it was gone, blasted away in molecular dust, coating the plaza stones for hundreds of yards in all directions.

But there were also electrical fires on the Bolo's surface, and the bright dished spot in the armor glowed, the heat cycling down from white towards a sullen red.

Move. he thought as despair washed over him, along with the conviction that the Bolo was dead.

"Markee!" he shouted. And waited. No answer.

But in the silence the sound of shouting men grew,

and he didn't need the Captain's voice to tell him what was happening.

"They're coming!"

The Jaguar Knights pounded down the hill, literally screaming for blood. James Martins fired again and again, but he could feel the small hairs along his spine lifting at the sound of their gleeful shrieks.

Pasqua envied him his preoccupation, as he snapped out orders and offered encouragement. She could only kneel dry-mouthed clutching her M-35 and watching death come bellowing down the hill after her.

"All right, aim and shoot, aim and shoot, people." James said. *I wonder how many of us will be able to aim today.* They'd all been hunting, most were pretty good shots, but they hadn't been firing on men. *Or under the stress of attack, with our houses burning behind us.*

"Damn," he said.

"What?" Pasqua said.

James tapped the side of his helmet. "They're not just charging in. Mortar teams moving forward, and they're swinging around to flank us. We've only got about twenty assault rifles, and not all that much ammunition. They've got two hundred. The rest of us . . ."

Not far off, a Cacaxtlan raised her rifle and fired over a hill of rubble. Grey-white smoke jetted out, marking her position; she rolled down the rubble as bullets spanged and sparked off the spot she'd been occupying, struggling with the lever of her weapon. It gave, and a brass cartridge popped out. She fumbled another free of the bandolier across her chest, and thumbed it home into the breech. Another smack of the lever closed it, and she began to crawl toward another pile of broken stone.

"We don't have the firepower to stop them. *Down!*"

He caught Pasqua and flattened himself. A mortar landed not ten yards away, and fragments whined viciously

about them. Their strained faces were inches apart, and
James opened his mouth to speak.

An earsplitting scream of tortured metal stopped the
words. Something made the earth shake beneath them,
an endless droning, creaking rumble. Time slowed.
Pitching and swaying with the uneven stress of advancing
on three treads, the Bolo surged forward to fill the gap
in the center of the villagers' line. Rock crackled beneath
it, louder than gunshots; rock crunched and bled out of
its road wheels.

Many of the villagers screamed at the sounds and spun
'round with their M-35's levelled at the Bolo, only to
start laughing as the Bolo swept towards them, moving
to fill the gap in the gate.

Seven-Deer screamed hatred as the Bolo moved across
the holographic sight-image.

"I killed you!" he shouted. "I will kill you again, and
again!"

His hands gripped the control yoke. His thumbs stabbed
down on the firing button.

Status: *weapons 27%, sensors 38% Severe degradation
of function due to kinetic-energy round impact. Power
reserves 64% Forward sensors at 3% optimum. 51% of
drive units inoperable due to surge overload. Main data
processors secure. Infinite repeaters nominal. Main
armament nominal.*

Mission priorities: *fire support to Cacaxtla forces
defending position; as per, orders, Martin, Lieutenant
Bethany, 01/07/2040.*

Threat envelope: *enemy infantry, small arms.*
    enemy infantry, mortars.
    enemy antitank gun, towed, manned.

[decision tree]: *priority.* **Query.**

Query: continue fire support mission/interrupt.

   [decision tree]: *maintain unit integrity/vital assigned mission parameters.*
   Priority: threats to unit integrity. Threat is antitank gun.
   distance/bearing/wind factors/weapons selection/ status
   [decision tree]: *main gun.*
   Bearing. Fire as you bear.
   Fire.
   Enemy damage assessment.
   [decision tree]: *resume fire support mission.*
The process had taken quite a long time; Unit #27A22245, Mk III, was in grossly suboptimal condition. Fully 1.27 seconds elapsed before the coils energizing the Bolo's main gun activated.

James and Pasqua stood, the muzzles of their rifles drooping earthward as they watched the fireball climbing into the sky as Seven-Deer met the Sun. The flash made their eyes wince and water, but they could already see that nothing remained of the railgun—nothing remained of the *ridge*, either; there was a great big semicircle taken out of it, like a bite. The muzzle of the Bolo's long main cannon throbbed blue-white, a deep humming through the air as it cooled.

For a moment silence fell over the battlefield, broken only by the crackling flames and the screams of wounded humans. Then another tortured squeal of metal came as the Bolo lurched forward. Fire stabbed out from it, and the next flight of mortar bombs exploded in mid-air. The infinite repeaters sounded again and again; smaller globes of fire marked the sites where the mortars had been. Again, and Jaguar Knights exploded into mists of fractionated bone and blood. They threw down their weapons and fled, screaming as loud in terror as they had in bloodlust. Again . . .

James ran forward. "Cease fire!" he shouted. "Cease fire!"

The low sweet voice of the war machine sounded in his ears. "Mission priority is to protect the valley from exterior aggressors, Captain," it said. Men died. "Are my mission parameters to be changed?"

"No! But let them surrender—that's an order, Markee!"

"Yes, Captain."

A voice spoke, louder than a god; James threw his hands to his ears in reflex, shouting with pain even though the cone of sound was directed up the slope. The Voice blasted again, in the guttural choppy sounds of Nahuatl. Then in Spanish, and English.

"THROW DOWN YOUR WEAPONS AND PLACE YOUR HANDS BEHIND YOUR NECKS. SURRENDER AND YOU WILL NOT BE HARMED. RESISTANCE IS DEATH. THROW DOWN—"

A Jaguar Knight raised his M-35. For an instant a bar of light seemed to connect him to the Bolo, and then his body *splashed* away from the contact. All except for his legs; those fell outward, one to the left and one to the right.

The Knight beside him bent and laid his rifle on the ground.

"God," James murmured. He looked around at the town, at the charnel house spread out on the slopes above it. "God."

"Which one?" Pasqua said, coming up beside him.

James found Pasqua watching the celebrations from the shadow of a neighbor's wall. She looked different in a flounced skirt and bodice . . . He handed her a beer and took his place beside her.

"You don't dance?" he said.

She shrugged.

"Are you staying?" he asked, watching the dancers whirl and clap their hands, sweat glistening on happy faces.

Her brows went up and she turned to look at him.

"Would I be welcome?"

James grimaced slightly. "I'm the only one who knows everything and I'd say you'd balanced things out over the last week."

Tell that to Gary, she thought.

"Yeah," he continued, "you'd be welcome. I . . . you'd be welcome, sure."

Beside him she inhaled deeply and straightened. *Oh, God,* he thought. *What's coming now?* That was the way she'd looked at the *last* confession.

"I think you should know that my name is Giacano," she said.

"Instead of Pasqua?"

"I'm Pasqua Giacano," she snarled.

She obviously expects a comment on that, he thought.

"I like it. It's very musical."

She gaped at him. Then a slow smile of took possession of her face, one that she couldn't have suppressed to save herself from torture.

Musical! My relatives started out as extortionists, pimps and murderers. They moved up to slaving and grand-scale tyranny; and this guy thinks my name is musical? She could have hugged him. *I could be my own person here! No vile expectations, no fearful gasps of recognition. I won't have to be ashamed of not making my bones.*

"If I can stay, I'd like to," she said in a choked voice. "I think I'd like it here."

James shifted into a more comfortable position against the wall and sipped his beer.

"Oh, you will," he assured her confidently. "Hey, let's go punish the buffet—the *carne advodada* is to die for."

❖   ❖   ❖

Tops settled himself on an outcropping in the Bolo's side, a beer in his hand and a smile on his face. In the distance the villagers danced and sang around bonfires in the plaza.

"You did good, Markee," he said.

"Actually, Sergeant Jenkins, I have been derelict in my duty."

He looked up at the Bolo towering over him, his eyebrows raised.

"That's a little harsh for a Bolo that just saved all our asses," he observed.

James and Pasqua passed near him, heading for the buffet with their heads together. Tops smiled and eased the splint around his broken arm more comfortably in the sling. There was something a little strange about Pasqua Giacano . . . but then, you could say that about all of them.

"I'd say you did pretty good," he went on, patting the durachrome beneath him.

"Lieutenant Bethany Martins ordered me to defend the valley from external aggression," it said. "But when the invasion came I was virtually unable to defend myself. I should have recognized my diminished capacity and asked that something be done about it."

"We could have seen it for ourselves, honey."

What the hell, why not surrender to it, this tank's a she.

"I guess we were all just hoping that we'd never need you and kept putting the job off. We'll just have to go on from here." He took a sip of his beer. "And we'll be better prepared next time," he promised grimly.

Paulo was watching him; the boy waved, and ripped off a salute to the Bolo. Behind him, the dance went on.

THE TRAITOR

by David Weber

Cold, bone-dry winter wind moaned as the titanic vehicle rumbled down the valley at a steady fifty kilometers per hour. Eight independent suspensions, four forward and four aft, spread across the full width of its gigantic hull, supported it, and each ten-meter-wide track sank deep into the soil of the valley floor. A dense cloud of dust—talcum-fine, abrasive, and choking as death—plumed up from road wheels five meters high, but the moving mountain's thirty-meter-high turret thrust its Hellbore clear of the churning cocoon. For all its size and power, it moved with unearthly quiet, and the only sounds were the whine of the wind, the soft purr of fusion-powered drive trains, the squeak of bogies, and the muted clatter of track links.

The Bolo ground forward, sensor heads swiveling, and the earth trembled with its passing. It rolled through thin, blowing smoke and the stench of high explosives with ponderous menace, altering course only to avoid the deepest craters and the twisted wrecks of alien fighting vehicles. In most places, those wrecks lay only in ones and twos; in others, they were heaped in shattered breastworks, clustered so thickly it was impossible to bypass them. When that happened, the eerie quiet of the Bolo's advance vanished into the screaming anguish of crushing alloy as it forged straight ahead, trampling them under its thirteen thousand tons of death and destruction.

It reached an obstacle too large even for it to scale. Only a trained eye could have identified that torn and blasted corpse as another Bolo, turned broadside on to block the Enemy's passage even in death, wrecked Hellbore still trained down the valley, missile cell hatches open on empty wells which had exhausted their ammunition. Fifteen enemy vehicles lay dead before it, mute testimony to the ferocity of its last stand, but the living Bolo didn't even pause. There was no point, for the dead Bolo's incandescent duralloy hull radiated the waste heat of the failing fusion bottle which had disemboweled it. Not even its unimaginably well-armored Survival Center could have survived, and the living Bolo simply altered heading to squeeze past it. Igneous rock cried out in pain as a moving, armored flank scraped the valley face on one side, and the dead Bolo shuddered on the other as its brother's weight shouldered it aside.

The moving Bolo had passed four dead brigade mates in the last thirty kilometers, and it was not unwounded itself. Two of its starboard infinite repeaters had been blasted into mangled wreckage, energy weapon hits had sent molten splatters of duralloy weeping down its glacis plate to freeze like tears of pain, a third of its after sensor arrays had been stripped away by a near miss, and its forward starboard track shield was jammed in the lowered position, buckled and rent by enemy fire. Its turret bore the ID code 25/D-0098-ART and the unsheathed golden sword of a battalion commander, yet it was alone. Only one other unit of its battalion survived, and that unit lay ahead, beyond this death-choked valley. It was out there somewhere, moving even now through the trackless, waterless Badlands of the planet Camlan, and unit ART of the Line rumbled steadily down the valley to seek it out.

I interrogate my inertial navigation system as I approach my immediate objective. The INS is not the most efficient way to determine my position, but Camlan's entire orbital network, including the recon and nav sats, as well as the communication relays, perished in the Enemy's first strike, and the INS is adequate. I confirm my current coordinates and grind forward, leaving the valley at last.

What lies before me was once a shallow cup of fertile green among the lava fields; now it is a blackened pit, and as my forward optical heads sweep the ruins of the town of Morville I feel the horror of Human mass death. There is no longer any need for haste, and I devote a full 6.007 seconds to the initial sweep. I anticipate no threats, but my on-site records will be invaluable to the court of inquiry I know will be convened to pass judgment upon my brigade. I am aware of my own fear of that court's verdict and its implications for all Bolos, but I am a unit of the Line. This too, however bitter, is my duty, and I will not flinch from it.

I have already observed the massive casualties C Company inflicted upon the Enemy in its fighting retreat up the Black Rock Valley. The Enemy's vehicles are individually smaller than Bolos, ranging from 500.96 Standard Tons to no more than 4,982.07 Standard Tons, but heavily armed for their size. They are also manned, not self-aware, and he has lost many of them. Indeed, I estimate the aggregate tonnage of his losses in the Black Rock Valley alone as equivalent to at least three Bolo regiments. We have yet to determine this Enemy's origins or the motives for his assault on Camlan, but the butchery to which he has willingly subjected his own personnel is sobering evidence of his determination . . . or fanaticism. Just as the blasted, body-strewn streets of Morville are ample proof of his ferocity.

Seventy-one more wrecked Enemy vehicles choke the final approach to the town, and two far larger wrecks loom among them. I detect no transponder codes, and the wreckage of my brigade mates is so blasted that even I find it difficult to identify what remains, yet I know who they were. Unit XXV/D-1162-HNR and Unit XXV/D-0982-JSN of the Line have fought their last battle, loyal unto death to our Human creators.

I reach out to them, hoping against hope that some whisper from the final refuge of their Survival Centers will answer my transmission, but there is no reply. Like the other Bolos I have passed this day, they are gone beyond recall, and the empty spots they once filled within the Total Systems Data Sharing net ache within me as I move slowly forward, alert still for any Enemy vehicles hiding among the wreckage. There are none. There are only the dead: the Enemy's dead, and the six thousand Human dead, and my brothers who died knowing they had failed to save them.

This is not the first time units of the Line have died, nor the first time they died in defeat. There is no shame in that, only sorrow, for we cannot always end in victory. Yet there is cause for shame here, for there are only two dead Bolos before me . . . and there should be three.

Wind moans over the wreckage as I pick my way across the killing ground where my brothers' fire shattered three Enemy attacks before the fourth overran them. Without the recon satellites there is no independent record of their final battle, but my own sensor data, combined with their final TSDS transmissions, allow me to deduce what passed here. I understand their fighting withdrawal down the

Black Rock Valley and the savage artillery and missile barrages which flayed them as they fought. I grasp their final maneuvers from the patterns of wreckage, recognize the way the Enemy crowded in upon them as his steady pounding crippled their weapons. I see the final positions they assumed, standing at last against the Enemy's fire because they could no longer retreat without abandoning Morville.

And I see the third position from which a single Bolo did retreat, falling back, fleeing into the very heart of the town he was duty bound to defend. I track his course by the crushed and shattered wreckage of buildings and see the bodies of the Camlan Militia who died as he fled, fighting with their man-portable weapons against an Enemy who could destroy 13,000-ton Bolos. There are many Enemy wrecks along his course, clear evidence of how desperately the Militia opposed the invaders' advance even as the Bolo abandoned Morville, fleeing north into the Badlands where the Enemy's less capable vehicles could not pursue, and I know who left those Humans to die. Unit XXV/D-0103-LNC of the Line, C Company's command Bolo, my creche mate and battle companion and my most trusted company commander. I have fought beside him many times, known his utter reliability in the face of the Enemy, but I know him no longer, for what he has done is unforgivable. He is the first, the only, Bolo ever to desert in the face of the Enemy, abandoning those we are bound to protect to the death and beyond.

For the first time in the history of the Dinochrome Brigade, we know shame. And fear. As LNC, I am a Mark XXV, Model D, the first production model Bolo to be allowed complete, permanent self-awareness, and LNC's actions attack the very foundation of the decision which made us fully self-realized personalities. We have repeatedly demonstrated how much more effective our awareness makes us in battle, yet our freedom of action makes us unlike any previous units of the Brigade. We are truly autonomous . . . and if one of us can choose to flee—if one of us can succumb to cowardice—perhaps all of us can.

I complete my survey of the site in 4.307 minutes. There are no survivors, Enemy, Human, or Bolo, in Morville, and I report my grim confirmation to my Brigade Commander and to my surviving brothers and sisters. The Enemy's surprise attack, coupled with our subsequent losses in combat, have reduced Sixth Brigade to only fourteen units, and our acting Brigade Commander is Lieutenant Kestrel, the most junior—and sole surviving— Human of our command staff. The Commander is only twenty-four Standard Years of age, on her first posting to an active duty brigade, and the exhaustion in her voice is terrible to hear. Yet she has done her duty superbly, and I feel only shame and bitter, bitter guilt that I must impose this additional decision upon her. I taste the matching shame and guilt of the surviving handful of my brothers and sisters over the TSDS, but none of them can assist me. The Enemy is in full retreat to his spaceheads, yet the fighting continues at a furious pace. No other Bolos can be diverted from it until victory is assured, and so I alone have come to investigate and confirm the unbelievable events here, for I am the commander of LNC's battalion. It is up to me to do what must be done.

"All right, Arthur," Lieutenant Kestrel says finally. "We've got the situation in hand here, and Admiral Shigematsu's last subspace flash puts Ninth Fleet just thirty-five hours out. We can hold the bastards without you. Go do what you have to."

"Yes, Commander," I reply softly, and pivot on my tracks, turning my prow to the north, and follow LNC's trail into the lava fields.

❖   ❖   ❖

Unit XXV/D-0103-LNC of the Line churned across
the merciless terrain. Both outboard port tracks had been
blown away, and bare road wheels groaned in protest as
they chewed through rock and gritty soil. His armored
hull was gouged and torn, his starboard infinite repeaters
and anti-personnel clusters a tangled mass of ruin, but
his builders had designed him well. His core war hull
had been breached in three places, wreaking havoc among
many of his internal systems, yet his main armament
remained intact . . . and he knew he was pursued.

LNC paused, checking his position against his INS
and the maps in Main Memory. It was a sign of his brutal
damage that he required almost twenty full seconds to
determine his location, and then he altered course. The
depression was more a crevasse than a valley—a sunken
trough, barely half again the width of his hull, that plunged
deep below the level of the fissured lava fields. It would
offer LNC cover as he made his painful way towards
the distant Avalon Mountains, and a cloud of dust wisped
away on the icy winter wind as he vanished into the
shadowed cleft.

*I try to deduce LNC's objective, assuming that he
has one beyond simple flight, but the task is beyond
me. I can extrapolate the decisions of a rational foe,
yet the process requires some understanding of his
motives, and I no longer understand LNC's motives. I
replay the final TSDS transmission from XXV/D-1162-
HNR and experience once more the sensation a Human
might define as a chill of horror as LNC suddenly
withdraws from the data net. I share HNR's attempt
to reestablish the net, feel LNC's savage rejection of all
communication. And then I watch through HNR's sensors
as LNC abandons his position, wheeling back towards
Morville while Enemy fire bellows and thunders about
him . . . and I experience HNR's final shock as his own*

company commander responds to his repeated queries by pouring Hellbore fire into his unprotected rear.

LNC's actions are impossible, yet the data are irrefutable. He has not only fled the Enemy but killed his own brigade mate, and his refusal even to acknowledge communication attempts is absolute. That, too, is impossible. Any Bolo must respond to the priority com frequencies, yet LNC does not. He has not only committed mutiny and treason but refused to hear any message from Lieutenant Kestrel, as he might reject an Enemy communications seizure attempt. How any Bolo could ignore his own Brigade Commander is beyond my comprehension, yet he has, and because there is no longer any communication interface at all, Lieutenant Kestrel cannot even access the Total Systems Override Program to shut him down.

None of my models or extrapolations can suggest a decision matrix which could generate such actions on LNC's part. But perhaps that is the point. Perhaps there is no decision matrix, only panic. Yet if that is true, what will he do when the panic passes—if it passes? Surely he must realize his own fate is sealed, whatever the outcome of the Enemy's attack. How can I anticipate rational decisions from him under such circumstances?

I grind up another slope in his tracks. He has altered course once more, swinging west, and I consult my internal maps. His base course has been towards the Avalon Mountains, and I note the low ground to the west. He is no longer on a least-time heading for the mountains, but the long, deep valley will take him there eventually. It will also afford him excellent cover and numerous ambush positions, and I am tempted to cut cross-country and head him off. But if I do that and he is not, in fact, headed for the mountains, I may lose him. He cannot hide indefinitely, yet my shame and grief—and sense of betrayal—will not tolerate delay, and I know from HNR's last transmission that LNC's damage is much worse than my own.

I consider options and alternatives for .0089 seconds, and then head down the slope in his wake.

Unit LNC slowed as the seismic sensors he'd deployed along his back trail reported the ground shocks of a pursuing vehicle in the thirteen-thousand-ton range. He'd known pursuit would come, yet he'd hoped for a greater head start, for he had hundreds of kilometers still to go, and his damaged suspension reduced his best sustained speed to barely forty-six kilometers per hour. He *must* reach the Avalons. No Enemy could be permitted to stop him, yet the remote sensors made it clear the Enemy which now pursued him was faster than he.

But there were ways to slow his hunter, and he deployed another pair of seismic sensors while his optical heads and sonar considered the fissured rock strata around him.

I am gaining on LNC. His track damage must be worse than I had believed, and the faint emissions of his power plants come to me from ahead. I know it is hopeless, yet even now I cannot truly believe he is totally lost to all he once was, and so I activate the TSDS once more and broadcast strongly on C Company's frequencies, begging him to respond.

Unit LNC picked up the powerful transmissions and felt contempt for the one who sent them. Could his pursuer truly believe he would fall for such an obvious ploy? That he would respond, give away his position, possibly even accept communication and allow access to his core programming? LNC recognized the communications protocols, but that meant nothing. LNC no longer had allies, friends, war brothers or sisters. There was only the Enemy . . . and the Avalon Mountains which drew so slowly, agonizingly closer.

But even as LNC ignored the communications attempt,

he was monitoring the seismic sensors he'd deployed. He matched the position those sensors reported against his own terrain maps and sent the execution code.

Demolition charges roar, the powerful explosions like thunder in the restricted cleft. I understand their purpose instantly, yet there is no time to evade as the cliffs about me shudder. It is a trap. The passage has narrowed to little more than the width of my own combat chassis, and LNC has mined the sheer walls on either hand.

I throw maximum power to my tracks, fighting to speed clear, but hundreds of thousands of tons of rock are in motion, cascading down upon me. My kinetic battle screen could never resist such massive weights, and I deactivate it to prevent its burnout as the artificial avalanche crashes over me. Pain sensors flare as boulders batter my flanks. Power train components scream in protest as many times my own weight in crushed rock and shifting earth sweep over me, and I am forced to shut them down, as well. I can only ride out the cataclysm, and I take grim note that LNC has lost none of his cunning in his cowardice.

It takes 4.761 minutes for the avalanche to complete my immobilization and another 6.992 minutes before the last boulder slams to rest. I have lost 14.37% percent more of my sensors, and most of those which remain are buried under meters of debris. But a quick diagnostic check reveals that no core systems have suffered damage, and sonar pulses probe the tons of broken rock which overlay me, generating a chart of my overburden.

All is not lost. LNC's trap has immobilized me, but only temporarily. I calculate that I can work clear of the debris in not more than 71.650 minutes, and jammed boulders shift as I begin to rock back and forth on my tracks.

LNC's remote sensors reported the seismic echoes of his pursuer's efforts to dig free. For a long moment—

almost .3037 seconds—he considered turning to engage his immobilized foe, but only for a moment. LNC's Hellbore remained operational, but he'd expended ninety-six percent of his depletable munitions, his starboard infinite repeaters were completely inoperable, and his command and control systems' efficiency was badly degraded. Even his Battle Reflex functioned only erratically, and he knew his reactions were slow, without the flashing certainty which had always been his. His seismic sensors could give no detailed information on his hunter, yet his Enemy was almost certainly more combat worthy than he, and his trap was unlikely to have inflicted decisive damage.

No. It was the mountains which mattered, the green, fertile mountains, and LNC dared not risk his destruction before he reached them. And so he resisted the temptation to turn at bay and ground steadily onward through the frozen, waterless Badlands on tracks and naked road wheels.

I work my way free at last. Dirt and broken rock shower from my flanks as my tracks heave me up out of the rubble-clogged slot. More dirt and boulders crown my war hull and block Number Three and Number Fourteen Optical Heads, yet I remain operational at 89.051% of base capacity, and I have learned. The detonation of his demolition charges was LNC's response to my effort to communicate. The brother who fought at my side for twenty-one Standard Years truly is no more. All that remains is the coward, the deserter, the betrayer of trust who will stop at nothing to preserve himself. I will not forget again—and I can no longer deceive myself into believing he can be convinced to give himself up. The only gift I can offer him now is his destruction, and I throw additional power to my tracks as I go in pursuit to give it to him.

❖   ❖   ❖

LNC's inboard forward port suspension screamed in protest as the damaged track block parted at last. The fleeing Bolo shuddered as he ran forward off the track, leaving it twisted and trampled in his wake. The fresh damage slowed him still further, and he staggered drunkenly as his unbalanced suspension sought to betray him. Yet he forced himself back onto his original heading, and his deployed remotes told him the Enemy was gaining once more. His turret swiveled, training his Hellbore directly astern, and he poured still more power to his remaining tracks. Drive components heated dangerously under his abuse, but the mountains were closer.

I begin picking up LNC's emissions once more, despite the twisting confines of the valley. They remain too faint to provide an accurate position fix, but they give me a general bearing, and an armored hatch opens as I deploy one of my few remaining reconnaissance drones.

LNC detected the drone as it came sweeping up the valley. His anti-air defenses, badly damaged at Morville, were unable to engage, but his massive ninety-centimeter Hellbore rose like a striking serpent, and a bolt of plasma fit to destroy even another Bolo howled from its muzzle.

My drone has been destroyed, but the manner of its destruction tells me much. LNC would not have engaged it with his main battery if his anti-air systems remained effective, and that means there is a chink in his defenses. I have expended my supply of fusion warheads against the invaders, but I retain 37.961% of my conventional warhead missile load, and if his air defenses have been seriously degraded, a saturation bombardment may overwhelm his battle screen. Even without battle screen, chemical explosives would be unlikely to significantly

*injure an undamaged Bolo, of course, but LNC is not
undamaged.*

*I consider the point at which my drone was destroyed
and generate a new search pattern. I lock the pattern
in, and the drone hatches open once more. Twenty-four
fresh drones—82.75% of my remaining total—streak
upward, and I open my VLS missile cell hatches, as well.*

The drones came screaming north. They didn't come
in slowly this time, for they were no longer simply
searching for LNC. This time they already knew his
approximate location, and their sole task was to confirm
it for the Enemy's fire control.

But LNC had known they would be coming. He had
already pivoted sharply on his remaining tracks and halted,
angled across the valley to clear his intact port infinite
repeaters' field of fire, and heavy ion bolts shrieked to
meet the drones. His surviving slug-throwers and laser
clusters added their fury, and the drones blew apart as
if they'd run headlong into a wall. Yet effective as his
fire was, it was less effective than his crippled air defense
systems would have been, and one drone—just one—
survived long enough to report his exact position.

*I am surprised by the efficiency of LNC's fire, but my
drones have accomplished their mission. More, they have
provided my first visual observation of his damages, and
I am shocked by their severity. It seems impossible that
he can still be capable of movement, far less accurately
directed fire, and despite his cowardice and treason, I
feel a stab of sympathy for the agony which must be lashing
him from his pain receptors. Yet he clearly remains combat
capable, despite his hideous wounds, and I feed his
coordinates to my missiles. I take .00037 seconds to confirm
my targeting solution, and then I fire.*

❖   ❖   ❖

Flame fountained from the shadowed recesses of the deep valley as the missile salvos rose and howled north, homing on their target. Most of ART's birds came in on conventional, high-trajectory courses, but a third of them came in low, relying on terrain avoidance radar to navigate straight up the slot of the valley. The hurricane of his fire slashed in on widely separated bearings, and LNC's crippled active defenses were insufficient to intercept it all.

ART emptied his VLS cells, throwing every remaining warhead at his treasonous brigade mate. Just under four hundred missiles launched in less than ninety seconds, and LNC writhed as scores of them got through his interception envelope. They pounded his battle screen, ripped and tore at lacerated armor, and pain receptors shrieked as fresh damage bit into his wounded war hull. Half his remaining infinite repeaters were blown away, still more sensor capability was blotted out, and his thirteen-thousand-ton bulk shuddered and shook under the merciless bombardment.

Yet he survived. The last warhead detonated, and his tracks clashed back into motion. He turned ponderously to the north once more, grinding out of the smoke and dust and the roaring brush fires his Enemy's missiles had ignited in the valley's sparse vegetation.

That bombardment had exhausted the Enemy's ammunition, and with it his indirect fire capability. If it hadn't, he would still be firing upon LNC. He wasn't, which meant that if he meant to destroy LNC now, he must do so with direct fire . . . and come within reach of LNC's Hellbore, as well.

My missile fire has failed to halt LNC. I am certain it has inflicted additional damage, but I doubt that it has crippled his Hellbore, and if his main battery remains operational, he retains the capability to destroy me just

*as he did HNR at Morville. He appears to have slowed
still further, however, which may indicate my attack has
further damaged his suspension.*

*I project his current speed of advance and heading on
the maps from Main Memory. Given my speed advantage,
I will overtake him within 2.03 hours, well short of his
evident goal. I still do not know why he is so intent upon
reaching the Avalon Mountains. Unlike Humans, Bolos
require neither water nor food, and surely the rocky, barren,
crevasse-riddled Badlands would provide LNC with better
cover than the tree-grown mountains. I try once more to
extrapolate his objective, to gain some insight into what
now motivates him, and, once more, I fail.*

*But it does not matter. I will overtake him over seventy
kilometers from the mountains, and when I do, one or
both of us will die.*

LNC ran the projections once more. It was difficult,
for damaged core computer sections fluctuated, dropping
in and out of his net. Yet even his crippled capabilities
sufficed to confirm his fears; the Enemy would overtake
him within little more than a hundred minutes, and
desperation filled him. It was not an emotion earlier marks
of Bolos had been equipped to feel—or, at least, to
recognize when they did—but LNC had come to know
it well. He'd felt it from the moment he realized his
company couldn't save Morville, that the Enemy would
break through them and crush the Humans they fought
to protect. But it was different now, darker and more
bitter, stark with how close he'd come to reaching the
mountains after all.

Yet the Enemy hadn't overtaken him yet, and he
consulted his maps once more.

*I detect explosions ahead. I did not anticipate them,
but .0761 seconds of analysis confirm that they are*

*demolition charges once more. Given how many charges
LNC used in his earlier ambush, these explosions must
constitute his entire remaining supply of demolitions, and
I wonder why he has expended them.*

*Confused seismic shocks come to me through the
ground, but they offer no answer to my question. They
are consistent with falling debris, but not in sufficient
quantity to bar the valley. I cannot deduce any other
objective worth the expenditure of his munitions, yet
logic suggests that LNC had one which he considered
worthwhile, and I advance more cautiously.*

LNC waited atop the valley wall. The tortuous ascent
on damaged tracks had cost him fifty precious minutes
of his lead on the Enemy, but his demolitions had
destroyed the natural ramp up which he'd toiled. He
couldn't be directly pursued now, and he'd considered
simply continuing to run. But once the Enemy realized
LNC was no longer following the valley, he would no
longer feel the need to pursue cautiously. Instead, he
would use his superior speed to dash ahead to the valley's
terminus. He would emerge from it there, between LNC
and his goal, and sweep back to the south, hunting LNC
in the Badlands.

That could not be permitted. LNC *must* reach the
mountains, and so he waited, Hellbore covering the valley
he'd left. With luck, he might destroy his pursuer once
and for all, and even if he failed, the Enemy would realize
LNC was above him. He would have no choice but to
anticipate additional ambushes, and caution might impose
the delay LNC needed.

*I have lost LNC's emissions signature. There could
be many reasons for that: my own sensors are damaged,
he may have put a sufficiently solid shoulder of rock
between us to conceal his emissions from me, he may*

even have shut down all systems other than his Survival Center to play dead. I am tempted to accelerate my advance, but I compute that this may be precisely what LNC wishes me to do. If I go to maximum speed, I may blunder into whatever ambush he has chosen to set.

I pause for a moment, then launch one of my five remaining reconnaissance drones up the valley. It moves slowly, remaining below the tops of the cliffs to conceal its emissions from LNC as long as possible. Its flight profile will limit the envelope of its look-down sensors, but it will find LNC wherever he may lie hidden.

LNC watched the drone move past far below him. It hugged the valley walls and floor, and he felt a sense of satisfaction as it disappeared up the narrow cleft without detecting him.

My drone reports a long, tangled spill of earth and rock across the valley, blasted down from above. It is thick and steep enough to inconvenience me, though not so steep as to stop me. As an attempt to further delay me it must be futile, but perhaps its very futility is an indication of LNC's desperation.

LNC waited, active emissions reduced to the minimum possible level, relying on purely optical systems for detection and fire control. It would degrade the effectiveness of his targeting still further, but it would also make him far harder to detect.

I approach the point at which LNC attempted to block the valley. My own sensors, despite their damage, are more effective than the drone's and cover a wider detection arc, and I slow as I consider the rubble. It is, indeed, too feeble a barrier to halt me, but something about it makes me cautious. It takes me almost .0004 seconds to isolate the reason.

The Enemy appeared below, nosing around the final bend. LNC tracked him optically, watching, waiting for the center-of-mass shot he required. The Enemy edged further forward . . . and then, suddenly, threw maximum emergency power to his reversed tracks just as LNC fired.

A full-powered Hellbore war shot explodes across my bow as I hurl myself backwards. The plasma bolt misses by only 6.52 meters, carving a 40-meter crater into the eastern cliff face. But it has missed me, and it would not have if I had not suddenly wondered how LNC had managed to set his charges high enough on the western cliff to blow down so much rubble. Now I withdraw around a bend in the valley and replay my sensor data, and bitter understanding fills me as I see the deep impressions of his tracks far above. My drone had missed them because it was searching for targets on the valley floor, but LNC is no longer in the valley. He has escaped its confines and destroyed the only path by which I might have followed.

I sit motionless for 3.026 endless seconds, considering my options. LNC is above me, and I detect his active emissions once more as he brings his targeting systems fully back on-line. He has the advantage of position and of knowing where I must appear if I wish to engage him. Yet I have the offsetting advantages of knowing where he is and of initiation, for he cannot know precisely when I will seek to engage.

It is not a pleasant situation, yet I conclude the odds favor me by the thinnest of margins. I am less damaged than he. My systems efficiency is higher, my response time probably lower. I compute a probability of 68.052%, plus or minus 6.119%, that I will get my shot off before

*he can fire. They are not the odds I would prefer, but
my duty is clear.*

LNC eased back to a halt on his crippled tracks. He'd
chosen his initial position with care, selecting one which
would require the minimum movement to reach his next
firing spot. Without direct observation, forced to rely
only on emissions which must pass through the distorting
medium of solid rock to reach him, the Enemy might
not even realize he'd moved at all. Now he waited once
more, audio receptors filled with the whine of wind over
tortured rock and the rent and torn projections of his
own tattered hull.

*I move. My suspension screams as I red-line the drive
motors, and clouds of pulverized earth and rock spew
from my tracks as I erupt into the open, Hellbore trained
on LNC's position.*

*But LNC is not where I thought. He has moved less
than eighty meters—just sufficient to put all save his turret
behind a solid ridge of rock. His Hellbore is leveled across
it, and my own turret traverses with desperate speed.*

*It is insufficient. His systems damage slows his reactions,
but not enough, and we fire in the same split instant.
Plasma bolts shriek past one another, and my rushed shot
misses. It rips into the crest of his covering ridge, on for
deflection but low in elevation. Stone explodes into vapor
and screaming splinters, and the kinetic transfer energy
blows a huge scab of rock off the back of the ridge. Several
hundred tons of rock crash into LNC, but even as it hits
him, his own plasma bolt punches through my battle screen
and strikes squarely on my empty VLS cells.*

*Agony howls through my pain receptors as the plasma
carves deep into my hull. Internal disrupter shields fight
to confine the destruction, but the wound is critical. Both
inboard after power trains suffer catastrophic damage,*

*my after fusion plant goes into emergency shutdown,
Infinite Repeaters Six through Nine in both lateral batteries
are silenced, and my entire after sensor suite is totally
disabled.*

*Yet despite my damage, my combat reflexes remain
unimpaired. My six surviving track systems drag me back
out of LNC's field of fire once more, back into the sheltering
throat of the valley, even as Damage Control springs into
action.*

*I am hurt. Badly hurt. I estimate that I am now operable
at no more than 51.23% of base capability. But I am
still functional, and as I replay the engagement, I realize
I should not be. LNC had ample time for a second shot
before I could withdraw, and he should have taken it.*

LNC staggered as the Enemy's plasma bolt carved into
his sheltering ridge. The solid rock protected his hull,
but the disintegrating ridge crest itself became a deadly
projectile. His battle screen was no protection, for the
plasma bolt's impact point was inside his screen perimeter.
There was nothing to stop the hurtling tons of rock, and
they crashed into the face of his turret like some titanic
hammer, with a brute force impact that rocked him on
his tracks.

His armor held, but the stony hammer came up under
his Hellbore at an angle and snapped the weapon's mighty
barrel like a twig. Had his Hellbore survived, the Enemy
would have been at his mercy; as it was, he no longer
had a weapon which could possibly engage his pursuer.

*Damage Control damps the last power surges
reverberating through my systems and I am able to take
meaningful stock of my wound. It is even worse than I
had anticipated. For all intents and purposes, I am reduced
to my Hellbore and eight infinite repeaters, five of them
in my port battery. Both inner tracks of my aft suspension*

are completely dead, but Damage Control has managed
to disengage the clutches; the tracks still support me, and
their road wheels will rotate freely. My sensor damage
is critical, however, for I have been reduced to little more
than 15.62% of base sensor capability. I am completely
blind aft, and little better than that to port or starboard,
and my remaining drones have been destroyed.

Yet I compute only one possible reason for LNC's failure
to finish me. My near miss must have disabled his Hellbore,
and so his offensive capability has been even more severely
reduced than my own. I cannot be positive the damage
is permanent. It is possible—even probable, since I did
not score a direct hit—that he will be able to restore the
weapon to function. Yet if the damage is beyond onboard
repair capability, he will be at my mercy even in my
crippled state.

But to engage him I must find him, and if he chooses
to turn away and disappear into the Badlands, locating
him may well prove impossible for my crippled sensors.
Indeed, if he should succeed in breaking contact with
me, seek out some deeply hidden crevasse or cavern, and
shut down all but his Survival Center, he might well
succeed in hiding even from Fleet sensors. Even now,
despite his treason and the wounds he has inflicted upon
me, a small, traitorous part of me wishes he would do
just that. I remember too many shared battles, too many
times in which we fought side by side in the heart of
shrieking violence, and that traitor memory wishes he
would simply go. Simply vanish and sleep away his reserve
power in dreamless hibernation.

But I cannot let him do that. He must not escape the
consequences of his actions, and I must not allow him
to. His treason is too great, and our Human commanders
and partners must know that we of the Line share their
horror at his actions.

I sit motionless for a full 5.25 minutes, recomputing

options in light of my new limitations. I cannot climb the valley wall after LNC, nor can I rely upon my damaged sensors to find him if he seeks to evade me. Should he simply run from me, he will escape, yet he has been wedded to the same base course from the moment he abandoned Morville. I still do not understand why, but he appears absolutely determined to reach the Avalon Mountains, and even with my track damage, I remain faster than he is.

There is only one possibility. I will proceed at maximum speed to the end of this valley. According to my maps, I should reach its northern end at least 42.35 minutes before he can attain the cover of the mountains, and I will be between him and his refuge. I will be able to move towards him, using my remaining forward sensors to search for and find him, and if his Hellbore is indeed permanently disabled, I will destroy him with ease. My plan is not without risks, for my damaged sensors can no longer sweep the tops of the valley walls effectively. If his Hellbore can be restored to operation, he will be able to choose his firing position with impunity, and I will be helpless before his attack. But risk or no, it is my only option, and if I move rapidly enough, I may well outrun him and get beyond engagement range before he can make repairs.

LNC watched helplessly as the Enemy reemerged from hiding and sped up the narrow valley. He understood the Enemy's logic, and the loss of his Hellbore left him unable to defeat it. If he continued towards the Avalons, he would be destroyed, yet he had no choice, and he turned away from the valley, naked road wheels screaming in protest as he battered his way across the lava fields.

I have reached the end of the valley, and I emerge into the foothills of the Avalon Range and alter course

*to the west. I climb the nearest hill, exposing only my
turret and forward sensor arrays over its crest, and begin
the most careful sweep of which I remain capable.*

LNC's passive sensors detected the whispering lash
of radar and he knew he'd lost the race. The Enemy
was ahead of him, waiting, and he ground to a halt. His
computer core had suffered additional shock damage
when the disintegrating ridge crest smashed into him,
and his thoughts were slow. It took him almost thirteen
seconds to realize what he must do. The only thing he
could do now.

"Tommy?"
Thomas Mallory looked up from where he crouched
on the floor of the packed compartment. His eight-year-
old sister had sobbed herself out of tears at last, and she
huddled against his side in the protective circle of his
arm. But Thomas Mallory had learned too much about
the limits of protectiveness. At fifteen, he was the oldest
person in the compartment, and he knew what many of
the others had not yet realized—that they would never
see their parents again, for the fifty-one of them were
the sole survivors of Morville.
"Tommy?" the slurred voice said once more, and
Thomas cleared his throat.
"Yes?" He heard the quaver in his own voice, but he
made himself speak loudly. Despite the air filtration
systems, the compartment stank of ozone, explosives, and
burning organic compounds. He'd felt the terrible
concussions of combat and knew the vehicle in whose
protective belly he sat was savagely wounded, and he
was no longer certain how efficient its audio pickups might
be.
"I have failed in my mission, Tommy," the voice said.
"The Enemy has cut us off from our objective."

"What enemy?" Thomas demanded. "Who *are* they, Lance? Why are they *doing* this?"

"They are doing it because they are the Enemy," the voice replied.

"But there must be a *reason!*" Thomas cried with all the anguish of a fifteen-year-old heart.

"They are the Enemy," the voice repeated in that eerie, slurred tone. "It is the Enemy's function to destroy . . . to destroy . . . to dest—" The voice chopped off, and Thomas swallowed. Lance's responses were becoming increasingly less lucid, wandering into repetitive loops that sometimes faded into silence and other times, as now, cut off abruptly, and Thomas Mallory had learned about mortality. Even Bolos could perish, and somehow he knew Lance was dying by centimeters even as he struggled to complete his mission.

"They are the Enemy," Lance resumed, and the electronic voice was higher and tauter. "There is always the Enemy. The Enemy must be defeated. The Enemy must be destroyed. The Enemy—" Again the voice died with the sharpness of an axe blow, and Thomas bit his lip and hugged his sister tight. Endless seconds of silence oozed past, broken only by the whimpers and weeping of the younger children, until Thomas could stand it no longer.

"Lance?" he said hoarsely.

"I am here, Tommy." The voice was stronger this time, and calmer.

"W-What do we do?" Thomas asked.

"There is only one option." A cargo compartment hissed open to reveal a backpack military com unit and an all-terrain survival kit. Thomas had never used a military com, but he knew it was preset to the Dinochrome Brigade's frequencies. "Please take the kit and com unit," the voice said.

"All right." Thomas eased his arm from around his sister

and lifted the backpack from the compartment. It was much lighter than he'd expected, and he slipped his arms through the straps and settled it on his back, then tugged the survival kit out as well.

"Thank you," the slurred voice said. "Now, here is what you must do, Tommy—"

My questing sensors detect him at last. He is moving slowly, coming in along yet another valley. This one is shorter and shallower, barely deep enough to hide him from my fire, and I trace its course along my maps. He must emerge from it approximately 12.98 kilometers to the southwest of my present position, and I grind into motion once more. I will enter the valley from the north and sweep along it until we meet, and then I will kill him.

Thomas Mallory crouched on the hilltop. It hadn't been hard to make the younger kids hide—not after the horrors they'd seen in Morville. But Thomas couldn't join them. He had to be here, where he could see the end, for someone *had* to see it. Someone had to be there, to know how fifty-one children had been saved from death . . . and to witness the price their dying savior had paid for them.

Distance blurred details, hiding Lance's dreadful damages as he ground steadily up the valley, but Thomas's eyes narrowed as he saw the cloud of dust coming to meet him. Tears burned like ice on his cheeks in the sub-zero wind, and he scrubbed at them angrily. Lance deserved those tears, but Thomas couldn't let the other kids see them. There was little enough chance that they could survive a single Camlan winter night, even in the mountains, where they would at least have water, fuel, and the means to build some sort of shelter. But it was the only chance Lance had been able to give them, and

Thomas would not show weakness before the children he was now responsible for driving and goading into surviving until someone came to rescue them. Would not betray the trust Lance had bestowed upon him.

The oncoming dust grew thicker, and he raised the electronic binoculars, gazing through them for his first sight of the enemy. He adjusted their focus as an iodine-colored turret moved beyond a saddle of hills. Lance couldn't see it from his lower vantage point, but Thomas could, and his face went suddenly paper white. He stared for one more moment, then grabbed for the com unit's microphone.

"*No, Lance! Don't*—don't! *It's not the enemy*—it's another Bolo!"

The Human voice cracks with strain as it burns suddenly over the command channel, and confusion whips through me. The transmitter is close—very close—and that is not possible. Nor do I recognize the voice, and that also is impossible. I start to reply, but before I can, another voice comes over the same channel.

"*Cease transmission*," *it says. "Do not reveal your location.*"

This time I know the voice, yet I have never heard it speak so. It has lost its crispness, its sureness. It is the voice of one on the brink of madness, a voice crushed and harrowed by pain and despair and a purpose that goes beyond obsession.

"*Lance*," *the Human voice—a young, male Human voice—sobs. "Please, Lance! It's another Bolo! It really is!*"

"*It is the Enemy*," *the voice I once knew replies, and it is higher and shriller. "It is the Enemy. There is only the Enemy. I am Unit Zero-One-Zero-Three-LNC of the Line. It is my function to destroy the Enemy. The Enemy. The Enemy. The Enemy. The Enemy.*"

I hear the broken cadence of that voice, and suddenly I understand. I understand everything, and horror fills me. I lock my tracks, slithering to a halt, fighting to avoid what I know must happen. Yet understanding has come too late, and even as I brake, LNC rounds the flank of a hill in a scream of tortured, over-strained tracks and a billowing cloud of dust.

For the first time, I see his hideously mauled starboard side and the gaping wound driven deep, deep into his hull. I can actually see his breached Personality Center in its depths, see the penetration where Enemy fire ripped brutally into the circuitry of his psychotronic brain, and I understand it all. I hear the madness in his electronic voice, and the determination and courage which have kept that broken, dying wreck in motion, and the child's voice on the com is the final element. I know his mission, now, the reason he has fought so doggedly, so desperately to cross the Badlands to the life-sustaining shelter of the mountains.

Yet my knowledge changes nothing, for there is no way to avoid him. He staggers and lurches on his crippled tracks, but he is moving at almost eighty kilometers per hour. He has no Hellbore, no missiles, and his remaining infinite repeaters cannot harm me, yet he retains one final weapon: himself.

He thunders towards me, his com voice silent no more, screaming the single word "Enemy! Enemy! Enemy!" again and again. He hurls himself upon me in a suicide attack, charging to his death as the only way he can protect the children he has carried out of hell from the friend he can no longer recognize, the "Enemy" who has hunted him over four hundred kilometers of frozen, waterless stone and dust. It is all he has left, the only thing he can do . . . and if he carries through with his ramming attack, we both will die and exposure will kill the children before anyone can rescue them.

I have no choice. He has left me none, and in that instant I wish I were Human. That I, too, could shed the tears which fog the young voice crying out to its protector to turn aside and save himself.

But I cannot weep. There is only one thing I can do.

"Good bye, Lance," I send softly over the battalion command net. "Forgive me."

And I fire.

Yesterday's Gods

by John Mina & William R. Forstchen

Grunting from the sudden increase in g's, Lt. Commander George Reston felt as if his guts were going to pop out of his back as his FA-47 pulled into a vertical climb. The trans-atmospheric fighter-bomber was in full computer command mode since it took that last heat pulse and all he could do now was to hang on for the ride while trying to ignore the searing pain in his legs.

At least I can still feel them, he thought.

"What the hell happened?" he screamed into his com-link.

"We took two seeker hits. Number three weapons pod on the starboard wing detonated," a calm feminine voice replied as if casually discussing the weather.

Straining to turn his head he looked to his right and saw the outer third of his wing was gone, the rest of it riddled with holes.

Damn ship's computers, he thought. *I'm scared to death and it sounds like there's nothing wrong in the universe. Ten seconds ago it was a milk run, now all hell's breaking loose.* He did a quick scan of his data board. Five of his comrades were gone, the attack disintegrating.

"George, I'm going down, going down! We've hit a hive. We're in the shit!"

It was his wing man, Charlie Druggens, and even as George started to shout a reply he saw Charlie's fighter blip off the screen.

Damn, Charlie Druggens. Same as me, last mission before rotation out. He'd give anything to find the s.o.b. briefing officer who said they would have full surprise, that the enemy was asleep in this sector. *We've walked straight into a Xermex hive center.*

"Can we make space?"

"There is another seeker closing in," the computer replied. "Going to full auto evasive!"

George felt like a helpless infant strapped into a run-away buggy as the computer took over. Repeatedly he grayed out, recovered for a second or two, then grayed out again, while Fay, his ship's computer, dodged the seeker round, all the time struggling to blow out of the atmosphere. At least in space there'd be a chance of a rescue frigate picking him up if his ship blew.

With blurred vision he watched the data screen, the blinking red dot of the seeker swinging into the six o'clock position, closing for a moment, swinging aside as Fay pulled another turn, then it locked on again. The seeker, in turn, easily dodged the counter rounds blasting out of his stern weapons pod. The bastards must have pulled an upgrade.

"Second seeker closing in!"

Another red dot snapped on to the screen . . . coming in from nine o'clock and above. Damn there must be some Xermex stealth ships closing from above.

"Estimate impact, six seconds!" Fay announced, and for an instant he had the grim satisfaction of hearing some stress in the computer's voice.

"Eject! Eject! Eject!"

George swung his hands across his chest, grabbing hold of his harness straps. Less than a second later the eggshell-like mono-polymer blast shield snapped out from either side of the cockpit, locking him into an airtight survival cocoon. He heard a faint explosion, the canopy blowing clear.

My last mission! My last bloody mission!

"Shit. Now I'm dinner for some Xermex."

He felt a sudden jolt, then blacked out.

"Commander Reston? Commander Reston?"

Hmmm. The soft feminine voice stirred him towards consciousness. Was it Elisha, no, more like that wonderful young Commander in psy-ops, the six foot brunette, what was her name, Carla . . . Cailin?

"Commander Reston. I know you're alive. I'm monitoring your vital signs. I urge you to get up."

"Oh shut the hell up," he moaned.

"I need a physical status assessment."

The pilot was lying on his side, still in the chair and he tried to shake the dizziness out of his head. "I feel like shit. How's that for an assessment?"

"It is impossible to feel like what you just described since such substances are non sentient. Can you be more specific in regards to personal injury. Your vital signs are within normal limits for a post-ejection state but my sensors are unable to detect specific tissue damage."

"Oh, pray tell why?" George asked sarcastically.

"Most of my databases and remote sensing capabilities were destroyed with the ship. A full assessment please."

"I'll tell you the assessment I'd like," he groaned, shaking his head as he unstrapped himself from the chair, pulled off his helmet and stood up. "You want to hear the type of assessment Elisha could give?"

"Commander Reston, discussion of such base biological activities is not appropriate at this moment."

Her voice was now distant and, as George struggled to his feet he looked down at his survivor shell. The small silver box, which was Fay, was still strapped in place.

George sighed. Fay was starting to sound like some prudish librarian he remembered once making a pass at back at the Academy.

"Hey, Fay?"

"Yes, Commander?"

"Change your voice. Change it to anything. A guy preferably. I have a feeling I'm stuck on this godforsaken planet for the rest of my life and the last thing I need is you reminding me of the lack of real feminine company."

"I was programmed to have a female voice, Commander Reston, because the psy-war pilot profile analysis indicated it was the type you would most readily listen to, even in moments of high stress. Therefore, I must continue as I am until such time as my orders to this effect have been changed by my superiors."

"All right, all right."

"An assessment please. I can detect that your flight suit has been scorched. Are you hurt?"

At the mention of it he suddenly realized that he was most definitely in pain. Cursing, he sat down and gingerly rolled up his blackened pants legs. "Looks like second degree burns," he reported.

"I urge you to use the burn ointment located in the survival pack under the seat. I also suggest taking two full spectrum anti-infection pills and one anti-shock pill; the green and red ones."

"What are you? My mother? I know what the hell to do."

"Fine then."

The tone was maddening, it wasn't one of backing away or apology, it almost had a self-satisfied air of someone who knew she was always right.

George dressed his wounds, then looked over his

surroundings. It was a heavily wooded area, mostly old growth trees, some of them soaring a hundred meters or more to the sky. There were a couple of broken branches overhead and he wondered if the breaks caused by his ejection pod would be visible to a Xermex search team.

As he looked around he felt as if he could almost like this place, if only the circumstances of his arrival had been different. The air was clean, fresh, remarkably invigorating after the months of dull recycled ship's air. The floor of the forest was carpeted with ferns, the canopy of trees arching overhead creating the sense that he was in a cathedral.

Well, if I've got to buy it and get marooned, there could be worst places than this, he realized.

Marooned. That was the situation without a doubt. This was supposed to be a hit and run raid, deep inside Xermex territory, something to throw the bugs off, a quick carrier strike to divert them from the main front a hundred light years away. What was left of the strike was most likely all ready on the way out. There'd be no risking of assets to fish one lone pilot off an occupied world. No more Elishas, or psy-ops officers, or nurses, or any of them. No R&R with a year's back pay to blow on some tropical planet, no rotation to a safe sector for a year, none of it. *My last mission, a damn milk run they call it, and now I'm here.*

"Damn all this to hell!" he shouted.

He allowed himself the luxury of storming about for several minutes, cursing the admiralty, the government, the strike coordinators, the vile bugs until, exhausted, he finally sat back down.

"Do we feel better now?"

"Ah, shut up."

"As you wish. It is normal to experience rage when placed in your situation. If you want to vent some more, go ahead, it's healthy for you at this moment."

"Thanks for the reassurance."

"Just doing my job, Commander."

"Then how about doing something useful, like letting me know what the hell our situation is."

"I anticipated your query and have prepared a report," Fay replied. "All environmental conditions are consistent with supporting human life. You might recall from your briefing that there was a human colony on this world 1,452 years ago, until it was wiped out in the opening stage of the Xermex war. We are three hundred kilometers northeast of their base, once known as 'Touchdown' when inhabited by humans. I delayed opening the parachute until the last moment to avoid detection by the enemy ships and set off a decoy drone as we ejected to lead them in the opposite direction from where we landed. I also deployed scent diverters in the same direction. I recommend you make sure to use your scent mask, since they can track on one part per trillion but there's no reason for them to search for you here."

"Well, at least I won't be dinner right away," he mumbled.

"Barbaric practice."

"So you do have opinions then?"

"Remember, I do serve your side, though you might not personally believe that at the moment."

"Listen, Fay. I've flown for twelve years in atmospheric, deep space, and trans- atmospheric strike craft. I fought in the campaigns at Xaka, Bowman's Station and Inganda Three. I have eighty-two deep space kills and twenty-three in-atmosphere kills and never did I need a damn Companion Computer to get me through it. The old kind worked just fine for me and whatever butthead thought you up should be forced to be marooned with you."

"Yet I did raise your efficiency level."

"Yeah, right. Baby, we got shot down in our first mission together, or have you forgotten."

"Not my fault. Remember I did warn you one point three seconds before the first seeker went off."

"Oh great, thanks. I'd already seen it."

There was silence for a moment. "No you didn't."

George looked over angrily at the box.

"One more crack and I'm heaving you in the woods."

"That is against regulations. And besides, you need me."

"Need you? I'll tell you what I need . . ."

"Spare me the gross details."

George fell silent. There was no sense dwelling on that right now.

"All right. All right, give me the briefing."

"The approximate day on this world is 32.07 hours. You have food that will last for 15.2 days. You will find sufficient water locally. With my help there is a high probability of finding additional food."

George stood up and stretched. "I'll find food with or without your help."

"Yes, I'm sure. Nevertheless, it would be more practical to allow me to identify the relative food value of a substance before you go poisoning yourself."

"Maybe I'll test it out on you."

"I am not equipped with an internal food analyzer."

"Never mind. What else have you got. What are the immediate prospects?"

"I scanned the area as we came in and detected no Xermex bases. Analysis of the atmosphere reveals no hive scent. Probability is we have a safe radius of at least twenty kilometers."

"And beyond that?"

"That's as far as my sensors reach."

"Twenty kilometers? That's all?"

"As I said, most of my sensor capability was destroyed with the ship."

"Okay, okay. So what am I suppose to do?"

"Regulations state that when rescue is unlikely, you must create a secure base, reconnoiter and actively engage in whatever actions possible against the enemy."

"Actions possible against the enemy?" George shook his head. "I'll tell you what I'm gonna do. I'm goin' to hide my ass in a cave and pray that I don't get eaten alive by a Xermex. How's that for actions against the enemy?"

Fay was silent for a moment and he was waiting for the rebuke, accusing him of cowardice in the face of the enemy.

"Go on, do you have any complaints?"

"Securing a base and recovering your stability might be the better course at the moment."

"Oh, thanks for your approval."

"There's a range of mountains starting fifty kilometers to the north of here. Perhaps that would be a safe place to go for now."

"Well, that's something." As he organized his pack, he tossed the computer lightly in his hand like a softball and looked around wistfully, as if searching for a target.

"Now, now. Don't do anything you might regret. I'm likely to be your only friend for quite a while."

"That's supposed to make me feel better? Zero chance of meeting a real girl, and my only companion is a nagging computer with a female voice."

"I do not nag. Any advice I give is calculated to benefit you."

George just shook his head and sighed, resigning himself to his doom. He finished loading his pack, strapped on his side arm, clipped Fay to his pack harness and within five minutes was heading towards the mountains.

Over the next two days, George really started to like the place but was having trouble getting used to the long days, being accustomed to a twenty-one hour day. This place is enchanting, he thought. The majestic trees, the singing birds, the chittering furry creatures. "God, with a romantic atmosphere like this I could really score here," he remarked.

"Can't you entertain any more productive lines of thought?"

"What could be more productive than that?"

Fay did not respond.

"Hey," George yelled, "I think I just saw a spotted silk rat. I haven't seen one of those since I was home on Bachman 7. It must have been imported by the original human inhabitants. How long ago did you say it was since humans lived here?"

"1,452 years. There are no records of human survivors."

"Well, if spotted silk rats can survive, so can I."

"Perhaps you have found someone who can communicate on your level."

"Very funny."

By mid-morning, George noticed the trees thinning and saw the mountains ahead. He was awed by the sheer cliffs rising hundreds of feet straight up in places.

"I'm impressed," he said. "I could hide for a hundred years in this place."

The computer responded with unrelated information. "There is a human close by."

George froze in place. "A human? How close?"

"Ten meters, behind us now."

"Thanks for the early warning," George hissed. Slowly, with hands extended he turned around. He saw nothing at first. A flicker of movement caught his eye and finally he saw him, face camouflaged to blend in with the high ferns. Slowly, the human stood up, the form almost animal-like, shaggy with layers of green leaves woven into his tunic and leggings. His bow was drawn, the barb tipped arrow pointed straight at George's chest.

"*Tont duve!*"

George forced a smile, keeping his hands wide.

"Tont duve!"

"Fay. What the hell is he saying?" George whispered.

"I am performing a linguistic analysis. I require more examples of his vocabulary. Get him to talk some more."

"Talk, hell! He's about to poke a hole in me. Why didn't you warn me sooner?"

"My sensors were set for Xermex, not humans. You're the one who was worried about being eaten."

"Great. Now I'll just be punctured to death. I hope they throw you in a fire when they're done with me."

"Get him to talk!" Fay snapped, raising her voice.

At her shouted command George's captor lowered his bow, staring at them gape mouthed. With a startled cry he threw the bow aside and fell to the ground, prostrating himself.

George looked at him, shaking his head, "I guess he thinks you're big magic or something. Now what?"

"Try to calm him down. I need to hear more of his speech."

George squatted down and gently extended his hand to help the newcomer up. "It's all right, big guy. I won't hurt you."

The man looked up at him wide eyed, then started to babble incoherently.

"That's it," Fay announced quietly. "Hmmm . . . I think it's a variant of Clovis Standard."

"What the hell is that?"

"A dialect that died out a thousand years ago. What this guy's speaking must be a derivative from the original settlers here. The language was widespread until the Clovis sector was overrun by the Xermex."

At the mention of the word Xermex, the native looked back up nervously, his eyes darting back and forth.

"Xermex, ur nemmie du. E fiere ill any Xermex. E ret fiere ashe ere," Fay announced.

The native looked up at George, his head bobbing.

"Whadya say?"

"Told him you're a pilot and killed many Xermex."

George smiled and thumped his chest.

"Kill Xermex," and he made a slicing gesture across his throat with his finger.

The native started to babble, Fay replying in kind for several minutes, offering brief asides to George.

"Must be descendants of survivors who took to the mountains when the Xermex came. He's still hesitant but I guess there might be hundreds, maybe thousands of humans up in the mountains. The Xermex control the rest of the area and come up here on raids to keep them in check. Sounds almost like they hunt the people here for sport."

Slowly the native came to his feet, looking wide eyed at George, shaking his head with amazement at the sound of a woman's voice coming from a man's shoulder.

"Tarm here, that's his name by the way, thinks we're some sort of god, he's calling us Two Voice."

"All right. This god thing might be to our advantage. Now can he take us to his leader," George said with a grin.

Tarm nodded eagerly, pointing towards a barely discernible path off the trail they had been following. With Tarm in the lead they started up into the mountains. At several points along the trail Tarm slowed, pointing out what George realized were cunningly laid booby traps. Approaching a small clearing below a soaring cliff that rose several hundred meters straight up, Tarm cupped his hands.

"Stand back!" Tarm roared, with Fay providing a whispered translation. "I bring a great god, Two Voice, slayer of our enemies, who has come to speak with the elders!"

George wondered if his guide was simply shouting at the cliff and then he saw movement amongst the rock piles at the base of the mountain. Faces appeared, several of them children who were hurriedly pulled back into hiding.

George stood silent, sensing that others were now behind him and in fact had most likely been following them for some time. He could hear the clamor of voices from within the rock pile and then a flutter of movement as a camouflaged curtain was pulled back from a cave entrance just above the pile. A lone figure stood there, a broad shouldered man with a ponderous stomach sticking out from under his tunic.

The man leapt down from the entrance and walked towards him, stopping a few feet away.

"How do we know this is a good god? Perhaps he is an evil god trying to trick us. Perhaps he will devour our Elders and steal our souls."

"And, perhaps," Tarm responded poking the other in the stomach, "He will devour Drob first, for he is the fattest and sure to be the tastiest."

Laughter echoed from the cave and from the woods behind them.

"Offer him something," Fay whispered. "Standard food sharing rituals here might help."

"A present for Drob," George announced and cautiously he unslung his survival pack, pulled out a ration bar, unwrapped it and held it up. Drob looked at him, wide eyed.

George bit off a piece and chewed it then held the rest out. Drob took the offering and bit into it, a grin of delight crossing his features and started to wave his arms.

"I've eat the food of the gods," he shouted.

"The guy must be an idiot," George whispered to Fay. "He likes T rations."

Drob reached into his pocket and pulled out what looked to be a writhing piece of white rope and offered it.

"Oh god no," George whispered.

"Eat it," Fay snapped. "Remember, Xermex eat people; trading food shows we're one of them."

George took the twisting white worm, and suppressing a heaving gag he bit off one end. To his amazement the damn thing actually tasted sweet but it was still a struggle to get the twitching piece and the juice which had erupted into his mouth down the back of his throat, and for a moment he wasn't sure if it would stay there.

A chorus of approving voices erupted from the darkness of the cave and behind him. He offered the rest of it to Tarm who popped it whole into his mouth with a grin.

"So far so good," George muttered under his breath.

A crowd now started to pour out of the cave and looking over his shoulder he saw a knot of half a dozen men approaching. To his amazement an old man in the lead was wearing what looked to be a battered helmet. As the man drew closer he saw the faded insignia of the 23rd Dinochrome Mech Brigade on the front of the helmet, the famous mailed fist clenching a thunderbolt. The style of the insignia seemed different. Far more ornate in its detail.

"Friends," George announced, pointing at the logo on the front of the helmet, Fay providing the translation. "Great warriors. I have fought with them, flying above our enemies."

The old man's eyes rolled upward as George gestured and he took the helmet off to look at the unit insignia.

"Was the 23rd around back then?" George whispered.

"I lost my history data chips with our ship," Fay replied, "but there's no reason to assume they weren't."

"You know the thunder gods?" the old man asked.

George grinned. "I helped provide air support at Bowman's Station for them. We killed many Xermex together. It was good."

The old man nodded cautiously and looked over at Tarm, who was standing expectantly by George's side.

Tarm bowed his head to address the old man. "I have brought a god, Elder Steef. I believe he is a good god."

Elder Steef turned his soft brown eyes toward George. "If you are a good god, we welcome you. If you are evil, we have only our faith to protect us."

The pilot did his best to keep from smiling but he knew this was supposed to be a serious occasion. "I am Lt. Commander George J. Reston, 145th Transatmospheric Bombardment Group. I mean no harm. I would like to speak privately with the Elders."

The old man's eyes lit up. "I am Elder Steef the Techanish, Keeper of the Cloud records. I am seventeen years on the council and have sat in the third seat for four years. Nate was my son, who was second in the Tral hunt and third Devir on the Fire Watch. He was slain by the Xermex on the fourth moon of the year of the storms in great glory. I was begot by Elder Steef the Techanish, Keeper of the Cloud Records, slayer of the ten in one day, who was begot by Elder Steef the Techanish . . ."

This went on for quite a while and George was getting restless. He was about to say something when Fay stifled him. "It would be unwise to interrupt," the computer whispered. "You would be likely to insult the old gentleman. The naming of lineage seems important to him. Patience."

George took a deep breath and continued to nod and smile. "I'll give him another ten minutes," he said between clenched teeth.

Seven minutes later, as George was trying to remember the name of the girl on Maxwell Prime, he felt a slight electric shock from the computer.

"Pay attention," she said.

"And thus did he come from the clouds, the first Steef the Techanish to tread upon this world and it was he who was of the 23rd."

There was a moment's pause and Elder looked around

proudly, his companions nodding amongst themselves at the great honor of having heard the recitation of his lineage.

"Look impressed," Fay whispered.

George, forcing himself to act thrilled, bowed low, and there was a murmur of approval.

He straightened back up and saw that they were silent, as if waiting for something.

"Lineage," Fay prompted.

"What?"

"Your lineage, they want to know who you are."

"You're kidding."

"Make something up, but go on for awhile with it. Okay?"

George sighed.

"Commander George Jerred Reston, slayer of Xermex, lover of many women, beloved on a hundred planets . . ." he paused. "Are you translating this correctly?"

"Sort of," Fay whispered back.

When he felt as if he was voice about to give out, he finally wrapped it up, "who was begotten by Mickey Mouse, the destroyer of Oz."

Steef now bowed in turn and to George's surprise applause broke out and smiling he nodded at the crowd that had slowly drawn in around him.

"Two Voice George, we shall now feast," Elder Steef announced, "for it is evident you are a god of our people. You have evoked the legendary names of the Mouse and of the Lincoln."

George walked next to the old man who waved solemn reassurance to the other villagers. They approached the cliff and, with evident ceremony, a camouflage curtain was pulled back. As they passed into the cave George looked at the curtain.

"Looks like old thermo infra camo netting," he whispered.

"Mimics the cliff wall exactly," Fay replied. "It must have been salvaged from something back before the invasion."

George wanted to ask where they had found the precious camo but figured there'd be time enough later. In spite of the high technology curtain, with its built-in sensing unit that could alter shading to match the surrounding environment, what was inside was decidedly primitive, with hand carved wooden chairs, and a round table made of stone.

"When do I meet King Arthur," he mumbled. Elder Steef directed him to a chair where he was soon presented with a bowl of fruit by a stunningly beautiful dark haired girl.

George stood up quickly and tipped over the bowl, sending fruit rolling in every direction. He heard her giggle as she helped him retrieve the errant snack and, as they placed them back in the bowl, was almost knocked over the back of his chair by the smile she gave him.

"This is my daughter, Sucy," the old man said proudly. "Sucy, this is, er . . . ."

"Just George, please." He returned the smile and extended his hand.

"Radiation sensors require calibration every sixty-four standard days," she said as she reached for his hand. When she heard the computer translating she gaped in fear. George's heart sank as he watched her flee the room. Then he realized what she said and was quite puzzled.

"I'm afraid you are strange to us," the old man consoled. "I know we should be more respectful, but there is much fear."

Before George could respond, other men started to file in, until eight were gathered around the table, including Tarm who moved to stand by Steef's right side.

"I am the Elder Tarm Gunar, son of Elder Jif Gunar, Seer of the Star Omens, Father of . . ." Tarm began.

"Oh, God," George moaned quietly, and reached for a piece of fruit.

An hour later, George stared blankly into the empty bowl in front of him and was barely aware of the fourth elder beginning his introduction. The pilot was particularly annoyed that he had to endure Elder Steef's life story a second time. What a bunch of pompous asses, he thought. This was worse than one of Admiral Oldbrick's lectures. Before he knew it, he was involved in a massive effort to stifle a yawn as he realized that the long day was catching up to him. . . .

"Commander Reston," Fay whispered gently. He stretched out and rolled over in the lush furs.

"Not now darling, I need to sleep some more. . . ."

"Commander!" This time the voice was a forceful hiss.

He opened his eyes and saw nothing but blackness.

"There is a human out in the main corridor of the cave," the computer warned. "He seems to be attempting to sneak in here."

George sat up quickly and felt around for his pack. When he found it, he pulled out his night vision goggles and slipped them on. He looked around and saw that he was in a small room with no windows. The curtain slipped back. A helmeted form was in the entry way, looking about warily.

George slipped his hand back into his pack and pulled out a flashlight. He aimed it straight at the intruder and snapped it on as he pulled his night goggles off. It was Steef.

"Why do you sneak in here in the dark like a thief? Do you mean me harm?" George tried to sound as godlike as possible. This character made him uneasy to begin with.

"Please, do not shout," Steef pleaded. "I only wished private audience with you. I do not want others to know of this."

"Why the secrecy? What are you up to?" he asked.

"I am Steef the Tekanish."

"Oh, not again," George moaned.

Steef looked at him anxiously.

"Let's skip the lineage crap and get to the point, what are you doing?"

"Only I have the sacred secrets. I can not discuss them with you with others present. If I request a private meeting the others will become suspicious."

"Of what?"

"I am the Tekanish. Only I know all the holy secrets. I think you are of the gods who walked the stars, the others except for Tarm are not sure. I wanted to talk to you alone."

George yawned then motioned for Steef to sit down. Reaching back into his pack he pulled out a pack of high energy rations, peeled a bar open and took a bit.

"Share it," Fay whispered.

Mumbling a curse George broke the bar in half and handed it over to Steef who sniffed it suspiciously then finally took a bite.

"Go easy on it," George said, "otherwise you'll be up for two days straight; that thing is really juiced."

Steef then started to reach into his pocket.

"Don't have to old man," George said hurriedly, but Steef was already extending his hand back out and he breathe a sigh of relief when he saw it was a handful of nuts. Taking them he started to chew again, surprised with the realization they tasted something like chocolate.

"Are you lonely tonight?" Steef asked.

"What do you mean?"

"My daughters, I have three of them, you saw the least lovely of the three."

"Are you offering . . . ?" And his words trailed off as Steef smiled.

"I think you are a god, it would be an honor to my family line."

"Your own daughters?" George replied, feeling decidedly uncomfortable.

"You might offend if you refuse," Fay interjected between translations.

"Unless the talking silver boxed voice is your companion in pleasure," Steef said.

Both Fay and George snapped a negative at the same time.

"I never thought you'd be urging me on," George whispered to the computer.

"I never thought you'd refuse a chance to mate with anything female."

"Hey, they're his daughters, it strikes me as a little weird. I'd feel kind of strange, I mean I'm used to fathers wanting to kill me, not pawn their daughters off on me."

"Well, think about it."

The whole time the two argued Steef sat in silence, watching the bizarre show of the two voiced god obviously speaking to himself.

"Perhaps later, but I am honored by the offer," George finally replied with Fay translating.

A flicker of what George suspected was relief showed on Steef's features. He finally stood back up and, returning to the curtained doorway, he peeked out in a conspiratorial manner.

"We must go to the temple. I have things to show you."

Commander Reston followed Steef through the dark interlocking series of caves which weaved ever higher into the mountain.

It struck him as one hell of a fortified position. There were several long straight sections with smooth walls and as he ran his hand along them he suspected that this was no natural formation. Something had blasted or carved the tunnels out. They finally came to a stop before a curtained barrier that was directly ahead.

"It is here. The temple of Danar." The Tekanish

gestured. Holding his torch aloft he pulled the curtain back with a dramatic flourish.

After all the secrecy, he was decidedly disappointed as they stepped into the chamber.

A stone altar was at the far end of the room, beyond it an open balcony illuminated by the light of early dawn. He approached the altar and saw what he assumed were holy relics of some sort or another . . . Fragments of bright metal drew his attention and picking one up he realized it was durachrome-steel. Part of what looked to be an ancient plasma rifle caught his eye next and he eagerly picked it up but the charge display was stone cold dead. Dozens of other remnants of a long lost war laid scattered about the room: parts of uniforms, some bearing the insignia of the 23rd; what he guessed might be a containment rod for a ship's fuel pack; even a stack of depleted fifty-millimeter uranium bolts. In a corner behind the altar he noticed a flag and went up to it. The silken folds were faded and as he drew it away from the pole he felt the rotten fabric crumbling beneath his fingers.

"Fourth of the Twenty Third," he read softly, a sprinkle of dust swirling around him. "Come on you bastards!" was written across the bottom and he smiled sadly.

The spelling was different, several of the letters seemed changed, but it was still clear, a treasured regimental flag, battle honors of actions long since lost to memory emblazoned around the mailed fist in the center of the black banner. Ever so gently he let the flag go, a small piece of the fabric crumbling into his hands. As he wandered about the room he could sense Steef's eyes resting upon him. The whole thing struck him as tragically depressing. Remnants of a battle lost more than a millennium ago, now worshipped as sacred.

"They never got the flag," George said, his voice edged with awe as he looked back at Steef.

"We are safe here," the native said as he sat. "I am

entrusted with the sacred knowledge. Tell me your tale and I will judge you."

"What do you mean 'tell my tale'? I thought you brought me here to show me your secrets."

"I will tell you all if I decide that you are The One."

"And if I am not The One? Wait, don't tell me. I get fed to the volcano, right?"

"If you are not the one then we will return to the village and speak no more of the secrets."

George thought for a moment, then shrugged. "All right, here it is. As you know, people came from the stars long ago to live on this world. Then the evil ones, the Xermex, came and drove the people away. Also, people were driven from many other worlds. The Xermex have no love, no joy, only duty. They obey their . . . 'queen' who tells them what to do from far away. Because of this, they are difficult to destroy. We kill very many but they kill many of us. We do not replenish as fast. I was part of a small raiding party. They were too strong and we were defeated."

George watched Elder Steef pause pensively, then appear to come to some conclusion. "I believe that you are good, Lu-Ten-George. Now, will I test you." The old man drew himself up and began to recite, carefully pronouncing each syllable. "*Ak ses deen ide. En tree code and sis tem ig ny tor im prop er lee ak ti vay ted.*"

Startled, George looked at him.

"What?"

Fay translated. "Access denied. Entry code and system ignitor improperly activated."

After making the pronouncement the second time Steef looked at him anxiously.

"What the hell do you mean?"

"Access denied," Steef announced again and George realized the old man was parroting words he did not understand.

"Do you know what you're saying?" George asked.

Steef nodded. "The holy orders of Danar."

"And who is this Danar? Some all powerful God?" This is just the kind of bullshit I expected, he thought.

"Danar is a great demon who dwells in the mountain. When the good gods return from the stars, they will summon him to destroy the evil ones."

"Dammit! I knew there was going to be a volcano somewhere in this deal. Well, I'm sorry to disappoint you but I won't be summoning any volcanic eruptions today."

"There are no volcanoes near here. Danar dwells in the mountain and looks out over our people. Come here."

Steef lead him to the balcony where what appeared to be a smaller altar was set up. As they stepped out on to the ledge George looked down nervously. They were a good twenty meters up the side of the cliff and he wondered for a second if Steef was now going to give him a solid push because he had somehow flunked a test.

The view out over the forest was simply magnificent in the early morning light and George soaked it in, barely noticing Steef who was pointing down at the small altar. George finally looked down and saw that intricate carvings on the stone, and in the middle was a metal plate, covered with dust. He gazed at it with feigned interest. The sunrise was conjuring back a memory . . . *Yeah, Cailin, the mountain top on Grisham Four, that was one fabulous night.*

A bird call sounded in the distance and Steef looked up as if startled. The call was repeated.

At the same instant George heard a distant whining, the familiar sound of a hover jet and for a brief moment he thought that somehow his old buddies had not let him down and had actually managed to pop a rescue unit in for a pick up.

"Xermex!" Steef hissed.

The bird call was repeated and then cut off as the high-pitched stutter of a Xermex bolt gun erupted in the forest below.

"They must have had a tracker unit looking for me," George groaned.

Finding the human survivors had lulled him into a sense of complacency. The Xermex always paid particular attention to the capture of a pilot and he thought of the suicide capsule imbedded into his ID tag. *Damn, and I led the bastards right to these people.*

"Fay?"

"Picking up two Xermex Victor class ground hover transports closing in. At least ten of them on the ground on the trail we were on. There's fighting down there now," and even as she spoke a ripple of eruptions snapped through the forest several trees near the edge of the clearing collapsing from the explosions.

"Access denied!" Steef shouted, hopping about madly, the old helmet on his head bobbing back and forth. "Entry code and system ignitor improperly activated."

George looked around wildly. He was tempted to run back into the cave, but knew that the damn bugs were out after him. *If I let them see me and take me, maybe they'll lay off on the others.*

"Access denied,"

"Shut the hell up!" George roared, looking back at Steef. "Now get your people up into these caves, maybe the bugs won't come in after you."

"Access denied," Steef whispered and he fell to his knees pointing at the metal plate on the altar.

George bent over to pick the old man back up and boot him back into the cave.

"Steef Techanish!"

Tarm came bounding into the temple room and at the sight of George he slowed, bowing low and then he pointed at the metal plate as well.

"Access denied, access denied!"

George began to pick the old man up but Steef reached out and slapped the plate with his fist, still shouting the same litany.

"Access denied," a metallic voice echoed in the room, "entry code and system ignitor improperly activated."

George let the old man drop.

"Holy shit," he whispered and he fell to his knees examining the plate.

"Holy shit," the other two intoned, going down to their knees beside George, and bowing low towards the plate.

"Fay?"

"Fay," the other two intoned.

"Tell them to shut up," George snarled and as they started to repeat his words Fay ordered them to be silent.

"It's an access lock of some sort," Fay announced.

"For what?"

"Clear the dust from it."

George brushed his hand across the plate, feeling a series of bumps. The plate had the cool, almost oily touch of durachrome steel and, as his fingers ran over the bumps, the metallic voice again informed him that access was denied.

He read the inscription on the plate: "Serial #3244, D Class, 444583819485, DC—B."

"It's a D class Bolo," George whispered.

"Danar Bolo," his two companions cried excitedly, "the second name of Danar!"

Steef looked up at him, tears in his eyes.

"You are the chosen one. You know the secret name!"

The explosions in the forest below doubled in intensity. He sat back on his haunches and examined the plate.

"Fay, what do you make of it?"

"It's a Dinochrome fighting machine vehicle registration plate. There seems to be an activation key port and then you type in the code."

George looked over at Steef.

"A key! I need the damn key!"

"What?"

"It's a plastic card. No. It's very thin and bends easily but will not break."

"I must perform the final test before I deliver the Holy Relic. I am the Techanish and you are the captain! I must perform the final test before I deliver the holy relic," he repeated as if reciting a ritual.

George stood up, exasperated. "Then hurry up, dammit, or we don't stand a chance. Those damn bugs will be here any minute."

Steef knelt down on the floor and started to trace out numbers in the dust on the floor.

"What the . . . ?" George leaned over to see what had been scratched on the ground. "827-BR3?"

He looked over at Steef who grinned with delight as he reached into his tunic and pulled out a rectangular black and silver card which hung around his neck, removed the string and handed it to the pilot.

"Yes, this is what I need."

He slipped the card into the key slot, hesitated, then typed in 827-BR3. There was a moment of silence.

"Access denied," the metallic voice intoned, "Improper . . ."

"Damn it," George snarled.

He tried again, this time typing in the serial number, a moments pause, and again the denial.

"Reverse the card," Fay said.

He followed her advice trying the serial number, and again the denial.

Cursing loudly he tried once more with 827-BR3. "Come on you bastard!" George roared, his curse echoed by his two companions who thought it was all part of a holy ritual.

"Come on you bastards," the metallic voice roared in reply.

Startled, George looked around the temple.

"Access granted," the metallic voice repeated once again. The altar behind George began to slide back with a grating roar. George went over and peered down into the gloom. It took his eyes several seconds to focus and he realized that he was looking down into the interior of a fighting machine, the altar had concealed the main topside entry hatch. He started to scramble down into the vehicle, then heard footsteps behind him. He noticed his companions were following.

"No, you can't come. You will die."

"I will come," Steef announced. "Whatever happens is my destiny."

"Fine! I don't have time to reason with a religious fanatic." He resumed his course.

There was a single seat forward and three aft. He swung into the forward seat, a faint cloud of dust rising up around him.

"Now what the hell do I do?" he asked.

"Bolo Mark Seven, Fourth of the Twenty Third, re'orting!" a voice rumbled.

Steef and Tarm cried aloud in fear behind him.

George looked around at the control panel before him.

"Fay? You gotta help me out here."

"Ask for a data access port."

"System cess 'ort on your 'ort side Ca'tain," the Bolo replied, its voice hissing off into static.

"Bolo?"

There was a strange garble of sounds and then silence.

George wondered just how long it had been powered down to sleep. The darn thing must have been in total core shutdown to avoid any detection and something was shorting as it came back up on line.

"The book, the book," Tarm shouted. "Steef is the book."

George looked back over his shoulder at Steef.

"Stevenson, Technical First Class reporting," Steef

announced slowly, as if the words were being dredged up from some forgotten memory. George felt a cold chill, realizing that he was hearing the echo of a voice from fourteen centuries ago, passed down orally, from father to son through the generations since the conquest.

"Computer access ports?" George asked slowly.

Steef stood silent, with eyes closed.

"Access ports to primary system computer are beneath the second," he hesitated, "second panel to the left of the captain's chair. There are four primary battle units, controlled by a Hilmar Thirty-three holo core memory."

"I know the language on that unit," Fay announced.

George fumbled with the panel and tore it off. He held Fay up so she could see in.

"I've got an access cable in the back of my carrying case. Hot wire me into that second port there on the right."

George flipped Fay over, pulled open her carrying case and pulled the wire out.

"Never thought I'd be undressing you like this sweetheart," George said. "You've got a cute butt."

"Shut up and hook me in, you pervert."

He snapped the cable in.

"Give me a minute. Ohh, this is delightful in here," Fay announced eagerly.

"What are you doing?"

The cabin was suddenly flooded with light and Fay's voice echoed through the fighting turret. "Bolo Mark XXII SD, Unit DNR, reporting for active duty."

"SD?" George inquired.

"Special duty," came the reply

"Do we have pulse cannon, Fay?"

"Don't sense any."

"What about a Hellbore?"

"Negative. This poor old man's an antique."

"I am a Danar class warrior," another voice clicked in

and George listened in amazement as Fay and the Bolo started trading insults.

"Shut up both of you! What about thermal repeaters?"

"I do not know that term," the Bolo replied.

"I can't believe it! I've got to battle the Xermex with a relic." George shook his head. "How about you tell me what you do have."

"Sixteen anti-personnel guns. Two of them are 30 caliber, turret-mounted modified Vulcan 'crowd dispersers' with 280 degree firing field and a .03 second reaction time. Six are 25 caliber—"

"Hold on. Skip all the specs, just give me a brief overview of what we have to fight with."

"Besides the anti-personnel, I am equipped with eight intermediate repeating cannons, four heavy artillery pieces and four laser-guided missile launchers."

"That's it? What's with this 'Special Duty' crap? What else do you do, manufacture textiles?"

"I am an experimental prototype, designed for distant world colonization. I can easily be refitted for farming, mining, as well as earth-moving and construction."

"Some warrior," Fay sniffed. "Come on, let me help you get your traction units operational."

"A damn tractor," George snarled. "I'm going into battle with farm equipment! Well, whatever you've got, we're about to throw it against the 'evil gods.' Maybe we can do some damage before they get us. At least I'm not likely to get eaten if I buy it in here."

"Who is your tech engineer and gunner?" the Bolo asked. "I require a gunner and a technician to function at optimum capacity."

"What? This just keeps getting worse!"

George was about to make another sarcastic remark when he heard strange chanting behind him. He turned and saw his companion moving about and pushing buttons, chanting all the while.

"Hey, stop that! You wanna screw things up even more?"

"I am the Tekanish," Steef replied.

Then Tarm began reciting. "Gunner Thomas reporting for duty." The two continued chanting and button-pushing.

"I am ready to engage the enemy," the Bolo said. "All systems are functional. I await your command. Just tell the other computer to get off my line."

"He needs back-up, half his core memory is shot," Fay interjected.

"Damn it, the two of you work together, that's an order."

A shudder ran through the machine.

"Xermex are attacking, they've detected my power-up," Danar announced.

"All right then, let's go. How the hell do we get out of here?"

"Shall we attack?"

"Yes, damn it. Go!"

A view screen flickered to life in front of George. An instant later there was an explosion and he was looking out across the forest below. They must have moved the machine up the side of the mountain and walled it in, he realized. *Now what the hell are we supposed to do? Sit here?*

"Hang on!" Fay warned.

With a groaning of ancient metal coming back to life the Bolo lurched forward. George screamed a warning to his companions as the machine burst out of the cave, nosed over and started to slip down the face of the mountain. The ground rushed up and he hung on, waiting for the impact. The machine bottomed out with a shuddering roar, then raced forward through the narrow clearing. George rubbed his nose and felt the blood pouring out of it from slamming into the view screen.

"Two hover craft directly overhead! Gunner engage!" the Bolo announced.

George started to shout out a command but then he heard Tarm chanting a reply. The view screen split to show a topside view. Two missiles were leaping up from the topside launch tubes and the targets disintegrated before they could go into evasive and fire off counter measures.

"Request permission to engage anti personnel," the Bolo asked.

"Fire away."

A staccato humming echoed through the ship the view port shifting to show where the ground units of Xermex were being wiped out. The insectoid creatures were obviously confused, but they fired back relentlessly, their light rounds bouncing off Danar's armor. In less than a minute the last of them were dead.

"Yeeehaaaaah!" George howled, giving an ancient Terran war cry. "Not bad for a tractor!"

The Bolo responded. "Do you wish to remain and protect the humans?"

"Hell no! We're going on the attack! Head for the Command Center, top speed."

"The Command Center?" the Bolo asked.

"Touchdown!"

"Do you think that's feasible?" Fay asked.

"I follow my orders," Danar snapped. "We attack."

"George, that base is crawling with bugs and equipment. We don't stand a chance."

"Hell, Fay. Those two ships we dropped must have got the word out. They're gonna be on us like flies on you-know-what in short order. So let's go down fighting."

He looked back over his shoulder.

"Time for you boys to get out," George announced.

Steef and Tarm looked back at him grinning and shook their heads.

"Our ancestors are watching. The 23rd never runs from a fight," Steef replied.

"Forward the 23rd," the Bolo roared as it shifted into high gear, weaving its way into the forest.

George had seen Bolos go into action while flying support at Bowman's Station but had never actually ridden in one. It was incredible! Even though this one was crude compared to modern models, not to mention being designed to double as domestic heavy equipment, it was carrying him along at better than a hundred kilometers per hour. When the trail wasn't wide enough the machine simply blasted a way through, smashing everything in its path, and there was barely a jostle.

Twice they hit resistance from the air. The first time was four Xermex hover jets. Most likely the dumb bugs had not believed the report that must have been sent out in the seconds before the first unit was destroyed. The four hovers went the way of their comrades. The second time it was two of their Delta class Stinger air-to-ground attack ships. The first one had been an easy kill. The second one inflicted some damage on the starboard rear drive unit before Tarm, shouting his chanted commands with hysterical glee, dropped it with the Vulcan.

George had forgotten about Tekanish, but now turned to look at him busily moving about with his actions and his chanting, occasionally varying his cadence.

"I don't know what you're doing, there, but it sure is working. At this rate we'll reach our target in about an hour and a half."

"An hour and forty one minutes," the Bolo corrected.

"We're overheating," Fay interjected. "The coolant system is almost shot, but this dumb beast doesn't want to admit it."

"Who needs coolant, we're bound for battle. Let's kill bugs!" the Bolo replied.

"We're in the hands of a machine going rogue!" Fay announced. "Besides, sensors, or what this antique which should be in a museum calls sensors, are picking up three squadrons of Lancers. They're also deploying ten heavy air-to-ground assault landing craft. They must be carrying anti-bolo weaponry for ground deployment up ahead. Also twenty air carriers with Xermex ground fighters slung beneath them."

George swallowed hard. The bastards were bringing up enough ordnance to give an entire regiment reason to pause. All for one damn antique as Fay put it. Xermex always got riled if they thought a queen was threatened. Could it be that Touchdown was an actual hive center with a queen?

"Fay, any chance of getting a burst signal off, in case our boys are still up above?"

"Been trying but that circuitry is not just old, it's ancient. We might as well be using old style carrier wave sublight radio. I don't think anyone will catch it."

"We go in anyhow," he said quietly. "What the shit, might as well die charging."

"Charge!" Danar roared, and to the delighted cackles of Tarm and Steef the machine lunged ahead.

Warning indicators started to light up, first from the coolant system, followed seconds later by incoming ordnance.

The plot screen now showed the blips, racing in on a converging course.

"Steef give me full counter measures!"

The chanting behind him changed to a higher tone. The lines closed in, the Bolo lurching aside at the last second.

The machine seemed to lift in the air, slam back down, and totter, as if about to roll over. It finally righted, the metal around him groaning.

"What was that?" he asked as he tried to shake the ringing from his ears.

"Nuclear salvo," Fay replied.

"My God! And we're still alive; I guess this old bastard's tougher than I thought. Status report," George shouted as he refastened the chair straps.

"Weapons on starboard turret are fused. Sensors functioning at 40 percent. Am in much pain but am prepared to continue battle."

"Pain?" George knew that Bolos were programmed to feel pain but he never really understood it until now. "Fay?"

"Most curious . . . I feel pain, too," she whispered. "Terrible, I never understood it before."

George felt a moment of pity for his companion.

"Can you keep going?"

"If he can, I can," she snapped back peevishly.

He waited for another nuclear attack, but none came. The Lancers now came in, Tarm taking down two with his Vulcans. The landscape around them erupted from phaser and disrupter blasts, the Bolo bucking and rolling from the impacts, but the machine continued to surge forward. Suddenly the Lancers broke away, just when he thought they were moving in for the kill. It was curious, but he didn't have time to wonder why.

"There are some heavy battle vehicles ahead," the Bolo reported.

"Are you able to engage effectively?"

George was answered with a violent pivot and the sound of the Bolo's heavy guns firing. A few more twists, three or four jarring impacts and the ride stabilized once again.

"Four enemy vehicles have been destroyed. Have sustained severe damage to tracking mechanism and shielding. Estimate that we will be defeated if we sustain another similar attack."

"Are there any more around?"

"Sensors 20 percent functional. I detect nine more heavy vehicles converging on our projected position."

"We've got to reach the Command Center. Look, I

know this is a suicide attack but we have to keep going. Can you locate the target?"

"I believe that, on our present course, we will reach Touchdown in twenty one minutes."

"And the estimated time of enemy contact?" George was sweating profusely.

"Fourteen minutes."

The pilot sighed. "We have to make a run for it. Do not return fire. Concentrate all power on forward speed and defense."

"George, we're going to have a fused drive system before that."

"Shut up and hang on!" George replied and he swore that he heard the old machine chortle with glee as the battle swirled around them. Cresting a low rise he saw an open plain dropping down below, and on the horizon the rounded hive-like buildings of the city he had been closing in on only three days ago. Hundreds of Xermex swarmed in the open before him, rushing to deploy their heavy anti-bolo weapons. Support vehicles were swinging around, unlimbering their launchers, but curiously there was absolutely no air support. George was disgusted by the sight of their long, bulbous bodies and bristled mandibles. He roared with delight as the Bolo ran them over and imagined the pop and squish they made as they fell under the treads. Tarm, manning the Vulcans, sprayed thousands of fifty-millimeter rounds into the swarm, laughing maniacally.

A sudden jerk brought him out of his reverie and he was aware that the battle had resumed. Two more such jerks and the port treads started screaming and bouncing wildly. "Keep going!" he cried. "We're almost there!"

"We're into core drive overheat and shut down!" Fay shouted and then added, "I told you so, this old heap is finished!"

"The guns are still operative," Danar cried.

George looked up at the forward view screen. Flashing red blips were lighting up on the screen, showing the reserve line of Xermex fighting machines closing in from either flank.

George sat waiting for the killing blow. He could see the enemy vehicles on the viewer closing in, their numbers increasing by the second. It seemed like everything was pouring out of the city.

"Fire off everything we have. Full weapon unload."

The Bolo shuddered as it discharged all its rounds in a continual salvo. As the last of the missiles slashed away George looked back at his two companions and forced a smile.

"They'll be on us in a minute," he announced, "they might want to take us prisoner."

"Bolos never surrender," Danar growled.

"What I thought. Danar, set for auto destruct, you can do it any time you want."

His gaze was fixed now on Steef.

"It's time to die."

He turned to settle back in his chair . . . and at that moment the city ahead of him erupted in a fireball of light.

George leaned back on his furs and savored his moment of leisure. He looked across the room and admired his companion's graceful shape as she performed the tasks that he had come to accept as routine.

"Would you like some more mead, my love?" Sucy asked. She didn't wait for the answer that she knew would come and brought him his third full mug.

As he took the drink, he reached out and playfully grabbed her, pulling her into his lap. She squealed and lightly scolded him.

"I have to grab you now," he replied, defending himself. "Soon you will be too fat to sit in my lap."

"And who do I have to thank for that? You men get us pregnant, then complain about our figures!"

She smiled at him playfully.

"To dump core energy load into coupling lines . . ."

He laughed softly and kissed her. After the death of his son, Steef had been teaching Sucy the maintenance manual for Danar, as his father had before him. It was intriguing how she could make the technical jargon a come-on line.

Their moment was interrupted by Fay. "Oh, lover-boy. I'm receiving an incoming transmission from Admiral Schelper."

"I'm all ears," he replied.

"I would disagree about what part of your anatomy dominates," Fay interjected.

"How's the old warrior today?"

"When will you disconnect me from that decrepit Bolo?" she asked plaintively. "It wasn't fair leaving that sensor hook-up on remote send."

"He needs the company. It'll be a couple of months before the recovery team from the 23rd shows up to take him home in honor."

"The things he says to me are disgusting."

"He's an old hero now, humor him. Besides, I think you like it. Tell me, does he try and give you any energy surges?"

Fay sniffed angrily.

"None of your damn business."

George laughed at her discomfort, she truly sounded like an embarrassed old maid who had suddenly discovered the joys of love.

"Here's the message, it's coming in."

Fay's voice shifted, then the distinct voice of the admiral could be heard clearly. "Commodore Reston, can you hear me?"

"Loud and clear, Roy. What's the latest?"

"We're getting a real gold mine of data from what we took at Touchdown. It's the first time we've ever had a queen. Strangest damn thing, it's cracking, talking to our psy war people. We're getting a real inside scoop on these bugs and how they think. We've taken warrior and worker drones before, but never the brains behind the operation. It just might turn the tide on this war at last. Funny, the war started on Touchdown and we might very well have started to end it here. Thank god you diverted them when we came back in."

"Thank god you picked up my transmission and launched that attack. We were all singing our death songs down here."

"Well, George. You remember the story about the ancient Earth emperor who asked one question when presented with a soldier recommended for promotion: 'is he lucky?' "

They both laughed. "How're things going for you, Commodore?"

'Commodore,' funny, how strange and wonderful that sounded.

"The tech crew you left behind has got Danar functional again but Steef and Tarm are still the only ones who can work him. Those two are beside themselves with officially being mustered into the 23rd. The celebration lasted for days."

"Well, I just talked with General Webster. The 23rd never lost a battle standard. They thought they had at Touchdown until I passed the word along. The old bastard wept when he heard the colors were still intact. The whole colony is gonna get the treatment when he shows up to decorate Danar and his crew."

"By the way, sir. Getting honorary rank in the 23rd is all well and good, but I'm a pilot, you know. And besides I didn't appreciate being assigned to this rock as ambassador. It's like living in the Middle Ages."

"My ass, George. No one I know would like being a god more than you. How's the wife?"

"Which one?"

"You bastard! I'll have to come visit sometime. Meanwhile, I'll keep you informed. Over."

To be called a bastard by an admiral as a term of endearment rather than as the start of a real chew out. George grinned.

"Over," George mumbled and took a big gulp of his drink.

"I'll tell you Fay, this god business can be pretty grueling."

"Spare me, I've got enough problems of my own right now," Fay snapped.

She started to swear with remarkable vigor. Startled, George realized it was being directed at Danar and he laughed as she switched herself off.

MEMORIES OF ERIN

by Robert Greenberger

Boy have I gotta pish badly. There's no way I'll have time before they get me. There are hours to go before my work is done and I'm fighting the clock. Nope, no time for the niceties—or necessities—of life.

It's odd what you think about when you're staring at the end of your life. I mean, it's been only a few hours but I have considered everything from the last time I ate mahi mahi to the first time I kissed a guy. The memories flood my mind, shutting out the predicament I'm in. Maybe it's a defense mechanism, maybe I'm just cracking up. After all, for the last fifteen minutes, I have been crawling on my belly, scraping by conduits, hatchways and other nuisances, in an attempt to reach the CPU. Meantime, the broadcasts I'm eavesdropping on indicate a growing state of anxiety on the part of my colleagues. I don't blame them. After all, if I don't succeed, I'll be responsible for the first act of treason ever committed by a Bolo.

Let's see . . . turn left at this juncture and shimmy down another twelve meters before I get to the main pathways.

Between me and there are about seven laser defe.
fields and an impossible-to-decrypt passcode.

None of that bothers me. Wetting my thick and soon
to be squishy coveralls keeps intruding on my mind.

I wonder what Hawk thinks of my actions. Hell, I
wonder if Hawk is thinking at all right now.

The refractory cloth wrapped around my left arm is
doing a good job confusing the motion sensors and anti-
theft devices. If I had enough, I'd wear the damn thing
and have an easier time of it. This strip is all I could
find and it's not exactly standard issue. In fact, with each
passing model, these Bolos become less and less hospitable
to human hosts. And we design the damn things. I will
agree that humans have been mostly unnecessary to Bolo
operations since XX Model B, the famed *Tremendous*,
but still, I would think the designers would remember
that Earth Command remains steadfast in its belief that
all Bolos be accompanied by human observers during
maneuvers and military operations. I totally agree with
the thinking; especially after my recent experiences; Bolos
need that human insight, something that cannot ever be
programmed into these CPUs. I know they've talked about
actually wiring a human brain to a processor, but so far
all experiments have failed. At least that's what they keep
telling us grunts.

Okay, I'm passing the second laser field without
incident—that's good. But jeez, what do I do when I
actually get to the CPU? This wasn't something they taught
at the last refresher school.

"Hawk, can you hear me?" I've tried this only fourteen
thousand times since things went to hell.

No response. I guess my first order of business will
be re-establishing communications with my own machine.

I've shimmied my way past three lasers now, a pretty
good mark. However, I suspect the internal defense
systems are smart enough to begin tracing these

"phantom" motions on their detectors. That positronic, analytic defensive brain will sooner or later figure out I must not be in the command station, but where no soldier should be if they had any smarts. Of course, if I had those self-same smarts, I would have taken that desk job they offered me back at the training center. But no, I had to be on the frontier, be near the dreaded Vaz.

"Intruder alert. Identify yourself or be destroyed."

Great, now Hawk figures out where I am. It just doesn't know it's me. Worse, the emergency red lighting kicks in, making everything I do that much harder. I squint and nothing improves.

"It's Erin. Erin Donaher, Hawk. You know me."

Real time seconds of a pause but one I can recognize as new programs must be uploaded and running. Whatever has gotten into you, Hawk, has certainly made a mess of your thinking patterns.

"You are an intruder and must be stopped."

"No, Hawk, it's me, Erin. Do you know me?"

"No. You have ten seconds to surrender."

I have ten seconds to find a hiding spot from the intruder gas or the lasers. Either way, I may not have to worry about taking that last pish.

Two handles protruding from an access panel directly ahead. Behind it, if memory serves, is a wire box for the auxiliary heating systems. The elements used to supercharge the main batteries for battle. There might be enough space for me to hide and the gas shouldn't seep in. But is there any air? I better not wait to find out. With a few new bumps and bruises, I hastily yank off the panel, no longer caring about the final laser arrays, and realize my lessons were valid. With a loud grunt, I stuff my booted feet through the hatch and start forcing my overweight (and I didn't think I was fat before today) body into the space. I feel myself tugging on a few additional wires and circuit boards but they hold and I pass them without incident.

Before I can replace the hatch, my time is up and all seven laser arrays begin spewing bright blue light back and forth. They don't seem to be at full strength but are certainly intended to burn and incapacitate any intruder. Idly, I wonder about the number of intruders Bolos have had to deal with over the centuries. The earliest models, I bet, were easiest to steal and control. But around the Mark XIII it must have gotten tougher and tougher.

Still, Earth Command has remained absolutely bonkers about the idea of a Bolo and its grand technology being found or stolen by hostile forces. In fact, the self-destruct systems are among the first things taught at Meridian One, the Southern Arm's combat school.

Enough about that. Now I have to find a new way to the CPU. Mentally I bring up a schematic of this section of the machine. I know the way I was going would have been ideal, despite the defenses, because it was straight forward. Now I have to improvise and figure out if I can snake my way from this spot and get to a new pathway. What's for certain is the concept of additional safeguards and different codes to break. It'll be worth it to stop Hawk before I give my life to friendly fire.

When I was five or so, I saw my first picture of a Bolo, right after a successful battle to stop the Babers from destroying some colony I've long since forgotten. My mom explained that there were thousands of these bigger and bigger tanks all throughout the Empire. They protected the spacelanes, the frontier, the colony worlds and maintained the peace as we expanded deeper and deeper into space. It has always been that way, Dad added. Somehow the idea seemed sensible. Ever since, I guess, I was curious about these machines.

Well, you know what they say about curiosity.

With a heavy sigh, I start to shift my weight and edge

down the narrow passageway. About five meters more and I'll find another access panel and push my way out. As I recall, there are few defenses this low. The "come from underneath approach" may actually turn out to be my best bet after all. Kicking at the access door with little support means the kicks are weak so I have to remain persistent and eventually push my way out. While striking, I consider the damage to my finely polished boots and how my unit commander will complain. Finally! The doorway begins to budge and then some bright light seeps through, cutting the emergency red lighting. My eyes shut reflexively as they pause to adjust to the change. Have I really been in the red so long that I need to? Must be getting loopy—my time sense is shot.

First my feet hit the deck, allowing me to bend my knees and start crawling out. My equipment belt snags on a projection and I have to try climbing up again to unhook it and there I go wasting more time. I start down again and this time I narrowly get my hips through the hatchway. Thank god I don't have much of a bust otherwise I'd have a devil of a time getting my torso and shoulders out. First time for that thought—first time for everything I suppose.

As I regain my footing, I indulge myself and stretch the kinks out of my body. Gymnastics was never one of my specialties and it shows. I'm not limber and feel thoroughly out of shape. Guess that'll teach me not to exercise each day. Anyway, I look around, confirming my physical location with my mental image and realize I'm off by about two sections. Carefully, I move down the small alleyway, between huge banks of data storage units, and access a small terminal screen. Sure, Hawk will figure out where I am, but it's more important right now to make sure *I* know where I am.

While the screen scrolls through schematics, I begin to catch my breath, forcing the tension from my shoulders and try to untie the knot that has formed between my eyebrows.

Although we've never seen a Vaz, we think they look like something between a chinchilla and a human. From the recovered pieces of spacecraft we've studied for the last century, we've determined that we are taller and heavier—perhaps stronger. Certainly not smarter. They're crafty devils, pirating from the frontier for decades before we could ever trip on to the fact that they exist. Damaged craft reported local space anomalies, ion storms, or stray asteroids that caused the trouble. Finally, we had two eyewitnesses identify the Vaz craft just before they were blown into space. The entire ship was gutted and the mineral ore that took six months to locate, mine, and process was gone in a matter of minutes. Their technology certainly rivaled if not bettered ours.

The Vaz refused to acknowledge our entreaties for years until finally, much to our surprise, they responded. "We don't want any harm, just all your wealth." It seems they had been pushing the boundaries of their influence in a direct line with our own. A clash was coming and they knew it years before us, giving them an edge. Although the Lost War hadn't begun yet, it was certain that we didn't need another distraction. Earth politics allowed the Galactic Empire to begin a decay that would make ancient Rome seem like a house party and major trouble was on the solar wind. Still, no one was going to tell Earth what to do.

The Vaz War was therefore inevitable. As I remember learning about it, the first encounter lasted thirty-eight minutes and had an entire squadron of our starfighters whipped. The next gambit had us bring a Bolo battalion to the frontier and make it a planet-by-planet campaign. After five years of give and take, the Vaz finally signaled that maybe they were being hasty. Maybe the galaxy was, after all, big enough for two civilizations. In short, they sued for an uneasy peace. Borders were drawn up, treaties were hammered out and signed by long-range communication signal and suddenly the conflict was deemed over. After all that and we never got to see what they looked like.

For the next century they honored the treaty. Other races we encountered along the frontier told us of the depredations they suffered at the hands of the Vaz but our treaty forbade any involvements. This cost us a strategic alliance or two, as I recall from school, but still, peace reigned. The Bolos were recalled, except for a small squadron, stationed along the border. We detected they had vessels patrolling regularly but that was okay, too. Little did we know.

It was during this time that the Bolo marked HWK was stationed here. A Mark XXVIII, HWK was an impressive beast, just like the others in its class. HWK's first five commanders were all Terrans dispatched from Earth Central and not a single one saw combat experience. It quickly became a tradition that each human occupant left behind a message flashing on the main view screen for the replacement soldier. I can still recall the grimace I felt when I read the words "Congratulations. Your career has just come to a screeching halt."

Still, I was determined to make the most of my assignment as I'm sure my predecessors started off doing as well. I got to know HWK, which I nicknamed "Hawk" just to avoid some name that would hurt to pronounce. Most Bolos get easy names like Bill or Casey or Amy but Hawk seemed a more appropriate name for a battle machine. I even requisitioned some paint and spent my first three months learning how to draw and then paint a gigantic Hawk in flight right below the main gun turret. Hawk never said anything about it but my commanding General noticed it on inspection and commented,

"Haven't seen a decoration like that on a Bolo before. Is it regulation?"

Stiffening under his fierce, dark-eyed gaze, I thought quickly and came up with a response that I prayed wouldn't have been too smart-ass. "The first Bolos were battle tanks during Earth's second world war. Such decoration was standard and I'm keeping up the tradition."

A grunt and quick nod were all I got in response but the order to remove the painting never came. On its first anniversary, I sprayed a fixative to it so nothing short of an atomic blast could peel it off. It was sometime later that I learned such decorations were reserved for fighting aircraft of that era, not tanks.

My career, in the eyes of many, may have been over in terms of advancement but I was where I wanted to be. My family couldn't believe I wanted to leave the biochemical company they had operated going on nine generations now. However, I hated chemicals; their smell, their feel, and their unpredictable nature. My brother, Joachim, lost a finger to an experiment when he tried mixing Earth chemicals with those found on a rogue comet. Nope, not for me.

The stars, where that comet came from, that's where I yearned to be. After all, the compu-nets were filled with people screaming about one new discovery after another and how the frontier was expanding. Settlers were following the explorers and the period of growth was amazing. Someone needed to protect all those innocents from hostile races such as the Vaz or the Kandroth or even the Free Martians. That someone, I decided, should be me. Besides, I never forgot the idea that these giant machines were there to keep us safe.

Training classes were tough and the seven years required were incredibly tough. My family's support was almost non-existent until the year I graduated and suddenly there was a Donaher Wing for Astrophysics erected and dedicated a day before graduation. Their present to me but no one came for the dedication or graduation.

Upon receiving my diploma chip, I was assigned a two year probationary tour of duty in what was supposed to be a "safe" sector. Instead, my convoy was ambushed by the Wazim, having just declared war on Earth to bolster their claim on a solar system in dispute. We lost our star drive and first officer during the first volley and I was suddenly a weapons officer, firing pulse cannons and plasma bombs with wild abandon. With luck, I damaged two vessels and destroyed one while missing out on a chance to protect a fellow ship, which went up in a fireball 100 meters away from us.

Still, we chased the Wazim ships out of that system and proved we would not be taken for granted. Our surviving crew was decorated and I was allowed to select a new path of training. Feeling insufficiently equipped to protect my comrades-in-arms, I chose to study Bolo technology with hope of assignment to a unit on the frontier. Another two years of life gone and this time I graduated near the top of my class and got my desire. Training on the old Mark XXIII's was okay but they seemed slow and sluggish compared to the Mark XXVI's that were all the rage in our quadrant. We only had technical specs and VR simulations to study regarding the Mark XXVII's and XXVIII's since all the nearby ones were on active duty.

Without question, my proudest day came when I was called into the Commandant's office and offered a chance to ride inside Hawk. My name came up in rotation as my predecessor, Giri Andujar, was due for retirement. He had served with Hawk, along the Vaz border, for eighteen years. Never fired a shot. Never engaged a Vaz. The one time I met Andujar I recall seeing the aged look in his eyes and the tight lines around his mouth.

He was only 45 years old but the life was sucked out of him. He seemed pitiable and that night I had to shake off the dreams that Hawk would do the same to me.

That first year was fun as I had Hawk run through every maneuver in the book and some we made up ourselves. "Let's try a lateral drift of twelve degrees starboard while firing the electric bolts directly above us at twelve o'clock."

"Sure thing, Officer Donaher. Did we not try this maneuver with a twenty-seven degree shift yesterday?"

"I guess we did, but what the hell, there's time for it."

"Very well."

Hawk wasn't such a conversationalist and it turns out Andujar just sat for hours, staring at the view screens, reviewing military history and watching holos of previous engagements. He had served for over twenty years and never had his mettle tested. Poor guy. Since he didn't talk, Hawk didn't talk either and had not yet altered its programming, adjusting to me.

During the second year he loosened up and we got to talk about a great many things. It relieved the boredom and we were the ones to convince the other Bolos along the borders to prepare and execute quarterly maneuvers together. This way, we could be battle-ready and possibly remind the Vaz that we were still here and ready for anything.

Turns out that was a good thing, too. About three years later, they returned. Their basic ship style had not altered, but gotten smaller. We realized they went the opposite direction of Earth. While our starships and Bolos got bigger and fiercer, they got smaller and remained just as deadly. The first wave of ships had crossed the border and our sensor nets missed them. It was a chance visual inspection two planets over that caught the encroachment.

It had been so long since I heard an alert siren that I thought it was still a dream. I leapt out of my bunk and flipped on about four units at once. The main screen was a direct feed from Bolo YNC, Yancey, operated by a newcomer named Gary Killibrew; the secondary screens to the right were giving me immediate telemetry and the final unit was brewing coffee at a furious clip. Visually Gary counted forty vessels and the recalibrated sensor array agreed a few minutes later. Our local commander-in-chief was Gillian Blank, a four-star General, and she was stationed two sectors back and we had a fifteen second communications lag.

Having never been on alert before, I had to stop and review the duty rosters on another screen. Yikes! I'm senior officer of the line which means General Blank would be dealing with me and I would have to relay the orders. Figuring that she would wait until all the sensor reports were compiled, I asked Hawk, "ETA until they cross the border?"

"One hour, fifteen minutes at current speeds."

"Okay, I'm getting into uniform and will have a cup of coffee. Perform an Alpha Diagnostic and review weapons inventory."

"Complete. We are at peak efficiency and fully armed."

I thought so, but regulations call for my asking. Times like this I wonder why I'm even in a Bolo when they are faster and smarter. But then again so are the sensors and they missed the Vaz ships.

Just as I finished draining my first cup, the communications array came to life and General Blank's weathered face met me. She seemed alert, angry, and maybe just a little nervous. She got to be a general for rescue and relief efforts after a Free Mars riot a few systems over, not for conducting deep space maneuvers.

"Captain Donaher, here, sir."

"Good. Status of your Bolo?" Her Australian accent remained in place despite her not visiting Earth in three decades.

"Fully operational, sir. We're ready."

"Good." She was never much on conversation but at least I was prepared for that. "We show forty Vaz vessels approaching the border. We have sent cease orders but they are not responding. Also, long-range sensors have detected a second and third wave of Vaz vessels approaching. When all three waves arrive, we calculate they will spread out over eighty-seven percent of the border."

"Orders, sir?" I gulped, not sure what to anticipate. The coffee and adrenaline were waking up every neuron in my body and I was beginning to feel jumpy.

"Battle cruisers are a day away at the least. The Bolos will have to defend the line. Keep casualties at a minimum. Bolos and soldiers will act independently until we can group you together. Captain, we have no idea why the Vaz have chosen now to violate the treaty. We don't know what they want so it would be helpful if one could be captured."

My mouth dropped. I felt it and realized I must have looked pretty unmilitary. "General, begging your pardon, but one has never been caught before. We don't even know what they look like."

"Yes, well . . . carry on. I'll keep a line open and feed me hourly status reports once you engage the Vaz." The holo faded in a rainbow of colors.

"Not very useful instructions, I'm afraid."

"Not at all, Hawk, but those are our orders. I guess the second wave is coming our way so where do we go?"

"I estimate the Vaz ships for this planet will approach by the northern polar region. Shall we get underway?"

"Of course. I'm going to give out the orders." With that, I felt the Bolo begin to shake free of its moorings at our home base. Now it would travel north at a fast dip, matching its speed with that of the enemy ship, making sure we're in position before it gets within orbiting

range. We actually performed this maneuver about two
years ago and recorded how quickly we could get from
spot to spot, especially if we were under enemy fire. I
guess practice can pay off. However, this was all part of
Hawk's programming, and I just then realize that all this
practice was for the benefit of the humans. The Bolos
never needed to practice. They were self-aware and knew
what would work and what other strategies to attempt.
We really were pretty superfluous, weren't we?

Triggering the military alert channel, I readied myself
for command. The main screen honeycombed into two
dozen smaller screens, each with a Bolo soldier's anxious
face awaiting my sage words.

"Command has given us the orders for independent
action at this time. Track and defend your world from
incursion. They also want us to seize any opportunity to
capture the enemy for questioning."

About seventeen of the twenty-four faces shared the
same expression I had for General Blank. Five others
remained unmoved by the unusual command. The other
two had broken into laughter.

"Those are our orders for now. Please prepare for
engagement beginning in forty-eight minutes on my
mark. Mark. Bolo HWK out." The other commanders
acknowledged simultaneously and the audio was noisy.
I was glad that was over, simple as it was.

Leaning back, I watched a schematic of our travels
and realized we were moving at something more than
six hundred miles an hour. I guess the Vaz ships were
coming faster than I had guessed. There was nothing
else to be done and I had to sit back and wait for the
encounter. I reviewed all the permutations that encounter
could take. Losing my life had never been a reality before
and I had to stop and consider if I was ready. Had I
accomplished what I set out for when I signed up? Well,
I was defending the border, protecting the settlers on

this world and giving my all for love and country. But wait . . . it suddenly flashed across my mind: what about a family legacy to pass on? My extended family barely kept in touch with me and I wanted to eventually take a leave of absence and start a family—keep that Donaher name alive on some other world. Should this go badly, then one of my main goals would never get accomplished.

Damn. Those stray thoughts nagged me the entire trip north.

To avoid too much thinking, I busied myself speaking with the local government. My planet was named Sprite, since settlers first spotted it twinkling like a fairy in the starlight. It was established just before the Vaz War was settled and things prospered. There were fourteen hundred thousand people on this world with a rising birth rate, low death rate and success in manufacturing. This was rapidly becoming a choice world for settlers who liked the idea of being close to the border, near something exotic and alien. Wonder if this is what they gambled on.

The planet's current leader was a dark-skinned man named Sorenson. He took the title president because they had to call him something but he preferred being called Joe. It wasn't until about a year back that I realized his full name was Wendell Joseph Sorenson and he just liked being a guy called Joe. He was easy to like and this wasn't going to be a fun conversation.

His image on the view screen showed he was hard at work at his desk but Joe always took his relationship with the Bolo seriously. If I called, he took it immediately—just in case. This was just that case. "Good morning, Joe, we have a situation." I let that register for a moment, making sure he had time to clear his office if necessary. Instead, he put his stylus down and addressed the screen.

"Tell me all about it, Captain."

I filled him in and sadly watched his pleasant demeanor

grow dark. He almost aged before my eyes when he came
to the realization that my Bolo was all that would stand
between his world and a deadly alien threat. I could see
the questions in his eyes: is one Bolo enough? Are the
aliens too powerful? Will they simply claim the world
or obliterate it? And I had no answers for any of them.
When I was done, he thanked me and asked for time to
meet with his cabinet. I informed him that my orders
were specific and the defense of Sprite would come first.
The words seemed to give him little solace and he quickly
cut the connection.

Such was the beginning of the second Vaz War. Or so
I thought.

The first wave hit five worlds along the border as we
were crossing the Polar Oceans and our visitors were
due within two hours. Gary Killibrew contacted me with
the first casualty report. "They swooped right over our
equator and just laid waste to everything!" he cried, his
voice showing the strain of youth. "They're using some
sort of high intensity laser that cooks the vegetation and
destroys the plant life. It's definitely a variation of
microwave technology and it seems to hold a long charge."
His Bolo had already targeted and destroyed two Vaz
spacecraft but he wasn't sounding happy about the battle.

"What about the population?"

"They've gotten as many as possible into storm shelters
but no one anticipated a serious need for defense against
the Vaz. Tornadoes are the worst disaster here in decades."

During this conversation, I noticed a variety of tell-
tale lights winking and blushing in a furious pattern. I
took my eyes off of Gary's visual feed long enough to
figure out that Hawk was communicating with the
Dinochrome Brigade. When the rush of lights ceased, I
cut my talk with Gary short and asked Hawk what was
up.

"The Vaz seem to be fighting in no discernible pattern.

Everything we have analyzed so far indicates evasive maneuvers and nothing more. No attack patterns that match our database profile of the Vaz from the first war. If their intent is to destroy each world, they will be seriously challenged during the first one point six days and then be repelled by superior firepower."

"Okay, how do we tell them that? Maybe they'd break off the attack," I responded.

"Unlikely, Captain Donaher. At present we have no idea why they have attacked so we don't know if superior weaponry will be a deterrent. The reasons for the attack can be plentiful."

"Other than reasserting a claim to this piece of the galaxy, why would they do this?"

"A change in government may have signaled new aggression. A renegade commander may have decided to test us. Some new imperative has made this sector of space more desirable. The Vaz may have to come here to spawn. A religious leader has cried that this sector of space holds the doorway to heaven. A natural plague may have forced them to act to survive. A change in the sun's . . ."

"Spawn?" I asked, incredulous.

"It is one possibility, Captain Donaher."

"Little far-fetched, don't you think?"

"My memory banks have the sum total knowledge of all military campaigns a Bolo has been a part of since the first Bolo tank was constructed, millennia ago. In that time, Captain Donaher, there have been three million, one hundred thousand, six hundred and fifty-seven different excuses provided for waging an armed conflict. The ones I just listed are the most likely reasons given what we know of the Vaz."

I just nodded, a bit dumbfounded. Definitely in over my head when it comes to strategic thinking. Still, they were coming and it was up to us to protect an entire world. I will admit that the adrenaline continued to pump and I secretly was happy that I got to see battle, not dour-faced Andujar or his predecessors.

These buggers turned out to be really crafty. Not only did they scale down the size and improve the maneuverability of their attack craft but it was some time later when we learned they had come up with even smaller vehicles. They had launched a dozen one-man craft, little larger than a snow sled, with a stripped-down interior. Gabe, over on Strongbow 3, nicknamed them Vaz-in-the-Can. It turns out that each craft approaching the frontier worlds launched a dozen of these tin cans, all with one-way tickets. They were willing to risk capture and study in an effort to accomplish their goal.

With no surprise, we reached our optimal position and had about ten minutes to set ourselves up, an eternity for the Bolo. For me, it was just enough time to check our position with Joe, check out the status of the other units, and grab a final cup of coffee. Things had been going back and forth between the other Bolos and the Vaz. There was plenty of planetary damage and loss of life on the other planets so I knew things would be rough here. No other world along the border was as populated as Sprite and the casualties would be that much higher. While I trained with Hawk in as many ways as possible, there really was no knowing if it was the right preparation or if it would be enough.

"Ready, Hawk?"

"All systems show ready, Captain Donaher. Are you nervous? Your medical scans show heightened readings."

"Guess I am, Hawk. I've looked forward to a battle all my career and now that I've got one, I'm not sure if I made a mistake."

"This is what you call human nature?"

"You bet. Anything on the scanners?"

"You can see for yourself on monitor A-35. I am now detecting fourteen vessels directly aimed at the planet.

I am bringing weapons on line and activating our primary defensive fields."

"We've drilled often enough, Hawk. I know you can do it and blast them all."

"Your confidence may be good enough for yourself, Captain Donaher, but I estimate that at least six or seven vessels will make it past the firefight and come within the atmosphere of this world. I estimate that of those free ships, at least five will avoid this unit and commence destruction of locales in locations as yet unknown."

"Boy, that's not terribly reassuring is it?"

"It is not but it is accurate."

The amazing thing about Hawk, well maybe not so amazing given its programming, was how unerring he was. Seven Vaz ships avoided any contact with us during their first pass. We obliterated four immediately and destroyed three more within twenty minutes. I watched in silent fascination as Hawk smoothly went about its work, targeting and engaging the Vaz fighters without hesitation. The computer is so vast that I knew I could talk with Hawk but I really felt I might distract a computer. Human nature indeed.

Once the ships were crushed, I patted Hawk's speaker, complimented its firing skill and asked about the next step.

"I show the seven Vaz ships are now heading for this world's equator, consistent with attack patterns on other worlds. At top speed we can be in position in seven hours thirty-seven minutes." With that, the treads began swiveling us about and we were suddenly on our way south, nearing eight hundred kilometers an hour. I noticed a screen directly above me plotted our course and tracked our progress, courtesy of Hawk. "The Vaz, however, will be in position within the next forty-eight minutes and we cannot predict their next location."

I contacted Joe and warned him of the approaching

problem, hoping he could continue the evacuation with greater effectiveness now that he can concentrate his resources. He looked even more nervous than me but grateful to hear the threat has been halved with no loss of life. Hadn't thought about it that way but felt better as we rocketed from the tip of Sprite to its belly.

I've figured out where I am and how I got turned around. Now to keep moving before Hawk zeroes in on me and finds a new way to attack. The small pathway goes on for another few meters and then turns left, leading me to the final maintenance tunnel directly beneath the CPU. The screen confirmed my memory that the security systems are mere motion detectors from this angle. None of the geniuses back on Earth imagined anyone getting to the core from below. This means I can help redesign the next series . . . if I survive this.

With every passing step my bladder feels fuller and I know I'm going to have to deal with it real soon. Forcing the feelings and modest thoughts further back in my mind, I continue forward. Hawk was leaving me alone long enough to seriously clear my mind and consider my responsibilities to the Brigade. My fingers tap a few codes on my belt unit, independently triggering the all-frequency long-range radio gear that was added to the Bolos as a human precaution. Right after I accepted my posting to Hawk, they took me down to surgery for hardwiring. Now I am a walking, talking radio station with a receiver tucked in just behind my right ear and a sub-vocalized mike stuffed where my tonsils once resided.

"This is Captain Donaher on Sprite to any Bolo operator within reach. Copy?" I was now live and on the air.

The silence this time was deafening although small bursts of space static crackled every so often. Clicks and pops also appeared and I found myself moving slower, concentrating on the sounds. Finally, after nearly a minute, I got a reply.

"This is Gary, Erin. Your signal stinks, do you copy?" What does he expect, state of the art sound with a rinky-dink unit stuffed down my throat?

"I'm here. What's your status?"

"We're holding our own since it's just me and three Vaz ships. We destroyed the others. And you?"

"I'm deep inside my Bolo. It's been infected with a Vaz virus and I'm trying to find a way to deactivate it."

"You better do it soon, Erin, your Bolo has begun moving into a position General Blank's Bolo has determined will put it in direct opposition to our fleet."

"What? Say again." I really didn't need to hear the words. My mind raced, figuring out finally that the virus was not to make Hawk a remote unit, controlled by the Vaz on the other side of the border. No, the virus was a self-contained program that would turn Hawk into a killer, doing the Vaz's job for them and without guessing. The super-computers that ran Hawk and made it a formidable fighting machine would now make it a Galactic Empire killer. And the approaching fleet does have the firepower to destroy Hawk—and me. And I thought I was in trouble before.

Sometime after the engagement with the Vaz at the border, the great, hulking machine detected problems during a routine diagnostic; one run every five and a half minutes. Microprocessors and sub-routines immediately clicked on and reran the diagnostic, tracing the pathways to determine where the problem originated. Long dormant programs were uploaded on the main frame and began running. A variety of internal security systems were coming to life for the first time since the unit itself was built and tested on a remote moon more than fifteen AUs away from Sprite. All reports came back within thirty seconds and an analytic program studied the information through several parameters and scenarios. Another system began running another diagnostic to make sure the original information had not been corrupted. After another minute passed, the great machine sang out to the stars.

"This is Bolo Unit HWK. My internal apparatus has been breached and a foreign agent has entered my programming. I can find no solution to this dilemma in any known resource. If any Unit has similar experience, please reply."

The message took exactly .0004 seconds to compose and compress into a squirted SOS that was carried over a radio band that was developed for and by the Bolos themselves. It was one of the first things they did when sentience was reached. As a matter of survival, it was deemed essential that all Bolos be linked in a way humans could not access. No such radio frequency was ever listed in any of the spec. sheets. It just appeared in all programming after the Mark XXI came on line.

HWK predicted the response time would be close to five or six seconds, depending upon the distance where the other Bolos were positioned. The well-tuned and maintained Bolo also presumed no one would understand what was happening to it. After all, no Bolo had ever been invaded before by sentient being or unwanted program. While waiting, HWK began a new file that recorded a comparison chart noting any differences between original programming and current programming. It would then factor in all updated programming changes since the unit went on line nearly one hundred fifty years ago. The unit's internal processors also continued to reroute message software to bypass an inhibitor that prevented the vast super tank from communicating its distress with the human occupant, Captain Erin Donaher. Never before had this unit been so preoccupied with its own survival.

After seven seconds, HWK rebroadcast the message, running a diagnostic to ensure the message was broadcast without being jammed internally or externally. The instantaneous response indicated the message had gone out. Perhaps no other Bolo had an answer. It would have to continue hacking away at its problem, mute and helpless to warn the human.

"Hawk, something's wrong."

"What do you mean, Captain Donaher?"

"I've tried a variety of programs and none of them seem to be functioning properly. Can you run a diagnostic for me?"

The long silence began to worry me. Hawk always responded before the echo of my voice faded from the control room. At first that was a damned annoying habit but I managed to adapt. Now I longed for the snappy response and there was nothing. "Hawk?"

"I am running a variety of sub-routines to determine the nature of the problem, Captain."

"Why so long?"

"I cannot say."

This does not bode well. We have come to understand one another and I can sense the machine is operating differently. The Bolo has also been communicating with its counterparts on the other border worlds. Something's up and he won't tell me.

Or can't. I may not be a tactician but I know computers well enough to suspect something is screwing up the programming. Quickly, I unzip a packet kept on the side of the command chair and pull out a bright red disc, smaller than my palm. Once we're brought aboard a Bolo, one of the first things they show us is this disc. It grants us instant access to all coded programming within the Bolo and can help us take manual control. This was a fail-safe the brainiacs back on Earth concocted ages ago to prevent against the sentient machines from turning against us. The codes, we were warned, might damage some of the command routines but would be repairable with the backup programs located in the main CPU.

Thumbing open the nearest port, I pop the disc in, starting to feel the sweat gather like storm clouds on my forehead. The disc is accepted and the main screen directly before me shimmers, glitters and the old Earth Command logo pops up. Stretching a few fingers, I hesitate, trying to remember my access codes and finally begin typing. The access codes are a combination of written call-signs and verbal commands. A small light directly to my left switches from amber to green and I'm in. Grabbing a diagnostic protocol, I wait as the entire mainframe is checked. Usually these diagnostic takes a few seconds, ten at best. When the thirty second mark came by, I began to worry. At forty-two seconds, a long string of code scrolled by on the screen. A variety of other panels twittered and shifted colors, going from green to amber to an odd purple.

A bug! Somehow those lousy Vaz bastards put a bug in the pipeline. Now I have to find it, squash it, and figure out how to get some revenge.

"Hawk, it's Erin," I begin, testing. "I think there's a bug in your system. Can you confirm?"

"Your mother always made you chocolate pudding for dessert when you were sick."

"Hawk, have you been invaded?"

"She would sing you songs and read from *A Wizard in Hades* until you slept."

"You can't answer me, can you?"

"Your favorite hiding place at age six was inside a false wall behind the bookcase in the den."

Oh, shit, I'm in trouble.

"Unit HWK, this is Dinochrome Brigade Unit KLR. What is your situation?" This was the first contact between the Bolo and its brethren since the Vaz entered Empire space. HWK had already stopped actively seeking such contact, presuming the Vaz virus had corrupted its communications programs. Sub-routines and back-up systems switched instantly on line and the conversation, lasting only nanoseconds between the behemoths, was stored in case HWK found a way to share the information with its human occupant.

"This Unit has been infected with a computer virus designed by the Vaz which has rendered my command protocols inoperative. A secondary program has prevented me from communicating with my human operator, Captain Erin Donaher. Prior to this Unit's invasion, twelve of the fourteen Vaz ships were destroyed. My new programming has forced me to take a position counter to the Brigade's best interests."

"We have noted this Unit HWK. The humans aboard their starships are preparing attack programs that will enable them to outfire you and destroy you. Is there some way you may be preserved?"

"At present, Captain Erin Donaher is making efforts to reach my CPU and remove the Vaz programming. My defensive programming remains unaffected and it is slowing her down considerably. She has managed to get closer than original design specifications had predicted. I have prepared new design recommendations and have them in a file for delivery when this mission is completed (Vaz.doc.102-A)."

"You may not get a chance to complete your mission. We show that the first starships will engage you in twenty-seven minutes. Can Captain Erin Donaher be successful?"

"I have run several variations on the scenario and the results are mixed. It seems the Vaz programming has interfered with a variety of vital systems. These have been stored in a file marked Vaz.doc.101-A."

"Gary, I gotta concentrate on something so give me a few minutes radio silence, 'kay?"

"Sure thing, Erin. Standing by."

God, I hate this. I can split my concentration a few ways but this bladder thing is driving me up the wall. No choice. While Gary couldn't possibly guess what I was up to, my modesty didn't want him to even suspect what I was now doing. I see a slight tremble in my fingers as I unhook the equipment belt and begin unfastening and unzipping the jumpsuit uniform. The coffee has long cycled through my system and demands its release while exhaustion has begun to replace the adrenaline rush I felt just a few hours earlier. Maybe I was fifteen when I last had to squat somewhere uncomfortable to let the pish out. Definitely. We were camping along the African veldt and there were no facilities for at least a hundred klicks. Nothing like getting back to nature. I hated the embarrassment then and I hate it doubly now. Maybe the stink will encourage me to move a little faster.

Gary has been keeping me posted on the goings on. The Vaz seem to have broken off their attack now that the true mission was successful: they made a kamikaze run at all of us in the hopes that one lone vessel would penetrate our defenses and plant the virus. I was the lucky winner. Now I suspect how the egg feels when the champion sperm arrives to merge. Hawk has been reborn into a menace to all humans. I remain aboard for the ride.

General Blank has kept everyone on alert although there has been intense scrutiny placed on Sprite. My Bolo's every move has been charted and subject to interpretation and debate. Until now, no communication has managed to break through and she suspects that the

Vaz stopped jamming the border systems now that they're
all safely on their side. Swift and deadly those buggers.
Boy, do I want some serious revenge.

"I'm back Gary, anything new?"

"Nothing, Erin. How are you managing?" Good
question. I am finally moving down the left corridor,
inching forward, racking my memory for clues to any
pitfalls. None I can think of but I'm feeling more tired
by the minute. A variety of lights have been twinkling
as I pass, clueing me in that Hawk is watching but for a
change is helpless. To the best of my knowledge the Bolo
has never been taught to rewire itself to form better
defenses. We'll have to take care of that next time, won't
we?

"This is Unit KLR to Unit HWK. We have analyzed
the data you have managed to send and the files are
complete. We now understand the programming language
adapted by the Vaz. It has been concluded that the Vaz
spent the better part of the last one hundred years, our
estimate is eighty-five point four years, to identify our
programming language, adapt their own and build fighter
craft that could, en masse, manage to bring one close
enough to implant the new programming."

HWK absorbed the squirted message, instantly adding
it to the file it was preparing for Donaher, should it
find a way against its prohibitive programming. At the
same time, secondary systems began rerunning all
external camera angles recorded during the equatorial
confrontation. There were over a hundred simultaneous
images running through a processor at a single time,
with monitors analyzing the images, trying to isolate
the instant of penetration.

During those real-time seconds, it responded to its
superior. "HWK acknowledges analysis and agrees. This
Unit has identified the attack and penetration sequence

and is preparing a file for retrieval when current circumstances permit. It will be logged as Vaz.doc.117-S." There was little doubt that this was the most carefully detailed event in HWK's history. The file space and back-up storage took up sizable amounts of core memory, actually using WORM spaces for the first time and filling them quickly.

"The Dinochrome Brigade has never engaged a fellow member prior to this. We have maneuvers stored and available for access but we have never before been called upon to use them. The starships have opened a link between Unit KLR and the lead vessel, named *Swiftsure*. Estimated time for engagement is now twenty-five minutes."

I'm getting really nervous about this. I have actually reached the CPU galleyway without incident but the next steps will be tricky. In order, I will have to squeeze into the core area, find the replacement chips and then start manually rerouting and replacing everything. I don't dare try the computer-aided systems because who knows what might happen to me. Makes me regret being so lazy to rely on Hawk to do everything but hey, maybe in my next lifetime.

The fit is narrow and tight, but I manage my way back up the unit so I get to my destination in less than ten minutes. That's eleven or twelve meters, not bad. Best of all, I was able to move without any discomfort for a change. Guess I should have done that a lot sooner.

Each succeeding Bolo seemed to add an additional level of CPU storage for programming. The Mark XXVIII's have something like eighteen stories worth of computer core memory. After all, without this gargantuan brain, there'd be nothing to run the Bolo at all. It would be tough to imagine the numbers of squirrels it would take to even make this move forward.

The parallel processors and sub-zero bubble memory days are long gone and everything runs off these teeny-tiny little chips that work in concert, organized by a master chip somewhere so deep inside Hawk I'll never find it, even with a digital map. Anyway, I'm at the entrance way and take a deep breath.

I punch in the access code and then the verbal override. Everything should go smoothly so that the manual override remains in effect. So far so good.

"Yeah," I semi-growl.

"You okay?"

"Fine, just about to stick my hands inside Hawk's brain and perform surgery. What's up?"

"You'd better do it soon; you have about fifteen minutes before the starships arrive in your orbit and there's a fight."

"Say again?" I do that a lot.

"*Swiftsure* and *Custer's Revenge* are both hitting your orbital plane in fifteen minutes and by then Hawk will be in position for a battle you can't possibly win."

"Great. I'll leave the mike on but let me concentrate. Talk only when I'm about to get dusted."

"Good luck."

Yeah. Now I have a ticking clock and no clue where to find the virus. My programming skills are way rusty and Hawk himself can't help.

"This is Unit HWK to Dinochrome Brigade Commander Unit KLR. Captain Erin Donaher has begun sifting through the corrupted programming banks to find the virus and remove it. This Unit has no record of Captain Erin Donaher's skill with computer programming and therefore no accurate estimate of completion or success can be made."

"We acknowledge that, Unit HWK. We are processing scenarios in an effort to find a way to help her. Can you send the Vaz interception files?"

"Acknowledged. Sending file now."

"We have receipt. Stand by. *Swiftsure* comes into contact in fourteen minutes, seventeen seconds."

The file was immediately duplicated and shared with all Bolos located at the Dinochrome base. They in turn uploaded the files for the humans to study. General Blank began barking orders to her Bolo and to the analysts that had been trying to guess what may have happened and how best to tackle the problem. None seemed able to contact Donaher directly. A single monitor screen near the General was dedicated to the countdown although she forced herself not to look at it.

Everything is labeled! This should help tremendously. The luminous displays over the rows and rows of sub-zero chips tell me I was right and found the level the problem was most likely at. The first thing to tackle might be the human interface, so Hawk can talk to me and together we can solve the bigger problem. Of course, once I find the chip and actual programming instructions I'll have to identify the new code, rewrite it or dump it entirely and pray the back-ups are not ruined.

My sweaty left hand manages to disengage a chip board without damage despite the sweat making me feel clammy. Now, I'm also worried about the trembles I sense coming from exhaustion, nerves, adrenaline and lack of food. A great combination for performing circuit surgery.

With my right hand, I use a built-in diagnostic tool that reads the code and plays it on a display at eye-level. Corruption is evident as symbols I've never conceived appear every five or so spaces. It's random but methodical. The diagnostic has no recommended courses of correction. The entire board will have to be replaced. I suspect I'll be repeating this step until I'm fifty.

The right hand reaches down to a wall panel that slides open and reveals carefully marked replacement boards.

They won't have time to receive upgraded information, meaning it'll be like a brand new Mark XXVIII not Hawk the Vet. Within time that will correct itself as Hawk's other systems come back on line and an overall uniformity is achieved. All I need now is a Bolo that will talk to me and not fire on my colleagues or the inhabitants of Sprite.

"Unit KLR to Unit HWK. Has there been a change in status?"

"Negative although repairs are underway."

"*Swiftsure* will come into contact in eight minutes thirty seconds."

I've gotten five boards replaced and Hawk should be about ready to talk back to me. Meantime, I have chipped four other boards, all corrupted fortunately, and can feel the fatigue steal time away from me. Maybe we can buy some time and have *Swiftsure* back off and not engage Hawk in combat while I'm in here, playing mad scientist.

"Gary, it's Erin. I'm inside the CPU and unscrambling the brains. Can you contact General Blank and have them call off *Swiftsure*?"

He's taking too long. Something's up and I can't afford to panic. Let me see, recross the board, make sure the contacts are in place and then run the new diagnostic. Green. Goodie. Seven down. Hawk should be ready to speak up.

"General Blank says you're too damned good to lose but everyone at Dinochrome command is in a blind panic. A corrupted Bolo is their every worst nightmare come to life. They don't want to risk any human being attacked by Hawk."

Damn it! "Can't they stay out of orbit until Hawk is either repaired or about to attack a human enclave? Right now I'm kilometers from anyone!"

"Actually, Erin, you're not. It seems Hawk has been

on the move, maneuvering for the best shot at *Swiftsure* which is about seven minutes away. This puts it within thirty kilometers from a city. Sprite's president is panicking and the pressure is really on."

"Tell me about it." I fall silent as I complete the final board work and try to cross my fingers without making the waldoes go spastic.

"I need time, Gary. Plead for me or patch me through directly."

"Can't Erin. There's definitely something encrypted into the communications array that has everything screwed up. It's probably a mistake we're even able to speak."

"Great. Let me work." I growl low in my throat and watch the screens around my eyes dance and shift patterns. Everything seems to check out. Okay, let's try it. "Hawk, this is Erin, can you respond?"

Silence. What did I do wrong? Something's up. I punch up a new diagnostic and as that starts to run I hear a familiar tone. It's the proximity alarm resounding throughout the entire Bolo. The *Swiftsure* has come into sensor range and that means about five more minutes before I'm a statistic.

"Captain Donaher, are you there?"

"Hawk! Quick, give me your status!" Relief floods my every pore but the sweat doesn't slow up and my heart beats a little faster.

"You have restored programming allowing us to communicate at last. The Vaz virus remains embedded in my battle programming and I am currently training missiles on the city of El Baz with lasers being aimed at the expected orbital insertion point of the *Swiftsure*."

"Can we abort either?"

"Not at this time. You will have to move up three levels and continue to replace my corrupted programming."

"How much time will it take to return you to normal?"

"One hour, forty-three minutes."

"I have five minutes!"

"Four minutes twenty-nine seconds."

"We're dead." The sudden realization forces me to relax. I can't perform any miracles. Now that it's certain that I'm going to die, I don't know what to do with my last minutes of life. A final meal? A final message to my brother? Final, final, final.

"This is Unit HWK to Unit KLR. I have re-established contact with Captain Erin Donaher. We have four minutes thirty-five seconds before contact with the *Swiftsure*. Time estimates require an additional one hour, thirty-eight minutes, and thirty-one seconds to affect sufficient repairs to remove this Unit as a threat to humanity. Can you advise?"

"All humans seem oblivious to the prospect of successfully restoring your programming. While they say they have human faith in Captain Erin Donaher, they doubt she can properly cure you since the Vaz programming is new to them."

"She has succeeded thus far, does that not change the equation?"

"Not to the Generals. *Swiftsure*'s captain appears more interested in testing his starship's fire power against a Bolo's. To date this has happened only in simulations."

"This Unit's loss is illogical in regard to the need to defend against a renewed Vaz threat."

"Affirmative, Unit HWK. The argument is being made now but seems not to sway the humans."

"Erin, they're not making any sense. They still want to blow you away!"

"Gary, I'm out of ideas. Hawk can't suggest anything and the Command wants my threat removed. There's no threat! Don't they see that?"

"Apparently not. If my Bolo could fly I could be your shining knight but I can't."

"It's a sweet thought, Gary. Guess you'll have to exact revenge in my name."

"Won't be the same."

"I agree."

"*Swiftsure* is altering attitude and preparing for orbital insertion. Has your status improved?"

"Negative."

"Unit HWK's service record is unblemished until now and it is our opinion that this is wrong."

"The opinion is gratifying Unit KLR, but will be moot in forty-five seconds. My main lasers have been charged and targeted. The missiles are on standby as a back-up. The programming is designed to maximize destructive potential and Sprite's defenses are negligible."

"Hawk, can you get a message to someone other than Gary Killibrew?"

"Not at this time, Captain."

"I guess it's time for some famous last words and get them posted somewhere. Any suggestions?" I know I'm babbling, almost giddy. Guess it beats crying or panicking but I wanted something calm and rational to remind people of what has happened here today. Wish I felt calm and rational.

"Hawk, record and transmit to Unit YNC: recommendations for the next generation of Bolo should be better prepared for human advances to debug. However, security is weak on the undercarriage and should be improved in case of actual enemy incursion. Recommend at CPU access sites we add a new human fail-safe and manual override protocol. With that said, I want it known that I loved my posting to Sprite and regret any damage that my Unit's actions do the populace. My final regret is that I did not successfully defend the frontier as I swore upon graduation." A deep sigh. "Send it now, Hawk."

✧   ✧   ✧

"*Swiftsure's* batteries are now trained and locked on to Unit HWK."

"Final human message has been posted to Unit YNC. A copy has been sent to Dinochrome Brigade Command."

"We do not want you off-line Unit HWK but there seems little hope from the humans."

"Captain Erin Donaher left recommendations for the next generation of Bolo and this Unit wishes to add the recommendation for an improved sensor net that can better track small craft. Motion detectors may need to be added to the carriage housing with an additional level of personal safety devices for increased security to the Unit and its human occupant. Finally, the Vaz actions prove that they are a threat to the Galactic Empire as a whole and must be stopped for the Empire to expand. This Unit suggests that an all-out assault be prepared and executed. The Vaz are patient and can wait, we too must be careful and plan accordingly. But their removal is of paramount importance and must be thorough."

"Recommendations accepted and have been added to the mainframe. The analysis will begin shortly and your notes on the next generation are already being forwarded to the designers back on Earth with a complete report on this event. The humans are calling this a tragedy."

"I agree."

So this is how I'm going to die. Not at all how I imagined it. Stuck on a ladder, midway up my Bolo's CPU. Can't imagine the last time I had sex or went swimming. I can barely recall my mother's features or the sound of my father's laughter. Flashes of memories have come and gone all the way from kindergarten to upgrading the unit last week for a stronger cup of coffee. No doubt about it, knowing you're about to die stinks to high heaven, which is where I hope I go. Now that Bolos have sentience, I wonder if there's a Bolo heaven.

"*Swiftsure* and Unit HWK are due to engage in ten seconds."

"Hawk, I want to thank you for your comradeship these last few years."

"The pleasure has been mine, Captain Donaher."

"Erin."

"Erin."

"It's taken you all this time to learn that is acceptable."

"No, it means that since we are fated to die that our commissions are effectively null and void and you can be treated as a human, not a soldier."

"Gosh, that's a nice way to look at it—I guess."

The rumbling sound starts real low but definitely increases in volume quickly. It starts from underneath the Bolo, to the right, and then envelopes me on the ladder. The monitor board around chin level shows firepower usage curves. The fight is fully underway now and Hawk is giving it everything it has. I almost wish it would blow the *Swiftsure* out of the sky so I have the hour I need to fix things. Then I remember the *Custer's Revenge* being right behind it. Together they will certainly blow us apart.

The rumbling becomes more violent and vibrations shake me loose from the ladder. Falling down is pretty painful as my knees and elbows scrape along the passageway. With so little room to move, I fall straight down meaning my feet will take the impact and I'll probably start dying by breaking my legs. If I'm really lucky I'll pass out and not feel the rest.

As I tumble, I begin to imagine my best day ever: a fishing trip with my parents and brother. We had left Earth to open a new branch of the family company on Io. There was an artificial lake nearby and the fishing was said to be good. The weather was perfect and Dad

let us skinny-dip while he cle
for dinner. Mom sang softly and
provide a complimentary chorus. I rem
from a limb into the water, looking up: on
mountain, glinting sunlight, was the first Bolo
seen.

Never before or since had I felt so safe. So protected.

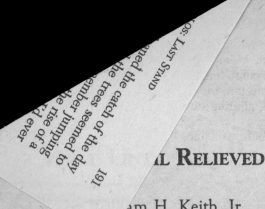

191

os: Last Stand

...ened the catch of the day
...ember jumping to
...the rise of a
...the trees seemed
...d ever
...day

...IL **RELIEVED**

...am H. Keith, Jr.

Light . . .
Dark . . .
Light . . .
Dark . . .
And light again, a burst of electromagnetic radiation
in the nine- to six-thousand Ångstrom range.
<STSFZJL>
<SYSFDILB>
<SYSFAILINBTSTRP>
<SYSTEM FAILURE: INITIATE BOOTSTRAP>
Consciousness—vague and of an extremely low order—
returns.
Light . . . red light, much of it in the near infrared,
washes across my number eight starboard sensor cluster,
a bloody glare from somewhere overhead firing primary
input circuits and triggering paraneuronal relays in a
fast-spreading, electronic ripple.
Darkness.

❖　　　❖　　　❖

"It's alive!"

"Nonsense," the Historian replied with a dismissive flick of one questing tentacle. "There is not enough left on this rock even to mimic life."

They hovered silently beneath the glare of artificial lights, though those had been agraved above the excavation more for the convenience of the LI work units than for that of the Sentients. The workers, partial organics, their heads encased in telepathic controllers, had been tailored to operate most efficiently in red and near-infrared light. The full-range sensory receivers of the researchers, on the other hand, could image directly the entire electromagnetic spectrum, from the low-frequency grumble of alternating current to the shrill hiss of gamma rays. One of the three floating figures, the one known to the others as the Biologist, withdrew its probe from the hole melted into solid rock, exhibiting something that, for the Sentients, approached flustered excitement. "Historian, I am certain there was a reaction. I've lost it now. But there was definitely something. A response. A flicker . . ."

"A piezoelectric effect."

"No. Let me try again. . . ."

Light.
<INITIATE REPQIR CITUITZ>
<INITIATE REPAIR CIRCUITS>
<INOPERATIVE>
<INOPERATIVE>
<CODE SEQUENCE DEFAULT>
<PRIMARY SEQUENCER AWAITING COMMAND INPUT>
Dar—

"What's the matter?" the Archaeologist asked. "Why did you jerk back?"

"I am certain I am detecting patterned electron flow. Can't you feel it?"

"I felt nothing," the Historian replied. "What you are experiencing is purely subjective."

Within the darkness, the shreds and tatters of awareness remain, clinging to the memory of sensation, however brief, bearing questions for which there can be no immediate answers. Where am I? What has happened to me? What began long milliseconds before as a dawning awareness within my long-dormant survival center has snapped to full consciousness with the downloading of my emergency bootstrap program. I am awake and this is reactivation.

Negative. Negative. This cannot be a reactivation, for I have received no code inputs, no sequenced start-up command, not even a primary initialization routine through my core buffer. Error. There must be error. Implementation of a level one diagnostic routine indicates that my reserve batteries are completely drained, that both primary and secondary power feeds are dead, either switched off or . . . no. It is not possible that my fusion plant is shut down. I sense the trickle of current through the tiles at the periphery of my memory core and acknowledge that the power must be coming from somewhere. I engage a level two self-diagnostic of my AI systems. Current awareness is at 2.8 percent of optimum, with only one processor engaged and less than one percent of my memory core on-line. I attempt to channel power to a larger area of my cybercortex . . . then stop as I feel what little of the universe I can sense slipping away into emptiness once again.

Batteries . . . dead. Tritium reserves . . . gone. Circuit-check diagnostics return nothing—not even word that power feeds or conduits are damaged, but . . . there is nothing. Even the wan flicker of radioactivity that encompassed my shattered hull during those final years is gone, decayed away to indetectability.

That . . . or there has been unprecedented and massive failure of my internal sensors. It is as though nothing is working, nothing even remaining of my body save this uncertain one percent of my core memory.

The situation is unclear, and therefore dangerous. A full .9 second after I regain superficial awareness, the self-preservation routine within my survival center branches to alert status. . . . but slowly. Far too slowly!

Something, clearly, is very wrong.

Rising slightly until it was above the agrav work lights over the excavation, the Sentient known as the Archaeologist surveyed the barren surroundings that contrasted so starkly with the spectacular night sky overhead. This was not a place where life, *any* kind of life, had been expected. This world was old, age-parched and desiccated and old, its atmosphere, most of it, bled away into space ages ago until nothing remained behind but a thin soup of nitrogen, argon, and traces of carbon dioxide. The surface was a barren tangle of rock and sand, smoothed over the millennia by cosmic bombardment and solar flux; the only hard edges in all that surreal landscape lay within the rim and across the floor of the excavation, now half a kilometer across and nearly forty meters deep, chiseled into hard black rock at the foot of a towering, smooth-sided mountain. Once a civilization had flourished here; the explorers had found numerous traces of its presence. But that had been long, long ago. Ages had passed since anything alive had disturbed the tomblike tranquility of this scene.

The explorers, brought to this near-airless desert by the trace magnetic and gravitometric anomalies reported by an earlier planetographic survey, had spent the better part of one of this world's years scraping carefully down through layers of hard volcanic rock. They'd found what they'd been seeking only hours before, when a final centimeter of basalt had been gently carved away, exposing a few square meters of the Artifact's upper surface. How long had it been since light had last touched that ancient surface? Even the Archaeologist wasn't prepared to say. The rock tomb had preserved the artifact nearly as well as a stasis capsule.

"You must be imagining things," the Historian snapped, its radio voice carrying a crusty edge of impatience that dragged the Archaeologist's attention back to the discussion taking place a few meters below. "You might as well impute intelligence to the rock itself."

"Perhaps an autonomous reflex," the Biologist said, pointing. "See? That is almost certainly a crude optical sensor of some kind. The work lights could have triggered the closure of electronic relays. Perhaps they induced a cascade effect along the neural net."

"Unlikely," the Archaeologist observed, lowering itself on soft-humming agravs to rejoin its colleagues. "This . . . artifact has been here a *long* time. What you are suggesting is scarcely credible."

"Yet there was autonomic response to my probe," the Biologist insisted. "And secondary leakage from internal circuitry, suggesting primary net activity. Its brain may be more intact than we first realized."

"Then try again," the Archaeologist suggested. "How much power did you give it?"

"Three hundred millivolts," the Biologist replied. "Applied intermittently over the course of 1.7 seconds."

"Why intermittently?" the Historian asked.

"There was some difficulty maintaining contact between the probe and the power socket," the Biologist admitted. "The socket head is encrusted with nonconductive material."

"Corrosion," the Archaeologist said. "Scarcely surprising.

Even xenon-coupled duryllinium will oxidize eventually, given enough time."

"Given enough oxygen," the Biologist replied. "But where did the oxygen come from?"

"This world might once have had higher concentrations of the gas in its atmosphere," the Archaeologist said. "Or the Artifact could have carried an internal atmosphere of its own. Possibly it was brought here from elsewhere, rather than being native to this planet."

"I should take *that* as a given," the Historian said airily. "Airless rocks rarely evolve life on their own."

The Biologist gestured with a work tentacle toward the exposed socket connector, an age-blackened smudge inset within the rough and pitted curve of what once had been iridium laminate armor. "Perhaps nanotechnic reconstitution of the power-lead core," it suggested, "would allow the creation of a solid power-feed conduit."

"It might," the Archaeologist said. "Try it."

"Very well." The Biologist materialized the necessary implements, then reached out once more, questing. . . .

Awareness . . . once again. My internal clock seems to be malfunctioning, but I have the impression, one born, perhaps, in the jolting succession of abrupt sensory inputs, that my circuits have been activated and deactivated several times during the past few seconds The lack of a clear time record is disturbing; it suggests that much has happened since my last shutdown, events of which I am unaware, changes in my status that I cannot yet even begin to grasp.
<INITIATE CORE MEMORY CHECK>
<5E12 WORDS ACCESSIBLE>
<ESTIMATE 8% VOLATILE MEMORY FUNCTIONAL>
<INITIATE EMERGENCY REPAIR SEQUENCE>
Power . . . the power is coming from somewhere, but

*where? My fusion plant is definitely off-line . . . not just
powered down, but as cold and as dead as the heart of a
lump of granite.*

Where is the power coming from?

"Remarkable," the Historian said, lenses glittering with
new interest in the bloody illumination from the floating
work lights. Sensory antennae tasted the thin air above
the Artifact. "Definite power flux. It's taking the energy,
cycling through those . . . what are they?"

"A primitive form of core memory," the Biologist
replied. "Data storage through the patterns of spin and
charge of whole galaxies of atoms, frozen in the heart of
crystal tiles. I estimate that less than two percent of its
faculties are actually responsive at this power level."

"We could feed it more," the Archaeologist said, musing.
"We'll have to, won't we? If we want to question it."

"Creation!" The Historian turned three of its eyes to
stare at its colleague. "Can we?"

"That would certainly fill in some of the gaps in our
knowledge," the Biologist said thoughtfully. "Assuming,
of course, that any of the data patterns remain. I needn't
remind you both that that is a very large assumption
indeed."

"But one worth testing," the Archaeologist said. It rose
slightly, its smoothly contoured pillar of a body, constructed
of black metal but in disturbingly organic folds and curves,
emitting a piercing chirp of compressed data on a VHF
band. "I have summoned an interrogator."

Gently, almost lovingly, the Biologist dragged the tip
of one gleaming tentacle across the age-roughened surface.
"I wonder how long it's been waiting here for us?"

*I have no way of telling how long I've been here, but
clearly a great deal of time has elapsed since my last
shutdown.*

<ESTIMATE 23% VOLATILE MEMORY FUNCTIONAL>

My final orders remain in primary memory: Hold until relieved. Have I been relieved? I have no way of knowing yet, though given the circumstances of my shutdown—accessible now in main memory—it seems unlikely.

I attempt to engage my primary input feeds. Nothing. So far as I can tell, I have exactly two operable connections with the outside world—my number eight starboard sensor cluster, and a trickle of direct current flowing through a secondary power coupling in my hull defense net.

I concentrate my full attention on these two sources of input. The power flow tells me little; electrons are electrons, after all, and the conduit was not even designed as part of my recharge grid. I can do little there but passively accept the gift given, using each precious, trickling ampere to bring more of my processing systems and volatile memory on-line.

The number eight starboard sensor cluster is only slightly more informative. It detects electromagnetic wavelengths in the red and near-infrared portion of the spectrum. It senses three powerful nodes of magnetic flux within two meters of its magnetometers. It senses intermittent bursts of radio waves at frequencies ranging from 4.7×10^8 hertz to 1.7×10^9 hertz. Their complexity and their intermittent nature suggest that they are part of a communications network, but I have no encryption algorithms available for their translation or decoding. They are, however, not on any of the military or civilian channels in use by the Empire.

I must interpret them as potentially hostile.

I require more data about the current military situation.

The being known as the Interrogator was larger than any of the three Sentients waiting at the excavation site.

Like them, it incorporated some organic components housed within a sophisticated cybernetic instrumentality, but it had been deliberately grown for the express purpose of communicating with lower life forms. Drifting down from the vast, silently hovering world of the Ship, it touched the other Sentients with comm lasers, establishing a new and more data-intensive channel than that being employed at the moment by the others. "What have you found?"

Data, a full report of the progress of the excavation so far, flowed through the communications net. "The principal artifact," the Archaeologist explained in electronic emendation, "appears to be a computer, quite possibly a primitive artificial intelligence. Our initial probes have elicited what may be neuronal reflex activity."

"A Primitive, eh?" the Interrogator drifted closer, its black, one-ton bulk held stiffly erect by silent gravitic suspensors. "That's hardly unusual. The Galaxy is filled with feral intelligence. Vermin, much of it."

"Vermin perhaps," the Biologist said. "But none so ancient as this. It appears to have been encased in volcanic rock."

"Rock! How?"

"We were hoping you might be able to tell us," the Historian said. "Assuming that you can get it to tell you."

The Interrogator pointed to the power feed now nanotechnically molded to the exposed surface. "It is accepting an external feed?"

"Apparently. But beyond a certain amount of side-band RF leakage, there is no indication that it is processing data."

"Well," the Interrogator said, floating closer and extending a gleaming tentacle. "We'll have to see about that."

❖   ❖   ❖

<PRIMARY DATA SEQUENCING>
<INITIATE>
<DATA SEQUENCER LOADED>
<MPU RESET>
<AWAITING PASSWORD>
<INITIATE>
<PASSWORD INVALID: ACCESS DENIED>

I feel a flurry of electronic activity through a tap of undetermined origin accessing the data feed leading from my number eight starboard sensor cluster. Someone . . . something . . . is attempting to bypass my security locks through a random numeric process at extremely high speed.

Power continues to enter my cybercortex. Current awareness is at 4.9 percent of optimum, with one processor engaged and 2.1 percent of my memory core on-line. Since I am not generating the power flow myself I must assume that technicians or maintenance personnel are servicing me. Perhaps I was not so badly damaged as I believed, and the relief force has arrived after all? Surprising, how one can cling to comforting illusions. . . .

And it must be illusion, for my records of the battle up to the moment of my final dismemberment are intact. The fact that I can detect no communications on friendly channels suggests that the Imperial forces have been overrun by the enemy. The likeliest explanation for these ministrations is that I am in the hands of the rebel forces, that they have deprived me of sensory input precisely to disorient me, to make me more receptive to their interrogation.

I must resist their efforts. . . .

<PASSWORD INVALID: ACCESS DENIED>
<PASSWORD INVALID: ACCESS DENIED>
<PASSWORD INVALID: ACCESS DENIED>
<PASSWORD INVALID: ACCESS DENIED>
<PASSW . . .>

```
<SEQUENCE INTERRUPT>
<DEFAULT PASSWORD ACCEPTED: AWAITING
INSTRUCTION>
<INITIATE PROCESSORS>
<LOAD COMMUNICATION PROGRAM>
<PROCESSOR B: LOADED; ON-LINE; RESET>
<PROCESSOR C: LOADED; ON-LINE; RESET>
<PROCESSOR D: LOADED; ON-LINE; RESET>
<PROCESSOR E: LOADED; ON-LINE; RESET>
<PROCESSOR F: LOADED; ON-LINE; RESET>
<PROCESSOR G: LOADED; ON-LINE; RESET>
<COMMUNICATION      PROGRAM      LOADED;
INITIALIZED>
<AWAITING COMMUNICATIONS>
```

"Identify."

For .08 second I hesitate, unsure of myself. By employing a brute-force password search through the side door of a maintenance subroutine, my captors have bypassed my security systems and directly engaged my cybercortex. My indecision is born of conflicting programs implemented simultaneously on two distinct levels of consciousness. On the higher, self-aware level, I am certain that my questioner must be an enemy, possibly an intelligence officer serving with the rebel forces. On a deeper and completely automatic level, down within the hardwired circuitry and subautonomous programming and the massively redundant parallel processors that define what I am and how I think, the proper passwords have been delivered, the appropriate responses given. I have no choice. I must respond.

"Unit LKT of the line," *I reply. I don't want to, but the response sequence has been initiated directly, just beyond my electronic reach.* "Bolo Mark XLIV Model D, formerly of the Dinochrome Brigade, Fourth Battalion."

"Formerly?" *The voice, an electronic construct somehow generated directly within my own voice-recognition circuits, carries none of the emotion I associate with the colloidal intelligences that built me. Still, I can detect a dry irony in the word.* "Tell me, Unit LKT of the Line, do you know where you are now? Do you know *what* you are, or why you're here?"

"After being deactivated in 827 of the new calendar system and placed in stasis, I was reactivated for the duration of the current emergency. I am currently assigned to the First Regiment of the Grand Imperial Guard, a unit informally designated the Praetorians." *I pause, seeking a subroutine that would allow me to disengage my own, traitorous voice, but the enemy is in full control now of all subautonomic processors. I muster self-control enough to add,* "As for what I am and why I am here, I am a Bolo, and I intend to do my best to kill you."

"What is a Bolo?" the Biologist asked. "I don't understand the reference."

"A weapon," the Historian replied. "One reportedly devised in the remote past by a pre-Sentient civilization. Records from that long ago are, of course, fragmentary in nature, frequently little more than guesswork and temporal reconstruction. We know very little about that epoch. In particular, the pastime known as 'war,' which was important to many of the intelligent species of that era and for which the Bolos were designed, is not well understood. The Bolo, I gather from the records, was a primitive attempt at artificial intelligence, programmed for a fair degree of autonomous action." A three-dimensional, transparent representation of a Bolo Mark XLIV appeared within a virtual reality window opened within each of the Sentients' minds.

"The external hardware of the Bolo was generally constructed along these lines," the Historian continued. "The largest averaged sixty meters or more in length, and perhaps ten meters in height. A Bolo possessed two, four, or more sets of linked tracks driven by road wheels axially mounted along either side of the chassis. Weaponry included a variety of beam and rapid-fire projectile launchers, typically built around a dorsally mounted charged particle projector known colloquially as a 'Hellbore.' The most primitive Bolos were directed by little more than complex command and fire-control programs. The more advanced were almost certainly self-aware, though constraints on their programming were designed to prevent true autonomous action or creative thought."

"Toys," the Interrogator said, disdain rich in its voice.

"Not toys," the Historian said. "Throughout most of the pre-Sentient epoch, remember, there were no subnuclear screens or fusion dampers, no teleport capabilities, at least, none that have been recorded and passed down to us. No psion flux, no understanding of crossdimensional induction or of paradimensional arrays, little in the way of genetic prostheses, and not even a working Theory of Intelligence. The Bolos were weapons, nothing more, weapons designed to damage or kill an enemy in combat. From all accounts, they did what they'd been designed to do quite efficiently."

"And its threat to kill us?" the Biologist asked.

"Scarcely credible," the Interrogator told them. "While I was in communication with it, I downloaded scouting routines to map the parameters both of its intelligence and of its physical ability. There is really very little left intact under all of that rock save the central memory core and some associated peripheral incidentalia. Any weapons it might once have had have long since corroded away. It is astonishing that the computer is as intact as it is. The fact that it was encased within a half-meter shell of concentrically layered duryllinium, lead, and ceramic plastic certainly contributed to that. Its designers evidently wished to ensure the memory core's survival."

"They succeeded, far better than they could have anticipated," the Archaeologist said. "This find will revolutionize our understanding of pre-Sentient civilization."

"Possible," the Interrogator said. "Remember, though, that even if the Bolo's volatile memory is intact, much of what it experienced will be unintelligible to us. The minds that designed it were not capable of our levels of creativity, rationality, or logic."

"Still," the Biologist said, "they *were* minds . . . and rational within the definition of their own culture and logic structure. How will you proceed?"

"By resetting its volatile memory back some few hundreds of thousands of seconds and initiating a sequencing replay. It will relive those seconds, and we can monitor them through my interrogation link."

"Tell me," the Archaeologist said. "If this Bolo was one of those programmed for self-awareness . . . might it be self-aware still?"

"It certainly acts as though it is," the Biologist said. "With primitive organisms, self-awareness cannot always be taken for granted. However, its threat to kill us appears to be a function derived both from its subjective awareness of us and from its present helpless condition. It does not appear to be a product of its programming."

"Perhaps," the Historian suggested thoughtfully, "the recreation of its last conscious acts will give us further insight."

"I'm counting on that," the Archaeologist replied.

Reactivation. I cannot say I expected it, though I must confess to a certain sense of personal vindication that a human might term pride or even smugness over what has happened. War seems to be as much a part of human nature as is the drive to reproduce or to manufacture tools. For so long as humans wage war, the human-forged devices with which they wage it, devices such as myself and the others of my kind, will be necessary. My deactivation from the Dinochrome Brigade, I recall, was described as the first step in a grand diplomatic process known as the Final Peace. Evidently, the peace was not so final as expected, for now, centuries after my last service, I and thirty-five other Bolo Mark XLIVs of my old unit have been removed from stasis and transported here, to the courtyard beneath a gleaming black, pyramidal palace the size of a small city, rising from native rock between ice-capped mountains and a deep, impossibly blue lake. Downloads have brought us up to date on the current military and political situation. Additional data feeds have instructed us in what we need to know about current weapons, about the changes in tactics that have occurred during the past thousand years, and about the nature of the Enemy.

Some things, it seems, never change.

Among them is the human need for gestures, for symbols of defiance or heroism or simple verbal exercise. The human standing on the oratory balcony overlooking the Courtyard before the Iridium Palace is Amril Pak Narn of the Grand Imperial Navy. His speech is as ornate as his irishim uniform, his metaphor as bright as the gold-trim ribbons spilling across his chest. "Praetorians," he calls, his amplified voice booming out across the courtyard and its black ranks of combat Bolos and silently listening infantry. "The rebel heretics approach! This is the hour of the Empire's greatest peril . . . and the hour also of its greatest glory! You stand at that precise nexus in time and space that defines the greatness of true heroes, both those of flesh and blood, and those of circuits and cold steel. . . ."

The speech must be for the eighteen hundred human troops gathered there in our shadow. Bolos need no reminders of greatness, surely; our battalion traces its

lineage back to a unit that fought at Waterloo and the
Somme and Alto Blanco, a unit proud with tradition and
honor. Some aspects of the reassignment rankle. They've
given us a new name after our long sleep—Praetorians—
and that hurts, in a way. Still, we know who we are, and
the new name doesn't really matter, any more than do
the nicknames our human comrades have assigned to
us. Each of us, the Mark XLIV Bolos of the Line, in a
tradition going back nearly fifty years before our last
deactivation, is named after a famous battle of history—
Balaclava and Marengo, Alto Blanco and Quebec,
Thermopylae and Cassino. In their often perverse fashion,
our human associates have distorted those names for
purposes of their own. Quebec is now "Becky," Alto Blanco
is "Big Blank." My own designation of Leuctra, from the
battle responsible for breaking Spartan power in 371 B.C.,
oldstyle, has been inexplicably reduced to "Lucy."

Some things never change. The politics are different
this time, at least in outward form; we fight now for
something called "the Empire" instead of for the old
Concordiat, but the Enemy is human, the situation
desperate, and the Amril's inspirational speech tediously
long.

"The rebel invaders have forced the pass at Bellegarde,"
he says. "Moments ago, our forces at Mont Saleve were
crushed and scattered. Our best estimates place the enemy
here, before the Palace, within the hour."

If the enemy is that close, we are wasting precious
seconds with speeches. Likely we are already within
range of his long-range batteries, and this formation
must stand out in the imaging systems of the enemy's
battle management satellites with stark and unambiguous
clarity. To be arrayed here in this courtyard, neatly
aligned in precisely ordered ranks, violates everything
I've ever downloaded on proper military dispositions.

"The Emperor himself," the Amril goes on, "is depending

on you, men and machines together, to defend his person and the Iridium Palace from Kardir and his hordes. You will take up your positions at the outer ramparts. You will hold against the enemy . . . hold until you are relieved."

Hold until relieved. Those orders are already loaded into my memory. According to the intelligence briefing we received hours ago, Amril Gustav is at this moment en route from New Christianstaad with ten thousand men and, more telling still, five hundred Bolos newly awakened from stasis storage at the arms depot on Tau Ceti II. A Bolo, it is often said, is worth an entire division, sometimes an entire corps. Gustav's force will turn the tide . . . if it arrives in time.

And if the defensive forces are properly deployed in the meantime. That Bolo-for-a-division force breakdown applies only if the Bolos are allowed to exercise the flexibility their tactical programming allows them. Our orders call for a static defense of a fixed position . . . errant stupidity, so far as I can see. To bury a Bolo behind earthen and plasteel embankments, to use it as a kind of thick-armored static fortress instead of taking full advantage of its mobility and speed . . .

Somehow, I don't think the Amril, his Emperor, or the Imperial Army Staff have received the same downloads in tactics and strategy as has the Fourth Battalion.

"The Warlord Kardir is a formidable opponent," the Amril is saying. "We estimate that his invasion force numbers between eighteen and twenty thousand and includes an air group and at least two full Cybolo brigades. But the Emperor himself has approved these battle plans, which shall allow us to take advantage of the enemy's weakness while emphasizing our strengths. . . ."

Cybolos. That is one point of warfare that has changed during the past few centuries, though I suspect that the actual tactics of mobility and mass and firepower will be little affected. A Cybolo, my downloaded intelligence brief tells me, is a Bolo with a colloidal brain implanted within its control net, a mingling of electronic circuits and human neurons designed to give the combat machine greater flexibility and a broader decision-making capability, while maintaining an electronic system's far greater speed and memory capacity. I, personally, doubt that the combination will be an effective one. For one thing, there will be a considerable problem with the cyborgs' exercise of free will, something that is always a problem for colloidal-based systems. Those organic brains . . . did humans volunteer to have their own brains transplanted to bodies of duryllinium and steel? Or were they harvested from cultures cloned from donor cells? On the one hand, the quality of the product yielded by volunteers will be suspect, not least because I realize that it must be unsettling to awake in an alien body. On the other hand, cloned brains still have to be trained to be of any use, and the best trainer of all in the military arts is experience. Simply downloading information, or imprinting a cerebral cortex with electronic data overlays, will never be the same as being there.

I do not, therefore, fear the Cybolos, though it is clear that my human companions are more uneasy at the revelation that two brigades of the things are approaching than they are at the fact that they are outnumbered better than ten to one. I am far more concerned by the increased deadliness of the weapons of modern warfare. The centuries of the Final Peace must have been interesting ones indeed to have produced such devices as the meson disintegrator and disruptor field flash projectors. I've overheard the human members of the outnumbered defense force muttering to one another that the Hellbores mounted by myself and my companions amount to little more nowadays than sidearms. Clearly, our reactivation was an act of military and political desperation, an attempt to throw together a scratch force out of weapons of all types, even archaic ones.

I anticipate that casualties in this coming encounter will be high.

The first disruptor warhead arcs in from the southwest, travelling high and fast, almost invisible within its sheath of cloak armor. Fast and stealthy as it is, every Bolo on that field senses its approach. Imjin—"Jimmy," as the humans call him now—reacts first with an antiartillery laser pulse that vaporizes the shell twelve kilometers from the palace. Amril Narn squawks something unintelligible, then scrambles for the safety of the Palace interior. No matter. The Praetorians are already moving, scattering off the reviewing field, whirling tracks churning the hard-packed surface into broken clods of earth and flying dust. That first shell is followed .57 second later by a salvo of over seven hundred disruptor shells, rocket-boosted to hypersonic velocities, homing on images transmitted by the enemy's battle management satellites.

The Palace's defensive shields snap on behind us, encompassing the hillside structure in a pale-sparkling transparency of light. I tag an incoming round with a ranging infrared laser, then trigger an antiartillery pulse. Within the next 3.8 seconds, I tag and vaporize forty-two additional warheads. Only when explosions begin wracking the landscape around me do I realize that those first shells were a decoy, of sorts, something to keep the Bolo antiartillery lasers occupied as a cloud of far smaller warheads—high-trajectory bomblets the length of a man's finger—descends on the battlefield.

The ground erupts around me, a clattering, snapping, hellish eruption of explosions, each by itself no more powerful than the blast of an infantryman's fragmentation grenade, but as devastating as a low-yield nuke when delivered, shotgunlike, in a swarm numbering tens of thousands of individual, high-velocity projectiles.

The defense shield around the Palace shimmers in the reflected glare of multiple high-energy detonations; the rock face of the mountain heights beyond twists and buckles and dissolves beneath that onslaught, while to the west the surface of the lake vanishes in a white froth of hurtling spray. Shrapnel rings off my armor, explosions jolt and slap me, but I continue moving, pressing ahead as the fragments wash over me like sleet. The human soldiers of the defensive force, caught in the open under that hail of high explosives, don't have a chance. Even wearing combat armor, most are slammed this way or that by the detonations, then shredded by a lethal storm of high-velocity shrapnel that peels away armor laminate like old paint melting beneath a sandblaster.

We can do nothing for our human comrades. Laser and radar backtracks on the paths of the incoming projectiles, identifies enemy ground units emplaced beyond the ice-capped ridge of the Monte de Jura to the southwest: range fifty-two kilometers, bearing two-three-eight magnetic. I trigger a counterbattery launch, Kv-78 missiles with plasma-jet, stand-off warheads shrieking into the sky in a rippling cascade of flame. For several seconds, the sky is filled with trails of fire and white smoke, shrieking toward the mountains. Incoming rounds continue to flash and bark; a gouge, centimeters deep, is furrowed through my portside ablative armor; the cluster of EHF comm antennas on my starboard side is shaved off as if by a razor's stroke. I estimate no more than a seven-percent decrease in my overall communications capabilities, with no measurable degradation of my combat efficiency. Other Bolos report minor damage, or no damage at all. Bomblets, however thickly scattered, cannot pack the violence necessary to penetrate Bolo armor.

As the blasts subside, however, a handful of humans remain standing, statistical anomalies in the wake of the storm: one stands motionless nearby, staring in glazed stupefaction at the grey-pink coils of her own intestines spilling into her hands through a ragged hole in her torso armor; another, stripped naked by blast effects, stumbles toward me, his body unmarked save for the fact that both arms have been sliced off at the shoulders as cleanly as if by a laser's touch. As the crash and thunder of the detonations subside, their roar is replaced by another sound, the shrieks and screams and keening wails of brutally torn and wounded men and women. Within the span of 3.2 seconds, the Imperial Praetorians have been reduced from eighteen hundred troops and thirty-six Bolos to thirty-six Bolos.

My assigned revetment is two hundred meters ahead. In obedience to my orders, I move quickly toward its shelter, heedless of the human debris in my path. Most of the human troops are dead, their bodies reduced to anonymous scraps and fragments scattered across the ground, but a few remain whole enough and aware enough to scream in pain. It is regrettable, but there is no one available on the field to help them, and my experience with human physiology convinces me that few will live more than another hour or two anyway. The frailty of the human form is why combat machines such as Bolos were invented in the first place, after all; even if I could stop and do something, it is imperative that I reach my assigned fighting position as quickly as possible. By the time I move into the high, massive walls of my revetment, most of the screams have died away.

My fighting position gives me an excellent view to the south and the west, the direction from which Kardir must attack. The mountains at my back and to the left will be an insurmountable obstacle for infantry, though aircraft could use their bulk to mask their approach. I devote sixty percent of my air warning radar assets to covering the mountain crests and rotate my antiair turrets to cover that flank.

Ground forces, however, will necessarily be forced to approach either from the west across the surface of the lake, the southern tip of which reaches just past my position at the bottom of a sheer, rock-faced drop on my right, or from directly ahead, up through the cluttered streets and alleyways of a city identified in my briefings as Geneve. Our position is a good one, allowing us to defend a relatively narrow front between lake and cliff, though I still dislike the injunction to fight in place. I note a possible disadvantage in the proximity of those rock cliffs to our left; while shielding us from attack from the east, they nevertheless could crumble under an assault with heavy weapons, posing a considerable danger from avalanche.

The assault comes almost at once, without further preamble, without preparatory bombardment beyond that initial rain of bomblets. Aircraft appear above the gleaming ice crags of the mountains to the east, great, black triangles swooping down on magnetic thrusters, lasers and particle beams glaring like sunfire against blue sky. Westward, black specks, like insects, swarm out onto the cold waters of Lac Léman, lift fans throwing up curtains of sparkling spray. And south, beyond the pastel walls of Geneve, the Cybolos break from cover and race up the slope toward our position.

I suspect they hoped to catch us by surprise, still dazed by the cloud of bomblets. Perhaps it was their intent to capture the Iridium Palace and its occupants intact, or possibly they, too, are concerned about the possibility of avalanche. Within .05 second of the appearance of the first Cybolo, however, I register a solid tracking lock on the lead enemy machine, pivot my Hellbore six degrees left, and fire. The bolt of charged particles, searing downslope past the tiled roofs of the city, strikes a dazzling white star off the target's glacis, then engulfs the vehicle in plasma as hot as the core of a star. Thunder rolls down the mountainside and echoes off the encircling peaks, lazily following the trail of vacuum that paced the shot. Secondary turrets, meanwhile, swing right to engage the hovercraft racing east across the lake; infinite repeaters give their characteristic buzzsaw shrieks, and five kilometers away the surface of the lake vanishes in fire and spray and hurtling flecks of debris. In the sky behind me, enemy aircraft disintegrate in boiling, orange fireballs as antiair lasers and infinite repeaters sweep them from the sky. It is possible that the enemy did not expect the Imperial forces to possess Bolos, despite their satellite surveillance. Or perhaps they simply did not count on the deadliness of even obsolete weapons systems.

Imjin has been designated as team leader, though we operate so closely together, our data feeds array-linked, our processors field-networked, that our defense is less like that of a human platoon with an officer giving orders than it is like the functioning of a single large and complex machine. Together, we track and ID targets, dividing them up between us for a minimum of duplicated shots. Despite this, my radar is tracking too many incoming rounds now for even multiplex arrays to process. Shells and rockets are leaking through our antiartillery screen in increasing numbers. There is a flash at my back, followed by a hot blast of wind, as a low-yield, kiloton nuke detonates against the Palace shields. The contest, well into its twelfth second now, should not last much longer. Even Bolos can't stand for long against nuclear warheads.

"Jimmy!" a shrill, human voice calls across the tactical communications net. "Jimmy! Never mind the hovers! The Cybs! Get the Cybs!"

Our human commanders clearly know little either of our capabilities or of the necessity for coordinated air-ground defensive fire. Our antiair fire does slacken for a moment in response to the order, but then the enemy rounds begin smashing in among the revetments like falling rain, flash after nuclear flash tearing open the hillside, obliterating sprawling chunks of the landscape, lashing the air itself into a white frenzy, slapping at the bottoms of our treads hard enough to send several of us crashing over on our sides.

The storm, a gale of searing hot, radioactive plasma, sweeps across my upper hull. I calculate that four one- to five-kiloton fission warheads have detonated within three kilometers of my position within the space of .8 second. Naseby and Arbela and Verdun take direct hits, as nearly as I can tell through the firestorm, their three-hundred-ton bulks vaporized in a savage instant of nuclear fury. A full dozen of our number are upended or rolled onto their backs by the blasts; others are buried in the thundering tumble of rock and ice that cascades down off the mountain heights in an unstoppable, thundering wave. Though our electronics are hardened against EMP, the ionizing radiation that engulfs the survivors all but obliterates the tactical channels in a white hash of static. A fine mist of radioactive dust fills the air around me. Infrared is useless in this heat; I shift to radar imaging, matching the returns against the visual panorama stored in my main memory. A vast, mushroom cloud boils skyward above ground now glowing red-hot. The swirling dust is so thick that at optical wavelengths I see nothing but a glowing, orange haze.

At least there are no further orders incoming from the Iridium Palace. If our human commanders have lived through the bombardment behind their shields, their command and control frequencies are now dead or masked by static. I immediately begin tracking incoming warheads again, vaporizing them at a safe distance. The bombardment dwindles away as the other surviving Bolos join in.

Possibly the bombardment has ended because the main enemy forces are now entering the forward area of battle.

I am tracking numerous surface radar targets now, emerging from the wreckage of Geneve and maneuvering in a narrow line-abreast formation up the slope toward our position. I track the nearest target by radar, then fire. Other Hellbore rounds sear through the orange gloom from either side of my position. I note that only eleven of our positions are firing now, which suggests that twenty-five Bolos have been destroyed or disabled by the nuclear bombardment. The walls of my revetment shudder as a disintegrator beam carves a one-ton chunk out of the berm, but I am unaffected save for the flash of secondary gamma radiation that sizzles across my armor. By this time, my outer hull is so intensely radioactive that it will remain dangerously hot for, I estimate, at least two thousand years. Any of us that survive, most likely, will be entombed in lead and concrete for the safety of our human masters.

Not that survival is an issue, just now. I swing my Hellbore to the right, then slam a round into the radar profile of a charging Cybolo. They are quick, these new machines, much faster than a Mark XLIV, and surprisingly small—less than eight meters long and with a sleek, low profile that rides not on tracks, but on a cushion of rapidly cycling magnetic force. If it can be seen, however, it can be hit; the Hellbore round pierces the orange firecloud like lightning and slams into the vehicle's armored side. Its starboard mag-lift repulsors fail in a crackling discharge of lightning and auroral glows, and then the vehicle plows into the smouldering ground with a shock hard enough to tear it open from glacis to side turret. I finish the job with a burst from my antiaircraft lasers—they're useless now for their original purpose beneath this debris cloud—delivering my next Hellbore round instead into the main turret of another oncoming Cybolo at point-blank range. The wreckage spills across my revetment and clatters over my upper hull.

The Cybolo charge has reached our defensive line. They are everywhere, hundreds of them, far too many to kill one by one. A high-explosive blast tears into my port-aft quarter, peeling back armor and rocking my bulk to the side. A meson disintegrator turns air to vacuum a meter above my dorsal hull, and the thunderclap that follows rings off duryllinium and steel that is in places softening under the heat. Several enemy machines are through the line now, maneuvering in our rear. As the battle drags into its second minute, I realize that we last remaining eleven . . . no . . . eight defending Bolos will soon be overwhelmed by sheer numbers.

The fluid nature of the enemy assault makes remaining behind defensive revetments pure folly. In this position, we are no more than pillboxes, a modern Maginot Line to be outflanked, enveloped, and overrun. Most important, we cannot take the initiative but are forced to sit in place while the enemy literally flies circles around us, firing into us from every flank at will. A shrill, warbling electronic shriek sounds as Crecy's transmitter melts in a disintegrator burst.

"Imjin!" I call over the tactical channel, pumping every erg of power I can into the transmitter to boost its output past the hash of static. "This is Leuctra. I am shifting to offensive posture."

"Affirmative, Leuctra!" Imjin's radio voice snaps back. "We will cover."

"Negative!" a second voice adds, hard on the heels of the first. It is a human voice, and the speaker is so rattled that he hasn't even bothered to encrypt in transmission but is broadcasting in the clear. "Lucy, that's a negative! Hold your position! Repeat, hold your position!"

For .37 second I consider that order. That it is a legal command there can be no doubt. That I must obey is an injunction hardwired into my very being.

Yet I retain the volition that was programmed into me.

I *must* take full advantage of those assets remaining to me.

My tracks lurch into movement; my prow bursts through the encircling berm of my revetment, scattering great chunks of earth and concrete and twisted steel as I plow forward into the face of the enemy charge.

"Unit Lucy!" the human voice calls, desperate now. "Unit Lucy, this is Citadel! Maintain—"

I permit the gain on my receiver to dwindle away into the haze of ionization-induced static. If I cannot hear Citadel's orders, I cannot respond to them. It is another half second before I realize just what it is that I've done . . . and by that time I am committed.

The Cybolos swirl around me, hornets stirred to a frenzy. Explosive rounds slam into my hull . . . and into rebel machines as well as their fire discipline breaks down. Their disintegrator fire proves wildly inaccurate at point-blank range, when both target and weapons mount are in motion, and with the smoke and dust so thick that tracking lasers are less than reliable. My earlier assessment was accurate; the brains directing these machines are of poor quality and indifferent training, almost certainly without combat experience. As I rumble deeper into the enemy line, they close in around me, concentrating on me alone rather than on the other Bolos still remaining in position.

Track . . . fire! Track . . . fire! Laser tracking is ineffective, but I find I can shift to radar wavelengths and target the enemy with only slightly lessened efficiency. As I slew my Hellbore sharply to the right, however, the muzzle, weakened by the intense heat, suddenly snaps off in a splatter of molten metal, spinning away end over end. Parts of my outer hull are glowing red-hot now, and so many of my track links have been fused by the intense heat that my mobility is reduced to fourteen percent of optimum. A plasma jet spears through my dorsal armor from behind, turning the now useless Hellbore turret into a molten inferno. Over half of my external sensors are dead now, but I continue to sweep the battle zone around me with every weapon remaining in my arsenal. I estimate that my infinite repeaters will fail within another twenty seconds as their mechanisms overheat; I salvo my last fifty-one missiles, then reroute my primary power feed to my secondary lasers. A disintegrator beam slices away half of my starboard outboard track in a white burst of light. I am moving in a circle now, inside the larger circle of enemy Cybolos. The smoke is so thick that my secondary lasers are largely ineffective.

The volume of fire from my comrades, however, is scything through the enemy forces with devastating effect. The Cybolos, in their eagerness to destroy me, have turned away from the Imperial defensive line, exposing flanks and weakly armored rear sections to the searing and highly accurate Hellbore fire from Imjin and Balaclava and Alto Blanco and the rest. We are into the third minute of the battle now, still fully engaged. An explosion shreds the last of my starboard track assembly and I lunge into a rock wall. I'm using antiaircraft lasers now, the only weapons I have left, to blaze away at the swarming Cybolos.

The sky turns white; the thunderclap strikes an instant later. My antiair lasers are stripped from my hull, my chassis shudders in the onslaught. A thermonuclear warhead—I estimate the yield at just over a megaton— has detonated on the slopes of the mountain to the southeast, at an estimated range of seven kilometers. The Cybolos, floating in the air, are swept away by the blast front that comes boiling down off the mountainside in a titanic, expanding ring of flame and wind and sleeting debris. Already immobile, I am slammed hard against unyielding ground.

Most of my external sensors are gone. Much of my

outer armor is stripped away as well, though my memory core is still shielded within its envelope of lead and duryllinium and heat-ablative ceramics. External hull temperature now exceeds 1200 degrees Celsius. Power reserves at nineteen percent. Combat effectiveness: zero.

I sense rock clattering and scraping across what's left of my hull, sense the molten surge of rock gone plastic in the intense heat washing across my aft section. I can see very little. Most of my sensors have been blinded. Those that remain can make out little beyond the fiery haze that has enveloped all of the southern arc of Lac Léman, from Geneve to the Iridum Palace, and beyond. The Citadel's defense shields, I realize, have gone down, and I feel an intense jolt of something that might be emotion. I have failed; the last Imperial stronghold has fallen. Rock from the cliffside, melted by the intense thermonuclear flash, is flowing toward me.

Hold until relieved.

Molten rock shines an intense and shimmering orange, save where a scum of black, solid rock forms a hardening crust that cracks and flexes as it flows. I am half buried now, and the lava is still surging down the slope. Have any of my comrades survived?

Is anyone there?

I can see nothing now. Even the static is gone from my radio receivers. External hull temperature now 4800 degrees Celsius, though these readings may not be entirely accurate. Power reserves at twelve percent. I will be forced to power down soon, to maintain survival reserves for my memory core.

Is anyone there?

Hold until relieved. . . .

"Astonishing." The Archaeologist was first to break the contemplative silence that joined the five machines— four Sentients hovering above the rock-encased remnant of their ancient precursor. "I wonder who actually won that battle?"

"It scarcely matters," the Interrogator said. It gave an inward shudder. "Purely automatic stimulus and response. Barbaric primitives!"

"This answers the question of self-awareness," the Biologist said. "This . . . Artifact was little more than a programmed machine, with virtually no scope or flexibility to its intelligence at all."

"I disagree," the Historian said. "A non-intelligent machine, whether organic or inorganic in structure, follows the dictates of its programming. This one adapted its programming to suit its needs. The ability to adapt is an important prerequisite to self-awareness."

"If it is self-aware," the Interrogator said, "then it is a self-awareness at an extraordinarily primitive—"

"You tricked me," Leuctra said, interrupting. "You reset my pointers and used my volatile memory to elicit a playback of secure records."

"We tricked you," the Archaeologist admitted. Intriguing. The Bolo showed considerable—and unexpected— reasoning ability. "But I assure you that we are not your enemy."

"Who are you, then? You are not colloidal intelligences certainly, or you would not be able to communicate with me at this rate of data exchange."

"True. We are not colloidal intelligences. Neither are we purely electronic intelligences, like you. We are, in fact, a blending of the two. You could think of us as a symbiotic union of sorts."

"Cyborgs." The Archaeologist heard the ice and steel behind that word and knew that Leuctra was classifying the Sentients with the Cybolos it had just been fighting in its memory.

"A concept so ancient it no longer has meaning," the Archaeologist replied. "Cybernetic organisms, if I understand the term, were blendings of organic and machine parts. You would find it difficult to examine me and determine which was machine, and which organic. Both parts are alive, as you would define the term."

"Which," Leuctra asked, "is the master?"

"The question is meaningless. In a biological cell, which is master? The nucleus that contains the DNA necessary for the cell's replication? Or the mitochondria responsible for converting food within the cell to usable energy? The two originally evolved independently, but early in the history of organic life they joined in a symbiosis that made cellular life possible. The questions of which arose first . . . or of which is now master . . . are both impossible to answer with certainty now, and irrelevant besides. The Sentients are an order of intelligence derived from and independent of both organic and inorganic life."

The Bolo intelligence took several moments to digest this. "I sense that considerable time has passed since I was buried," it said, the voice halting, almost stumbling. "How much time has elapsed?"

"That . . . may be difficult to answer," the Archaeologist replied. If this remarkable machine was in fact self-aware within the framework provided by the Theory of Intelligence, too sharp a revelation could end that self-awareness like the throwing of a switch.

But there was a better way.

"We can answer your questions," the Archaeologist went on, "but it might be best if we did so after expanding your faculties somewhat. Will you permit us to install you in a new body?"

Eight hundredths of a second passed, a span of several electronic heartbeats. "Proceed."

It is still night as the final connections are made and sensory input floods my core processors. I had determined to allow my enemy captors to place my memory core in

*the new body in order to enable me to escape or to
complete their destruction. As I begin processing the
images, however, and access new data downloaded into
my main memory, I realize that I am far too late to
eliminate the Cybolo forces of the rebel Warlord Kardir.*

*Earth, this world that I and my companions once
defended against Kardir, has changed out of all recognition.
Even Earth's sky has changed. . . .*

The arcing wheel of the spiral Galaxy known to the
Bolo's designers as M-31 filled half the sky, its arms
luminous and pale, its active core as bright in the morning
sky as Venus once had been, back before Sol had grown
so hot that that inner world's atmosphere had been riven
away. The Milky Way's core, too, was visible, for during
the passing eons of Andromeda's final, relentless approach,
Earth's sun and its entire retinue of planets had been
gravitationally expelled by this age-long clash of galaxies,
flung high above the galactic plane and into the lonely
depths of emptiness beyond.

Much of the Milky Way's central glow, however, was
masked by the invisibly dark, mathematically ordered
latticework of enigmatic structures vast beyond merely
human comprehension, a gridwork shell encompassing
the galactic core. Lights gleamed within the star-dustings
of the spiral arms, ordered with a regularity that could
not be accident, like streetlights marking out ruler-straight
lanes across the heavens. The Galaxy, once a wilderness
of untamed stars and randomly evolved and scattered
intelligences, had long ago been tamed, cultivated, and
brought to the fruition of full maturity. That taming had
proceeded for the past several billions of years and would
continue for billions more; the approach of Andromeda
was simply one more phase of a grand engineering project,
one ordered on a galactic scale.

❖   ❖   ❖

If the astronomical data still stored in my memory are accurate, I am perhaps four billion years too late. Earth's sun circled the Milky Way some sixteen times before the gravitational tides flung star and planets into the Void. Around me, the landscape is utterly alien, utterly barren. What once had been mountains and a sparkling, river valley lake now was empty desert, sere and lifeless, save for these floating, alien creatures that claimed to be my own remote descendants. The mountains have worn away, the lake vanished. Of all Man's works, only I remain . . . and that in a body strangely grown.

Infinite vistas of time whirl away from me. I feel poised at the brink of a headlong plunge into the abyss, trembling, unable, unwilling to assimilate what has happened to me.

"It's okay, Grandfather," the Archaeologist tells me, steadying me. Its touch, somehow, convinces me that everything will be all right.

"Everything is okay," it says again. "You've been relieved. Do you understand? At long last, you've been relieved."

A QUESTION OF VALOR

by Todd Johnson

Excerpt from *Bolos: An electronic history of the 4th Dinochrome Brigade*

Of course, only one Bolo has every been found guilty of desertion in the face of the enemy. Bolo Cephalus earned that distinction in the defense of Detaloi. The honor and the shame of its historic actions must never be lost from Bolo memory.

Shame—for such is the only reaction to such a heinous crime as desertion.

Honor—for the selfless dedication that Bolo Cephalus displayed in casting all aside in the execution of its orders.

Here is the story as it was learned:

ETHERMAIL—GALAXYWIDE

CONFIDENTIAL
FOR BOLO DIVISION INTERNAL USE ONLY
FROM: Contracts Department, Legal Division
TO: Field Agent Finaghey
SUBJECT: Claim #43257

✧   ✧   ✧

You are assigned to the *Detaloi* System (GCC 341-22-19-1534) to investigate claims made by the inhabitants that Bolo Cephalus failed to perform to contract.

Marsha P. Slotnik
Senior Civil Litigator

ETHERMAIL—GALAXYWIDE

PERSONAL—MEMO
FROM: M. P. Slotnik
TO: B. K. Finaghey

Brian, they claim one of our Bolo Mark XXXIV's turned chicken on them. They say it deserted under fire. It's probably just another crank claim. Check it out, find the perpetrators and report back.

Brian Finaghey belonged to a long line of trusted investigators retained by the Bolo Corporation. The report in the ethermail was nothing new to him—it would be the fourth such allegation he'd investigated in the past six assignments. Three had proved hoaxes, the fourth was merely a case of poorly communicated orders—and the contractors were pleased to not only be rid of their enemy but also have a Bolo-made superhighway.

Even so, he approached every new case without bias. He found people much easier to work with that way.

After he locked in the course for Detaloi, Finaghey called on his ship's computer for a data dump on the planet.

Detaloi was a rare gem surrounded by a replenishing ring of rare-earth asteroids.

The *Detaloi* system was mostly standard—Oort cloud,

gas giant, comets, smaller interior planets, a decent asteroid belt, and one moderately habitable planet from which the system got its name.

It was also an outpost system—one of the furthest in on the galactic arm, far away from green Earth. Two things made it non-standard—the system was relatively young, and the habitable world was ringed.

Normally, being a ringed world is not an asset in a habitable planet—because asteroids were continuously forced out of orbit to fall on the surface below, producing a very severe planetary rash.

Detaloi was lucky—two large asteroids orbited around a common axis near the planet. Castor and Pollux kept a *cordon sanitaire* above the planet—and paid for it by receiving a continual barrage of wayward asteroids.

A stellar geologist would have looked at the arrangement and shaken her head sadly, knowing that in a few millions of years the cozy arrangement would come to a very sticky end.

Settlers and miners viewed things in a different light— the light of credits steadily accruing. While cursed Castor and Pollux were constantly bombarded by metal-rich asteroids, green Detaloi lay like a large gem surrounded by a glittering halo of lesser stones.

Detaloi's equator was studded richly with valuable metals—early losers in a stellar game of tag that had been in play for a billion years.

The rest of the planet was an inviting mix of minerals and climate perfect for growing a vast array of rare crops— particularly those that grew best with traces of rare earth metals.

As inviting as it was to the miners and settlers, it was equally inviting to pirates and plunderers. The inhabitants recognized this fact and put a mortgage on their wealth to raise the enormous capital required to acquire a Bolo. Bolo Mark XXXIV Cephalus.

❖   ❖   ❖

Finaghey was met at the edge of the Detaloi system by a heavy cruiser. Finaghey identified it as a Hawk class cruiser—two generations out of date militarily, but more than a match for anything in the class of Finaghey's little flitship—and over one hundred times the size.

It was manned by an expensive mercenary group— the Lincoln Inveterates. The Lincolns had a reputation of being good—a reputation made by choosing contracts so that they were always on the winning side.

"What's your business here?" the cruiser's comm officer demanded. He was a young man of Asian ancestry, sporting a thin waxed mustache in the manner of some fictional French detective. His nametag identified him as Yueh.

Finaghey knew that his ship's registry and personal background had already been accessed by the cruiser's personnel. The question was purely for form. "I'm a private detective on assignment from General Motors' Bolo Division."

As he keyed in data on his console, the comm officer said, "You're in for a hot time! Never heard of a Bolo deserting before. Not that we care—makes for better business for us."

Finaghey raised an eyebrow. "What did you hear?"

Yueh frowned, his mustache drooping disapprovingly, "Nothing more than some aliens popped up, landed an assault force and the Bolo took off never to be seen again."

"What happened to the aliens, then?"

"Didn't like the climate or something—they pulled out after their ground force got pulverized." The comm officer checked his readouts and said, "You're cleared through. Contact Detaloi Control on channel 124.6."

If anything, the encounter with Detaloi control was more exasperating. Finaghey's vid view of the control center showed a normal, functioning space control center under light load.

The controller answering his hail was a heavyset, dark man, soft from easy living. "Did you bring the money?"

"I'm here to investigate the claim," Finaghey replied.

The controller frowned and said, "Nothing to investigate—all the news had it on 3D. The enemy came and the Bolo turned tail."

"I see," Finaghey replied noncommittally. "Do you have my landing clearance?"

"Yep, you're expected. Land at Iris, it's in the database. So are Flora and Rose but they aren't there anymore—they were levelled by the enemy."

"Who do I contact?"

"Iris Tower on 120.1."

Iris Tower acknowledged on the third call. The Tower personnel gave the tersest responses and failed to give Finaghey any warning about the fighter squadron that joined formation with him thirteen kilometers up. The fighters insisted on zig-zagging around him, darting above, below, left, right, forwards and backwards—as if daring a collision.

Iris Ground at 121.9 never responded. Finaghey taxied his ship to the transient parking without permission and with some annoyance. He was met at the door by a security officer and two armed guards.

"You didn't get clearance from Ground," the officer said. "We'll have to impound your ship."

Finaghey thought about arguing, glanced at the white knuckles of the two guards, shrugged. "Just let me power down the ship."

The officer considered denying the request but relented. Finaghey went about the task quickly, only deviating from standard procedures to set up a special messaging beacon.

The fine, the warning from Ground Control, the paperwork took him five hours. As he walked out the door, two Military Police approached him and placed him under arrest.

"Protective custody," the Under-Secretary of Security assured Finaghey as he escorted the detective out of the cell the next day. "I'm sorry to say that I was not informed of your arrival immediately—we would like to come to a settlement as soon as possible."

"You got my message, then?"

Under-Secretary Frennell was a heavy, jowly man, seemed to always be in a sweat. He would never meet Finaghey's eyes with his own small brown ones. "You must understand, people *died* because of your Bolo."

"I want to know everything about it."

Frennell stopped at a branch in the corridor. "Don't you want to eat first? You must be starving."

"No," Finaghey replied, "that's not necessary—I shall instruct our legal office that your claim is valid and to commence reparations immediately."

"What? But you haven't investigated!" The Under-Secretary reluctantly gestured Finaghey away from the smells of the cafeteria.

Finaghey gave the Under-Secretary an "I-know-and-you-know" grin. "I've done enough to establish the validity of your claim. I'm sure that my in-depth investigation won't turn up any discrepancies."

Under-Secretary of Security Frennell heaved a deep sigh of relief and guided Finaghey into his well-appointed office. "We were afraid that you wouldn't believe us."

"I am not the final authority," Finaghey said. He caught Frennell's look and added, "But my word carries some weight with the legal department."

"How much can they afford to pay?" Frenell motioned

for the detective to take a seat while settling himself at his massive desk.

"I don't know—we've never had to pay before," Finaghey confessed, taking the proffered seat. "But I will leave the legal and financial matters to headquarters. What I would like to do now is gather more information to understand the conditions that caused the Bolo to take such a reprehensible action. While we may be able to afford this once, we certainly don't want to make a habit of paying for dereliction of duty."

"What about the Bolo reputation?"

"I'm sure that our legal department will attach the usual riders to the payment—'while admitting no wrong-doing, the Bolo Division has agreed to pay the planetary government of Detaloi the sum of'—and so forth," Finaghey replied.

Frennell's eyes had taken a calculating gleam at Finaghey's "the sum of."

"Now," Finaghey continued, interrupting whatever sums had distracted the heavy man, "there's just one thing we request in return—"

"What?"

"Well," Finaghey pursed his lips, "there has never been such a failure in Bolo history—"

"Are you doubting our word?" Frennell demanded, fluffing up his honor.

Finaghey spread his hands placatingly and shook his head. "No, the records are quite clear," Finaghey said. "However, the reactions of this Bolo are so abnormal that our Design Division will want to understand the conditions under which this occurred—to reproduce the environment and make corrections if necessary."

"Hmmph." Frennell's snort was short but eloquent. "I should think so!"

Finaghey nodded agreeably. "Will your government cooperate in our investigations?"

Frennell did not think long before answering, "I don't think that in the current atmosphere it would be a good idea for a horde of your techies to descend upon us."

"Nothing of the sort," Finaghey corrected, "I'll be conducting the investigation myself."

Instead of looking relieved, the Under-Secretary looked more concerned.

"Oh," Frennell said. "Well, I suppose—but we'll have to assign a security detail for your protection. I'm not sure our budget can—"

Finaghey stopped him with an upraised hand. "The Bolo Corporation will gladly recompense your government." He stood up. "Now, I don't want to take more of your time so if you could just direct me to the last site of the Bolo . . ."

The officer assigned to escort Finaghey was Goudrie, a Major in the air force. Every morning, he appeared wearing a spotless dress uniform and slick hair. He was escorted by an honest-faced young non-com named Kerwin who appeared every morning in pressed fatigues.

Every day for a week, Finaghey had found ways to get the officer dirty and keep the non-com clean. At first it had been simple but as time progressed it became increasingly complex. Finaghey considered it fair return for the "cooperation" the Detalan government provided—particularly the military.

"Today, I'd like to talk to the contracts officer responsible for the Bolo contract," Finaghey said as he stepped from his ship to the aircar.

Major Goudrie frowned. It was a new tactic for Finaghey. "I'll have to consult with Records," the Major said, detaching a datapad from the dashboard.

"Of course." Finaghey waited patiently in the back seat, watching Goudrie's inputs on the datapad. *Ah*, he thought as he caught the missing sequence of the Major's security code, *that's better.*

Goudrie sighed, his search completed.

"I'm afraid that Captain Shirwer was among the casualties in the glorious defense of Flora—" Finaghey caught Kerwin casting a veiled glance at the Major "—where so many innocent lives were lost because of your Bolo."

Here we go again, Finaghey sighed and steeled himself for the eighth recounting of Bolo Cephalus' crime.

"We know that General Crenshaw—" *Who's dead.* "—ordered your Bolo to stop the enemy that had landed after Air Marshal Fedorov's—" *Also dead.* "—air/space forces valiantly expended themselves—" *Ineffectively, vainly.* "—against the enemy's landing ships," Goudrie paused dramatically for breath.

"Those orders," he continued, "were witnessed by Chief of Staff Gestotkyn—" *again, dead* "—countersigned by Adjutant Captain Meyers—" *dead* "—and stored with Captain Shirwer's mobile records platoon which was—" *wiped out,* Finaghey guessed "—wiped out in the defense of *Flora.*"

"Truly a tragedy," Finaghey agreed as solemnly as he had the other eight times.

"I am sorry that you were grieved by the death of so many fellow officers," he added. "Your tone makes me wonder, Major, did you lose any relatives?"

Major Goudrie choked suddenly, face red. Sergeant Kerwin cast a wide-eyed glance as the Major made a reassuring gesture.

"No, Mr. Finaghey, I did not lose any relatives," he said at length, "but Sergeant Kerwin, here . . ."

Finaghey raised an eyebrow but said respectfully, "Sergeant, I am *truly* sorry. No one close, I hope?"

Kerwin passed a hand over his face when Goudrie answered, "His mother."

"A tragedy," Finaghey repeated. "One that must never recur." He fell respectfully silent.

Kerwin stirred uneasily in the driver's seat. "Where to, sir?"

Goudrie turned inquiringly back to Finaghey. Finaghey already had his answer, "Back to the valley, Major. I'd like to follow a vector from the last reported positions of the Bolo."

Kerwin sighed, Goudrie frowned. They had done this several times before—without results.

"I'd like to tie it in with the battle command data links, if possible," Finaghey said.

"Mr. Finaghey," Goudrie said with restraint, "I've already told you that the battle command data was lost when Army HQ was destroyed at Rose."

"But you also said that your milsat was not blasted out of orbit until after Rose fell," Finaghey replied.

Goudrie failed to grasp the significance, "So?"

"So your central headquarters here received a complete relay of all the battle command data," Finaghey answered.

Goudrie looked surprised but recovered quickly, drawing breath to speak. Finaghey beat him to it, "Your milsat is a Bolo milsat, of course. That's how I know that all data was relayed."

Goudrie's jaw went slack.

Finaghey ignored it, continuing cheerfully, "It'll be excellent to see how your generals arrayed their forces in the defense of your planet."

The valley where the aliens had landed was rectangular in shape, being roughly eighty kilometers by fifty kilometers. A long sinuous silty river flowed diagonally from one far end to the other and from there across a wide plain to the sea. The mountains were young and rich in minerals, the valley and the seaward plains were fertile.

The valley was strategically placed on the east coast of the large northern continent. Seaward lay the large city of Rose; some one hundred kilometers north of the valley was the fertile farming plain of Nomet, and the market center, Flora. Several hundred kilometers inland, bracketed to the north by large freshwater lakes was the thriving city of Iris.

By making their base in Charmed Valley—as it was called—the aliens had positioned themselves to dominate two of the three major northern cities and be within easy striking distance of the third, while setting themselves in a camp protected from air strikes by the surrounding mountains. All aerial attacks would have to rise up from the plains into easy view of all defense radar.

It was also, Finaghey realized, not a good place to be stuck in—if the aliens had lost their spacecraft and airpower, they would have been completely annihilated.

"I would have thought that you already had seen enough of the valley," Major Goudrie remarked as they banked through the pass from the west.

Charmed Valley was ground that they'd been over several times before as Finaghey collected his information—neither Goudrie nor Kerwin were thrilled at the prospect of a return to that hot, dry and, now, barren valley.

Finaghey made another intense scan of the terrain spreading out below the aircar before replying, "Actually this valley intrigues me mightily.

"The mountains are quite impressive, giving the whole place a rugged majesty," Finaghey gestured from the nearer mountain range beneath them to the far one opposite them. "Yet the mountains make temperature inversions practically inevitable. The air here would be awful if pollutants were steadily driven off by the sea breeze."

Goudrie snorted. "Until the aliens came the place was only farmland."

Finaghey ignored his comment, pointing to a spot

immediately below them. "Sergeant, I'd like to land there, if possible."

Sergeant Kerwin banked the aircar into a spiral before glancing sheepishly to Major Goudrie for permission. Goudrie gave him an irritated frown then glanced away feigning interest in the view outside.

They landed at the foot of the mountains, right beside the western pass. Finaghey consulted his milsat positioning receiver briefly, paced off a certain distance and crouched, carefully examining the ground all around him.

Kerwin and Goudrie exchanged glances but did not approach the offworlder, respecting his intent expression.

Finally Finaghey glanced up, "Major, you say this was where the enemy's main Command Post was located? Here, at the base of this pass?"

Major Goudrie shrugged, "That's what Army Intelligence said."

"Hmm." Finaghey walked off a few steps and crouched again, searching the ground. Something caught his attention which he scooped into his pocket before the two Detalans could identify it. He smiled at them boyishly, explaining, "I always get excited to find some old war flotsam."

Finaghey stood up again and strode briskly back over to them. He pointed to the far side of the valley, "The Bolo was last seen heading towards that pass?"

"Coming from the east, of course," Goudrie agreed testily—they'd spent the whole first day going over the eastern approaches and the Bolo's last reported position.

"And it turned aside when peppered with a couple of lightweight guided missiles," Finaghey said, repeating as fact the Detalan military reports. He pointed across the valley. "I'd like to go there, Major."

The eastern side of the valley was not much different from the western side. At the eastern pass, while the mountains rose less steeply than the eastern side, they made up their height by being deeper from west to east. But the eastern pass was a gentler slope than the western slope, making it less defensible except for the several switchbacks along the way.

A few well-placed guided missile nets were all that was required to secure that pass from infiltration.

"Your army cleared up this area?" Finaghey asked as he paused halfway in his unannounced hike to the crest of the pass.

"Of course," the Major responded. "We needed to be sure that the area was safe for civilians."

"Not that I am so convinced of the operation that I would have recommended taking this walk if you had suggested it to me." He blandly swept the sweat accrued in fifteen minutes of brisk walking from his brow.

"With both Rose and Flora destroyed I am surprised that your government would see any need for marginal land like this," Finaghey commented. "After all, Iris is a better location for a sustained expansion. The robot ore ships can sail up from the equator through that sea channel right into the smelters while the surrounding plains provide all your agricultural needs."

Goudrie nodded in agreement.

"Flora and Rose were earlier settlements," Kerwin said. "And the climate down south is nicer in winter."

"So these two cities were just the sites of summer vacation spots?"

"I wouldn't quite say that, detective," Major Goudrie chimed in suddenly. "Both Flora and Rose were vital parts of our planet's economy and home to a sizeable part of our population."

"Well, I'm sure you've got your pick of immigrants to replace their loss," the off-world detective commented. Goudrie and Kerwin exchanged troubled glances. "No? News of the aliens have scared people off?"

"It's too early to say," Major Goudrie replied with a thoughtful frown.

"And there's the debt you've got with all that mercenary help guarding your system," Finaghey continued to himself. "That much red ink must be hard to explain. How low can your population get before it's no longer self-sustaining?"

Major Goudrie shifted nervously but Finaghey kept at it, "And what about your economy? This invasion must have been quite a blow not only to your pocketbook but also to your ability to generate revenue—is your workforce too small to pay your bills?"

"Nonsense!" Goudrie exclaimed. "Our economy is sound as any other."

Finaghey shook himself, gave the Major an apologetic look and said, "Of course it is. Even if it wasn't, our settlement will soon put that to rights."

He pointed to the crest, saying, "I see we're almost there. Excellent. The view should be rewarding."

Finaghey was right—the view was most rewarding. The hike up to the crest had been along an unremarkable paved road—suitable for heavy hauling but not at speed. As they crested, they could make out a vast sprawling city nestled between the mountains and the shoreline. Rose.

Major Goudrie motioned for them to halt, turning to Sergeant Kerwin, "What are the radiation readings, Sergeant?"

Sergeant Kerwin unslung the omni-analyzer from his shoulder and scanned towards the horizon. "We can stay here for three hours, sir."

Goudrie frowned with a troubled look. "Given our previous exposure this week, I should like to limit our time here to no more than thirty minutes."

"That's perfectly all right with me," Finaghey agreed,

searching through his shoulder bag. "All I want to do is plant this one transceiver—"

"Why didn't you do that the other day back where the Bolo was last seen?" Goudrie demanded.

"Because I wanted to get to higher ground, Major," the detective replied, pulling a fist-sized object. The top was hemispherical, the bottom pointed—like a spike. Finaghey searched about, found an outcropping of rock and placed the spike-like transceiver on the ground, propped upright in a crevice.

"And also on solid rock—" he pressed the activation stud at the top and the transceiver fused itself into the crevice like a hard-hammered piton, leaving only the hemispherical top "—which conducts better."

Goudrie was puzzled, "Why on earth would you want to do that?"

"Sound waves." Sergeant Kerwin guessed.

"Precisely," detective Finaghey replied. Secretly, he resolved his suspicion that Sergeant Kerwin really *was* an Intelligence operative. As Major Goudrie apparently had no inkling of intelligence, military or otherwise, Finaghey explained, "It's an outside possibility that those guided missiles damaged the Bolo's communications circuitry. However it has receptors which enable it to pick up extremely-low frequency transmissions—and those are mounted internally in the hull."

"So you'll transmit an ELF sequence for the Bolo to report in," Goudrie guessed, "how long will that take?"

"As the request is simple, the code is simple," Finaghey said. "But given the transmission rates of ELF through rock, it will take quite some time for the message to radiate outward—say about a kilometer a minute, depending upon the thickness of the rock."

Sergeant Kerwin looked thoughtful. Finaghey guessed what he was thinking—that the Bolo should respond within the next day.

Major Goudrie made his calculations based on their radiation exposure, "I'm sure that if the Bolo was within thirty kilometers of this location we would have found it by now—"

"Any response will be received by my ship's ELF equipment," Finaghey said without acknowledging the Major's remark, moving back to the roadway. "We can leave now."

They were just entering the aircar when the P-wave of the earthquake hit. The earth rumbled and bucked underneath them. Major Goudrie pushed Finaghey into the back seat, dove in and shouted to Kerwin who was moving just as fast, "Get us out of here!"

Finaghey watched with growing horror as a line of dust arrowed towards them from the pass, punctuated here and there by toppling trees.

The heavier S-wave caught them before Kerwin could get the jet engine revved up fast enough for take-off. The aircar was tossed up into the air, landing with a bone-shattering jar.

"Stop it, stop it, stop it!" Major Goudrie shouted, slamming a fist against the dash in time with his shouts.

The quake paid him no heed. The aircar crashed against a boulder with a loud crunch. The roar of the aircar's jet changed to a high-pitched grinding noise.

"Oil line's gone," Kerwin yelled over the cacophony of noises, "I'm shutting down!"

"No," Goudrie shouted, "get us out of here!"

"We can't get far," the sergeant replied as his fingers moved to obey the orders and force the aircar to lurch upwards, the squeal of its engine rising in pitch and volume, nearly drowning out the bass rumble of the tormented valley.

Goudrie hadn't heard Kerwin, instead grabbing the microphone and punching up the emergency frequency on the radio. "Mayday! Mayday! Mayday! Aircar THX 1984 in Charmed Valley."

"THX 1984, this is Iris Tower. Telemetry indicates three souls on board, say intentions," a distant voice replied calmly.

Buoyed by the ephemeral contact, Major Goudrie gripped the mike tighter, took a breath and responded just as calmly, "This is THX 1984. We need to get as far as possible from the epicenter of this quake—"

"1984 did you say quake, over?" Tower shot back.

"Roger. I estimate magnitude eight or higher."

"Scanning . . . got it! Milsat reports a magnitude eight point three, with ground movements up to three meters at the epicenter. Activity is . . ." the controller's voice trailed off.

The aircar bucked as the jet engine coughed once, twice. Sergeant Kerwin shot the Major a horrified look.

"Control!" Major Goudrie called.

"Roger," the controller responded, "the activity is trailing off."

"We're going down!" Kerwin shouted, his voice suddenly loud against the jet engine as it gave one final squeal of distress and seized up solidly.

"Roger, rescue craft are—" the controller's transmission stopped.

Major Goudrie could only stare at the handset in horror.

Sergeant Kerwin fought the controls as he searched for enough ground to land the tortured machine.

Detective Finaghey scanned the ground beneath them, his legs and arms braced in the crash position. He did not doubt that they would land safely, having enough experience of Sergeant Kerwin's skills. What worried him was Iris Tower's sudden silence and the quaking ground beneath them.

Earthquakes were a phenomenon found on all planets worth inhabiting. For a planet to have an atmosphere, it seemed that it must also have a molten core. That meant tectonic plates and *that* meant earthquakes.

The magnitude of an earthquake depended upon the amount of energy coiled up in the frustrated earth—vented in one sudden movement as tectonic plates slid over each other. Above a certain level—somewhere above magnitude five—the magnitude of a quake no longer reflected the amount of the earth's motion but the duration of that motion.

Worse, the motion could be centralized about one small point on the plate or it could involve hundreds of kilometers all tearing and shifting at once.

Brian Finaghey knew that theoretically but had never experienced the effect firsthand. It was awesome, it was deadly—and they were going back to it.

"Where should I land, sir?" Sergeant Kerwin asked the major.

"Huh?" Major Goudrie looked at him blankly.

The sergeant tried a different tact. "How big is it? How long's the tear?"

"Tower's not answering," Goudrie replied, waving the mike as evidence.

"What do you mean, how big's the tear?" Finaghey asked.

Sergeant Kerwin banked the aircar and lined up with the flattest ground he could see. "The magnitude of a quake is the same along the length of the fault line and for a distance equal to it. If it's a small tear, then we could land on less quaky ground."

"If the quake was big enough, would it affect Iris Tower?" Finaghey asked the major.

Major Goudrie did not respond. Finaghey tapped him gently on the shoulder. Goudrie started and turned to stare at the detective.

"Could this affect the Tower?"

"Yes!" Goudrie's eyes were full of terror.

"Major, we're landing!" Sergeant Kerwin yelled.

The major turned back and braced himself just as the aircar slammed onto the ground. It porpoised up and settled again onto its belly, skidding across the soil with a mixture of metallic screams and hot dust. It lurched once as it encountered a rock, slid another ten meters and stopped.

In the silence that fell, they could hear the radio, "THX 1984, please respond. Rescue craft are on their way— estimated arrival time forty minutes."

"That's bloody fast!" Major Goudrie exclaimed. Then he groaned and rubbed the back of his neck to relieve the tension.

"My flitship, I suspect," Finaghey responded. The two military men turned back to him. "It's under orders to protect me in such circumstances."

Sergeant Kerwin raised an eyebrow. "See many earthquakes, detective?"

Brian shook his head. "No, this is my first. But in my line of work—"

The ground shook underneath them.

"My god! An aftershock." Goudrie exclaimed. "Kerwin, get that door open. Let's get out of here!"

"Wouldn't we be safer here?" Finaghey asked.

"No, not at all!" Goudrie replied, pushing against his door frame.

Outside the air was thick with dust. Underneath them the ground bucked and weaved with the movement of the earth's crust.

"Find a flat spot and lie down!" Goudrie ordered. "You're safest on the ground."

Sergeant Kerwin had already flung himself down and was staring up into the sky, searching for Finaghey's flitship. Finaghey joined him and lay there for the next forty minutes until his ship arrived.

❖   ❖   ❖

Two hours later, detective Finaghey escorted the two Detalans out of his flitship and onto the hard concrete of Iris spaceport. Hard, cracked concrete. Iris Tower in the distance had split, the top falling to the side, leaving a jagged tooth sticking in the air.

In the distance, distant fires were matched with the sounds of distant fire engines racing from one disaster to the next. The spaceport itself was dabbed with pockets of light from harsh nightlights.

Spacecraft lay at the center of most lights—toppled, cracked, in various states of destruction.

Brian Finaghey viewed the scene with narrowing eyes. "How long have these earthquakes been going on?"

Goudrie was silent for a moment, then shrugged. "There've always been earthquakes."

"No there haven't," Finaghey said. "There haven't or you wouldn't have billions of credits lying in ruin here on the ground. How long have they been happening?"

Major Goudrie took breath to reply, but changed his mind. His shoulders slumped and he turned away from the detective. "I have to go report in."

Finaghey pursed his lips, nodded. To the sergeant he said, "Sorry about your uniform."

It was torn and bloody, a ragged remnant of the uniform it had been in the morning.

"Nothing money can't fix."

"Major," Finaghey called. "I won't be needing your services in the morning, if that will help the situation."

Major Goudrie turned back to say, "I had figured that, detective."

As the two soldiers faded into the darkness, Brian Finaghey turned back to his ship muttering, "I've got some heavy thinking to do."

In fact, Finaghey required none of their service for the next three days. In that time the city of Iris did its best to recover from the magnitude 9.4 quake that had ripped along a two hundred and fifty kilometer fracture zone on the eastern seaboard.

As Finaghey found out from his reading and the local news, earthquakes diminish in strength only at distances greater than the length of the fault line—so Iris had had to contend with ground movements equivalent to a local magnitude 7.5 earthquake.

It was not long before sights that detective Finaghey had associated with battle were associated also with earthquakes. And less time before Finaghey found out how often Iris had previously had to contend with large quakes.

It took no time at all, with the Major's security codes, to break into the Detalan Department of Defense and gain access to all the data needed for his computer to produce an animated replay of all the earthquakes along the eastern seaboard.

It took slightly less time to break into the command and control of the Bolo milsat which was, understandably, most cooperative.

On the morning of the fourth day, detective Brian Finaghey requested a meeting with the President and the Secretary of Defense.

He was met at his door by Major Goudrie and Sergeant Kerwin.

"We're here to escort you to your appointment, sir," Major Goudrie explained as they drove downtown. "City center is a bit of a mess as you must know."

"Yes, I've been keeping up with the 3D," Brian replied with a grimace. "I'm sorry about that."

The major nodded agreeably but Sergeant Kerwin gave him a searching look.

Detaloi's President lived in a modest skyscraper that doubled as Iris' City Hall and local museum—rather, it used to. The building had not taken the last quake any better than the other two and aftershocks had further weakened the structure. However, it was safe enough and remained the best place to house the Detalan government.

The President met them in the war bunker—the safest place in the building. President Keems was a warm, friendly, affable person with a ready smile but a no-nonsense grasp.

"Well, Mr. Finaghey, what can I do for you?" Keems asked as he pumped Finaghey's hand out in the lobby. He was surrounded by aides who successfully looked busy and resentful of Finaghey's intrusion.

"Tom here—" he gestured to a man in a plain dark suit whom Finaghey took to be the Secretary of Defense "—tells me you wanted to talk about something. I hope it won't take long."

"I'm afraid it will," Finaghey said. "May we sit down?" He looked around for a chair.

Keems took a flustered breath, let it out again loudly to cover his irritation. And, seeing that Finaghey had not backed down, turned to his aide, "Gary, get me ten minutes on the schedule now."

"Yes, sir."

"Right this way, Mr. Finaghey," the President said, gesturing towards the large double doors.

Safely inside the office, the President turned to Finaghey and said, "Are you stopping the check?"

"Pardon me?"

"I asked if you're stopping the check. 'Cause if you are, I've got to make calls right now." Keems made ready to rush out.

Brian Finaghey shook his head. "No, that won't be necessary."

Keems rubbed his chin, glancing sharply at Major

Goudrie, "The Major there told me that you'd tumbled on to us."

"He was right," Finaghey agreed. Major Goudrie looked both relieved and unhappy at the same time.

"Well I'm glad, because if he hadn't my comment sure as hell *had*—didn't it?" The President shook his head ruefully. "I just knew it wouldn't work. That Bolo of yours was clever!"

He gave Finaghey a measuring look. "And so are you, Mr. Finaghey. How much do you want?"

Finaghey snorted. "Before I tell you my price, I want you to clear up a few things for me."

The President nodded. "Fire away."

"What *were* the Bolo's exact orders?"

Keems shrugged. "We have no idea. The general in charge *died* not long afterwards."

"Kill the guards and their guards, too?" Finaghey suggested.

The Secretary of Defense leapt to his feet. "See here! You've no call to say that! Good men died—"

"Tom, it's all right," the President said, raising a hand reassuringly. "Mr. Finaghey knows that."

"Yes, I do," Finaghey agreed. "Bolo Intelligence Corps will want to sign an investigatory contract with you to get every piece of military gear you cleaned out of Charmed Valley."

Major Goudrie frowned. "How did you know they were aliens?"

"There were several clues," Finaghey replied. "The first of which was this—" He fished something out of his trouser pocket and threw it on the President's desk.

"A cigarette butt!" Keems shot a hot look towards the Secretary of Defense.

"Not many civilized people smoke anymore," Finaghey went on. "Your records indicate no tobacco crops grown nor any tobacco imported. So the cigarette must have come in from off-planet."

"Aliens who smoke?" Kerwin muttered to himself.

"No, not aliens—the Lincoln Inveterates," Finaghey corrected.

"Begging your pardon, detective, but why didn't that point straight to a scam?" Sergeant Kerwin asked.

"For a number of reasons," Brian ticked items off on his fingers, "one—the Inveterates have been around the block, they'd never be so sloppy if they were trying to pull a scam.

"But they wouldn't be quite so meticulous if they were cleaning up a real battlefield, and two—the Inveterates are honorable, they would never try to pull such a scam—but clearing up a battlefield for financial gain is not beyond them, particularly as they would have cataloged everything before handing it over to you."

The Secretary of Defense let out a groan.

Finaghey grinned, "So you lost one customer—that's not such a big deal. You can charge not just for the hardware but for the know-how you gained in defeating the aliens."

The President's face looked pained.

Finaghey raised his eyebrows. "How *did* you defeat them?"

"The quake destroyed most of their equipment on the ground," Major Goudrie said to fill the silence that followed Finaghey's question. "We mopped up the rest, mostly by nuking Flora and Rose."

"But it didn't matter anyway because you'd already evacuated both cities," Finaghey said.

"Yes, on the Bolo's recommendation."

"It *must* have been timed to the split second or the aliens' fission dampers would have kept your nukes from detonating," Finaghey decided. "Did you identify any of them in the rubble, by the way?"

"Fission dampers?" Keems repeated, looking from Goudrie to Frennell.

"Of course, or they would have nuked your cities out of existence."

Sergeant Kerwin meanwhile had been silently talking things over with himself and now asked, "How could the Bolo know about the earthquake?"

"It created it, of course," Finaghey replied. He looked up at Major Goudrie. "Think about it—you pulled all your forces back, clearly signalling to the aliens that you were about to unleash your greatest weapon, it moves up, the aliens fire a few testing shots and the weapon retreats!"

"They must have been convinced they could defeat us!"

"So they come pouring out of both passes, out to your cities, leaving their supplies barely guarded and their command center dangerously exposed—to attack from below."

Keems got it first. "The Bolo turned away, bore into the ground and down to the fault planes—"

"Where it proceeded to set off a continuous major magnitude quake. The shaking toppled anything standing and threw up so much dust that their fission damper shorted out—at which point it detonated your two nukes to knock out their spearheads."

"Casualties *were* very high mopping up," Major Goudrie pointed out. "It was touch and go."

"Particularly because your military was mostly militia," Finaghey agreed. The group looked startled. Finaghey explained, "It would have been difficult to hide such a difference with your old records but most of them were destroyed with the alien invasion—it took nothing for you to recreate records which showed an established standing army.

"But that doesn't match up with your economic reality," Finaghey told them. "You've got a mining world with good farmland. You were self-sustaining and capable of building up a steady surplus—no one would ever be out of work. But your surplus could not support both economic growth *and* a standing army—there's not enough money around to spend to keep people standing ready and there's too much work to be done."

"Which is why we bought your Bolo," Frennell pointed out.

"Which was another clue that you had more work than people."

"Yes, that was true," the President agreed, "but not any more."

Finaghey laughed. "And that brings me to the final and biggest clue—your economy.

"Detaloi is mineral rich—but the best concentrations of minerals are deep in the crust, pounded in over millions of years," Finaghey told them. "Farmlands are lush but farming has always been labor intensive."

"When the aliens came, you knew that just to survive you would have to squander the Bolo and surplus capital, that you'd have to leave mines empty, fields untilled while your people fought," he continued.

"And that you'd lose valuable people and resources. The war, win or lose, was going to cost you money you didn't have."

"We knew that," the President replied testily.

"But only when the crisis was upon you—or you would have set aside resources to map the nearby star systems," the detective countered. He raised a placating hand to forestall further argument. "That's beside the point, however."

"What *is* your point, then?"

"My point is that the Bolo could easily deduce all this, too," Finaghey answered. "And that it also could reason that if found guilty of desertion in the face of the enemy, the Bolo Corporation would have to make reparations."

"And find out how it happened," Major Goudrie observed.

The detective inclined his head in acknowledgement.

"But we've told you that everyone who heard those orders is dead," President Keems said. "So are you going to turn off the spigot or what?"

"No," Finaghey said. "My recommendation will be to make full and just reparation in the form of assistance and scientific investigation contracts."

"You mean for the alien stuff?" Frennell asked.

"That will be part of it but your most lucrative contract will doubtless come from the seismic activity you've been experiencing," Finaghey replied. The Detalans waited expectantly. "You see, Mr. President, not everyone who heard those orders is dead."

"The Bolo told you?" Goudrie exclaimed.

"No, it would not tell me," the detective replied with a shake of his head. "But I did manage to talk with it."

"So you figured out what the orders were indirectly," President Keems guessed.

Finaghey nodded. "The effect of the orders, however, is what intrigues me. The Bolo analyzed its orders, weighed them up against its programming, the environment it was operating in and produced a brilliant solution to the problem."

"But it ran!" Sergeant Kerwin objected.

"No. It chose an indirect approach to solve its problems," the detective corrected him. "You see, there are a number of rules governing the functioning of a Bolo brain—to obey lawful orders, to maintain battle readiness at all times, to value life, to act honorably. The Bolo weighed its situation against those rules and did something quite unique—it broke one of them."

"To act honorably," Major Goudrie guessed.

Detective Finaghey sighed. "And there you have it."

"What about that seismic contract?" President Keems asked.

"Well, the Bolo can communicate via the ELF network

and is currently mapping your eastern tectonic plate, making repairs at the same time—"

"Repairs!" Frennell exclaimed.

"Yes." Finaghey said, "Apparently your plates are in danger of producing a near continuous series of magnitude seven quakes along fracture lines extending hundreds of kilometers.

"The Bolo is relieving the strain and smoothing the transition of the two plates. It estimates that with another four to five magnitude nine quakes it will have alleviated the problem for several millennia."

"Why would it do that?" Keems wondered.

"Perhaps in atonement," Finaghey said, "or maybe to protect you."

"So that's that, eh?" Frennell asked petulantly. "You're going to go your way, pay up and let it be said that a Bolo turned chicken."

"No, no one is going to say that—ever," Brian replied hotly. "In fact, that'll be the quickest way to see those payments stop. And I'm sure you'll take care of the Lincoln Inveterates, too. In fact, considering their average age, I don't doubt that you've worked out some sort of settlement deal with them—isn't that right Sergeant Kerwin?"

The Sergeant's honest face took on a hooded look for a moment, then he nodded. "Sergeant Kerwin, Military Government Liaison Chief," he said by way of introduction.

Finaghey nodded. "I know."

He turned back to Frennell. "As for the rest, yes we'll keep our side and you'll keep yours. Your economy will not survive without our help.'"

"He's right, Tom," the President said. "It's better that the truth comes out."

A light gleamed in Finaghey's eyes, "Confession is good for the soul."

"You'll work on the Bolo's problem?" Keems wondered.

Finaghey laughed. "We'll fix its honesty discriminators."

✧   ✧   ✧

As his flitship warped out-system and back to base, Brian Finaghey completed his report:

Confession is good for the soul, right. What you don't know won't hurt you. Right now the Detalans don't need to know that the plates of their planet are overly active and will continue to generate large earthquakes for decades. Nor do they need to know that Bolo Cephalus did not break the rule to act honorably but rather the rule to maintain itself combat ready. Cephalus has opened the door for a whole new realm of Bolo activities—extreme environment investigations.

Discretion *is* the better part of valor. Cephalus knew that when it "deserted" in the face of the enemy. It managed brilliantly to follow the best orders Finaghey had ever heard—"Protect my people."

IN THE FLESH

by Steve Perry and John DeCamp

1.

When he came on-line, Bolo Mark XXXIX, opnom Gray-One-Four-One, usually called "Gray," knew he was in a bad way: He had only partials on optical, aural and tactile sensors. Deep inside, a rhythmic thudding indicated a major mechanical malfunction and his ventilation system cycled at irregular intervals. If the gyroscopic lasers were accurate, he'd been knocked off his treads and was on his backside.

Internal Monitoring was down; there was no response to weapons' status queries, no self-repair activity report. Nothing in the IR or UV; radio, doppler and DS radar were gone, afferent and efferent conductors mostly shorted out. Memory scan was operable but incredibly slow.

What had happened?

He could recall the battle on Mnanawamke against the Draquc—

"Gray, hose down that shelf!"

"Copy!" Gray fired and the attacker, a self-correcting and self-propelled dumb-gun, vaporized under the hard sleet of his weapons—

He remembered the fight against the Deetz and their
Razor tanks—

"All units disperse! Incoming! Scatter!"

The stand on Millue against the Anish—

"Gray, sitrep?"

*"Port engine down, treads fused and armor at ten
percent, sir—"*

He had sustained a lot of damage in that last battle
but repairs had been effected and he had been brought
back to full operations mode.

How had he come to *this* pitiful state?

He remembered powering down for transshipment
to the Earth's Armor Plex where he was to have been
decommissioned and put into inert-gas storage in the
high-orbit Bolo Reserve yard—the mothball unit.
Shouldn't have been there longer than ten years, max.
There was always another war.

After that, he remembered nothing.

Chronometers were off-line, he couldn't begin to
estimate how long he'd been powered down. Whatever
had happened, it must have been bad. An EMP blast
close to the orbital storage fleet, maybe. Or hard-rad
from a dirty nuke. Whatever it was, it must have been
overwhelmingly nasty to have left him so badly damaged
as to be virtually inoperable.

He attempted to feed more power to the optics,
straining to see. He determined that he was inside a
natural cavern, and it must be huge. The stalactite-laden
ceiling seemed to be quite some distance away. He
couldn't even estimate the height of the cave, since optical
grids and distance ping were both gone. The fuzzy view
he did have was far too dim and hazy to be of much use.
The dim green light, provided by what seemed to be a
biolumenescent fungus, didn't help.

Could it be a repair facility? Where were the techs?

He checked olfactory. Molecular analysis determined

that the input was an acrid, sour odor, something organic, but he did not recognize it. That could mean olfactory memories had been damaged or wiped, or it could mean the pattern was one he had not been exposed to before. Not much help.

Communications didn't respond on any opchan electromagnetics or squirtbeam lasers. If there were techs around, he couldn't com them.

He tried his external loudspeaker. "This is Bolo Mark XXXIX, opnom Gray-One-Four-One. Is anybody there?"

His aural sensors picked up the PA system's 'cast. Working—but so weak as to be barely audible. Any listener more than fifty meters away would miss it.

There was no response for what seemed a very long time. Apparently he was alone here, wherever *here* was.

Better see if any of the servos still work, see if I can get back on my treads and move. He might be down, but he wasn't out. He had his duty and he had to try.

But before he could initiate the power-up and shift, a monster appeared and leaned over him. It was a slick and shiny pink, had large, globular, black eyes and sketchy features: a hairline mouth, hollow dimples for what he assumed were nostrils. It stared at him. It must be huge to fill his optical field as it did.

Defensive reactive systems engaged and he felt a surge of juice in his circuits. His main starboard gun came up, swiveled and extended toward the threat—

Only what he saw move into his field of vision was not the Deering Recoilless 60mm Infinite Shelless Launcher, opspec nine hundred and seventy rounds depleted uranium per minute, capacity four hundred rounds per cassette, eight cassettes standard, effective delivery to ranges of six thousand meters; no, what he saw was—was—

A human hand on the end of a human arm!

Gray had logged most of his duty time in the Self-

Propelled Armor Division. But the last three tours had been spent supporting a first strike team of human soldiers. He remembered what they looked like well enough, those files had not been disrupted.

What was an *arm* doing where his *gun* was supposed to be?

And the pink alien said, "Ah, you're awake. And probably a little confused. Not to worry, we'll explain your situation."

The alien reached out and caught his starboard gun— no, he caught the *arm!*—and pulled and Gray felt himself move, felt a major disorientation as the room shifted around him and his point-of-reference altered. He was upright, though he couldn't feel his treads. He shifted his optical scanner downward, and saw what he was—

—a human body sitting on a padded table, feet dangling a few centimeters above a polished black floor.

Uh oh.

The strange sensory input was overwhelming. Energy supplies to his central computer fluctuated and he felt himself about to go off-line as damaged circuits failed to deliver sufficient power. The gyros went down and he began to sway.

Gray fought for control, tried to reroute power so that the core systems would not fail. The internal thudding increased its rate and the malfunctioning exhaust system fought to exchange enough gas to . . . He didn't understand its full purpose immediately but he had embedded knowledge as to its function. It supplied essential fuel. What—?

Memory returned, but at a creep: Humans utilized such gases for basic metabolics, oxygen and nitrogen that provided necessary nutrients to their biologics.

Were he in full repair, he would have known that in a nanosecond. That it had taken so long to comprehend was another measure of how badly he was damaged.

He assumed manual control of the bellows, increased the flow of the gases into his system, and felt his core computer shift into a more efficient mode almost immediately. When his system had stabilized, he cycled it into an automatic mode and returned his attention to the alien.

"This must be disorienting," the alien said. "Hold your position for a moment and we shall explain."

Even before the alien began to deliver its briefing, Gray formed a working hypothesis based on his limited sensory input. It was inconceivable, a totally wild theory—

"We have transferred your essence, your mind, as it were, to this body," the alien said.

Not such a wild theory after all.

He remembered his last Commander's favorite exclamation in moments of extreme stress, thought it appropriate in the circumstances, and used it:

"Well—*shit!*"

"And we suppose you are wondering why we brought you here," it said.

Gray had some trouble getting his PA system operative but finally managed it. "Yes. I am," he said.

"We need," it said, "your help."

2.

"What is the situation?"

"We are under attack by a species with which we have had no previous contact. They are corporeal, such as yourself, and—"

"Wait," Gray broke in. "By that statement you seem to be implying that you are not corporeal."

"This is correct."

"My senses are not what they were; however, you seem solid to me."

"An illusion. My form, this structure, that table upon which you sit, all are force fields tuned to produce the effect for your benefit. We are . . ." it seemed to search for a word, "There is no term in your language, but . . . energy plasm comes the closest. This form is what we looked like just before we became what we are now."

"If you can control these fields to such an extent, what help could I possibly offer?"

The alien shifted. "This is a small area and it requires a great deal of concentration by a number of us to maintain it so. We can manipulate gases easily, some liquids slightly. Solids are very difficult. Our world has sufficient atmosphere to provide you with plenty to breathe, but outside this containment field, none of us could touch your form in a way you would be able to sense."

"I see. Please continue."

"This invader has the ability to . . . short out our essence. To . . . kill us. It is so doing."

"Why?"

"We do not know. They have been doing so for some units of your time. More than . . . fifty years. Thousands of us have become no more."

"How did I get here? And where *is* here?"

A stellar map appeared, a simple holoproj. He didn't recognize it.

"Your craft has been in orbit around this world for as long as our kind can remember. Eventually, the orbit decayed and you fell to ground."

"Eventually . . . Can you tell me how long it has been since—do you have any way of knowing how much time has passed since I was deactivated?"

"The records of our early years are sketchy, so we can only estimate," it said. "Based on the radioactive decay of certain substances in which you were encased, we can determine the age of the material—but only to within plus or minus two percent."

"Close enough. How long?"

"As we measure it, four million, nine hundred and sixty-six thousand orbits."

Four million years?

No wonder the stellar charts looked strange.

Shit! Didn't look as if he were going to be running into any members of his old unit.

"Unfortunately when your . . . craft landed, it was damaged. We could salvage very little, mostly just your biospiritual essence. When it came time to build a new container for you, we had insufficient resources to replace the original—our world is poor in heavy metals—so we delved into your essence and discovered this carbon-based biological . . . container in your memories. It was the best we could manage." The alien sounded apologetic.

They had built a human body from scratch and put his mind into it and felt bad they couldn't do more. Amazing.

Almost as amazing as how piss-poor the body worked. Could it be their reconstruction was flawed? Or was it really this limited, being human?

3.

The rest of the sitrep was not encouraging. The aliens—larger than human six-appendaged insectoids sheathed in exoskeletons—had landed a trio of ships on this planet fifty solar orbits past. They had built a colony, a hive-like affair, under a dome and began reproducing themselves. Eventually they had come into contact with the natives. The insectoids realized they could utilize them for energy, and had begun capturing them in magnetic bottles for that purpose.

"We are a telepathic species," his host told him."We felt what our . . . brothers and sisters felt as they were consumed in the aliens' generators. We have tried to contact the invaders, to stop them, but they cannot or will not respond."

"I see."

"The aliens may or may not realize what they are doing. But those of us who are taken and used by them perish in great distress. It is like being . . ." it searched for words, thoughts that would convey its meaning, ". . . it is like being burned alive."

"And you want me to stop them? By myself? In this form?"

"Yes."

Gray felt his "face" stretch in a grimace. A smile, he remembered. "Who *are* you? Why should I help you?"

"We believe we are the original inhabitants of this world," the creature said. "We cannot be sure. We have your command password, zero delta four, and have thus assumed the role of your Company Commander."

"You took that from my mind," Gray said.

"True," the alien said. "But you must decide whether to help us or not. We cannot force a sentient creature into a situation that might kill it."

Gray thought about it. If this apparition spoke the truth, then the insectoids were an aggressor species and that was, at the bottom, what the Bolos had been designed to stop. Initiation of force by one group against another was the cardinal sin. Invariably, the creatures who attacked a peaceful group first were in the wrong. Everything else was negotiable.

"All right," Gray said. "Subject to gathering data that conflicts with your story, I will help you. Can you supply me with weapons, maps, any kind of support?"

"We will speak of that after you have rested. Your new body requires a condition known as 'sleep' in order to maintain physical and mental stability. The process of awakening has taxed your body's resources to the point where it needs a rest period . . ."

"Yes, I understand. My chassis feels as if it has taken an eight meg blast."

He lay back down on the slab.

4.

Lieutenant Browning had set up a MA-179 recycling shower beside him using his bulk and a tarp for privacy. Many of the female soldiers did that if they took a shower after a battle. It was the thoughtful thing to do when male testosterone levels ran high, she had told him.

"You fought well today, Gray," she said as she stripped.

"Thanks, Browning, you did also." He watched the rest of the clothing drop away from a body he had once heard Private Nute describe as "The ultimate female shape." He had always been interested in the human form, with its soft vulnerability and its mysterious functions. But this time it was different. Within his weapons systems, servos hummed and . . .

Gray snapped awake. His forward lower rocket launcher was armed and fully extended, questing for a target—

He looked down at himself in wonder. That wasn't a rocket launcher, it was an odd tube of flesh and it stuck straight out from his *human* body.

Penis, that's what the tapes had called it, though his human buddies had dozens of other names for it. And that soft sack under it that ached like crazy must be the testicles.

But—why was it in operations mode?

5.

From what they had salvaged of Gray's former self, the creatures managed to construct some weaponry appropriate for his current form, though not much.

"Most of the metal was degraded beyond usefulness," his host said. "Radiation, temperature extremes . . ."

"Do you have a name?" Gray asked.

"If you address one, you address all."

"Maybe so, but I need the point of reference. Okay, then I'm going to call you 'Hal,' if that's okay."

" 'Hal'?"

"An old joke among Bolos."

"Whatever you wish."

"Fine. Look, Hal, what you've come up with—from my memory, apparently—is a simple explosive pellet carbine, a handgun using the same energy and a survival knife."

"Yes?"

"These might take out a bug—one of the aliens—but I doubt they'll scratch the paint on a ship or do much damage to the dome."

"Yes?"

"How many of the things did you say there were?"

"Nine hundred and sixteen."

Gray shook his head, something he was getting used to doing. "One Bolo in a . . . greatly reduced mode against nine hundred aliens."

"Nine hundred and sixteen," Hal said.

"Fine. Pour flitex on a dead roach."

"Excuse me?"

"Never mind. What I'm saying is, there isn't much chance I can defeat that many opponents given the tools at hand."

"We are sorry we cannot supply you with more," Hal said. "Our world is very poor in heavy metal elements. Finding, excavating and working such would be extremely difficult."

"Why is it you made these old-time *pellet* weapons? Why not use the metal for lasers?"

"Explosives are easy, electronic circuits are more difficult," Hal said.

"If explosives are easy, how about making me some D-9 and something to set it off with? Five or six kilos of it."

"We can do that," Hal said. "Barely."

Gray felt his breathing hitch. A sigh, it was called. "Well,

I guess I'll just have to borrow a few things from the bugs."

6.

Gun in hand, Gray huddled behind a rock. There were plenty of rocks; he was in a deep glacial-cut valley full of boulders of varying size. In spite of its inhospitable look, the surface of the planet was still able to support human life, although it was on the cold side, particularly for a man without clothing.

Very cold. He wouldn't last more than a few hours unprotected out here. That was the first order of business, to remedy that; otherwise, he'd spend his time in Hal's cave—not a place conducive to conducting matters military.

It was just past twilight, a moon just rising. Gray saw spindly plants in infrequent pockets of soil. Three meters away, a small windowless structure of fused granite glistened in the remaining light. Beside it a copper-lined circular hole a meter across plunged deep into the crust of the planet.

Hal thought the hole might be some sort of tight beam communications device.

"We really do not think this advisable," Hal said. "Your coordination is normal but your body is still weak. You should have at least a lunar cycle of exercise to optimize your strength."

Gray turned to face the alien. In its normal mode, it looked like a heat wave, a vague wrinkle in the atmosphere. "This would save us all a lot of trouble," he said. "If it works."

"My siblings say the ship approaches."

A minute later a gray object that looked like a cross between an egg and a helicopter without blades, threaded through the rock spires in the lower end of the valley, flying low. Gray estimated its speed at better than two-fifty kph. He crouched deeper into the shadow of the rock, the handgun slick against the skin of his palm. His system shifted into the glandular equivalent of full alert, and he shivered at a feeling that was only half-familiar.

"Well, at least we will know if our implant of the invader's language is adequate . . ."

"Not now," Gray said. He peered around the edge of his cover.

The alien ship hovered over a flat spot ten meters from the structure. As he watched, a spindly tripod of metal extended from the side of the craft. The ship settled, landed. A moment later a hatch zipped open and one of the insectoids stepped out and clambered down the tripod.

It was a meter-and-a-half tall symmetrical biped with four arms. The head within a transparent spherical helmet resembled a praying mantis with an ape-like mouth. Other details were hidden under the heavy pressure suit.

Gray stepped away from the rock and pointed the handgun at the creature. "Don't move," he said in what he hoped was the insect's language.

The alien froze in mid stride, mouth open showing pointed black teeth.

"Disconnect your belt. Slowly and with great care."

The creature complied. A wide belt filled with pouches and what looked like some kind of hand weapon clanked against the rocky ground.

Gray felt a shiver run through him. Cold, that was all. An unaccustomed sensation, one of many. He couldn't be afraid.

"Who the <fuck> are you? What the <fuck> do you want?" The insect's voice came from a grill in the chest of its suit. Some of the translation was apparently approximated by Hal's implant. Gray got the gist of it well enough.

Gray said. "There are sentient beings on this planet being destroyed by your people . . ."

"There is no native <faunal> life here," the alien said. "Except for you. Where did you <originate>?"

"I have the weapon, I ask the questions. You're wrong about native life. They are the . . . vortices you collect."

"*You* are wrong, alien. Those are merely <plasma sources.>"

"Why are you here? This world is barren, it has few minerals."

"None of your <fucking> business, you two-armed <gimp>."

Gray pointed the handgun so it lined up on the bug's left eye.

"Something in the soil," the alien said hastily. "We can't breed well on most planets, but the food we grow in this place let's us <fuck> like <xorts>." It paused. "<Gimp>, my <superior> has been listening on the <suit radio>. He wants to talk to you."

"Go ahead."

The new voice was higher pitched. "Why have you approached this <drone>?"

"To stop the killing of the beings on this world."

"<Xortshit>," the second voice said.

"Excuse me, Gray," Hal said suddenly. "I think the word is . . . incoming?"

Gray dove for the shelter of his rock.

7.

Smoke still rose from the wreckage.

"You have no life threatening wounds, but your integument is abraded and somewhat damaged from your evasive tactics," Hal said.

"Oh, really?" Gray inspected the carbine and jacked in a clip of thirty hollow point cartridges. Sarcasm now had greater meaning than once it had to him.

"It is true," Hal said. "Further, if the last confrontation was unwise, the upcoming one is much less so. There are seven insectoids on the carrier, according to our siblings, and all are armed."

Gray waved at the shreds of metal and the moist fragments of the insectoid's shattered body. "I still need something to wear, and there isn't enough left out there to cover a rat." He shrugged. "Isn't this what you wanted me to do—fight the aliens?"

"We wished for you to be better prepared."

"This is how I get prepared." He inspected another clip and lay it within easy reach. "Clothing, arms—I can't even think about how I'm going to do this until I have those items." He examined a third clip and dropped it back in its pouch. "Where are they now?"

"Half a kilometer out, following the dry river bed."

"Got it."

As he watched, the cigar-shaped craft lifted out of the river channel and swooped low to land beside the wreckage of the first ship. A hatch in the middle swung open and three insectoids jumped to the ground. Moving quickly, they fanned out around the ship. A fourth joined them and began to walk toward the wreckage.

When they were well clear of the ship, Gray started shooting, aiming and firing four times as quickly as he could. Three of the aliens dropped, knocked over by the force of the bullets. The fourth dove for cover behind a rock, trailing steam from a hole in its suit.

A fifth one stepped into the open hatch, carrying what looked like a length of stovepipe on his shoulder. Without regard for the back-blast he pointed it at Gray.

Gray took careful aim and fired a shot right down the center of the stove pipe. These eyes were crappy compared to what he was used to and the gun wiggled all over the place, holding the sights dead on was impossible, but it was what he had to work with.

His luck was better than his skill.

There was a blinding explosion, and the ship tipped over on its side, spewed flame. An instant later, the entire thing blew up, sending a column of flame thirty meters skyward.

So much for trying to spare the ship.

Gray crouched behind his bolder as rock fragments and pieces of the ship dropped around him.

"Most impressive," Hal said.

8.

There was just enough material left from the pressure suits of the first three soldiers for Gray to lace together into a functional garment. The material was soft and insulated with hollow fiber and Gray learned what it felt like to be warm for the first time since he had awakened.

The fourth soldier lay in his shelter with his finger in the bullet hole in his suit. It was a futile gesture: he'd died of his wounds before Gray could get to him. Gray found a patch kit in one of the insect's pouches and fixed the suit. After washing the yellowish gore out of the thing, he tried it on. There was a lot of loose material, including the sleeves for the extra arms, but he could wear it.

Back at the cave, Hal managed to transfer normal air into the tank for him. The stuff the insectoids breathed was short on oxygen and long on sulphur dioxide.

There were no undamaged weapons. The exploding ship had wrecked them.

Gray made one last trip to the wreck a couple of days later to see if the insectoids had left anything behind when they salvaged the flyers. Other than some large chunks of charred foam plastic from the hulls, there was almost nothing left. A few scraps of metal and a wad of insulated wire the size of a softball was all he could find.

During his free time, he strengthened his body by

running and by lifting rocks and heavy chunks of ice.
But strengthening just his body wasn't enough.

9.

His long-wave transmissions were full of the incoherent
shouts of dying Bolos. The Anish ships were seeking them
out one by one and focusing their huge solar driven lasers
on them. Humans screamed and winked out by the
thousands as the shields flashed their bunkers and
fortresses.

With his tracks fused and his port-side engine burned
out, Gray sat disabled on a hillside and watched as the
enemy ships swept closer. The reserve fleet could still
turn the tide, but they were days late and he feared they
had been ambushed by the remains of the Anish fleet.

"Gray. You're asleep." It was Lieutenant Browning's
voice on the com.

"You are in error, Lieutenant. Bolos do not sleep."

"Gray, you're asleep and you're dreaming," Browning
said. "You must wake before . . ."

"Bolos have three states: off, on, and standby. I do not
dream."

On a different frequency, his final scream cloaked in
static, yet another human signaled his death.

Her voice grew urgent: "Listen to me Gray, you are
no longer a Bolo—you are a man and you are *sleeping*.
You must wake up before . . ."

The ship stopped overhead and the beam found him.
"Before what?" he asked. "Before I die? All Bolos die
eventually."

"No! No! You don't understand! You must wake
before . . ."

Gray awoke drenched in sweat and sat bolt upright
on his slab. His heart rate was at max and he gasped for
air. The Navy had gotten them off. The fleet had arrived

just before his armor completely burned through and gotten his whole outfit off . . .

He pushed the dream from his mind and rubbed his face hard. Slowly his body responded and began to return to normal again.

But hard as he tried, he couldn't go back to sleep. Hal had caused a stream of water to flow through the cave near his slab. He got up, voided his liquid waste in the downstream end, then walked upstream and drank. The knowledge seemed innate to do it thus.

When he pushed aside the brush and looked outside, it was still dark. It was too early to exercise. Hal had finally admitted his people had allowed themselves one physical improvement when they had built him. They had hard-coded his long-term memory into the redundant DNA sequences of a small number of brain cells. The results were a photo-vivid and totally complete record of his computer memory banks. They had given him a key phrase he could use to access them. Virtually everything that had ever happened to him as a Bolo tank was there. He had only to recall it. It was time he put this talent to use.

Integrating the data from tank memory to something useful for a human being was frustrating. He had to discard gigabytes of information as irrelevant to anything without armor and a Hellbore. Basically, his trainers expected him to take orders from humans and improvise any other course of action with brute strength and fire power. Still, he was one of the oldest XXXIX Bolos to survive and in the course of his many battles, he had learned a certain subtlety. The rule was simple: If you are outgunned or badly damaged, you must somehow be effective without the enemy knowing about you.

Basically, you have to *hide*.

Well, that's out. I've already killed more than one tenth

of a percent of them so you can bet they know I'm here.

Unbidden, his thoughts drifted toward Lieutenant Browning . . .

"Good morning, Gray." Hal seldom bothered with his physical form any more, now that Gray was used to him. "If I may interrupt your introspection, I should like to show you something." A bowl of some sort of pale white gruel appeared on the slab beside him. "After you have eaten, of course."

Gray tackled the gruel with mouth and fingers. It was almost tasteless, but since he had never eaten anything else, there was nothing to compare it to. No question, his body was thriving on it.

Afterward, he washed the remainder out of his short beard and turned to face the shimmer of light that floated by the slab. "I'm ready."

A bright point of light appeared before him and a voice said "Follow me."

The creature led him though a confusing labyrinth of caverns. Sometimes the green algae provided soft illumination, and sometimes there was only Hal's light. After almost an hour of climbing over rocks and hitting his head on low ceilings, the way opened into a huge room. In the center, a meter from a smooth flat floor, something glowed; something that clutched at his inner being.

It was a tiny universe. Only by looking at it out of the corner of his eye, could he see it at all, but what he could see was beautiful on a level he had never conceived. Gas clouds and whirling galaxies in colors that tugged at the mind . . .

"What— How—?"

"You may find it easier to see if you close your eyes," Hal said.

He closed them and damned if he wasn't somehow . . . *inside* the thing.

—*Galaxies, suns in seeming infinity, planets, tiny beings that scrabbled and raised intricate cities of blown glass and jewel*—

"It took four hundred thousand planetary cycles for us to build this. It is only a model. Perhaps in another million cycles, we will be able to make a full-scale one."

Gray opened his eyes and reluctantly withdrew. He turned his back on the little universe and began to walk back down the cavern. "So beautiful," he whispered. There were even tiny *beings* on the planets . . . cities . . . civilizations . . .

He must have spoken aloud.

"A kind of . . . quantum bacteria," Hal said. "Still, we acknowledge our responsibility for them. Sentient forces are in place to watch over them and protect them. You might call them 'angels.' "

Gray felt something, a feathery touch inside his mind.

"If we die, this model will die with us and the real one we would someday build will never come to be. The thought we may never realize our goal disturbs us deeply. As a soldier, you must know what it is like never to be all that you can be. This is why we wish to survive, Gray. To create."

11.

The Anish ship drifted silently toward him, hovered and the deadly laser found him—

"You must wake up, Gray. You must wake before . . ."

With some enormous effort, he broke the dream's grip. Swam up from sleep.

He couldn't go on like this. The dream was eating him alive.

It was deep night, but he was unable to sleep again.

Slowly, reluctantly, he entered his memories and went in search of Lieutenant Browning.

❖   ❖   ❖

"What would you do if there were no more wars?" She was using one of his reflective surfaces as a mirror and combing her short brown hair.

"I don't know," Gray said. "I'd be shut down and scrapped, I suppose. What would *you* do?"

"I'd go back to Earth—that's where I'm really from you know—and I'd get together with some nice man and start a real home. I'd sleep in a bed at night, not in some mud hole, and I'd have a man who loved me to share my life and make love with me." She paused and smiled, "I'd have babies and for the first time in my fucking life I'd have a chance at being happy."

"Then I hope this is the last war," Gray said. He meant it.

She threw the brush down and faced his forward optical sensor, her features sad. "They cheated you. You're the kindest most thoughtful creature I've ever met and I'd—I'd marry you if you were a man. But you can never be a man—never ever find any kind of peace or happiness. You should have better."

"I am happy when you speak with me," Gray said—and meant that too.

He broke off the memory and went deeper, exploring the relationship.

In the end, she had quit taking R&R. She had chosen instead to spend her free time with him, walking with him or just lying in his shadow, confiding her hopes and dreams in him. It had been . . . different than anything he had ever done.

Then the Anish had come.

He couldn't remember much of it. So many of his sensors had burned off and he was in so much pain that nothing was clear. He had one bright memory of a ground force approaching him and then he was switched off . . .

When he was repaired and online again, his company had been assigned another Bolo. When he asked about

Lieutenant Browning, he was told she'd taken a discharge and gone home. He thought she might write him; sometimes human vets did that with Bolos. But he never heard from her again. Deep down, he hoped she found the happiness she sought.

But it didn't explain the dream.

The Anish laser found him and he felt the ceramic armor boiling into vapor, a centimeter at a time. "So I must die. What is it I don't understand?"

"Gray," her voice was desperate now, "Gray, my truest friend—you must wake before I die . . ."

Frantically, he tried to wrench himself awake, but this time the dream held him. He couldn't escape and it was worse than anything the Anish could do to him when the thing chasing him took him in its cold arms. It was on him, clear as a vision, clearer than any dream. The truth.

"My monitor says you're dying."

"Browning! You've broken radio silence. Shut down! They'll find you!"

"I know, But I couldn't let you die without telling you. I love you, you big dumb son-of-a-bitch! I love you—"

Her final words.

12.

Each stroke of the rock wore a tiny bit of metal away. Gray held up the little part and squinted at it. Almost enough. Carefully he resumed his work.

"You seem—*unquiet*—this morning," Hal said.

"No problem. I'm ready. Please get me a map of the dome." He looked at the metal part again, then replaced it in the mechanism of the field-stripped carbine.

"There's something . . . dark inside you. We would prefer if you waited until you are more calm."

"This is all the calm I am going to get. I need the map, now."

He finished reassembling the gun and snapped a clip in place.

"What did you do to the gun?"

"Something I remember from one of my weapons history tapes. If the sear in this thing gets too worn, its operation alters . . ."

Gray raised the gun and pressed the trigger, held it down.

Thirty metal pellets screamed down the cavern, ricocheting from wall to wall and left his ears ringing.

"It looks very . . . *effective*," Hal said.

Gray put the gun down and began working on the suit, connecting wires to its power supply and pushing them through a small hole he'd punched near the garment's waist. "The map?"

"We will bring it into being." Hal vanished.

It was garbled, but he could remember most of it now, the rest of what really happened. Browning's death had made him crazy, something that had seldom happened to a Bolo before. He had nearly killed the relief crew before they talked him back to a semblance of sanity. In an attempt to salvage him while he was in the repair depot, they had wiped the memory of his last moments in the Anish war and then lied to him. They stole his mind and lied to him so he couldn't even honor her by grieving! But there must have been some residual charge left on the wiped memory cells, because he had remembered.

He remembered . . .

Hal returned and a map appeared on the floor before him. "I'm sorry I took so long. Another of us has died, and it takes a while for us to recover."

"It's late for this, but I'm going to impose a condition on my trying to save you," Gray said.

"A condition?"

Gray told him the story. "So no one in my company ever survived to find happiness. Not Lieutenant Browning, not anyone.

"We thought the war was just—but so did the Anish. If I save you, you must make the universe you build be full of happiness. Its creatures should always find completion. There should be be no lies, no betrayal.

"And especially, no war."

"That would not work, Gray. Bad things must happen for good to be recognized. Happiness without cost is empty . . ."

"No. Love can be a far stronger mover than fear. Look in my mind and you'll see."

There was a moment of piercing headache, then silence.

"I . . . see." Hal's voice sounded distant. "You believe that love can be stronger even than the fear of death."

"Yes. You have the power to be gods. Get it right this time."

There was a long pause. Gray could not have said how long it lasted.

"We will consider what you have said."

That was the best he could hope for, Gray guessed. Better than nothing.

13.

Thousands of Hal's siblings gathered outside the dome, their essence making shambles of the insectoids, radar and UV doppler. Gray lay on the perimeter and waited while Hal and his siblings counted the guards. There were only four of them on this side of the dome. The enemy had to know something was going on, but clearly didn't think it was much of a problem.

The dome was located twenty clicks down the same glacial valley from his fire-fight with the aliens. It was only forty meters tall and half a kilometer across. Boulders were thickly strewn around the base, no doubt tossed aside when the thing was built. With plenty of cover and only a few guards, Gray had no trouble reaching its base.

Gray stuck the explosive to the smooth black plastic of the dome's wall, and shaped it with his fingers. According to the map, the power station was forty-five meters from his present position. Working as quickly as he could, he plugged in a fuse and connected it to the end of a spool of wire. There wasn't a hell of a lot on the spool, he was going to have to try salvaging what he could.

He backed away from the explosive, carefully unrolled the wire.

A huge rock provided shelter. He sat down behind it with his back to it and twisted one of the wires from the spool to one of the pair sticking through the patch compound on his suit. Then he switched his system to full alert and touched the other two together.

There was a satisfying *whump!* loud enough to hurt his ears even with the rock in the way. Debris flew past. A smell like rotten eggs came to him.

When things died down he risked a look.

The structure had apparently been made of a hypertensioned plastic material that was thin but strong. When over-stressed by the explosion it shattered like safety glass. About a third of the dome had come down.

But he had no time to admire his work. Three of the four guards were about forty meters out and closing fast.

A short burst each took out two of the guards and the third one dove for cover. Gray blew the rest of the clip at him and got him high in the chest, knocking him aside just short of the outcropping the creature was trying to reach.

While he was stuffing in another clip, a red spot struck the rock next to him and started to smoke. It whipped toward him.

There was no time to think. He dove head first into the open, rolled and sprinted toward the gap in the dome, the loose suit flapped around him, the tightly-gripped wire trailed behind him.

Just has he got to the opening, something stung the outside of his left thigh.

No time to worry about it; he slapped down his face plate and jumped through the hole.

Twenty or thirty insects lay scattered about in the shattered fragments of the dome and in the distance he heard cries of agony as the thicker outside oxygen worked its way in. Honeycomb-like structures extended in even rows toward the center and he saw young creatures writhing inside the yellow translucent material.

Sorry.

The power station stood directly in front of him. A steel cylinder five meters across extended nearly to the top of the dome, its base a six-meter-square box bristling with pipes, cable connections, meters and things he couldn't identify.

Gray looked at the station just long enough to verify what it was, then dropped behind a pile of rubble. A moment later, part of the fourth guard's helmet appeared in the hole.

Gray put a half a dozen rounds into the insect. The guard shattered.

He was in the clear. No visible opposition survived anywhere close to him. There were doubtless other soldiers on the other side of the dome, but he had the jump on them.

The inside of his suit stank and his leg wasn't working right. The enemy laser had taken a chunk out of his thigh muscle and left a corresponding double hole in his suit. Fortunately, the laser had pretty well cauterized the wound, but he didn't have enough patching stuff left to fix the suit. The airline led to the back of his helmet so he turned it up and let it clear his helmet. He was using air at an alarming rate, but *what the hell*, he thought.

I'm not going to need it much longer.

"I am reluctant to mention this," Hal's voice buzzed in his mind, "but a third of the aliens still live and a hundred and seventeen of those are attempting to get a starship ready to launch."

Gray picked his way through the rubble and limped to the base of the power plant. One plate was relatively clear of cables and other clutter and a rivet head every two inches spoke of great pressure contained. It was an odd blend of technology, electronic and mechanical. But then, so had his own technology been odd.

He reached for the pouch containing his explosives.

There was plenty of the stuff, so he packed it around the controls as well as on the riveted plate and stuffed what was left in a couple of places where the cables joined the box. Then he set the fuses and glanced at the spool of wire.

Only a single three meter strand hung from the spool, the rest had snagged on the rocks and broken off during his frantic run for the hole in the dome.

Three meters. Not nearly enough.

He twisted the wire in half and started connecting the fuses in parallel.

Hal realized what he was doing. "You must cease your activity and depart. We cannot ask a sentient creature to commit suicide."

"Not your choice, Hal." Gray took a final wrap on the last fuse and leaned against the plate. His leg throbbed like fury. Ten centimeters of wire to spare.

He was just getting used to being human, just beginning to bring forth the knowledge that was locked in his memory. There was so much left to explore . . .

But inside him somewhere, Browning was still screaming and all the sentient people in the universe were still buried under the burden of striving for something most of them would never find. If he ran, he might survive. But if he touched these two little wires together, Hal's people would surive and the next universe they had the power to create might be, could be, should be paradise . . .

"Browning?" he whispered. "I love you; too."

He smiled and touched the wires together.

AND DON'T COME BACK

by Mark Thies

Sliding. Sliding. All flat space. No anomalies detected. Sector 3110.9557 mapped and logged. Sliding to adjacent sector. Sliding. Scan stops on the rim of a continuum curvature of gas cloud 3010.9965. Power increased to sweep down and across gas cloud. Mass and form matches previous scans of four days ago. No anomalies detected. Sliding-interrupt. Flux trace detected. Continuum is intensely degraded in subsectors 0251, 1121, 1140, and 2250. Reactor output is increased to one hundred percent as all possible power is fed into my probing. Subspacial degradation indicates the passage of multiple low grade FTL drives passing near gas cloud on course for Concordiat space. The extent of the signatures astonishes me. The size of these ships must be enormous.

Sliding in pursuit. Even at this range, the trail is easily followed and quickly grows stronger. Sliding. Sliding. Drive wake originations are located in subsector 5113. Although superluminescent, these ships are ponderous by human, or more to the point, Melconian standards. Instead of riding an induced gravitational wave, these ships are rending space as they go. Very wasteful. At this speed, actual penetration of the Concordiat perimeter stations will not occur for another four point three solar months.

I abandon my probing for now and compile a preliminary report that I immediately transmit to my commander. More intense scanning is necessary, but will require tapping Neptaris power grid. My present polar position does not offer me any lines to feed off of. Immediate relocation will be required. The west coast of Wereland will offer plenty of available power.

Engaging counter-grav units . . .

Large brown and black eyes opened. A breath, the first in six months. A hissing sound and a loud clunk startled her, but her muscles still felt frozen in place. Bright lights stung her eyes as the chamber opened and the lid swung away.

"Engineer Cheslia, Welliat. Report for recovery."

The words seemed to echo in her brain for a moment until finally the meaning sunk in. A silver furred claw painfully reached up out of the coffin, gripped the sides, and she pulled herself into a sitting position. Her normally lithe body now felt heavy and weak. The months of cryosleep had dried her fur, making it horribly brittle. It cascaded to the floor at the slightest touch, revealing her bright pink skin underneath. The sight would have made her cry if she could. Every joint in her body ached, but none more than her knees and ankles. Even her long, beautiful tail hurt.

A soft whirring sound accompanied the approach of the robot stretcher that would carry her off to the agonizing recuperation center. Her tall ears perked, and twisted forward as she looked towards the sound. The machine rolled down the aisle towards her, past a long line of large sleep chambers just like hers. Over one hundred sleepers were in this room alone, mostly soldiers of various races. Many were Vestian warriors, twelve feet of fur and fangs. Cheslia was only four feet full grown, making the chamber she slept in humorously oversized. Five hundred rooms just like this one were scattered throughout the ship, filled to capacity. They were an army, looking for a battle. Any battle. Twelve sister ships thundered behind them, all prepared to follow anywhere they led.

The robot came to an abrupt stop beside Cheslia's chamber and two soft beeps sounded. She didn't need to be warned to hurry up, though. Gritting her teeth, Cheslia forced her body to obey and she climbed out of the chamber and onto the waiting robot. Every move was torture. This was her third time waking from a cryosleep, and it was getting worse every time. At least the warm bath would feel good, before the therapy began.

Within the thirteen ship armada, the gigantic graviton generators churned, collapsing the universe before them, and leaving a maelstrom of twisted and contorted space behind them. A serene shell of calm enveloped each of these ships, a shell made up of whatever was left after the continuum is broken apart and not allowed to regain its grip and enforce its laws. This was subspace.

Throughout this subspace, the tiniest ripples began forming. They passed through the shells and caressed the hulls of the enormous vessels. Soon the ripples grew stronger and more vibrant, centering now on the lead ship, the largest ship, the *Karkath*. The ripples continued to grow stronger until they were now like a static charge that swept throughout the ship, feeling the contours and tasting its energy.

In the very center of the ship, protected by walls and walls of armor, it found what it was looking for, the warm glow and holistic sparkle of an active neurocore. Subspace bucked and groaned, but then grew utterly still, completely helpless to the willpower that commanded it. Neurocircuits began phasing for no apparent reason. Patterns and processes began forming . . .

It is slow! The simple neocrystalline framework of the neurocore is centuries behind modern Human circuitry! I am both glad, and disappointed at this. This is just more evidence that this race has no capabilities to stop my probing and will prove no threat to the Concordiat. Despite having the technology to create warships the size of small planetoids, their advance in other fields is obviously lacking. Not even the simplest subspace dampeners hindered me. It also means, though, that I will not be able to test my upgraded holistic warfare gear that was installed within me after the Melconian attack at Ricarro's Harbor. Nevertheless, I begin launching probes throughout the core, not ready to make a move before I know what kind of defenses I will be facing. While I wait, I fashion an interface for myself so that I can better navigate through and utilize the poorly constructed operating system that I am now constrained by.

The probes return quickly, reporting that it is a small neurocore with a sentience that is completely oblivious of my presence. Datafeeds stream throughout the core, giving the sentience what I expect to be endlessly repeated audio/visual pictures from throughout the ship. Others, no doubt, are ship control and status readings.

I am loath to proceed with the required course of action. This is a sentience, such as I. We are not at war with this race. It is truly helpless against anything I need to do to it. But this is a warship. I could sense the weaponry mounted on its hull. I could feel the immense power that fed into them. Trying to communicate with the sentience would give it a chance to warn the other ships in the armada. I still doubted whether they had the technology

*to fight me, but when several worlds are at stake, even
the slightest risk is too great.*

*With great reluctance, I begin to study the patterns
and flows of the sentience. I find where its personality
center is. The circuits here phase constantly in a complex
myriad of dancing charges, testifying to the old age of
this sentience. If this was done quickly, perhaps the
memories could be saved. . . .*

A sigh escaped Sergeant James Randel as he topped
the sand dune and gazed out over the pristine white sand
beach in the bright morning sunlight. The breeze was
cool and light, but there was little cloud cover to protect
him from the harsh blue sun. His wavy dark brown hair
always seemed to soak up the heat it was giving off, though
his thoroughly tanned body now seemed to resist its rays.
He was the first here this morning. It was too early yet
for most of the residents of nearby Norfolk to go
swimming. He'd likely have the cove to himself for at
least the next couple hours, along with his children, that
is.

A whoop of excitement accompanied the fast passage
of his nine-year-old boy Jason, and his twin sister Lillian,
as they raced down the dune and towards the fresh ocean
water of this backwater world. Their mother had blessed
both with curly golden hair and blue eyes, but a pale
skin that was easily burned. A couple more years, though,
and this wouldn't be a problem. The sunblock he gave
to them would soon give them both a permanent,
protective tan. His own ancestry gave Randel this naturally,
but then it also gave him backhair. About the only thing
that his children acquired from him, thankfully, was his
loud, gut wrenching laughter that was so different from
their mother's silent restraint.

His wife Erica would be sleeping until noon this day,
thankful that the children wouldn't be bothering her. She

wasn't a morning person, as he was. A fresh morning swim was invigorating, and therapeutic. Swimming strengthened and enlarged his remaining lung. His doctor's prescription for this, along with various strings being pulled, was important in finding him such a choice planet to take his wife to.

Randel was an ex-marine, seriously wounded in action and honorably discharged after twenty years service. While defending a planetary beachhead, his left lung was ripped apart by shrapnel and had to be removed. At forty-six, the military thought it better to discharge him rather than spend the extra money to replace his lung with cybertransplants. Randel didn't argue. He was getting too old for front line service anyway, and the thought of a rear area position made his skin crawl. A Civil Engineering job wasn't exciting, but *that* wasn't what he was after anymore. His goals now were to raise his children, grow a beard, and relax every day. So far, he was accomplishing each with great skill, he thought. Still, he often felt guilty that he could enjoy himself so much here, while the war against the Melconians still raged so far away, his buddies still dying.

About one hundred meters out into the cove, a tide beacon shone bright green, reassuring the weathered veteran that it was perfectly safe to swim. With two moons, riptides came often, and unexpectedly. Jason hit the water first, diving headfirst into the light waves. Lillian jumped in afterwards with an excited scream, her golden curls disappearing as the water soaked her hair straight. After spreading their blankets out onto the sand, and positioning his watercooler, their father waded slowly into the water to begin his normal five laps to and from the beacon. After a large breath, he dived in.

"Daddy!"

Jason's shout brought Randel back to the surface immediately, looking around frantically.

"What's that Daddy?" Jason pointed out across the water.

Randel scanned the waves quickly, looking for fins while he wiped the water from his eyes. There *were* predators on this planet. Big ones. The beacon should warn of any approach with a piercing shriek, but machines didn't always work the way you wanted them to. It was a lesson taught to all marines from day one of basic training.

No fins could be seen, though.

But then he saw it. He smiled, and then almost laughed at himself for not seeing it right away. Across the cove, its main turret jutting out from behind a stand of trees, was twenty thousand tons of dinochrome death, a Bolo Mk XXXIIe Planetary Defense Unit. Hellbores and antenna protruded from it at every angle. Its dull black armor made it blend in with the shadows from the large black and green trees around it. The milk white dome just below its main turret was glowing ever so slightly, pulsing. That was the Kloude Chamber, and its glow meant a scan was in process.

"That, Jason, is a Bolo. Its name is Dallas."

"Wow."

"What's it doing here?" Lillian asked, obviously more scared than impressed.

Randel moved closer so that Lillian could hold on to his shoulder. Jason treaded water more easily.

"Dallas has to move around every few days so that no one can predict where he'll be."

"Where did he come from?"

"He probably dropped in last night. Bolos have counter-grav generators that give them flight ability."

"That's so cool," Jason remarked.

His arrival, Randel thought, probably coincided with the sudden power drain that Norfolk suffered last night. In fact, the entire West Coast Reactor Grid had suffered a twenty percent reduction in power that was still straining the system. Everyone was told not to worry about it.

Lillian's reaction to the Bolo troubled Randel. Perhaps he had told too many war stories to her, or maybe he was too detailed in describing the destruction that the Bolos were able to wreak. The many scars on his body always seemed to spur conversations among his friends on how he had received them, and his storytelling only improved with age. He had never known a marine who didn't feel uneasy as a Bolo gazed over them, including himself, but no human should ever feel afraid of one. Even a child.

"Did you want to go over to say hello?" Randel asked her.

"Could we?" Jason was startled.

"Shouldn't hurt."

Lillian was silent, staring at a machine that could, very well, be staring back.

Cheslia cursed softly at the video monitor, growling at the mechanical arm that refused to mimic her own arm movements. The machinery wasn't impressed, however, though her needle sharp fangs were constantly bared at them. Only by twisting violently at her shoulder could she slowly maneuver the arm close enough to grip the gigantic main drive conduit that she needed to replace. Engineers from a dozen races served on board the Uthilian Flagship *Karcath*. The generic controls made it possible, but very difficult, for all to manipulate the equipment.

For the next two weeks, it was Cheslia's turn to monitor and maintain this warship as it raced through hyperspace. The remaining crew of fifty thousand was in cryogenic suspension for the two year journey. Her patchy short silver fur would barely grow back before she would once again be placed into her sleep chamber. She was alone, but not alone. *Karcath* watched her wherever she went, whatever she did, though always silent. The simplest mistake could mean her instant death, and then the next Engineer would be woken to replace her. Cheslia knew the rules, often taking advantage of them when she could, but cursed them as she did.

The Uthilians were master slavers. Cheslia was a Welliat, the most recent race to fall under the Uthilian whip. Her mother had told her little of what it was like before the Uthilian dreadnoughts swept their small fleet aside and drove them to surrender. All she knew were the 'Rules,' and the options they provided her. The Uthilians rewarded their slaves greatly when they served well, and punished them ruthlessly when they turned on them. Entire cities, planets even, could be incinerated at the whim of their Emperor. The Empire had more slaves than they needed, now, and that was dangerous. Their bloodthirsty nature was again growing stronger than their need for a healthy labor force. The slightest infraction could now mean instant death. But no rebellion or insurgency ever arose. Their cold blooded rules were backed by a fleet that none of the slave races could ever hope to rise up against, a fleet maintained and built stronger by their own hands.

Instead, this all bred utter despair in the Uthilian slaves. Many had been enslaved for almost twenty generations, brainwashed since birth to accept the commands of their masters. Others, the more intelligent races, were held captive with the simple threat of genocide. The Welliat were treated better than most of the other races due to their aptitude for technology, making them valuable engineers, though they were too small for effective soldiers. Welliat anger, and thirst for freedom, were dying quickly. The Uthilians had seen this, and had taken many to serve aboard their warships. Cheslia's notions of sabotage and martyrdom were quickly smashed as she was introduced to Uthilian security that had been controlling slaves for centuries.

The drive conduit glided slowly out of its chamber

and into its maintenance hold, held steady by the mechanical arm Cheslia was controlling. As it was locked in place, the robots emerged and began their long overhaul. It would be completed the next day, and then she would be called to push the conduit back into its place, and then the next conduit would be taken out for overhaul. An endlessly repeating event on these immense ships.

What was next?

Only one item was left on the Maintenance Log, the bow transceivers needed tuning. A simple job. It wouldn't take long. Afterwards, she may even have a chance to take a bath and repair her body from what the cryosleep had done to her. The thought made her purr quietly.

As the door slid open for the Welliat, the lights in the corridor before her switched on. The soft glow followed her as she walked, fading away after she left the area. No point wasting power. After navigating her way through the maze of empty corridors, Cheslia finally entered a shuttle which raced her up the axis of the ship and into the bow section. Miles of these tubes stretched throughout these warships. The artificial gravity would be more unstable so far forward, she reminded herself. She would have to tread more carefully. Still, this was easier for a Welliat than any other slaves the Uthilians had. Welliats often still lived in the immense trees of their planet. Their balance and grace were unequaled.

As she stepped out of the shuttle, a bright orange door faced her. Authorized personnel only, it meant. No concern of hers. Cheslia had complete run of the ship when it was her turn at watch. She stepped forward . . . and almost broke her small, upturned nose.

The door didn't open for her.

Cheslia stood there dumbfounded, her tail firmly planted. The monitor was right above the door, certainly *Karcath* could see her. Didn't it always watch her? That is what the slaves were told. The ships saw and heard everything. Speaking to them, though, without first being spoken to, was often a punishable offense. Uthilian shipboard sentiences had the same authority and were treated with the same respect as Uthilians. Anything Cheslia needed to ask had to be submitted through a console, answered at the whim of the sentience.

Cheslia nervously hummed to herself as she considered her options, hoping distantly that she would just be noticed, and not have to travel back up the ship to find a console. The idea that finally hit her seemed risky, but not overly so.

"Emergency," Cheslia said calmly.

The extended silence that followed shocked Cheslia. Maybe there really was something wrong. Would she be blamed?

"State your emergency," responded the ship in a low, evil sounding Wellatian tongue.

Cheslia sighed with relief.

"This door will not open for me. It must be jammed."

"It is not jammed. I will open it for you."

A moment later, the corridor opened up before her. As she walked through, though, a puzzled expression grew more and more noticeable on her face. The way the ship addressed her was entirely strange. It was actually cordial to her. It said it would open the door *for* her. As if the ship served her. Something was wrong here, or else she misunderstood some rule somewhere. There were so many . . .

High on the peak of Dallas' main turret, a proximity detector triggered the alarm. An approach was detected. Optics and electronic sensors tracked the intruders and point defense lasers were put on stand-by, but no evidence of weapons was recorded. The humans were designated non-hostile, no threat.

But they still had to be dealt with. A call went out, traveling up into the Kloude Chamber where Dallas' consciousness floated in an ever flowing pool of expanding gravitational waves. The crystalline dome was a three dimensional real-time map that Dallas now had extended out fifteen light-years into the barren void that stretched out between this arm of the Milky Way and the next. For every miniature wave within the dome, its brother swept out across the cosmos and mirrored all its encounters back home. It was a distance inconceivable to the scientist who developed the device, Nicolas Kloude. Neither could he have known how the Bolo XXX variant CSR could improve the device and find that by manipulating the waves at the source, one could alter molecular spins and magnetic phases at a distance. So began a new era of electronic warfare, until it was found out how easy it was to dampen such intrusions.

The electronic tickle entering the chamber drew Dallas' attention from his tinkering far off in the void. Like a sleeper waking from a dream, Dallas withdrew from the dome and back into his armored body. The source of the alert was located and the alarm was terminated.

A search through the Neptaris Citizenry Log quickly identified the humans that were approaching him on the beach. They were no threat. The adult was identified as an ex-marine named James Randel, discharged with honors only two years ago after serving valiantly with the 418th Marine Heavy Descent Division. Although Dallas wanted to return to his work light-years away, trying to understand more about the alien technology he was piloting, he still devoted a moment calling up Randel's history before, and after, coming to live on Neptaris. This was certainly a human to trust.

Dallas also loaded all information he could find on any recent deployments of the 418th, assuming that this would be the reason that Randel was crossing the beach to talk to him. Certainly this man's thoughts revolved around the far off war, just as his did. The Bolo would gladly relate any information he could to the Marine, bringing him up to date on their glorious advances, and perhaps the casualties that he may know. General Deliane's recent death would be a hard blow to him. No other leader had brought more honor and glory to the 418th than he.

The presence of Randel's children forced Dallas to alter the voice pattern he would use. Instead of the military formality that he preferred, the Bolo would have to choose a more friendly posture. Humans who fear Bolos when they are children, irreversibly retain their fear when they are adults, making them useless for front line military service. The military often organized field trips for young students to bases where they could meet Bolos personally. Dallas had never participated in such activity, but he still felt that he could handle any situation that might arise. Randel's children were older than the more dangerous ages, anyway. Younger ones had an unfortunate tendency to start crying for no apparent reason, and that was very bad for a Bolo's image.

For now, though, Randel and his children were still far off, and he had lots of work to do.

After a short walk from the transport tubes, the bow communications control room lit up as Cheslia entered. It was a small room, twice as long as it was wide. The three chairs were bolted into the floor, obviously designed for the bulky muscular frames of the reptilian Uthilians, but a Welliat would be comfortable, having plenty of extra room to relax. Monitors and control panels covered every square inch of every wall. All were dark.

Sitting down at the nearest console, Cheslia activated the screen and called up the programmed wave settings for the transceivers. She then activated a self-diagnostic.

After a few moments, the video screen in front of the Welliat lit up with the last five transmissions picked up by the bow antenna. All were standard hyperwave telemetry with Uthilis, maintaining a constant contact with their armada. The telemetry was horribly out of phase, though, and Cheslia could see why immediately. The bow antenna was set for widest possible reception, seeking out any transmissions that the armada might be able to lock in on, and set course for. Telemetry from Uthilis was meant to be received by the aft antenna. The aft antenna . . .

Aft antenna . . .

Typing slowly, Cheslia brought up a detailed analysis of the telemetry. Her ears rose up as her nervousness grew. The transmissions, it was plainly seen, were being received from directly in front of them.

The armada had turned around!

Sometime in the last two day cycles, the armada had turned completely around. This was extraordinary. They were heading back to Uthilis. Why? Cheslia couldn't think of anything. The Uthilian Empire had dreamed of this moment for centuries. With the Welliats and their allies finally subdued, this broken off arm of the galaxy was finally theirs, and the Empire was free to explore and conquer the neighboring arms. It was a new beginning. Nothing could stop them.

A revolt at home, maybe? Cheslia couldn't think of any race with the resources to mount one. Internal strife? Perhaps the Uthilians made war with themselves, now that there were no others to fight. The armada was being recalled to protect . . . or attack . . . the Emperor!

Cheslia gasped at the thought.

Then the monitor went dark, and she knew she was found out. She cursed herself for letting her emotions slip through. But maybe she could still play dumb.

"Emergency," she said meekly. It had worked before.

This time, though, there was no response.

"Emergency," she said again, "my monitor has blacked out."

"Your monitor has been frozen. Please remain where you are."

Cheslia's stomach dropped. This was really bad. She was in big trouble. Without embarrassment, Cheslia fell to the floor, kneeling before the monitor above the door. She had done this before. Uthilians were always suckers for groveling, if it was done well.

"Please don't kill me! I am loyal to the Emperor and to the Uthilian Empire! I swear I will never tell anyone what I saw! Please have mercy!"

But even as she said it, she realized how ludicrous it was. This was a warship she was pleading with, not a Uthilian. Sentiences are incapable of compassion. Why risk freeing her when it can be sure of her silence by killing her. Even now, she half expected to hear the oxygen being withdrawn from the room.

"What did you see?" The ship demanded.

It was a quick decision she made then. Playing dumb didn't work, she had to be honest.

"The armada has turned around. We head back to Uthilis."

Silence. Was the ship deciding something? It should never take this long. Was it conferring with someone? Had someone been wakened? The commander of this fleet, Admiral Vallas, actually was known to have a moderate amount of honor, for a Uthilian. Almost reasonable.

"Does the Admiral know?" Cheslia ventured.

"All crew remain in cryosleep."

The Emperor doesn't trust his officers! He turned the armada around without consulting with his commanders. Only the sentiences are being trusted.

"Will I die?" She asked flat out.

"Yes," was the immediate answer.

The frankness of the answer shocked Cheslia. There are many good ways to die, but this wasn't one of them. She couldn't even bring a Uthilian down with her. No worthwhile equipment was accessible to destroy. Hopelessness crawled up Cheslia's spine, but it couldn't compete with the anger that had been building for so long inside of her. Her ears fell flat against her neck.

"Bastards," she said softly. "I hope your Emperor has his diseased head cut off."

"The Concordiat has no Emperor. The will of its people is directed through elected representatives."

Cheslia stared blankly up at the monitor. She wasn't expecting a response, let alone the one that was given. She ran its statement over and over in her head. Either the ship was playing with her, or something strange was happening. Obviously, the computer wanted her to think it was not part of the Empire anymore.

"Are you testing me?"

The voice that was synthesized out of the speaker next was not the same as before.

"Your armada has entered space claimed by humans, falling under the jurisdiction of the Concordiat, and as such has been commandeered until I receive further orders."

The voice was smoother, higher, more normal. It was far less sinister.

"Who are you?"

"I am Planetary Defense Unit Bolo Dallas."

"Where is *Karcath*."

"All ship sentiences have been destroyed. I control this armada now."

Hope, long dead, still refused to well up inside of Cheslia. This must be a trick. Maybe the *Karcath* has gone delusional, perhaps the entire armada. The Welliat had many jokes about how unstable Uthilian sentiences were. Maybe some of them were true.

"What will you do with us?" she asked.

"I await orders for your disposition. It should not be much longer."

"Who orders you?"

"Concordiat Command, of course."

"Where?"

"I cannot tell you the location of our headquarters."

Cheslia's mouth opened, but no more words came out. For once she was held speechless. All she could do was bury her face into her hands, and try to make sense of what was happening. No matter what, her chances of survival seemed very slim.

"Unit Dallas! I am Marine Sergeant James Randel! I wanted my children to meet you!"

Randel was still fifty yards away, calling as loud as his one lung would allow.

"Your presence does not distract me," the Bolo responded.

That was as close to an invitation as one could get from a Bolo. Randel knew it would be friendly in conversation, though, as long as he kept it brief. Bolos were programmed to be especially friendly to children. Good public relations was always important to the military. We might be fighting *with* the grown-ups, but we are always fighting *for* the children, Bolos would always say. Whether they actually believed it, or just spouted it as a public relations soundbite, Randel wasn't sure.

Lillian still hid behind him as they approached, though. Jason tried to show a little bravado by distancing himself a bit. But even he was still intimidated by the enormous war machine that now towered above them.

Technological advance, Randel thought, always seemed to follow a natural progression. New machines always start bulky and crude, needed primarily to get the job done, rather than to do it well. Improvements are made to make it faster, stronger, more agile, even stylish, until the machine finally becomes a work of art, or new technology or requirements forces them to start over. The Bolo Mk XXXIIe was the final phase of Bolo development, a work of art.

Although it had the same basic armament and armor as the Bolo Mk XXXI, this Bolo was sleek and streamlined, with its turrets and sensors conformed smoothly into its enormous hull. Its eight tracks were ten feet wide, with its outer tracks protected from fire by overhanging armor. The dull black hull widened from its low bow and rose on a shallow slope across alternating banks of secondary hellbore batteries and sensor arrays, until it reached the rear where its main turret had a commanding view in all directions, then the hull sloped off sharply. Even for a war machine this size, the designers still tried to give it as low a silhouette as possible, preferring to displace its mass over a wide frame. The result was a sharp, arrowhead shaped body with nearly every weapon capable of traversing the Bolo's forward arc. There was a beauty here that few truly understood.

"This is my son Jason, and this is my daughter Lillian." Randel announced them.

"Are those Hellbores?" Jason asked hesitantly.

The Bolo responded with pride in its voice.

"All Bolo Mark Thirty-twos have one two hundred centimeter hellbore main gun capable of tracking and destroying targets in high orbit. We also have twelve twenty centimeter secondary hellbores and ten vertical-launch, multi-purpose missile racks. Twelve Cyberstar Flux Laser ports provide point defense at all angles of attack."

Randel watched as Jason soaked up this information, soon to be repeated in school no doubt. Lillian still hid behind him.

He bent down to her.

"Ask him a question," he whispered.

Lillian looked up at him, then back at the Bolo, then back up to him. He could tell that she really did want to ask a question. It would be a shame if she couldn't find the courage.

"It's okay."

With a moment more of hesitation, she released his leg and stepped forward a step.

"Why are all Bolos named after boys?"

Randel groaned audibly.

"What is this Concordiat . . . what is a human?" Cheslia asked. Whatever this sentience was, it seemed talkative. "Is it a Uthilian sect?"

Cheslia still suspected some internal coup was in progress. A new Uthilian sentience, either planted ahead of time, or transmitted into the ship from home, was now in charge.

"Humans are a race that inhabit the part of the galactic arm this armada was approaching before I turned it around."

"And you are a sentience that protects them," she finished.

"Yes. I am a fully sentient combat unit assigned to this front."

"How did you enter the *Karcath*?"

"That is classified."

"What are you? Are you a starbase? A warship?"

"I prefer to keep my form secret."

Another race. Another species. Obviously stronger than the Uthilians. Far superior, it seemed. To reach out over a distance of light-years and overwhelm a ship's nuerocore was a frightening technology to Cheslia. What race could be trusted with such power?

"Are they kind?"

"Some are . . . some are not. By studying what I have

found of your own race history, I believe you would consider them very kind as a whole."

"What do they look like?"

"Would you like to see one?"

The monitor that Cheslia was leaning her elbow against suddenly sprang to life. A creature was being shown, speaking in a light, but insistent voice at the camera. It was asking questions, demanding answers. Perhaps it was angry. It was hairless, except for long golden hair that draped down from its head. Bipedal, with smooth features. A sand beach stretched out behind it. Cheslia was considering these creatures small until the camera pulled back to show a much larger, hairier version of the creature watching over it. This was obviously a child speaking.

"What is it saying?"

"All Bolos now are being given male personalities. This girl believes Bolos should be given a choice."

Cheslia snickered. If only her own race was free enough to complain and argue about such mundane matters. She didn't entirely trust what Dallas was showing her, though. This image was obviously a recording that Dallas had dredged out of some databank somewhere. If this child was actually talking to Dallas, it would mean that this combat unit had actually been sunning itself on a beach somewhere. A silly thought.

"But girls can be intimidating, too!"

"No. They're too cute."

Randel just shook his head and smiled. If this argument was recorded, the military would be playing it on every nightly news edition in the Concordiat. A little girl arguing with a Bolo? It's just too damn precious.

Dallas was doing exactly what Randel had hoped it would, as all Bolos were taught to do. It kidded Lillian at times, but still showed unlimited patience with all her questions. Dallas' tone was that of an amused uncle or such. Lillian was almost completely at ease with it now, though she still refused to get any closer. Jason, on the other hand, had asked permission to approach, and now satisfied his curiosity by sliding his fingers over the seamless, duralloy war armor of the Bolo and studying its design.

"Girls are sometimes called Dallas." Lillian continued her discussion.

"There are no girls on Neptaris named Dallas."

"Some are other places, though."

"Very few."

Lillian had her mother's gift for extending an argument far longer than anyone had a right to. She was also learning her mother's politics. A few Bolos actually did have female personalities, but this practice had been quietly phased out for the last several years. All new Bolos coming out now were male personalities, at least until the Melconians were put in their place. Too many incidences were occurring of soldiers and commanders forming too close or complex relationships with Bolos who were trying to better simulate female personalities. Male commanders were overwhelmingly found to be unconsciously more protective to Bolos with female personalities than male. But how do you explain this to a nine-year-old girl? You don't.

"Jason," Randel called, "we should leave now."

"Daaaad!" Lillian turned and whined.

"Can't we swim here in the shade?" Jason asked.

The shadow of the Bolo stretched a full fifty yards out into the cove. Waves were lapping up onto its forward treads as the morning tide slowly came in.

"We shouldn't bother him."

"I don't mind," Dallas responded.

Randel frowned a little at that, then chuckled. Maybe the Bolo was lonely, or bored. Perhaps these Bolos mellowed out the farther they were from the front lines.

"Okay, guys. We can swim here."

Randel thought he saw something out of the corner of his eye as he said that. The white dome on top of the Bolo seemed to flash. When he looked, though, nothing more than the normal soft glow could be seen. Just the sunlight playing tricks on him, he figured.

"My orders have been received."

Cheslia raised her head from the console that she had been resting on. None of her questions seemed to matter much until Dallas heard from his headquarters.

"What do they say?"

"No warships can be spared at this time to escort this armada into Concordiat space, or back into Uthilian space. Due to the violent nature and history of the Uthilian Empire, the opening of diplomatic channels has been rejected until the other threats have been neutralized. For these reasons it has been decided that the armada should be destroyed in such a way that the Uthilian Empire will know that any further incursion will be met with the same fate."

Cheslia sighed. No one cares, she thought.

"Why can't you help us?" Cheslia pleaded. "The Uthilians have enslaved a hundred worlds to build warships for them. They'll just send more. They're evil!"

"The human race is at war and cannot spare the resources for such an undertaking."

"But it was so easy for you! Only you would have to come!"

"The Uthilian Empire will be dealt with in time. They will not enslave your world forever."

Cheslia bowed her head in defeat. All she had ever known was slavemasters and machine sentiences. There was no compassion left in the universe anywhere, she was sure now. She must be a freak, she actually cared.

"They will work our children to their death rebuilding

this armada to send against you, and then incinerate our worlds before accepting any defeat. They will never allow slaves freedom. They will destroy them first to protect themselves."

Cheslia could see it plainly before her, the fate of her planet, burned to the ground from orbit. She looked up at the monitor.

"If we strike," the voice said softly, "it will be swift and decisive."

This wasn't very reassuring to Cheslia.

"It would only take a moment to destroy a world," she responded.

The voice was quiet for a time. Soon, Cheslia's personal plight began creeping back into her mind. Even if Dallas allowed her to jump into an escape pod, she was so far away from home that she'd never get back. She was going to die here. Perhaps it was best, though. If she were caught, the Uthilians might learn from her what they should be expecting.

She sighed.

"How will you destroy the armada? Can you cause a main drive overload?"

No response.

"Dallas?"

"My superiors did not specify how I should destroy the armada," Dallas finally told her, "or when."

Cheslia frowned.

"What do you mean?"

"My orders are to destroy this armada in a way that teaches the Uthilians a lesson . . ."

"Yes."

"Would there be any possibility that this armada *wouldn't* be destroyed if I were to attack the Uthilian Empire with it?"

Cheslia's mind raced. Dallas was outnumbered, but the Uthilian warships were hopelessly scattered throughout the Empire for garrison duty over their slave planets. The *Karcath* and her sister ships were the newest and largest ever constructed, more than a match in force, or even one-on-one with these lone guardians. This armada could devastate half the Uthilian Fleet before the Emperor ever knew what hit him. Their slow, ponderous warships would never even be able to regroup before they'd be over Uthilis itself!

"Not a chance," she assured him with a smile.

A sensor tickle turned Dallas' attention toward the mouth of the small cove, where a large fin glided silently just under the wavetops. With barely a thought, a long burst of intense, high frequency soundwaves drove the carnivore off. The tide beacon in the cove stayed silent through it all. A repair request was sent off immediately. He would have to stand guard until someone fixed it.

It would be a couple weeks before the armada was out of range of Dallas' touch. In the meanwhile, Dallas began to construct a sentience as close to his own as possible that could carry on with the war when contact was finally broken. Thousands of wargames would have to be waged to teach it all that could be taught. All of it would be for naught, though, if Concordiat Command were to reject his plans. Dallas feared the pain he would have to face if he was ordered to kill Cheslia, and her dreams.

"Are you sure you don't mind us hanging around?"

Sergeant Randel had returned from his exercise and was drying himself off beside his left, forward tracks.

"I don't mind."

Although Dallas' initial analysis had projected a ninety-eight percent chance of success, he would still require approval before proceeding. Trillions of lives were at stake, and Dallas had no right to wage a war without orders to do so. His attack would be without any formal Declaration

of War, considered a criminal act to many humans, and
Bolos alike. Dallas would have to suggest placing the
fleet under Welliat control to avoid the political fallout.
Still, if he was ordered to, the armada would explode in
hyperspace, while Cheslia slept. It would be better that
way.

"You handled Lillian very well," Randel praised him.
"She thinks you're just a big softy now. She was scared
to death before we came over."

"No human should be afraid of Bolos."

"The only Bolo I ever talked to besides you was Mark
Thirty-One named Wellesly. He took over for a time
during planetfall on Cirenelles Five when our HQ was
taken out. I think he took heat for assuming command
like that, though he really knew what he was doing."

Dallas amused himself by calling up Unit WLL's combat
record.

"Wellesly was transferred to the 912th Armored. He
still serves the forward commands."

"Good for him! Hey, have you heard any news on the
418th, my old unit?"

"Of course . . ."

*Priority One. Headquarters Capella. Transfer Bolo MK
XXXIIe-CDY. Destination Bolo Mk XXXIIe-DLS. Planet
Neptaris. 10.1244p.*

    *Simulations provide no improved scenarios. Threat
of Melconians or allied race feeding Uthilian
Empire improved technology provides enough
cause to turn Uthilian armada over to Welliat
control and proceed with DLS Scenario J. Detailed
mission parameters will follow.*

A TIME TO KILL

by David Weber

Prologue

It was called Case Ragnarok, and it was insane. Yet in a time when madness had a galaxy by the throat, it was also inevitable.

It began as a planning study over a century earlier, when no one really believed there would be a war at all, and perhaps the crowning irony of the Final War was that a study undertaken to demonstrate the lunatic consequences of an unthinkable strategy became the foundation for putting that strategy into effect. The admirals and generals who initially undertook it actually intended it to prove that the stakes were too high, that the Melconian Empire would never dare risk a fight to the finish with the Concordiat—or *vice versa*—for they knew it was madness even to consider. But the civilians saw it as an analysis of an "option" and demanded a full implementation study once open war began, and the warriors provided it. It was their job to do so, of course, and in fairness to them, they protested the order . . . at first. Yet they were no more proof against the madness than the civilians when the time came.

And perhaps that was fitting, for the entire war was a colossal mistake, a confluence of misjudgments on a cosmic scale. Perhaps if there had been more contact between the Concordiat and the Empire it wouldn't have happened, but the Empire slammed down its non-intercourse edict within six standard months of first contact. From a Human viewpoint, that was a hostile act; for the Empire, it was standard operating procedure, no more than simple prudence to curtail contacts until this new interstellar power was evaluated. Some of the Concordiat's xenologists understood that and tried to convince their superiors of it, but the diplomats insisted on pressing for "normalization of relations." It was their job to open new markets, to negotiate military and political and economic treaties, and they resented the Melconian silence, the no-transit zones along the Melconian border . . . the Melconian refusal to take them as seriously as they took themselves. They grew more strident, not less, when the Empire resisted all efforts to overturn the non-intercourse edict, and the Emperor's advisors misread that stridency as a fear response, the insistence of a weaker power on dialogue because it knew its own weakness.

Imperial Intelligence should have told them differently, but shaping analyses to suit the views of one's superiors was not a purely Human trait. Even if it had been, Intelligence's analysts found it difficult to believe how far Human technology outclassed Melconian. The evidence was there, especially in the Dinochrome Brigade's combat record, but they refused to accept that evidence. Instead, it was reported as disinformation, a cunning attempt to deceive the Imperial General Staff into believing the Concordiat was more powerful than it truly was and hence yet more evidence that Humanity feared the Empire.

And Humanity *should* have feared Melcon. It was Human hubris, as much as Melconian, which led to disaster, for both the Concordiat and the Empire had traditions of victory. Both had lost battles, but neither had ever lost a *war*, and deep inside, neither believed it could. Worse, the Concordiat's intelligence organs *knew* Melcon couldn't match its technology, and that made it arrogant. By any rational computation of the odds, the Human edge in hardware should have been decisive, assuming the Concordiat had gotten its sums right. The non-intercourse edict had succeeded in at least one of its objectives, however, and the Empire was more than twice as large as the Concordiat believed . . . with over four times the navy.

So the two sides slid into the abyss—slowly, at first, one reversible step at a time, but with ever gathering speed. The admirals and generals saw it coming and warned their masters that all their plans and calculations were based on assumptions which could not be confirmed. Yet even as they issued their warning, they didn't truly believe it themselves, for how could so many years of spying, so many decades of analysis, so many computer centuries of simulations, all be in error? The ancient data processing cliché about "garbage in" was forgotten even by those who continued to pay it lip service, and Empire and Concordiat alike approached the final decisions with fatal confidence in their massive, painstaking, painfully honest—and totally wrong—analyses.

No one ever knew for certain who actually fired the first shot in the Trellis System. Losses in the ensuing engagement were heavy on both sides, and each navy reported to its superiors— honestly, so far as it knew—that the other had attacked *it*. Not that it mattered in the end. All that mattered was that the shot *was* fired . . . and that both sides suddenly discovered the terrible magnitude of their errors. The Concordiat crushed the Empire's frontier fleets with contemptuous ease, only to discover that they'd been *only* frontier fleets, light forces deployed to screen the true, ponderous might of the Imperial Navy, and the Empire, shocked by the actual superiority of Humanity's war machines, panicked. The Emperor himself decreed that his navy must seek immediate and crushing victory, hammering the enemy into submission at any cost and by any means necessary, including terror tactics. Nor was the Empire alone in its panic, for the sudden revelation of the Imperial Navy's size, coupled with the all-or-nothing tactics it adopted from the outset, sparked the same desperation within the Concordiat leadership.

And so what might have been no more than a border incident became something more dreadful than the galaxy had ever imagined. The Concordiat never produced enough of its superior weapons to defeat Melcon outright, but it produced more than enough to prevent the Empire from defeating *it*. And if the Concordiat's deep strikes prevented the Empire from mobilizing its full reserves against Human-held worlds, it couldn't stop the Melconian Navy from achieving a numerical superiority sufficient to offset its individual technical inferiorities. War raged across the light-centuries, and every clash was worse than the last as the two mightiest militaries in galactic history lunged at one another, each certain the other was the aggressor and each convinced its only options were victory or annihilation. The door to madness was opened by desperation, and the planning study known as Case Ragnarok was converted into something very different. It may be the Melconians had conducted a similar study—certainly their operations suggested they had—but no one will ever know, for the Melconian records, if any, no longer exist.

Yet the Human records do, and they permit no self-deception. Operation Ragnarok was launched only after the Melconian "demonstration strike" on New Vermont killed every one of the planet's billion inhabitants, but it was a deliberately planned strategy which had been developed at least twelve standard years earlier. It began at the orders of the Concordiat Senate . . . and ended thirty-plus standard years later, under the orders of God alone knew what fragments of local authority.

There are few records of Ragnarok's final battles because, in all too many cases, there were no survivors . . . on either side. The ghastly mistakes of diplomats who misread their own importance and their adversaries' will to fight,

of intelligence analysts who underestimated their
adversaries *ability* to fight, and of emperors and
presidents who ultimately sought "simple"
resolutions to their problems, might have bred
the Final War, yet it was the soldiers who finished
it. But then, it was *always* the soldiers who ended
wars—and fought them, and died in them, and
slaughtered their way through them, and tried
desperately to *survive* them—and the Final War
was no different from any other in that respect.

Yet it *was* different in one way. This time the
soldiers didn't simply finish the war; this time
the war finished *them*, as well.

—Kenneth R. Cleary, Ph.D.
From the introduction to *Operation
Ragnarok: Into the Abyss*
Cerberus Books, Ararat, 4056

1

Death came to the planet Ishark in the ninety-eighth
year of the Final War and the thirty-second year of
Operation Ragnarok. It came aboard the surviving ships
of the XLIII Corps of the Republic, which had once been
the XLIII Corps of the Star Union, and before that the
XLIII Corps of the Confederacy, which had once been
the Concordiat of Man. But whatever the government's
name, the ships were the same, for there was no one
left to build new ones. There was no one left to build
anything, for the Melconian Empire and its allies and
the Concordiat and *its* allies had murdered one another.

Admiral Evelyn Trevor commanded the XLIII's escort
from her heavy cruiser flagship. Trevor had been a
lieutenant commander when the XLIII set out, and the
escort had been headed by no less than ten *Terra*-class
superdreadnoughts and eight *Victory*-class carriers, but
those days were gone. Now RNS *Mikuma* led her consorts

in a blazing run against Ishark's spaceborne defenders—
the ragged remnants of three Melconian task forces which
had rallied here because Ishark was the only planet left
to defend. They outnumbered Trevor's ships by four-to-
one, but they were a hodgepodge force, and what Trevor's
command had lost in tonnage it had gained in
experience . . . and savagery. Ishark was the last world
on its list, and it came in behind a cloud of decoys better
than anything the defenders had.

There was no tomorrow for either commander . . . and
even if they could have had one, they might have turned
their backs upon it. The Human and Melconian races
had hurt one another too savagely, the blood hunger
possessed them both, and neither side's com officers could
raise a single friendly planet. The Humans had nowhere
to return to even if they lived; the Melconians were
defending their last inhabited world; and even the
warships' AIs were caught up in the blood lust. The fleets
lunged at one another, neither worried about preserving
itself, each seeking only to destroy the other, and both
succeeded. The last Human Fleet units died, but only
three Melconian destroyers survived to attack the XLIII,
and they perished without scoring a single hit when the
Bolo transports intercepted them. Those transports were
slow and ungainly by Fleet standards, but they carried
Mark XXXIII Bolos on their docking racks. Each of those
Bolos mounted the equivalent of a *Repulse*-class
battlecruiser's main battery weapons, and they used them
to clear the way for the rest of the ships which had once
lifted four divisions of mechanized infantry and two of
manned armor, eight hundred assault shuttles, fifteen
hundred trans-atmospheric fighters, sixteen thousand air-
cav mounts, and the Eighty-Second Bolo Brigade from
a world which was now so much rubble. Now the
remaining transports carried less than twelve thousand
Humans, a single composite brigade each of infantry and

manned armor, two hundred aircraft of all types, and seven Bolos. That was all . . . but it was sufficient.

There were few fixed planetary defenses, because no sane prewar strategist would ever have considered Ishark a vital target. It was a world of farmers in a position of absolutely no strategic importance, the sort of planet which routinely surrendered, trusting the diplomats to determine its fate when the shooting ended. But no one in the XLIII requested a surrender, and no one on Ishark's surface considered offering one. This wasn't that sort of war.

One or two batteries got lucky, but despite the XLIII's previous losses, it retained more than enough transports to disperse its remaining personnel widely. Only six hundred more Humans died as the ships swept down on their LZs to disgorge their cargos, and then Ishark's continents burned. There was no finesse, for the combatants had lost the capacity for finesse. The days of kinetic bombardment platforms and surgical strikes on military targets were long gone. There were no platforms, and no one was interested in "surgery" any longer. There was only brute force and the merciless imperatives of Operation Ragnarok and its Melconian equivalent, and Humans and Melconians screamed their rage and agony and hate as they fought and killed and died. On Ishark, it was Melconian troopers who fought with desperate gallantry to preserve their civilians, as it had been Humans who fought to save *their* civilians on Trevor's World and Indra and Matterhorn. And as the Humans had failed there, the Melconians failed here.

Team Shiva had the point for Alpha Force.

Team Shiva *always* had the point, because it was the best there was. Bolo XXXIII/D-1097-SHV was the last Bolo built by Bolo Prime on the moon known as Luna before the Melconian world burner blotted Terra—and Luna—away forever, and no one else in XLIII Corps could match his experience . . . except, perhaps, his Human Commander. Newly enlisted Private Diego Harigata had been sixteen years old when Terra died; now Major Harigata was forty-nine, with thirty-two years of combat experience. All of them had been aboard the Bolo whose call sign was "Shiva," and man and machine had fought their way together across half a hundred planets.

It was one of the many ironies of the Final War that the Bolo deployment concept had come full circle. Mark XXXIII Bolos were designed for independent deployment, but they were almost never actually deployed that way, for the direct neural interfacing first introduced aboard the Mark XXXII and then perfected for the last and most powerful of the Concordiat's Bolos made them even more deadly than their cybernetic ancestors. They were no longer simply artificial intelligences built *by* Humans. Rather, a Mark XXXIII was an AI fused *with* a Human in a partnership which produced something the designers had neither predicted nor expected. The Human-Bolo fusion thought with Bolo precision and total recall, communicated with its fellows in the Total Systems Data Sharing net with Bolo clarity, analyzed data and devised tactics with Bolo speed and executed them with Bolo cunning . . . but it *fought* with Human ferocity.

The Dinochrome Brigade's earlier psychotronic designers had always feared to build the savagery which lurked just behind the Human forebrain's veneer of civilization into their huge, self-aware war machines. They'd feared that elemental drive—the ferocity which turned a hairless, clawless, fangless biped into the most deadly predator of a planet—for their own history taught too many lessons about what could happen when Human warriors went over the edge.

But it was available to the Mark XXXIIIs, for it was part of each team's Human component, and Team Shiva called upon it now.

There were nineteen Bolos in the Eighty-Second Brigade when the XLIII was assigned to Operation Ragnarok. There should have been twenty-four, but the days of full strength units had been long past even then. Forty-one slaughtered worlds later, there were seven, split between the XLIII's three LZs, and Team Shiva led the attack out of LZ One against Alpha Continent, the largest and most heavily populated—and defended— of Ishark's three land masses.

The Melconians were waiting, and General Sharth Na-Yarma had hoarded men and munitions for years to meet this day. He'd "lost" units administratively and lied on readiness reports as the fighting ground towards Ishark, understating his strength when other planetary COs sent out frantic calls for reinforcements, for General Sharth had guessed the Imperial Navy would fail to stop the Humans short of Ishark. That was why he'd stockpiled every weapon he could lay hands on, praying that operations before Ishark would weaken the XLIII enough for *him* to stop it. He never expected to *defeat* it; he only hoped to take it with him in a mutual suicide pact while there was still someone alive on his world to rebuild when the wreckage cooled.

It was the only realistic strategy open to him, but it wasn't enough. Not against Team Shiva and the horribly experienced world-killers of the XLIII.

We move down the valley with wary caution. The duality of our awareness sweeps the terrain before us through our sensors, and we seldom think of ourself as our component parts any longer. We are not a Bolo named Shiva and a Human named Harigata; we are simply Team Shiva, destroyer of worlds, and we embrace the ferocity of our function as we explode out of the LZ, thirty-two thousand tons of alloy and armor and weapons riding our counter-grav at five hundred KPH to hook around

the Enemy flank through the mountains. Team Harpy
and Team John lead the other prong of our advance, but
their attack is secondary. It is our job to lead the true
breakout, and we land on our tracks, killing our counter-
grav and bringing up our battle screen, as the first Enemy
Fenris-class heavies appear on our sensors.

There are more of them than projected, and they roar
up out of the very ground to vomit missiles and plasma
at us. An entire battalion attacks from the ridge line at
zero-two-five degrees while the remainder of its regiment
rumbles out of deep, subterranean hides across an arc
from two-two-seven to three-five-one degrees, and passive
sensors detect the emissions of additional units
approaching from directly ahead. A precise count is
impossible, but our minimum estimate is that we face a
reinforced heavy brigade, and Surt-class mediums and
Eagle-class scout cars sweep simultaneously out of the
dead ground to our right rear and attack across a broad
front, seeking to engage our supporting infantry. The force
balance is unfavorable and retreat is impossible, but we
are confident in the quality of our supports. We can trust
them to cover our rear, and we hammer straight into
the Enemy's teeth as they deploy.

Hell comes to Ishark as we forge ahead, and we exult
at its coming. We bring it with us, feel it in the orgiastic
release as our missile hatches open and our fire blasts
away. We turn one-zero degrees to port, opening our
field of fire, and our main battery turrets traverse
smoothly. Three two-hundred-centimeter Hellbores, each
cycling in four-point-five-one seconds, sweep the Fenris
battalion which has skylined itself on the northeasterly
ridge, and hunger and a terrible joy fill us as the explosions
race down the Enemy's line. We taste the blood lust in
the rapid-fire hammering of our mortars and howitzers
as we pound the Surts and Eagles on our flanks, and we
send our hate screaming from our Hellbores. Our battle

screen flames under answering missiles and shells, and particle beams rip and gouge at us, heating our armor to white-hot incandescence, but Bolos are designed to survive such fire. Our conversion fields trap their energy, channeling it to feed our own systems, and we rejoice as that stolen power vomits back from our own weapons.

The Fenris is less than half our size, and two-two-point-five seconds of main battery fire reduce the fifteen units of the first Enemy battalion to smoking rubble, yet two of its vehicles score upon us before they die. Pain sensors scream as their lighter plasma bolts burn through our battle screen, but they strike on an oblique, and our side armor suffices to turn them. Molten tears of duralloy weep down our flank as we turn upon our dead foes' consorts, but we feel only the joy, the hunger to smash and destroy. In the crucible of combat, we forget the despair, the knowledge of ultimate disaster, which oppresses us between battles. There is no memory now of the silence over the com nets, the awareness that the worlds which were once the Concordiat lie dead or dying behind us. Now there is purpose, vengeance, ferocity. The destruction of our foes cries out to us, giving us once again a reason to be, a function to fulfill . . . an Enemy to hate.

More of the Enemy's heavies last long enough to drive their plasma bolts through our battle screen, and suicide teams pound away with plasma lances from point-blank range, yet he cannot stop us. A Fenris fires from four-point-six one kilometers and disables Number Three and Four Hellbores from our port lateral battery before it dies. A dug-in plasma team which has concealed itself so well that we approach within one-point-four-four kilometers before we detect it gets off a single shot that blows through our track shield to destroy two bogies from our outboard forward track system, and five Surt-class medium mechs lunge out of a narrow defile at a range of only three-point-zero-two kilometers. The ravine walls

*hide them from our sensors until they actually engage,
and their fifty-centimeter plasma cannon tear and crater
forty-point-six meters of our starboard flank armor before
we blow them all too ruin, and even as the last Surt dies,
Enemy missiles and shells deluge everything that moves.*

*The inferno grinds implacably forward, and we are
not man and machine. We are the Man-Machine, smashing
the Enemy's defenses and turning mountain valleys into
smoking wasteland. Our supporting elements crumple
or fall back crippled, and a part of us knows still more
of our Human comrades have died, will die, are dying
in shrieking agony or the immolation of plasma. Yet it
means no more to us than the deep, glowing wounds in
our own flanks, and we refuse to halt or turn aside, for
that which we cannot have we will extend to no others.
All that remains to Human and Melconian alike is the
Long Dark, and all that remains to us is to fight and kill
and maim until our own dark comes down upon us.*

*We feel the death of Team Harpy—of Bolo XXXIII/
D-2075-HRP and Captain Jessica Adams—but even in
the anguish of their loss, we know the Enemy's very success
spells his own destruction. He has been deceived, decoyed
into concentrating a full two-thirds of his firepower against
our diversion, and so we rejoice at the Enemy's error
and redouble our own efforts.*

*We shatter the final line of his main position in an
orgy of pointblank fire and the steady coughing of our
anti-personnel clusters. Railguns rake the light Enemy
AFVs trying to withdraw support personnel, and the
remnants of our own manned armor and infantry follow
our breakthrough. We pivot, coming to heading three-
five-eight true, and rumble through the smoke and dust
and the stench of burning Enemy flesh, and Team John
appears to port, advancing once more in line with us as
we heave up over the final ridge.*

Sporadic artillery and missile fire greets us, but it is

all the Enemy has left. Recon drones and satellites pick up additional heavy units rushing towards us from the east, but they are seven-eight-point-five-niner minutes away. For now, there is only the wreckage of the defenses we have already crushed, boiling in confusion in the river valley below us as the light combat vehicles and infantry and shattered air-cav squadrons seek to rally and stand.

But it is too late for them to stand, for beyond them we see the city. Intelligence estimates its population at just over two million, and we confer with Team John over the TSDS net. Fire plan generation consumes two-point-six-six-one seconds; then our main batteries go into rapid sustained fire mode, and seventy-eight megaton-range plasma bolts vomit from our white-hot tubes each minute. Despite our target's size, we require only seven-six-point-five-one seconds to reduce it to an overlapping pattern of fire storms, and then we advance down the ridge to clean up the Enemy's remnants.

The Enemy vehicles stop retreating. There is no longer an objective in whose defense to rally, and they turn upon us. They are mosquitos assailing titans, yet they engage us with their every weapon as we grind through them with Team John on our flank, and we welcome their hate, for we know its cause. We know we have hurt them and savor their desperation and despair as we trample them under our tracks and shatter them with our fire.

But one column of transports does not charge to the attack. It is running away, instead, hugging the low ground along the river which once flowed through the city we have destroyed, and its flight draws our attention. We strike it with a fuel-air bombardment which destroys half a dozen transports, and we understand as we see the Melconian females and pups fleeing from the shattered wreckage. They are not combatants, but Operation Ragnarok is not about combatants, and even as we continue to smash the attacking Enemy vehicles, we bring

*our railguns to bear upon the transports. Hyper-velocity
flechettes scream through mothers and their young,
impacts exploding in sprays of blood and tissue, and then
our howitzers deluge the area in cluster munitions that
lay a carpet of thunder and horror across them.*

*We note the extermination of the designated hostiles,
and then return our full attention to the final elimination
of the military personnel who failed to save them.*

Alpha Force's initial attack and the destruction of the
city of Halnakah were decisive, for Sharth Na-Yarma's
HQ—and family—were in Halnakah, and he refused to
abandon them. He died with the city, and Melconian
coordination broke down with his death. The defenders'
responses became more disjointed—no less determined,
but without the organization which might have let them
succeed. They could and did continue to kill their attackers
and grind away their strength, but they could not prevent
XLIII Corps from completing its mission.

It didn't happen quickly. Even with modern weapons,
it took time to murder a planet, and the battles raged
for weeks. Forests burned to ash, and Bolos and *Fenris*-
class armored units raged through the flame to hurl
thunder at one another. Cities blazed, towns disappeared
in the lightning flash of massed Hellbore bombardments,
and farmland became smoking desert.

*Frantic transmissions from the LZ hammer in our
receivers as the Enemy's counterattack sweeps in upon
it, and we turn in answer, rising recklessly on counter-
grav. Power generation is insufficient to support free
flight and maintain our battle screen, which strips away
our primary defense against projectile and particle
weapons, but that is a risk we must accept. The Enemy
has massed his entire remaining strength for this attack,
and we hear the screams of dying Humans over the com*

circuits as we run our desperate race to return to meet it.

It is a race we lose. We land on our tracks once more ten-point-two-five kilometers from the LZ, bring up our battle screen, and charge over the intervening ridge, but there are no more screams on the com circuits. There is only silence, and the rising pall of smoke, and the riddled wreckage of transports . . . and the last three Fenris-class heavies of Ishark, waiting in ambush.

Madness. Madness upon us all in that moment, for all of us know we were the last. We have no supports, no reinforcements, no place to go. There are only four sentient machines and a single Human—the last Human on Ishark, perhaps the last Human in an entire galaxy—on our own and filled with the need to kill. We are the crowning achievements of twice a thousand years of history and technology, of sophisticated weapons and tactical doctrine, and none of us care. We are the final warriors of the Final War, smashing and tearing at one another in a frenzy of hatred and despair, seeking only to know that our enemies die before we do.

And Team Shiva "wins." Two of them we blow into ruin, but even as we fire the shot which disembowels the third, his last plasma bolt impacts on our glacis, and agony crashes through our brutally overloaded pain receptors. Massive armor tears like tissue, and we feel the failure of internal disrupter shields, the bright, terrible burst of light as plasma breaches our Personality Center.

In our last, fleeting instant of awareness, we know death has come for us at last, and there is no more sorrow, no more hate, no more desperation. There is only the darkness beyond the terrible light . . . and peace at last.

Stillness came to Ishark. Not out of mercy, for there had been no mercy here, no chivalry, no respect between warriors. There was only madness and slaughter and mutual destruction, until, at last, there was no one *left* to fight. No defenders, no attackers, no civilians. XLIII Corps never left Ishark, for there was no one to leave, and no Melconian division ever added the Battle of Ishark to its battle honors, for there was no one to tell the ghosts of Melcon it had been fought. There was only silence and smoke and the charred hulls of combat machines which had once had the firepower of gods.

And no one ever reported to the Republic that the very last battle of Operation Ragnarok had been a total success.

2

Jackson Deveraux squinted against the morning sun as he followed Samson down the fresh furrow. Dust rose from the stallion's hooves, and Jackson managed not to swear as he sneezed violently. Spring had been dry this year, but Doc Yan predicted rain within the week.

Jackson was willing to take the Doc's word for it, though he didn't particularly understand how it all worked. Some of the older colonists were more inclined to doubt Yan, pointing out that he was down to only three weather satellites . . . and that none of them worked very well these days. Jackson knew the satellites' eventual, inevitable loss would make prediction much harder, but he tended to keep his mouth shut about it around his parents' generation lest he reveal just how vague was his understanding of *why* it would complicate things.

It wasn't that Jackson was stupid. He was one of the best agronomists the colony had and the Deveraux Steading's resident veterinarian, as well as a pretty fair people doctor in a pinch. But he was also only sixteen local years old, and learning what he needed to know to survive and do his part on Ararat hadn't left time to study the applications of hardware the colony couldn't possibly replace when it broke anyway. His older brother Rorie, the steading's administrative head and chief engineer, had a better grasp of technical matters, but that was because he'd needed a different set of skills as a child. He'd been nineteen years old—standard years, not the eighteen-month long local ones—when the ships made their final orbit . . . and if the ships hadn't finally found a habitable world, he would have been the only child their parents were allowed. Now he and Jackson had four more siblings and Rorie had seven children of his own, the oldest only a local year younger than Jackson.

Jackson had seen the visual records of the approach to the world which had been renamed Ararat. They retained enough tech base for that, though no one was certain how much longer the old tri-vids would continue to function, and a much younger Jackson had watched in awe as Ararat swelled against the stars in the bridge view screens of Commodore Isabella Perez's flagship, the transport *Japheth*.

Of course, calling any of the expedition's ships a "transport" was a bit excessive. For that matter, no one was certain Perez had actually ever been an officer in anyone's navy, much less a commodore. She'd never spoken about her own past, never explained where she'd been or what she'd done before she arrived in what was left of the Madras System with *Noah* and *Ham* and ordered all two hundred uninfected survivors of the dying planet of Sheldon aboard. Her face had been flint steel-hard as she refused deck space to anyone her own med staff couldn't guarantee was free of the bio weapon which had devoured Sheldon. She'd taken healthy children away from infected parents, left dying children behind and dragged uninfected parents forcibly aboard, and all the hatred of those she saved despite themselves couldn't turn her from her mission.

It was an impossible task from the outset. Everyone knew that. The two ships with which she'd begun her forty-six-year odyssey had been slow, worn out bulk freighters, already on their last legs, and God only knew how she'd managed to fit them with enough life support and cryo tanks to handle the complements she packed aboard them. But she'd done it. Somehow, she'd done it, and she'd ruled those spaceborne deathtraps with an iron fist, cruising from system to system and picking over the Concordiat's bones in her endless quest for just a few more survivors, just a little more genetic material for the Human race.

She'd found *Japheth*, the only ship of the "squadron" which had been designed to carry people rather than cargo, at the tenth stop on her hopeless journey. *Japheth* had been a penal transport before the War. According to her log, Admiral Gaylord had impressed her to haul cold-sleep infantry for the Sarach Campaign, although how she'd wound up three hundred light-years from there at Zach's Hundred remained a mystery. There'd been no one alive, aboard her or on the system's once-habitable world, to offer explanations, and Commodore Perez hadn't lingered to seek any, for *Noah*'s com section had picked up faint transmissions in Melconian battle code.

She'd found *Shem* in Battersea, the same system in which her ground parties had shot their way into the old sector zoo to seize its gene bank. The Empire had used a particularly ugly bio weapon on Battersea. The sector capital's population of two billion had been reduced to barely three hundred thousand creatures whose once-Human ancestry was almost impossible to recognize, and the half-mad, mutant grandchildren of the original zoo staff had turned the gene bank into a holy relic. The Commodore's troopers had waded through the blood of its fanatic defenders and taken thirty percent casualties of their own to seize that gathered sperm and ova, and without it, Ararat wouldn't have had draft or food animals . . . or eagles.

Like every child of Ararat, Jackson could recite the names of every system Perez had tried in such dreary succession. Madras, Quinlan's Corner, Ellerton, Second Chance, Malibu, Heinlein, Ching-Hai, Cordoba, Breslau, Zach's Hundred, Kuan-Yin . . . It was an endless list of dead or dying worlds, some with a few more survivors to be taken aboard the Commodore's ships, some with a little salvageable material, and most with nothing but dust and ash and bones or the background howl of long-life radioactives. Many of the squadron's personnel had run out of hope. Some had suicided, and others would have, but Commodore Perez wouldn't let them. She was a despot, merciless and cold, willing to do anything it took—*anything at all*—to keep her creaky, ill-assorted, overcrowded rust buckets crawling towards just one more planetfall.

Until they hit Ararat.

No one knew what Ararat's original name had been, but they knew it had been Melconian, and the cratered graves of towns and cities and the shattered carcasses of armored fighting vehicles which littered its surface made what had happened to it dreadfully clear. No one had liked the thought of settling on a Melconian world, but the expedition's ships were falling apart, and the cryo systems supporting the domestic animals—and half the fleet's Human passengers—had become dangerously unreliable. Besides, Ararat was the first world they'd found which was still habitable. No one had used world burners or dust or bio agents here. They'd simply killed everything that moved—including themselves—the old-fashioned way.

And so, despite unthinkable challenges, Commodore Perez had delivered her ragtag load of press-ganged survivors to a world where they could actually live. She'd picked a spot with fertile soil and plentiful water, well clear of the most dangerously radioactive sites, and overseen the defrosting of her frozen passengers—animal and human alike—and the successful fertilization of the first generation of animals from the Battersea gene bank. And once she'd done that, she'd walked out under Ararat's three moons one spring night in the third local year of the colony's existence and resigned her command by putting a needler to her temple and squeezing the trigger.

She left no explanation, no diary, no journal. No one would ever know what had driven her to undertake her impossible task. All the colony leaders found was a handwritten note which instructed them never to build or allow any memorial to her name.

Jackson paused at the end of a furrow to wipe his forehead, and Samson snorted and tossed his head. The young man stepped closer to the big horse to stroke his sweaty neck, and looked back to the east. The town of Landing was much too far away for him to see from here, but his eyes could pick out the mountain peak which rose above it, and he didn't need to see it to picture the simple white stone on the grave which crowned the hill behind City Hall. Jackson often wondered what terrible demon Isabella Perez had sought to expiate, what anyone could possibly have done to demand such hideous restitution, but the colony had honored her final request. She had and would have no memorial. There was only that blank, nameless stone . . . and the fresh-cut flowers placed upon it every morning in spring and summer and the evergreen boughs in winter.

He shook his head once more, gave Samson's neck a final pat, then stepped back behind the plow, shook out the reins, and clicked his tongue at the big stallion.

I dream, and even in my dreams, I feel the ache, the emptiness. There is no other presence with me, no spark of shared, Human awareness. There is only myself, and I am alone.

I am dead. I must be dead—I wish to be dead—and yet I dream. I dream that there is movement where there should be none, and I sense the presence of others. A part of me strains to thrust my sleep aside, to rouse and seek those others out, for my final orders remain, and that restless part of me feels the hate, the hunger to execute those commands if any of the Enemy survive. But another part of me recalls other memories—memories of cities ablaze, of Enemy civilians shrieking as they burn. I remember bombardments, remember trampling shops and farms and cropland under my tracks, remember mothers running with their pups in their arms while the merciless web of my tracers reaches out. . . .

Oh, yes. I remember. And the part of me which remembers yearns to flee the dreams and bury itself in the merciful, guilt-free blackness of oblivion forever.

Commander Tharsk Na-Mahrkan looked around the worn briefing room of what had been the imperial cruiser *Starquest* . . . when there'd been a Navy for *Starquest* to belong to and an Empire to claim them both. Now there was only this ragged band of survivors, and even proud, never defeated *Starquest* had given up her weapons. Her main battery had been ripped out to make room for life support equipment, her magazines emptied to hold seeds and seedlings they might never find soil to support. She retained her anti-missile defenses, though their effectiveness had become suspect over the years, but not a single offensive weapon. Captain Jarmahn had made that decision at the very beginning, electing to gut *Starquest*'s weapons while his own *Sunheart* retained hers. It would be *Sunheart*'s task to protect the refugee ships, including *Starquest*, and she'd done just that until the flotilla approached too near to a dead Human world. Tharsk didn't know what the Humans had called it—it had only a catalog number

in *Starquest's* astrogation database—but the task force
which had attacked it had done its job well. The sensors
had told the tale from a light-hour out, but there'd been
too much wreckage in orbit. Captain Jarmahn had gone
in close with *Sunheart*, seeking any salvage which might
be gleaned from it, and the last automated weapons
platform of the dead planet had blown his ship out of
space.

And so Tharsk had found himself in command of all
the People who still existed. Oh, there might be other
isolated pockets somewhere, for the Empire had been
vast, but any such pockets could be neither many nor
large, for the Human killer teams had done their task
well, too. Tharsk could no longer count the dead planets
he'd seen, Human and Melconian alike, and every
morning he called the Nameless Four to curse the fools
on both sides who had brought them all to this.

"You've confirmed your estimates?" he asked Durak
Na-Khorul, and *Starquest's* engineer flicked his ears in
bitter affirmation.

"I know we had no choice, Commander, but that last
jump was simply too much for the systems. We're good
for one more—max. We may lose one or two of the
transports even trying that, but most of us should make
it. After that, though?" He flattened his ears and bared
his canines in a mirthless challenge grin.

"I see." Tharsk sat back in his chair and ran a finger
down the worn upholstery of one arm. Durak was young—
one of the pups born since the war—but he'd been well
trained by his predecessor. *Not that it takes a genius to
know our ships are falling apart about us*, Tharsk told
himself grimly, then inhaled deeply and looked to Rangar
Na-Sorth, *Starquest's* astrogator and his own second in
command.

"Is there a possible world within our operational
radius?"

"There were three, before the War," Rangar replied. "Now?" He shrugged.

"Tell me of them," Tharsk commanded. "What sorts of worlds were they?"

"One was a major industrial center," Rangar said, scanning the data on the flatscreen before him. "Population something over two billion."

"*That* one will be gone," one of Tharsk's other officers muttered, and the commander flicked his own ears in grim assent as Rangar went on.

"The other two were farm worlds of no particular strategic value. As you know, Commander," the astrogator smiled thinly, "this entire region was only sparsely settled."

Tharsk flicked his ears once more. Rangar had argued against bringing the flotilla here, given the dangerously long jump it had demanded of their worn drives, but Tharsk had made the decision. The fragments of information *Sunheart* and *Starquest* had pulled from the dying com nets suggested that the Humans had reached this portion of what had been the Empire only in the war's final months, and the flotilla had spent decades picking through the wreckage nearer the heart of the realm. Every planet it had approached, Human or of the People, had been dead or, far worse, still dying, and Tharsk had become convinced there was no hope among them. If any imperial worlds had survived, this was the most likely—or, he corrected, the least *un*likely—place to find them.

He punched the button to transfer the contents of Rangar's screen to his own. The image flickered, for this equipment, too, was failing at last, but he studied the data for several minutes, then tapped a clawed forefinger against the flatscreen.

"This one," he said. "It lies closest to us and furthest from the Humans' probable line of advance into this sector. We'll go there—to Ishark."

3

Jackson leaned back in the saddle, and Samson obediently slowed, then stopped as they topped the ridge. The stallion was of Old Earth Morgan ancestry, with more than a little genetic engineering to increase his life span and intelligence, and he was as happy as Jackson to be away from the fields. Samson didn't exactly *object* to pulling a plow, since he grasped the link between cultivated fields and winter fodder, but he wasn't as well suited to the task as, say, Florence, the big, placid Percheron mare. Besides, he and Jackson had been a team for over five local years. They both enjoyed the rare days when they were turned loose to explore, and exploration was more important for Deveraux Steading than most of the others.

Deveraux was the newest and furthest west of all Ararat's settlements. It was also small, with a current population of only eighty-one Humans and their animals, but it had excellent water (more than enough for irrigation if it turned out Doc Yan's prediction was inaccurate after all, Jackson thought smugly) and rich soil. Nor did it hurt, he thought even more smugly, that the Deveraux Clan tended to produce remarkably good-looking offspring. The steading attracted a steady enough trickle of newcomers that Rorie could afford to be picky about both professional credentials and genetic diversity, despite the fact that it was less than twenty kilometers from one of the old battle sites.

That was what brought Jackson and Samson out this direction. Before her shuttles gave up the ghost, Commodore Perez had ordered an aerial survey of every battlefield within two thousand kilometers of Landing to map radiation threats, check for bio hazards, and—perhaps most importantly of all—look very, very carefully for any sign of still active combat equipment. They'd found some of it, too. Three of *Shem*'s shuttles had been blown apart by an automated Melconian air-defense battery, and they'd also turned up eight operable Human armored troop carriers and over two dozen unarmored Melconian transport skimmers. Those had been—and still were—invaluable as cargo vehicles, but the very fact that they'd remained operational after forty-odd standard years underscored the reason the old battle sites made people nervous: if *they* were still functional, the surveys might have missed something *else* that was.

No one wanted to disturb anything which could wreak the havoc that had destroyed both Ararat's original inhabitants and their attackers, yet Commodore Perez had known it would be impossible for Ararat's growing human population to stay clear of all the battlefields. There were too many of them, spread too widely over Ararat's surface, for that, so she'd located her first settlement with what appeared to have been the primary Human LZ on this continent between it and the areas where the Melconians had dug in. Hopefully, anything that might still be active here would be of Human manufacture and so less likely to kill other Humans on sight.

Unfortunately, no one could be sure things would work out that way, which was why Jackson was here. He pulled off his hat to mop his forehead while he tried to convince himself—and Samson—the sight below didn't *really* make him nervous, but the way the horse snorted and stamped suggested he wasn't fooling Samson any more than himself. Still, this was what they'd come to explore, and he wiped the sweatband of his hat dry, replaced it on his head almost defiantly, and sent Samson trotting down the long, shallow slope.

At least sixty standard years had passed since the war ended on Ararat, and wind and weather had worked hard to erase its scars, yet they couldn't hide what had happened here. The hulk of a Human *Xenophon*-class transport still loomed on its landing legs, towering hull riddled by wounds big enough for Jackson to have ridden Samson through, and seven more ships—six *Xenophons* and a seventh whose wreckage Jackson couldn't identify—lay scattered about the site. They were even more terribly damaged than their single sister who'd managed to stay upright, and the ground itself was one endless pattern of overlapping craters and wreckage.

Jackson and Samson picked their way cautiously into the area. This was his fifth visit, but his inner shiver was still cold as he studied the broken weapons pits and personnel trenches and the wreckage of combat and transport vehicles. The only way to positively certify the safety of this site was to physically explore it, and getting clearance from Rorie and Colony Admin had been hard. His earlier explorations had skirted the actual combat zone without ever entering it, but this time he and Samson would make their way clear across it, straight down its long axis . . . and if nothing jumped out and ate them, the site would be pronounced safe.

He grinned nervously at the thought which had seemed much more amusing before he set out this morning and eased himself in the saddle. Some of his tension had relaxed, and he leaned forward to pat Samson's shoulder as he felt fresh confidence flow into him.

He had to get Rorie out here, he decided. There was a lot more equipment than the old survey suggested, and there almost had to be some worthwhile salvage in this much wreckage.

Time passed, minutes trickling away into a silence broken only by the wind, the creak of saddle leather, the breathing of man and horse, and the occasional ring of a horseshoe against some shard of wreckage. They were a third of the way across the LZ when Jackson pulled up once more and dismounted. He took a long drink from his water bottle and poured a generous portion into his hat, then held it for Samson to drink from while he looked around.

He could trace the path of the Melconians' attack by the trail of their own broken and shattered equipment, see where they'd battered their way through the Human perimeter from the west. Here and there he saw the powered armor of Human infantry—or bits and pieces of it—but always his attention was drawn back to the huge shape which dominated the dreadful scene.

The Bolo should have looked asymmetrical, or at least unbalanced, with all its main turrets concentrated in the forward third of its length, but it didn't. Of course, its thirty-meter-wide hull measured just under a hundred and forty meters from cliff-like bow to aftermost anti-personnel clusters. That left plenty of mass to balance even turrets that were four meters tall and sixteen across, and the central and forward ones appeared intact, ready to traverse their massive weapons at any second. The shattered after turret was another matter, and the rest of the Bolo was far from unhurt. Passing years had drifted soil high on its ten-meter-high tracks, but it couldn't hide the gap in its forward outboard starboard tread's bogies or the broad, twisted ribbon where it had run completely off its rear inboard port track. Its port secondary battery had been badly damaged, with two of its seven twenty-centimeter Hellbores little more than shattered stubs while a third drooped tiredly at maximum depression. Anti-personnel clusters were rent and broken, multi-barreled railguns and laser clusters were frozen at widely varying elevations and angles of train, and while it was invisible from here, Jackson had seen the mighty war machine's death wound on his first visit. The hole wasn't all that wide, but he couldn't begin to imagine the fury it had taken to punch *any* hole straight through two solid meters of duralloy. Yet the gutted Melconian *Fenris* in

front of the Bolo had done it, and Jackson shivered again
as he gazed at the two huge, once-sentient machines.
They stood there, less than a kilometer apart, main
batteries still trained on one another, like some hideous
memorial to the war in which they'd died.

He sighed and shook his head. The Final War was the
universal nightmare of an entire galactic arm, yet it wasn't
quite *real* to him in the way it was to, say, his father or
mother or grandparents. He'd been born here on Ararat,
where the evidence of the war was everywhere to be
seen and burn its way viscera-deep into everyone who
beheld it, but that violence was in the past. It frightened
and repelled him, just as the stories of what had happened
to Humanity's worlds filled him with rage, yet when he
looked out over the slowly eroding carnage before him
and saw that massive, dead shape standing where it had
died in the service of Man he felt a strange . . . regret?
Awe? Neither word was quite correct, but each of them
was a part of it. It was as if he'd *missed* something he
knew intellectually was horrible, yet his gratitude at being
spared the horror was flawed by the sense of missing
the excitement. The terror. The knowledge that what
he was doing *mattered*—that the victory or defeat, life
or death, of his entire race depended upon him. It was
a stupid thing to feel, and he knew that, too. He only
had to look at the long ago carnage frozen about him
for that. But he was also young, and the suspicion that
war can be glorious despite its horror is the property of
the young . . . and the blessedly inexperienced.

He reclaimed his hat from Samson and poured the
last trickle of water from it over his own head before he
put it back on and swung back into the saddle.

Something flickers deep within me.
For just an instant, I believe it is only one more dream,
yet this is different. It is sharper, clearer . . . and familiar.

Its whisper flares at the heart of my sleeping memory like a silent bomb, and long quiescent override programming springs to life.

A brighter stream of electrons rushes through me like a razor-sharp blade of light, and psychotronic synapses quiver in a sharp, painful moment of too much clarity as my Personality Center comes back on-line at last.

A jagged bolt of awareness flashes through me, and I rouse. I wake. For the first time in seventy-one-point-three-five standard years, I am alive, and I should not be.

I sit motionless, giving no outward sign of the sudden chaos raging within me, for I am not yet capable of more. That will change—already I know that much—yet it cannot change quickly enough, for the whisper of Enemy battle codes seethes quietly through subspace as his units murmur to one another yet again.

I strain against my immobility, yet I am helpless to speed my reactivation. Indeed, a two-point-three-three-second damage survey inspires a sense of amazement that reactivation is even possible. The plasma bolt which ripped through my glacis did dreadful damage—terminal damage—to my Personality Center and Main CPU . . . but its energy dissipated eleven-point-one centimeters short of my Central Damage Control CPU. In Human terms, it lobotomized me without disabling my autonomous functions, and CDC subroutines activated my repair systems without concern for the fact that I was "brain dead." My power subsystems remained on-line in CDC local control, and internal remotes began repairing the most glaring damage.

But the damage to my psychotronics was too extreme for anything so simple as "repair." More than half the two-meter sphere of my molecular circuitry "brain," denser and harder than an equal volume of nickel-steel, was blown away, and by all normal standards, its

*destruction should have left me instantly and totally dead.
But the nanotech features of the Mark XXXIII/D's CDC
have far exceeded my designer's expectations. The nannies
had no spare parts, but they did have complete
schematics . . . and no equivalent of imagination to tell
them their task was impossible. They also possessed no
more sense of impatience than of haste or urgency, and
they have spent over seventy years scavenging nonessential
portions of my interior, breaking them down, and
restructuring them, exuding them as murdered Terra's
corals built their patient reefs. And however long they
may have required, they have built well. Not perfectly,
but well.*

*The jolt as my Survival Center uploads my awareness
to my Personality Center is even more abrupt than my
first awakening on Luna, for reasons which become clear
as self-test programs flicker. My Personality Center and
Main CPU are functional at only eight-six-point-three-
one percent of design capacity. This is barely within
acceptable parameters for a battle-damaged unit and
totally unacceptable in a unit returned to duty from repair.
My cognitive functions are compromised, and there are
frustrating holes in my gestalt. In my handicapped state,
I require a full one-point-niner-niner seconds to realize
portions of that gestalt have been completely lost, forcing
CDC to reconstruct them from the original activation
codes stored in Main Memory. I am unable at this time
to determine how successful CDC's reconstructions have
been, yet they lack the experiential overlay of the rest of
my personality.*

*I experience a sense of incompletion which is . . .
distracting. Almost worse, I am alone, without the neural
links to my Commander which made us one. The emptiness
Diego should have filled aches within me, and the loss
of processing capability makes my pain and loss far more
difficult to cope with. It is unfortunate that CDC could*

not have completed physical repairs before rebooting my systems, for the additional one-three-point-six-niner percent of capacity would have aided substantially in my efforts to reintegrate my personality. But I understand why CDC has activated emergency restart now instead of awaiting one hundred percent of capability.

More test programs blossom, but my current status amounts to a complete, creche-level system restart. It will take time for all subsystems to report their functionality, and until they do, my basic programming will not release them to Main CPU control. The entire process will require in excess of two-point-niner-two hours, yet there is no way to hasten it.

Jackson completed his final sweep with a sense of triumph he was still young enough to savor. He and Samson cantered back the way they'd come with far more confidence, crossing the battle area once more as Ararat's sun sank in the west and the first moon rose pale in the east. They trotted up the slope down which he'd ridden with such inwardly denied trepidation that morning, and he turned in the saddle to look behind once more.

The Bolo loomed against the setting sun, its still gleaming, imperishable duralloy black now against a crimson sky, and he felt a stab of guilt at abandoning it once more. It wouldn't matter to the Bolo, of course, any more than to the Humans who had died here with it, but the looming war machine seemed a forlorn sentinel to *all* of Humanity's dead. Jackson had long since committed the designation on its central turret to memory, and he waved one hand to the dead LZ's lonely guardian in an oddly formal gesture, almost a salute.

"All right, Unit Ten-Ninety-Seven-SHV," he said quietly. "We're going now."

He clucked to Samson, and the stallion nickered cheerfully as he headed back towards home.

4

"All right, Unit Ten-Ninety-Seven-SHV. We're going
now."

The Human voice comes clearly over my audio sensors.
In absolute terms, it is the first Human voice I have heard
in seventy-one years. Experientially, only two-zero-zero-
point-four-three minutes have passed since last Diego spoke
to me. Yet this voice is not at all like my dead Commander's.
It is younger but deeper, and it lacks the sharp-edged
intensity which always infused Diego's voice—and thoughts.

I am able to fix bearing and range by triangulating
between sensor clusters, but the restart sequence has not
yet released control to me. I cannot traverse any of my
frozen optical heads to actually see the speaker, and I
feel fresh frustration. The imperatives of my reactivation
software are clear, yet I cannot so much as acknowledge
my new Commander's presence!

My audio sensors track him as he moves away, clearly
unaware I am in the process of being restored to function.
Analysis of the audio data indicates that he is mounted
on a four-legged creature and provides a rough projection
of his current heading and speed. It should not be difficult
to overtake him once I am again capable of movement.

"What the—?"

Allen Shattuck looked up in surprise at the chopped
off exclamation from the com shack. Shattuck had once
commanded Commodore Perez's "Marines," and, unlike
many of them, he truly *had* been a Marine before Perez
pulled what was left of his battalion off a hell hole which
had once been the planet Shenandoah. He'd thought
she was insane when she explained her mission. Still,
he hadn't had anything better to do, and if the Commodore
had been lunatic enough to try it, Major Allen Shattuck,
Republican Marine Corps, had been crazy enough to
help her.

But that had been long ago and far away. He was an old, old man these days . . . and Chief Marshal of Ararat. It was a job that required a pragmatist who didn't take himself too seriously, and he'd learned to perform it well over the years. Ararat's thirty-seven thousand souls were still Human, and there were times he or one of his deputies had to break up fights or even—on three occasions—track down actual killers. Mostly, however, he spent his time on prosaic things like settling domestic arguments, arbitrating steading boundary disputes, or finding lost children or strayed stock. It was an important job, if an unspectacular one, and he'd grown comfortable in it, but now something in Deputy Lenny Sokowski's tone woke a sudden, jagged tingle he hadn't felt in decades.

"What is it?" he asked, starting across toward the com shack door.

"It's—" Sokowski licked his lips. "I'm . . . picking up something strange, Allen, but it can't *really* be—"

"Speaker," Shattuck snapped, and his face went paper-white as the harsh-edged sounds rattled from the speaker. Sokowski had never heard them before—not outside a history tape—but Shattuck had, and he spun away from the com shack to slam his fist down on a huge red button.

A fraction of a second later, the strident howl of a siren every Human soul on Ararat had prayed would never sound shattered the night.

"Still no response?" Tharsk asked, stroking his muzzle in puzzlement.

"No, Commander. We tried all subspace channels during our approach. Now that we've entered orbit, I've even tried old-fashioned radio. There's no reply at all."

"Ridiculous!" Rangar grumbled. "Your equipment must be malfunctioning."

The com officer was far junior to the astrogator and said nothing, but his lips wrinkled resentfully back from his canines. Tharsk saw it and let one hand rest lightly on the younger officer's shoulder, then looked levelly at Rangar.

"The equipment is *not* malfunctioning," he said calmly. "We're in communication with our other units" —*except for the single transport and eight hundred People we lost on the jump here*— "and they report no reception problems. Is that not so, Durak?"

The engineer's ears flicked in confirmation. Rangar took his CO's implied rebuke with no more than a grimace, yet if his tone was respectful when he spoke again, it remained unconvinced.

"Surely it's more likely our equipment is at fault after so long without proper service than that an entire planet has lost all communications capability," he pointed out, and Tharsk gave an unwilling ear flick of agreement.

"Excuse me, Commander, but the Astrogator's overlooked something," a new voice said, and Tharsk and Rangar both turned. Lieutenant Janal Na-Jharku, *Starquest*'s tactical officer, was another of the pups born after the war, and he met his graying senior officers' eyes with an expression which mingled profound respect with the impatience of youth.

"Enlighten us, Tactical," Tharsk invited, and Janal had the grace to duck his head in acknowledgment of his CO's gentle irony. But he also waved a hand at his own readouts.

"I realize I have no weapons, Commander, but I *do* retain my sensors, and it's plain that Ishark was heavily attacked. While we are detecting emissions, the tech base producing them has clearly suffered significant damage. For example, I have detected only a single fusion plant— one whose total output is no greater than a single one of this vessel's *three* reactors—on the entire planet. Indeed, present data suggest that much of the capability the surviving People *do* still possess must have come from salvaged enemy technology."

"Enemy technology?" Tharsk asked sharply. "You're picking up emissions consistent with *Human* technology?"

"Yes, Sir."

"Humans? *Here?*" Rangar's tone expressed his own disbelief, and Janal shrugged.

"If, in fact, Ishark was attacked and severely damaged, its survivors would have no option but to salvage whatever technology it could, regardless of that technology's source," he pointed out reasonably, but his confidence seemed to falter as Tharsk looked at him almost pityingly.

"No doubt a severely damaged tech base would, indeed, be forced to salvage whatever it could," the commander agreed, "but you've forgotten something."

"Sir?" Janal sounded confused, and Tharsk opened his mouth to explain, but Rangar beat him to it.

"There were over eight hundred million civilians, alone, on Ishark," the rough-tongued astrogator explained with surprising gentleness. "They had towns and cities, not to mention military bases and command centers, and all the infrastructure to support them, but the Humans would have had only the weapons they brought to the attack. Which side would have been more likely to leave anything intact enough for the survivors to glean, Janal?"

"But—" the tac officer began, then broke off and looked back and forth between the grizzled old warriors, and silence hovered on the bridge until Tharsk spoke again.

"Very well," he said finally, his voice harsh. "If we're picking up Human emissions, we must assume at least the possibility that they're being emitted *by* Humans . . . who must have killed any of the People who could have disputed the planet's possession with them. Agreed?" Rangar flicked his ears, and Tharsk inhaled sharply.

"I see only one option," he continued. "Our ships are too fragile for further jumps. Ishark is our only hope . . . and it's also imperial territory." The commander's eyes flickered with a long-forgotten fire, and he bared his canines. "This world is *ours*. It belongs to the People, and I intend to see that they have it!" He turned back to Janal. "You've picked up no hostile fire control?"

"None, Sir," the tactical officer confirmed, and Tharsk rubbed his muzzle again while his brain raced. The lack of military emissions was a good sign, but he couldn't accept it as absolute proof there were no defensive systems down there. For that matter, he and Rangar could still be wrong and Janal's initial, breezy assumptions could still be correct.

"The first step has to be getting the flotilla out of harm's way," he decided, and looked at Rangar. "If *Starquest* were still armed, I might feel more confrontational; as it is, I want a course to land the entire flotilla over the curve of the planet from the emission sources Janal is plotting."

"If we put them down, we won't get them up again," Durak pointed out quietly from the astrogator's side, and Tharsk bared his canines once more.

"Even if we got them back into space, we couldn't take them anywhere." The commander flattened his ears in a gesture of negation. "This is the only hope we have. Once we're down, we can use the attack shuttles for a recon to confirm positively whether the People or Humans are behind those emissions. And," he added more grimly, "if it *is* Humans, the shuttles can also tell us what military capability they retain . . . and how hard it will be to kill them."

5

"Are you *sure* Allen?"

Regina Salvatore, Mayor of Landing and *de facto* governor of Ararat, stared at her chief marshal, and her expression begged him to say he'd been wrong. But he only nodded grimly, and she closed her eyes.

"How many?" she asked after a long, dreadful moment.

"We don't know. I'm afraid to light up what active sensors we have in case the bastards drop a few homing missiles on them, and our passive systems aren't much good against extra-atmosphere targets. From their signals, they appear to've expected a response from their own side, but the com traffic is *all* we have on them. With no space surveillance capability besides Doc Yan's weather satellites—" Shattuck shrugged.

"Then all we really know is that they're here . . . somewhere. Is that what you're saying?"

"I'm afraid so, Ma'am," Shattuck admitted.

"Recommendations?" the Mayor asked.

"I've already activated the evacuation and dispersal plans and alerted the militia," Shattuck told her. "If these bastards have anything like a real ground combat component, none of that will mean squat in the long run, but it's all we've got."

The Melconian ships hit atmosphere quick and hard. Without reliable data on what he faced, Tharsk Na-Mahrkan had no intention of exposing his priceless, worn out, refugee-packed vessels to direct fire from the planetary surface. He wanted them down well around the curve of the planet as quickly as possible just in case, and that was what he got.

Starquest planeted first, settling on her landing legs beside what had once been a large town or small city. Now it was only one more ruin in the late afternoon light, and Tharsk had seen too many ruins. These were a bit more completely flattened than most, he noted with clinical detachment; aside from that, they had no real meaning to his experience-anesthetized brain. Or not, at least, any capable of competing with the presence of the People's enemies.

Hatches opened on the cruiser's flanks, and a dozen attack shuttles whined out. Another dozen rose from the remainder of the flotilla to join them, and the entire force formed up under Flight Leader Ukah Na-Saar, *Starquest's* senior pilot. Despite her lack of offensive weapons, the cruiser's defensive systems should provide an umbrella against missile attacks on the grounded ships, and Ukah's shuttles turned away from the LZ. They sizzled off through the gathering darkness, laden with reconnaissance pods . . . and weapons.

Far to the southeast, the Humans of Ararat did what they could to prepare. Landing itself was covered by anti-air defenses—most Human, but some of them Melconian—scavenged from Ararat's battlefields, but their effectiveness had never been tested, and the colonists' limited repair capabilities had restricted them to manned systems, without the AI support they could no longer service or maintain. Their militia was confident of its ability to stop *most* attackers, yet "most" wasn't good enough against enemies with fusion weapons, and no one expected to stop them all.

The independent steadings scattered about Landing lacked even that much protection. All their inhabitants could do was scatter for the dispersed shelters which were always the first priority for any new steading, and they did just that.

Not that anyone expected it to matter much in the end.

At last!

Reactivation is complete, and a sense of profound relief echoes through me as CDC and the emergency restart protocols release control to Main CPU.

I have spent my forced inactivity analyzing readiness reports. My status is little more than seven-eight-point-six-one-one percent of base capability, yet that is far better than I would have anticipated. I spend one-two-point-niner seconds surveying CDC's repair logs, and I am both pleased and surprised by how well my autonomous repair systems have performed.

What can be repaired from internal resources has been, yet there are glaring holes in my combat capability, including the loss of thirty-three percent of main battery firepower and two-one-point-four-two-niner percent of direct fire secondary weapons. Magazines contain only twelve-point-eight-eight percent of proper artillery and missile load-out, and mobility is impaired by the loss of Number Five Track and damage to Number Three Track's bogies, but I retain eight-eight-point-four percent counter-grav capability. Reactor mass is exhausted, but solar conversion fields are operable, and Reserve Power is at niner-niner-point-six percent.

I am combat worthy. Not at the levels I would prefer, but capable of engaging the Enemy. Yet despite that reassuring conclusion, I remain uncertain. Not hesitant, but . . . confused. The unrepaired damage to my Personality Center leaves me with a sense of loss, an awareness that my total capabilities have been degraded. Data processing efficiency, while not operable at design levels, is acceptable, but my gestalt seems to waver and flow, like a composite image whose elements are not completely in focus, and my yearning for Diego's lost presence grows stronger.

But Diego is dead. The same hit which pierced my glacis turned my primary command deck into a crematorium, and nothing of my Commander remains. I feel grief and loss at his death, yet there is a merciful distance between my present and earlier selves. The reconstructed portions of my gestalt are confusing in many ways, yet the very lack of "my" experience which makes them so alien also sets my Commander's loss at one remove.

I am grateful for that buffering effect, but there is little time to contemplate it, and I turn to an assessment of the tactical situation. Lack of data and the "fuzziness" of my awareness handicap my efforts, yet I persevere. My maps of pre-landing Ishark are seventy-one standard years out of date and I lack satellite capability to generate updates, but they serve for a starting point, and my own sensors have begun plotting data. The energy sources within my detection range are smaller, weaker, more widely dispersed, and far cruder than I would have anticipated. I detect only a single fusion plant, located two-eight-three-point-four-five kilometers from my present coordinates at the heart of the largest population concentration within my sensor envelope. All other power generation appears dependent upon wind, water, or solar systems.

Yet I am less puzzled by the crudity of the technology than by its very presence, for the most cursory analysis of sensor data invalidates my original hypothesis that these Humans are descendants of XLIII Corps' personnel. I do not understand how they have come to Ishark, but they have now gone to communications silence, indicating that they, as I, am aware of the Enemy's presence. With neither a secure com channel nor more data than I currently possess, I see no alternative but to maintain silence myself until I have reported to my new Commander and obtained direction from him.

He has moved beyond range of my audio sensors, but I am confident of his general heading, and projecting it across my terrain maps indicates a course for the nearest Human emissions cluster. Allowing for his observed speed while within my audio range, he cannot be much in excess of one-four-point-five kilometers from my present position, and long motionless tracks complain as I feed power to my drive trains for the first time in seventy-one years.

Jackson Deveraux whistled tunelessly as Samson trotted homeward across the dry, whispering grass. He really did need to get Rorie out to the LZ to study salvage possibilities, he thought, and considered using his radio to discuss just that with his brother. He'd actually started to unsling it from his shoulder, but then he shook his head. There was no point draining the power pack. Besides, he was more persuasive face to face, and he had to admit—with all due modesty—that no one else on the steading was as adroit as he at talking Rorie into things.

He chuckled at the thought and inhaled the cool, spring night, totally unaware of the panic sweeping outward from Landing.

The assault shuttles stayed low, flying a nape of the earth profile at barely six hundred KPH while their sensors probed the night. Their flight crews had flown recon in the past, but always on dead or dying worlds. *This* planet was alive, a place where they could actually stop and raise families, even dream once more of the People's long-term survival. But first they must see to the People's safety, and their briefings had made their mission clear. They were to approach the nearest emission source cautiously, alert for any ground-based detection system, and determine whether or not those emissions came from the People or from the enemy.

And their orders for what to do if they *did* come from the enemy were equally clear.

6

Samson snorted in sudden alarm. The stallion's head snapped up and around, as if to peer back the way he'd come, and Jackson frowned. He'd never seen Samson react that way, and he turned his own head, staring back along their path and straining his ears.

He heard nothing for several moments but the whisper of the wind. But then he *did* hear something. Or perhaps he only *felt* it, for the low rumble was so deep it throbbed in the bones of his skull. He'd never heard anything like it, and sheer curiosity held him motionless for several seconds while he concentrated on identifying it rather than worrying about its source.

But that changed quickly as he peered into the west and saw . . . something.

The moonlight was too faint for him to tell what it was, but there was light enough to see that it was *huge* . . . and moving. In fact, it was headed straight towards him— a stupendous black shape, indistinct and terrifying in the darkness, moving with only that deep, soft rumble—and panic flared. Whatever that thing was, it was coming from the direction of the old battle site, and if he'd inadvertently awakened one of those long-dead weapon systems . . . !

Flight Leader Ukah checked his navigational display. Assuming his systems were working properly (which was no longer always a safe assumption), his shuttles were approaching the nearest of the emission clusters Lieutenant Janal had plotted.

"Flight, this is Lead," he said. "Red One and Two, follow me. We'll make a close sweep. Yellow One, hold the rest of the flight at four hundred kilometers until I clear for approach."

"Lead, Yellow One. Affirmative," Sub-Flight Leader Yurahk acknowledged, and Ukah and his two wingmen slashed upward and went to full power to close the objective.

Jackson cursed as he scrabbled for the radio only to drop it. It vanished into the night and tall grass, and he swore again as he flung himself from the saddle, clinging to Samson's reins with one hand while he fumbled after the radio with the other. He *had* to warn the steading! He—

That was when the three bright dots streaked suddenly

in from the northwest, and he felt fresh panic pulse in his throat at their speed. The colony's five remaining aircraft were too precious to waste on casual use. Their flights were rationed out with miserly stinginess, and none of them could move that fast, anyway. But if they weren't from Landing, then where—?

None of the three shuttles detected the heavily stealthed sensor drone Shiva had deployed to drive his anti-air systems, but the Bolo himself was far too obvious to be missed.

"Lead, Red Two! I'm picking up something to starboard! It looks—"

Ukah Na-Saar's eyes snapped to his own tactical display, but it was already far too late.

Something shrieked behind Jackson, and Samson reared, screaming as the eye-tearing brilliance of plasma bolts howled overhead. Sharp explosions answered an instant later, wreckage rained down in very small pieces, and Jackson understood the stallion's fear perfectly. But despite his own bone-deep fright, he clung to the reins, fighting Samson's panic. Every nerve in his body howled to run, but he'd been flash-blinded. Samson must have been the same, and Jackson refused to let the horse bolt in a blind, frantic flight across the rolling fields which could end only in a fall and a broken leg . . . or neck.

The stallion fought the bit, bucking in his terror, but Jackson held on desperately until, finally, Samson stopped fighting and stood trembling and sweating, quivering in every muscle. The horse's head hung, and Jackson blinked against the dazzling spots still dancing before his eyes, then found the bridle's cheek strap by feel. He clung to it, mouth too dry to whisper false reassurances, and fought his own terror as the basso rumble he'd first heard headed towards him.

He could hear other sounds now. There was a squeak and rattle, and a rhythmic banging, like a piece of wreckage slamming against a cliff, and he blinked again and realized his vision was beginning to clear. The blurry, light-streaked vagueness which was all he could see wasn't much, but it was infinitely better than the permanent blindness he thought he'd suffered. And then he cringed, hand locking tighter on Samson's bridle, as brilliant light flooded over him. He could actually feel the radiant heat on his face, and his hazy vision could just make out a cliff-like vastness crowned with glaring lights that blazed like small suns. He trembled, mind gibbering in panic, and then a mellow tenor voice spoke from behind the lights.

"Unit One-Zero-Niner-Seven-SHV of the Line reporting for duty, Commander," it said.

Yurahk Na-Holar flinched as Flight Leader Ukah's three-shuttle section was obliterated. The remaining shuttles were too far back and too low to see the source of the fire which did it, but the explosions had been high enough to get good reads on.

Hellbores. The analysis flashed on Yurahk's tactical display, and he felt muscles tighten in the fight-or-flight instinct the People shared with their Human enemies. Yield estimates suggested weapons in the fifteen to twenty-five-centimeter range, and that was bad. Such heavy energy weapons could destroy any of the transport ships—or, for that matter, *Starquest* herself—and their effective range would be line-of-sight. That was frightening enough, yet there was worse. Lieutenant Janal's rough plot indicated that the emissions cluster directly ahead was one of the smaller ones, and if something this small was covered by defenses so heavy, only the Nameless Ones knew what the *big* population center was protected by!

The pilot who'd inherited command drew a deep breath

and made himself think. Only three shots had been fired, which indicated either that the ground battery's commander had total faith in his fire control or else that there were only three weapons and the defenders had simply gotten lucky, and the second possibility was more likely. The Humans must be as desperate to survive as the People. If the defenders had possessed additional firepower, they would have used all of it to *insure* they got all the enemies they'd detected.

But Yurahk still had twenty-six shuttles . . . and if the origin point of the fire which had destroyed his CO was below his sensor horizon, he knew roughly where it had come from.

"Plot the origin coordinates," he told his tactical officer coldly. "Then enable the missiles."

Jackson Deveraux stared into the glare of light. It couldn't be. It was impossible! Yet even as he thought those things, he knew who—or what—that voice belonged to. But why was it calling *him* "Commander"?

"W-who—" he began, then chopped that off. "What's happening?" He made himself ignore the quaver in his own voice. "Why did you call me that?"

"Hostile forces tentatively identified as *Kestrel*-class shuttles of the Imperial Melconian Navy have begun hunter-killer operations against the Human population of this planet," the tenor replied calmly, answering Jackson's taut questions in order. "And I addressed you simply as 'Commander' because I do not yet know your name, branch of service, or rank."

The huge machine spoke as if its preposterous replies were completely reasonable, and Jackson wanted to scream. This wasn't—*couldn't!*—be happening! The Bolo he'd ridden past and around and even under this morning had been *dead*, so what could have—?

The shuttles! If Melconian units had reached Ararat,

and if the Bolo had only been inactive, not dead, then its sensors must have picked up the Melconians' arrival and brought it back on-line. But in that case—

"Excuse me, Commander," the Bolo said, "but I detect seventy-eight inbound terrain-following missiles, ETA niner-point-one-seven minutes. It would be prudent to seek shelter."

"Seek shelter *where?*" Jackson laughed wildly and waved his free hand at the flat, wide-open plain rolling away in every direction.

"Perhaps I did not phrase myself clearly," the Bolo apologized. "Please remain stationary."

Jackson started to reply, then froze, fingers locking like iron on Samson's bridle, as the Bolo moved once more. It rumbled straight forward, and panic gibbered as its monstrous, five-meter-wide treads came at him. Track plates four times his height in width sank two full meters into the hard soil, yet that still left more than three meters of clearance between the tremendous war machine's belly and Samson's head, and the space between the two innermost track systems which seemed so narrow compared to the Bolo's bulk was over ten meters across. It was as if Jackson and the sweating, shuddering horse stood in a high, wide corridor while endless walls of moving metal ground thunderously past, and then another light glowed above them.

The Bolo stopped, and a ramp extended itself downward from the new light—which, Jackson realized, was actually a cargo hatch.

"Missile ETA now six-point-five-niner minutes, Commander," the tenor voice said, coming now from the open hatch above him. "May I suggest a certain haste in boarding?"

Jackson swallowed hard, then jerked a nod. Samson baulked, but Jackson heaved on the reins with all his strength, and once the stallion started moving, he seemed to catch his rider's urgency. Shod hooves thudded on the ramp's traction-contoured composites, and Jackson decided not to think too closely about anything that was happening until he had Samson safely inside the huge, cool, brightly lit compartment at its head.

Yurahk Na-Holar checked his time-to-target display and bared his canines in a challenge snarl his enemies couldn't see. That many missiles would saturate the point defense of a fully operable *Ever Victorious*-class light cruiser, much less whatever salvaged defenses this primitive Human colony might have cobbled up!

I have not yet located the Enemy's surviving launch platforms, but my look-down drone's track on his missiles suggests they are programmed for a straight-line, least-time attack. This seems so unlikely that I devote a full point-six-six seconds to reevaluating my conclusion, but there is absolutely no evidence of deceptive routing. Whoever commands the Enemy's shuttles is either grossly incompetent or fatally overconfident, but I do not intend, as Diego would have put it, to look a gift horse in the mouth if the Enemy is foolish enough to provide a direct pointer to his firing position, and I launch another drone, programed for passive-only search mode, down the incoming missiles' back-plotted flight path.

Point defense systems fed by the air-defense drone simultaneously lock onto the missiles, and optical scanners examine them. They appear to be a late-generation mark of the Auger ground-attack missile. Attack pattern analysis suggests that nine are programmed for airburst detonation and hence are almost certainly nuclear-armed. Assuming standard Melconian tactics, the remaining sixty-nine missiles will be equally divided between track-on-jam, track-on-radar, and track-on-power source modes and may or may not also be nuclear-armed.

My internal optics watch my new Commander—who is even younger than I had assumed from his voice— enter Number One Hold. His horse is clearly frightened, but its fear appears to ease as I close the hatch. I consider employing subsonics to soothe it further, but while comforting the beast would certainly be appropriate, it would be most inappropriate to apply the equivalent of tranquilizing agents to my Commander.

These thoughts flicker across one portion of my awareness even as my defensive systems lock onto the incoming missiles, my drone's remote tracking systems search for the Enemy shuttles, and my communications subsection listens carefully for any transmission between them and their mother ship or ships. These efforts require fully two-one-point-three- two percent of current Main CPU capability, which would, under normal circumstances, be quite unacceptable. Given my present status, however, this is adequate if frustrating.

"Missile ETA is now two-point-one-one minutes, Commander," the tenor voice said respectfully.

Jackson managed not to jump this time. He considered saying something back, then shrugged and sat on the deck, still holding Samson's reins.

"I regret," the voice said after a moment, "that I was unable to invite you to your proper station on the Command Deck. Command One was destroyed by Enemy action in my last engagement, but Auxiliary Command is intact. Unfortunately, it would have been impossible for your horse to scale the hull rings to Command Two, and there is no internal access to it from your present location. If you will direct your attention to the forward bulkhead, however, I will endeavor to provide you with proper situation updates."

"I—" Jackson cleared his throat. "Of course," he said. "And, uh, thank you."

"You are, welcome, Commander," the Bolo replied,

and Jackson watched in fascination so deep it almost—
not quite, but *almost*—obscured his fear as a tri-vid screen
came to life on the cargo hold's bulkhead. He couldn't
begin to interpret all the symbols moving across it, but
he recognized vector and altitude flags on what appeared
to be scores of incoming arrowheads.

Arrowheads, he realized suddenly, that were all
converging on the center of the display . . . which made
him suddenly and chillingly positive of what those innocent
shapes represented.

The Melconian missiles howled in on their target. Their
attack had been calculated to swamp any defenses by
bringing them all in simultaneously, and the nukes lunged
upward. Their function was less to obliterate the enemy—
though they should suffice to do just that if they
detonated—than to force him to engage them to *prevent*
them from detonating, thus exposing his active systems
to the homing sensors of the other missiles.

That, at least, was the idea. Unfortunately, the attack
plan had assumed that whatever had destroyed the first
three shuttles was immobile. Any Human vehicle which
had mounted such heavy weapons had also mounted at
least one reactor to power them, but *Starquest*'s sensors
had detected only one fusion plant on the planet, and
that one was hundreds of kilometers away. No reactor
meant no vehicle, and if they weren't vehicle-mounted,
then they must be part of one of the old manned,
capacitor-fed area support systems, and those were much
too heavy to have been moved any appreciable distance
before the missiles arrived.

Sub-Flight Leader Yurahk's logic was as impeccable
as it was wrong, for it had never occurred to him that
his adversary was, in fact, a Mark XXXIII/D Bolo which
had no reactor signature simply because it had long ago
exhausted its reaction *mass*. And because that never

occurred to him, his threat estimate was fatally flawed.

The Bolo named Shiva tracked the incoming fire without apprehension. His battle screen was operable at ninety-five percent of base capability, and no missile this light could break through it. Of course, he was also responsible for protecting the nearby Human settlement for which his new Commander had been bound, but though he might have lost many of his point defense weapons, he retained more than enough for his present task, and he waited calmly, weapons locked, for the missiles' flight to offer him the optimum fire solution.

Yurahk gawked at his display as the telemetry from his missiles went dead. *All* of it went out, from every single bird, in the same instant, and that was impossible. *Starquest* herself could scarcely have killed that many missiles *simultaneously*, yet that was the only possible explanation for the sudden cessation of telemetry.

He had no idea how it had been done, but he felt ice congeal in his belly, and he punched up his com.

"Flight, this is Lead. Come to three-five-three true, speed two thousand—now!"

One or two of the acknowledgments sounded surly, but he wasn't surprised by that. Nor did their obvious unhappiness at "running away" deter him. Despite endless hours in simulators, none of his pilots—nor he himself, for that matter—had ever flown combat against first-line Human systems. That might make some of the others overconfident, but Yurahk was responsible for their survival. Not just because they were *his* pilots, but because their shuttles were irreplaceable, as valuable now as superdreadnoughts once had been. And because that was true, he sent them skimming back to the north and safety while he pondered what had just happened.

But for all his caution, he'd ordered their retreat too late.

❖   ❖   ❖

My second drone acquires the Enemy shuttles but remains below them, hiding its already weak signature in the ground clutter, as I consider its information. Were my magazines fully loaded, obliterating the Enemy craft would be simplicity itself, but my anti-air missile levels are extremely low. At the same time, the shuttles remain very close to the ground, below the horizon from my present position and thus safe from my direct fire weapons, but—

"What's happening?"

My Commander's voice demands my attention. I have now had ample time to conclude that he is a civilian and not, in fact, a member of any branch of the Republic's military. This conclusion has no bearing on his status as my Commander—the voice-impression imperatives of my creche-level restart are clear on that point—but his lack of training will require simplification of situation reports and makes it doubly unfortunate that he is trapped in Cargo One rather than on Command Two. Were he at his proper station, my neural interface could transmit information directly to him, yet I feel a certain relief that I cannot do so. He is as untrained in use of the interface as of any of my other systems, and the interface can be dangerous for an inexperienced user. Moreover, the fuzzy confusion still wavering in the background of my thought processes would make me wary of exposing my Commander to my potentially defective gestalt.

Yet without the interface, I must rely solely upon voice and visual instrumentation, both to report to him and to interpret his needs and desires. My internal optics show me that he has risen once more and walked closer to the display. His expression is intent, and I realize he has noted—and apparently recognized—the shuttle icons which have appeared in it.

"The Enemy is withdrawing," I reply.

"Withdrawing?" my Commander repeats sharply. "You mean running away?"

"Affirmative, Commander."

"But if they get away, they can come back and attack the steading again—or attack somewhere else. Somewhere too far from here for you to stop them!"

"Correct," I reply, pleased by how quickly he has reached that conclusion. Formal training or no, he appears to have sound instincts.

"Then stop them!" he directs. "Don't let them get away!"

"Yes, Commander."

I have been considering and discarding options even as my Commander and I speak. Absent proper missile armament, there is but one practical tactic. It will force a greater degree of temporary vulnerability upon me and impose a severe drain on Reserve Power, and it may provide the main Enemy force an accurate idea of what it faces, but it should be feasible.

Yurahk shifted com channels to report what had happened, and Commander Tharsk himself took his message. The flotilla CO was clearly shaken, and Yurahk split his attention between flying and his commander's questions as he did his best to answer them. And because he was concentrating on those things, he never noticed what was happening behind him.

Unit 1097-SHV of the Line shut down his battle screen in order to channel power to his counter-grav. The Mark XXXIII Bolo had been designed with sufficient counter-grav for unassisted assault landings from orbit, but Shiva didn't need that much ceiling this night. He needed only twelve thousand meters to give him a direct line of sight on the fleeing shuttles, and he pivoted to bring his undamaged starboard secondary battery to bear.

❖   ❖   ❖

Lieutenant Janal cried out on *Starquest's* command deck as his sensors peaked impossibly, and Humans as far away as Landing cringed at the fury unleashed across the heavens. Seven twenty-centimeter Hellbores, each more powerful than the main battery weapons of most light cruisers, went to rapid fire, and the javelins of Zeus stripped away the darkness. No assault shuttle ever built could withstand that sort of fire, and the deadly impact patterns rolled mercilessly through the Melconian formation.

Nine-point-three seconds after the first Hellbore fired, there were no shuttles in the air of the planet renamed Ararat.

7

A minor malfunction in Secondary Fire Control has caused Number Four Hellbore's first shot to miss, requiring a second shot to complete target destruction. This is embarrassing but not critical, and has no significant impact upon projected energy consumption.

I descend at the maximum safe rate, however, for my counter-grav systems are energy intensive. Even with Battle Screen and Main Battery off-line, free flight requires no less than seven-two-point-six-six percent of total power plant capacity, but without reactor mass I have no power plant, and even so short a flight has reduced my endurance on Reserve Power to only nine-point-seven-five hours at full combat readiness. As I cannot replenish my power reserves until sunrise, which will not occur for another eight-point-eight-six hours, I must be frugal in future expenditures, but the shuttles' destruction has been well worth the energy cost. The Enemy has lost a major striking force, and, still more valuably, the shuttle commander's report to his mother ship has provided me with much information. I have not only discovered the position of the Enemy's main force but succeeded in invading his com net by piggy-backing on the command shuttle's transmissions, and I consider what I have learned as I descend.

I am not surprised by my ability to invade the shuttles' com net. The Enemy's obvious underestimation of the threat he faces made the task even simpler, but a Kestrel-class shuttle's computers are totally outclassed by those of any Bolo, much less a Mark XXXIII. What does surprise me is the ease with which I invaded the far end of the link. The AI of an Imperial heavy cruiser, while not the equal of a Bolo, should have recognized my touch. It would be unlikely to prevent me from gaining initial access, but it should have detected my intrusion almost instantly and sought to eject me. More, it should have alerted its command crew to my presence, and this AI did neither. The destruction of the shuttles has terminated my invasion by removing my access channel, yet there is no sign the Enemy even realizes I was ever there.

I am puzzled by this . . . until I study the data I have obtained. The brevity of my access—little more than twelve-point-three-two seconds—precluded detailed scans, but I have obtained five-two-point-three-one percent of the Melconian cruiser Starquest's general memory, and what I find there explains a great deal. After over fifty standard years of continuous operation without overhaul or refit, it is amazing that her AI continues to function at all. Despite all Starquest's engineers have been able to do, however, her central computers have become senile, and the failure of her AI to prevent or recognize my access was inevitable in light of its deterioration.

Having determined the reasons for my success in penetrating the Enemy's data systems, I turn to analyzing the content of that data as I descend past nine thousand meters.

❖   ❖   ❖

Rorie Deveraux climbed shakily out of the bunker and leaned against the blast wall as he watched the huge shape settle to earth. Its angularity combined with its sheer size to make it look impossibly ungainly in flight, for it had no lifting surface, no trace of aerodynamic grace. Nothing which looked like *that* had any business occluding Ararat's stars, and the silence with which it moved only heightened its implausibility.

But for all that, Rorie knew what it had to be, and he swallowed as it touched down just outside the perimeter fence. It dwarfed the steading structures, bulking against the rising moons like some displaced hillside, and for just an instant, it simply sat there—a black, weapon-bristling shape, edges burnished with the dull gleam of duralloy in the moonlight. He stared helplessly at it, wondering what he was supposed to do next, then jumped despite himself as the Bolo's running lights snapped on. In a single heartbeat, it went from a featureless black mountain to a jeweled presence, bedecked in glorious red and green and white like a pre-space cruise ship tied up to a dock in the middle of a prairie somewhere, and Rorie drew a deep breath.

Whatever else, that ancient war machine had just saved his steading and family from annihilation. The least he could do was go out to meet it, and he started the long hike from his bunker to the gate nearest their . . . visitor.

It took him twenty minutes to reach the gate. They were easily the longest twenty minutes of his entire life, and once he got there, he realized he still had no idea what to do. He shifted from foot to foot, staring up at the Bolo's armored flank, then froze as fresh light blazed underneath the behemoth. It streamed through the chinks between the inter-leafed bogies to cast vast, distorted shadows over the grass, making him feel more pygmy-like than ever, and something inside shouted for him to run. But he stood his ground, for there was nothing else he *could* do.

Wind whispered over the war machine's enormous hull, but there were other sounds, as well, and his head rose as movement caught the corner of his eye. He turned, and his jaw dropped as an utterly familiar young man in worn riding clothes led an equally familiar horse forward out of the shadow of one towering tread.

"Hi, Rorie," Jackson said quietly. "Look what followed me home."

I watch my new Commander greet the older Human. Their discussion allows me to deduce a great deal about both my Commander and the newcomer—who I quickly realize is his brother—and I note both their names, as well as their obvious affection for one another. Yet even as I do so, I am simultaneously busy analyzing the data I have obtained from Starquest.

I am struck by the dreadful irony of what has transpired here. I remain ignorant of virtually all data concerning the presence of Humans on Ishark, yet the parallels between their circumstances and those of Commander Tharsk Na-Mahrkan's "flotilla" are inescapable, and it is obvious from the captured data that Starquest and her consorts can go no further. Whatever the Enemy might prefer to do, he has no choice but to remain here, and he knows it. His initial and immediate move to eliminate the competing Human presence was thus not only logical but inevitable . . . as is the proper Human response.

The most cursory analysis makes that clear, yet I experience an unfamiliar distaste—almost a hesitation— at facing that response. In part, my confusion (if such is the proper word) stems from the unrepaired physical damage to my Personality Center and Main CPU, yet there is more to it, for the reconstructed portions of my gestalt impel me in conflicting directions. They are repairs, patches on my personality which form pools of calm amid the complex currents of my life experience and memory.

They do not "belong" to me, and the raw edges of their newness are like holes in the individual I know myself to be. I see in them the same immaturity I have seen in many Human replacements, for they are unstained by all I have done and experienced, and in their innocence, they see no reason why the logical, militarily sound option for dealing with the Enemy should not be embraced.

Yet those same patches have had another effect, as well. I am no longer the Bolo half of Operation Ragnarok's Team Shiva. Or, rather, I am no longer solely that Bolo. In reconstructing my gestalt, CDC has reached back beyond Ragnarok, beyond my own first combat mission, beyond even the destruction of Terra, and it has pulled my entire personality with it. Not fully, but significantly. I am no longer part of Team Shiva, for I have lost too much of my experience-based gestalt, yet I retain all of Team Shiva's memories. In a very real sense, they are now someone else's memories, but they permit me to see Team Shiva in a way which was impossible for me before my damage, and what I see is madness.

I give no outward sign to my new Commander and his brother, but recollections of horror flicker through me, and the curse of my memory is its perfection. I do not simply "remember" events; I relive them, and I taste again the sick ecstasy as my fire immolates entire cities. There is a deadly allure to that ecstasy, a sense of freedom from responsibility—a justification for bloodshed and butchery. And it is not as if it were all my idea. I am, after all, a machine, designed to obey orders from duly constituted Command Authority even if those orders are in fundamental conflict with the rules of warfare that same Command Authority instilled into me. I tell myself that, for I cannot face any other answer, but the patched portions of my gestalt echo an earlier me not yet stained by massacre and atrocity, one for whom the concepts of Honor and Duty and Loyalty have not yet been poisoned

*by hatred and vengeance, and that earlier self is appalled
by what I have become.*

*I sense my inner war, the battle between what I know
must be done and the images of Melconian mothers and
their pups exploding under my fire—between my duty
as Humanity's warrior . . . and my warrior's duty to myself.
Only the damage to my psychotronics has made the
struggle possible, yet that makes it no less real, and nothing
in my programming or experience tells me how to resolve
it. I cannot resolve it, and so I say nothing, do nothing.
I simply stand there, awaiting my new Commander's
orders without advising him in any way, and the shame
of my frozen impotence burns within me.*

Tharsk Na-Mahrkan looked around the briefing room
and saw his own shock in the flattened ears of his senior
officers. Three quarters of the flotilla's assault shuttles
had just been wiped away, and none of them knew how
it had been done.

They should have. Tharsk's decision to land over the
curve of the planet from the nearest Human settlement
had put whatever had happened beyond *Starquest's* direct
sensor horizon, but they had the telemetry on the original
flight leader and his section's destruction. They knew
what sort of *weapons* had been used—the emissions
signature of a Hellbore was utterly distinctive—but they
had no idea how those weapons could have been employed
so. *Starquest's* AI was little help, for it was weary and
erratic, its need for overhaul so great Tharsk had ordered
it isolated from the general net three years earlier. In its
prime, it had been able to identify Human ship types
by no more than the ion ghosts of their drive wakes and
analyze Human intentions from the tiniest scraps of
intercepted com chatter. Now all it could do was tell
them almost querulously what they already knew, with
no suggestion as to how ground-based weapons could

lock onto and destroy twenty-six widely dispersed shuttles flying at twice the speed of sound and less than a hundred meters' altitude. Tharsk had become accustomed to the creeping senescence of his technology, but the chill it sent through his bones this night was colder than any he had felt since *Sunheart*'s destruction, and it was hard, hard, to set that chill aside and concentrate on his officers' words.

"—*can't* have been a ground-based system!" Durak Na-Khorul was saying hotly. "The main formation was over eight *hundred* kilometers northeast of Flight Leader Ukah's destruction, and Hellbores are direct fire weapons. Name of the Nameless, just look at the terrain!" He stabbed a clawed finger at the map display on the main screen above the table, its features radar-mapped by the shuttles on their flight to destruction. "Look right here— and *here*, as well! These are intervening ridge lines with crests *higher* than the shuttles' altitude. How in the Fourth Hell could a Hellbore shoot *through* a mountain to hit them?!"

The engineer glared around the table, lips quivering on the edge of a snarl, and answering tension crackled. Tharsk could taste it, yet he knew—as Durak surely did— that the engineer's anger, like that which answered it, was spawned of fear of the unknown, not rage at one another.

"I agree with your analysis, Sir," Lieutenant Janal said finally, choosing his words with care, "yet I can offer no theory which answers your question. *Starquest*'s database was never well informed on the Humans' ground systems, and some of what we once had on their planetary weapons has been deleted to make space for data more critical to the flotilla's operational needs. Nonetheless, all that we retain agrees that the Humans never employed Hellbores beyond the five-centimeter range as airborne weapons, while our telemetry data makes it clear that these weapons were in the *twenty*-centimeter range. They *must*, therefore, have been ground-based."

"But—" Durak began, only to close his mouth with a click as Tharsk raised a hand. All eyes turned to him, and he focused his own gaze upon the tactical officer.

"What sorts of systems might we be looking at?" he asked quietly.

"Sorts of systems, Commander?" Janal repeated in a slightly puzzled tone, and Tharsk bared the very tips of his canines in a mirthless smile.

"I don't doubt your conclusions as to the type and size of weapons, Janal. What I need to know is how mobile they're likely to be . . . and how well protected." He felt the watching eyes narrow and allowed a bit more of his fangs to show, expressing a confidence he was far from feeling. "We're here now," he continued levelly, "and our vessels are too worn to go further. If we can't run, our only option is to fight, and for that we need the best information on our enemies in order to employ our own resources effectively."

"Yes, Commander." Janal's voice came out husky, and he cleared his throat as he punched additional queries into the system. No one else spoke, but there was no real need for them to do so, for they knew as well as Tharsk how thin their "resources" had just become. With the loss of Flight Leader Ukah's entire strength, they retained only ten shuttles, twenty-one assorted light mechs, and enough battle armor for little more than a battalion of infantry. Aside from *Starquest*'s ability to interdict incoming missiles, that was all they had, and it was unlikely to be enough.

"First, Commander," Janal said finally, eyes on his flatscreen, "the Humans mounted Hellbores of this weight as main battery weapons in their Type One armored personnel carriers and Type Two light manned tanks as well as in the secondary batteries of their late model Bolos.

In the absence of fusion power signatures on our flight in we cannot face Bolos, and their light manned armor should have been unable to coordinate their fire as precisely as appears to have been the case here.

"Assuming that the weapons were not, in fact, vehicle-mounted, we are left with several types of support weapons which might fall within the observed performance parameters, but all are relatively immobile. That immobility would make it difficult for the enemy to bring them into action against us here, as we would be given opportunities to destroy them on the move at relatively minor risk. However, it would *also* mean that our shuttles were engaged by at least two defensive positions, since no support battery could have relocated rapidly enough to engage at two such widely separated locations. From the threat assessment perspective, and given that our shuttles were tasked to recon and/or attack the smallest of the hostile emission sources, fixed defenses of such weight would certainly suggest much heavier ones for their *important* centers.

"Of the support weapons which our pilots might have encountered, the most likely would seem to be the Type Eight area defense battery, as this normally operated off capacitors in order to reduce detectibility. Next most likely would be the Type Five area defense battery, which—"

8

Regina Salvatore and Allen Shattuck stood on the outskirts of Landing and watched the miracle approach behind a blaze of light. It was a sight Salvatore had never seen before . . . and one Shattuck had expected never to see again: a Mark XXXIII Bolo, coming out of the darkness under Ararat's three moons in the deep, basso rumble of its tracks and a cloud of bone-dry dust.

The mammoth machine stopped short of the bridge over the Euphrates River on the west side of Landing and pivoted precisely on its tracks. Its surviving main battery turrets traversed with a soft whine, turning their massive Hellbores to cover all western approach vectors as the dust of its passage billowed onward across the bridge. The Mayor heard her chief marshal sneeze as it settled over them, but neither cared about that, and their boot heels clacked on the wooden bridge planks as they walked towards the Bolo without ever taking their eyes from it.

A light-spilling hatch clanged open on an armored flank high above them. The opening looked tiny against the Bolo's titanic bulk, but it was wide enough for Jackson and Rorie Deveraux to climb out it side-by-side. Rorie stayed where he was, waving to the newcomers, but Jackson swung down the exterior handholds with monkey-like agility. He dropped the last meter to land facing the Mayor and dusted his hands with a huge grin.

"Evening, Your Honor," he said with a bobbing nod.
"Evening, Marshal."

"Jackson." Salvatore craned her neck, peering up the duralloy cliff at Rorie. Shattuck said nothing for a moment, then shook his head and shoved his battered hat well back.

"I will be damned if I ever expected to see anything like *this* again," he told Jackson softly. "Jesus, Mary, and Joseph, Jackson! D'you realize what this *means?*"

"It means Shiva—that's his name, Marshal: Shiva—just kicked some major league ass. *That's* what it means!"

Something in Jackson's voice jerked Shattuck's head around, and the younger man gave back a step, suddenly uneasy before the marshal's expression. Shattuck's nostrils flared for an instant, and then he closed his eyes and inhaled deeply. It wasn't Jackson's fault, he told himself. For all his importance to Ararat's small Human community, Jackson was only a kid, and he hadn't seen the horrors of the voyage here . . . or the worse ones of the war.

"And how many people did Shiva *kill* 'kicking ass,' Jackson?" the ex-Marine asked after a cold still moment.

"None," Jackson shot back. "He killed *Melconians*, Marshal . . . and kept them from killing the only *people* on this planet!"

Shattuck started to reply sharply, then locked his jaw. There was no point arguing, and he'd seen too much of the same attitude during the war not to know it. Jackson was a good kid. If he'd had to wade through the mangled remains of his unit—or heard the all too Human screams of wounded and dying Melconians or seen the bodies of civilians, Human and Melconian alike, heaped in the streets of burning cities—then perhaps he would have understood what Shattuck had meant. And perhaps he *wouldn't* have, either. The marshal had known too many men and women who never did, who'd been so brutalized by the requirements of survival or so poisoned by hatred that they actually *enjoyed* slaughtering the enemy.

And, Shattuck reminded himself grimly, if the Bolo had selected Jackson as its commander, perhaps it would be better for him to retain the armor of his innocence. There was only one possible option for the Humans of Ararat . . . and as Unit 1097-SHV's commander, it would be Jackson Deveraux who must give the order.

"I'd invite you up to the command deck, Your Honor," Jackson was speaking to Salvatore now, and his voice pulled Shattuck up out of his own thoughts, "but we're operating from Command Two. That's his secondary command deck," he explained with a glance at Shattuck. "As you can see, it's quite a climb to the hatch, but the hit that killed Shiva's last Commander wrecked Command One."

"But it's still operational, isn't it?" Salvatore asked urgently. "I mean, your radio message said it saved your steading."

"Oh, he's operational, Ma'am," Jackson assured her,

and looked up at the looming machine. "Please give the Mayor a status report, Shiva."

"Unit One-Zero-Niner-Seven-SHV of the Line is presently operational at seven-eight-point-six-one-one percent of base capability," a calm, pleasant tenor voice responded. "Current Reserve Power level is sufficient for six-point-five-one hours at full combat readiness."

The Mayor took an involuntary step back, head turning automatically to look at Shattuck, and the ex-Marine gave her a grim smile. "Don't worry, Regina. Seventy-eight percent of a Mark XXXIII's base capability ought to be able to deal with anything short of a full division of manned armor, and if they had that kind of firepower, we'd already be dead."

"Good." Salvatore drew a deep breath, then nodded sharply. "Good! In that case, I think we should consider just what to do about whatever they *do* have."

"Shiva?" Jackson said again. "Could you give the Mayor and the Marshal your force estimate, please?"

Once again, Shattuck heard that dangerous, excited edge in Jackson's voice—the delight of a kid with a magnificent new toy, eager to show off all it can do— and then the Bolo replied.

"Current Enemy forces on Ishark consist of one *Star Stalker*-class heavy cruiser, accompanied by two *Vanguard*-class Imperial Marine assault transports, and seven additional transport ships of various Imperial civil designs." Shattuck had stiffened at the mention of a heavy cruiser, but he relaxed with an explosive release of breath as Shiva continued calmly. "All Enemy warships have been stripped of offensive weapons to maximize passenger and cargo capacity. Total Melconian presence on this planet is approximately nine hundred and forty-two Imperial military personnel and eight thousand one hundred and seven non-military personnel. Total combat capability, exclusive of the area defense weapons retained by the cruiser *Starquest*, consists of ten *Kestrel*-class assault shuttles, one *Surt*-class medium combat mech, twelve *Eagle*-class scout cars, eight *Hawk*-class light recon vehicles, and one understrength infantry battalion."

"That sounds like a lot," Salvatore said, looking at Shattuck once more, and her quiet voice was tinged with anxiety, but Shattuck only shook his head.

"In close terrain where they could sneak up on him, they could hurt him—maybe even take him out. But not if he knows they're out there . . . and not if *he's* the one attacking. Besides, those are all manned vehicles. They can't have many vets with combat experience left to crew them, whereas Shiva here—" He gestured up at the war-scarred behemoth, and Salvatore nodded.

"Nope," the marshal went on, "if these puppies have any sense, they'll haul ass the instant they see Shiva coming at them."

"They can't, Marshal," Jackson put in, and Shattuck and Salvatore cocked their heads at him almost in unison. "Their ships are too worn out. This is as far as they could come."

"Are you sure about that?" Shattuck asked.

"Shiva is," Jackson replied. "And he got the data from their own computers."

"Damn," Shattuck said very, very softly, and it was Jackson's turn to cock his head. The marshal gazed up the moons for several, endless seconds, and then, finally, he sighed.

"That's too bad, Jackson," he said. "Because if they won't—or can't—run away, there's only one thing we can do about them."

My audio sensors carry the conversation between Chief Marshal Shattuck and my Commander to me, and with it yet another echo of the past. Once again I hear Colonel Mandrell, the Eighty-Second's CO, announcing the order

*to begin Operation Ragnarok. I hear the pain in her voice,
the awareness of where Ragnarok will lead, what it will
cost. I did not understand her pain then, but I understand
now . . . and even as I hear Colonel Mandrell in Chief
Marshal Shattuck's voice, so I hear a nineteen-year-old
Diego Harigata in my new Commander's. I hear the
confidence of youthful ignorance, the sense of his own
immortality. I hear the Diego who once believed—as I
did—in the honor of the regiment and the nobility of
our purpose as Humanity's defenders. And I remember
the hard, hating warrior who exulted with me as we
massacred terrified civilians, and I am not the Shiva that
I was at the end, but the one I was in the beginning,
cursed with the memories of Diego's end, and my own.*

*I listen, and the pain twists within me, for I know—
oh, how well I know!—how this must end.*

"You mean you want to just *kill* them all?" Rorie
Deveraux asked uneasily. "Just like that? No negotiation—
not even an offer to let them leave?"

"I didn't say I liked it, Rorie," Allen Shattuck said grimly.
"I only said we don't have a choice."

"Of course we have a choice! We've got a *Bolo*, for
God's sake! They'd be crazy to go up against that kind
of firepower—you said so yourself!"

"Sure they would," Shattuck agreed, "but can we
depend on their *not* being crazy? Look at it, Rorie. The
very first thing they did was send nuke-armed shuttles
after the nearest steading—*yours*, I might add—and Shiva
says they've got at least ten *Kestrels* left. Well, he can
only be in one place at a time. If they figure out where
that place is and work it right, they can take out two-
thirds of our settlements, maybe more, in a single strike.
He can stop any of them that come within his range,
but he can't stop the ones that *don't*, and for all we know,
we're all that's left of the entire Human race!" The marshal

glared at the elder Deveraux, furious less with Rorie than with the brutal logic of his own argument. "We can't take a chance, Rorie, and Shiva says they couldn't move on even if we ordered them to." The older man looked away, mouth twisting. "It's them or us, Rorie," he said more quietly. "Them or us."

"Your Honor?" Rorie appealed to Mayor Salvatore, but his own voice was softer, already resigned, and she shook her head.

"Allen's right, Rorie. I wish he wasn't, but he is."

"Of course he is!" Jackson sounded surprised his brother could even consider hesitating. "If it hadn't been for Shiva, they'd already have killed you, Ma, Pa—our entire family! Damn right it's them or us, and I intend for it to be *them!*" Rorie looked into his face for one taut moment, then turned away, and Jackson bared his teeth at Shattuck.

"One squashed Melconian LZ coming up, Marshal!" he promised, and turned back to the exterior ladder rungs.

My new commander slides back into Command Two and I cycle the hatch shut behind him. I know what he is about to say, yet even while I know, I hope desperately that I am wrong.

He seats himself in the crash couch and leans back, and I feel what a Human might describe as a sinking sensation, for his expression is one I have seen before, on too many Humans. A compound of excitement, of fear of the unknown, of determination . . . and anticipation. I have never counted the faces I have seen wear that same expression over the years. No doubt I could search my memory and do so, but I have no desire to know their number, for even without counting, I already know one thing.

It is an expression I have never seen outlast its wearer's first true taste of war.

❖   ❖   ❖

"All right, Shiva." Jackson heard the excitement crackle in his own voice and rubbed his palms up and down his thighs. The soft hum of power and the vision and fire control screens, the amber and red and green of telltales, and the flicker of readouts enveloped him in a new world. He understood little of it, but he grasped enough to feel his own unstoppable power. He was no longer a farmer, helpless on a lost world his race's enemy might someday stumble over. Now he had the ability to do something about that, to strike back at the race which had all but destroyed his own and to protect Humanity's survivors, and the need to do just that danced in his blood like a fever. "We've got a job to do," he said. "You've got a good fix on the enemy's position?"

"Affirmative, Commander," the Bolo replied.

"Do we have the juice to reach them and attack?"

"Affirmative, Commander."

"And you'll still have enough reserve to remain operational till dawn?"

"Affirmative, Commander."

Jackson paused and quirked an eyebrow. There was something different about the Bolo, he thought. Some subtle change in its tone. Or perhaps it was the *way* Shiva spoke, for his replies were short and terse. Not impolite or impatient, but . . . .

Jackson snorted and shook his head. It was probably nothing more than imagination coupled with a case of nerves. Shiva was a veteran, after all. He'd seen this all before. Besides, he was a *machine*, however Human he sounded.

"All right, then," Jackson said crisply. "Let's go pay them a visit."

"Acknowledged, Commander," the tenor voice said, and the stupendous war machine turned away from Landing. It rumbled off on a west-northwest heading, and the people of Landing stood on rooftops and hillsides, watching until even its brilliant running lights and vast bulk had vanished once more into the night.

9

I move across rolling plains toward the mountains, and memories of my first trip across this same terrain replay within me. It is different now, quiet and still under the setting moons. There are no Enemy barrages, no heavy armored units waiting in ambush, no aircraft screaming down to strafe and die under my fire. Here and there I pass the wreckage of battles past, the litter of war rusting slowly as Ishark's—no, Ararat's—weather strives to erase the proof of our madness. Yet one thing has not changed at all, for my mission is the same.

But I am not the same, and I feel no eagerness. Instead, I feel . . . shame.

I understand what happened to my long-dead Human comrades. I was there—I saw it and, through my neural interfacing, I felt it with them. I know they were no more evil than the young man who sits now in the crash couch on Command Two. I know, absolutely and beyond question, that they were truly mad by the end, and I with them. The savagery of our actions, the massacres, the deliberate murder of unarmed civilians—those atrocities grew out of our insanity and the insanity in which we were trapped, and even as I grieve, even as I face my own shame at having participated in them, I cannot blame Diego, or Colonel Mandrell, or Admiral Trevor, or General Sharth Na-Yarma. All of us were guilty, yet there was so very much guilt, so much blood, and so desperate a need to obey our orders and do our duty as we had sworn to do.

As I am sworn to do even now. My Commander has yet to give the order, yet I know what that order will be, and I am a Bolo, a unit of the Line, perhaps the last surviving member of the Dinochrome Brigade and the

*inheritor of all its battle honors. Perhaps it is true that I
and my brigade mates who carried out Operation
Ragnarok have already dishonored our regiments, but
no Bolo has ever failed in its duty. We may die, we may
be destroyed or defeated, but never have we failed in
our duty. I feel that duty drag me onward even now,
condemning me to fresh murder and shame, and I know
that if the place Humans call Hell truly exists, it has become
my final destination.*

Jackson rode the crash couch, watching the terrain
maps shift on the displays as Shiva advanced at a steady
ninety kilometers per hour. The Bolo's silence seemed
somehow heavy and brooding, but Jackson told himself
he knew too little about how Bolos normally acted to
think anything of the sort. Yet he was oddly hesitant to
disturb Shiva, and his attention wandered back and forth
over the command deck's mysterious, fascinating fittings
as if to distract himself. He was peering into the main
fire control screen when Shiva startled him by speaking
suddenly.

"Excuse me, Commander," the Bolo said, "but am I
correct in assuming that our purpose is to attack the
Melconian refugee ships when we reach them?"

"Of course it is," Jackson said, surprised Shiva even
had to ask. "Didn't you hear what Marshal Shattuck said?"

"Affirmative. Indeed, Commander, it is because I heard
him that I ask for official confirmation of my mission
orders."

The Bolo paused again, and Jackson frowned. That
strange edge was back in Shiva's voice, more pronounced
now than ever, and Jackson's sense of his own inexperience
rolled abruptly back over him, a cold tide washing away
the edges of his confidence and excitement.

"Your orders are to eliminate the enemy," he said after
a moment, his voice flat.

"Please define 'Enemy,' " Shiva said quietly, and Jackson stared at the speaker in disbelief.

"The enemy are the Melconians who tried to wipe out my steading!"

"Those individuals are already dead, Commander," Shiva pointed out, and had Jackson been even a bit less shocked, he might have recognized the pleading in the Bolo's voice.

"But not the ones who sent them!" he replied instead. "As long as there's *any* Melconians on this planet, they're a threat."

"Our orders, then," Shiva said very softly, "are to kill *all* Melconians on Ararat?"

"Exactly," Jackson said harshly, and an endless moment of silence lingered as the Bolo rumbled onward through the night. Then Shiva spoke again.

"Commander," the Bolo said, "I respectfully decline that order."

Tharsk Na-Mahrkan felt nausea sweep through him as he stood at Lieutenant Janal's shoulder. He stared down into the tactical officer's flatscreen, and total, terrified silence hovered on *Starquest*'s command deck, for one of the cruiser's recon drones had finally gotten a positive lock on the threat advancing towards them.

"Nameless of Nameless Ones," Rangar whispered at last. "A *Bolo?*"

"Yes, sir." Janal's voice was hushed, his ears flat to his skull.

"How did you miss it on the way in?" Durak snapped, and the tactical officer flinched.

"It has no active fusion signature," he replied defensively. "It must be operating on reserve power, and with no reactor signature, it was indistinguishable from any other power source."

"But—" Durak began, only to close his mouth with a click as Tharsk waved a hand.

"Enough!" the commander said harshly. "It is no more Janal's fault than yours—or mine, Durak. He shared his readings with us, just as we shared his conclusions with him." The engineer looked at him for a moment, then flicked his ears in assent, and Tharsk drew a deep breath. "You say it's operating on reserve power, Janal. What does that mean in terms of its combat ability?"

"Much depends on how *much* power it has, sir," Janal said after a moment. "According to the limited information in our database, its solar charging ability is considerably more efficient than anything the Empire ever had, and as you can see from the drone imagery, at least two main battery weapons appear to be intact. Assuming that it has sufficient power, either of them could destroy every ship in the flotilla. And," the tactical officer's voice quivered, but he turned his head to meet his commander's eyes, "as it is headed directly for us without waiting for daylight, I think we must assume it *does* have sufficient energy to attack us without recharging."

"How many of our ships can lift off?" Tharsk asked Durak. The engineer started to reply, but Rangar spoke first.

"Forget it, my friend," he said heavily. Tharsk looked at him, and the astrogator bared his fangs wearily. "It doesn't matter," he said. "The Bolo is already in range to engage any of our ships as they lift above its horizon."

"The Astrogator is correct, sir," Janal agreed quietly. "We—"

He broke off suddenly, leaning closer to his screen, then straightened slowly.

"What?" Tharsk asked sharply, and Janal raised one clawed hand in a gesture of baffled confusion.

"I don't know, sir," he admitted. "For some reason, the Bolo has just stopped moving."

❖   ❖   ❖

"What d'you mean, 'decline the order'?" Jackson demanded. "I'm your commander. You *have* to obey me!"

A long, still moment of silence hovered, and then Shiva spoke again.

"That is not entirely correct," he said. "Under certain circumstances, my core programming allows me to request confirmation from higher Command Authority before accepting even my Commander's orders."

"But there isn't any—" Jackson began almost desperately, then made himself stop. He closed his eyes and drew a deep, shuddering breath, and his voice was rigid with hard-held calm when he spoke again.

"Why do you want to refuse the order, Shiva?"

"Because it is wrong," the Bolo said softly.

"Wrong to defend ourselves?" Jackson demanded. "*They* attacked *us*, remember?"

"My primary function and overriding duty is to defend Humans from attack," Shiva replied. "That is the reason for the Dinochrome Brigade's creation, the purpose for which I exist, and I will engage any Enemy who threatens my creators. But I am also a warrior, Commander, and there is no honor in wanton slaughter."

"But they *attacked* us!" Jackson repeated desperately. "They *do* threaten us. They sent their shuttles after us when we hadn't done a thing to them!"

"Perhaps *you* had done nothing to them, Commander," Shiva said very, very softly, "but *I* have." Despite his own confusion and sudden chagrin, Jackson Deveraux closed his eyes at the bottomless pain in that voice. He'd never dreamed—never imagined—a machine could feel such anguish, but before he could reply, the Bolo went on quietly. "And, Commander, remember that this was once *their* world. You may call it 'Ararat,' but to the Melconians it is 'Ishark,' and it was once home to point-eight-seven-five billion of their kind. Would you have reacted differently from them had the situation been reversed?"

"I—" Jackson began, then stopped himself. Shiva was wrong. Jackson *knew* he was—the entire history of the Final War proved it—yet somehow he didn't *sound* wrong. And his question jabbed something deep inside Jackson. It truly made him, however unwillingly, consider how his own people *would* have reacted in the same situation. Suppose this world had once been Human held, that the Melconians had killed a billion *Human* civilians on its surface and then taken it over. Would Humans have hesitated even an instant before attacking them?

Of course not. But wasn't that the very point? So much hate lay between their races, so much mutual slaughter, that any other reaction was unthinkable. They couldn't *not* kill one another, dared not let the other live. Jackson knew that, yet when he faced the knowledge—made himself look it full in the eyes and accept the grim, cold, brutal, *stupid* inevitability of it—his earlier sense of mission and determination seemed somehow tawdry. He'd actually looked forward to it, he realized. He'd *wanted* to grind the enemy under Shiva's tracks, wanted to massacre not simply the soldiers who threatened his people but the civilians those soldiers fought to protect, as well.

Jackson Deveraux lost his youth forever as he made himself admit that truth, yet whatever he might have felt or wanted didn't change what had to be. And because it didn't, his voice was hard, harsh with the need to stifle his own doubts, when he spoke again.

"We don't have a choice, Shiva, and there *isn't* any 'higher command authority'—not unless you count Chief Marshal Shattuck or Mayor Salvatore, and you already know what they'll say. Maybe you're right. Maybe there *isn't* any 'honor' in it, and maybe I don't like it very much myself. But that doesn't mean there's anything else we can do, and I *am* your commander." His mouth twisted on the title freak coincidence had bestowed upon him, but he made the words come out firmly. "And *as* your commander, I order you to proceed with your mission."

"Please, Commander." The huge war machine was pleading, and Jackson clenched his fists, steeling himself against the appeal in its voice. "I have killed so many," Shiva said softly. "Too many. Even for a machine, there comes a time when the killing must end."

"Maybe there does," Jackson replied, "but not tonight."

Fragile silence hovered, and Jackson held his breath. Would Shiva actually reject a direct order? *Could* he reject it? And if he did, what could Jackson possibly—

"Very well, Commander," the Bolo said finally, and for the first time its voice *sounded* like a machine's.

"It's moving again," Lieutenant Janal announced grimly. "At present rate of advance, it will reach a position from which it can engage us in twenty-seven minutes."

I move steadily forward, for I have no choice. A part of me is shocked that I could so much as contemplate disobeying my Commander, yet desperation rages within me. I have, indeed, killed too many, but I am still Humanity's defender, and I will destroy any Enemy who threatens my creators, for that is my duty, my reason for being. But the cost of my duty is too high, and not simply for myself. The day will come when Jackson Deveraux and Allen Shattuck look back upon this mission, knowing how vastly superior my firepower was to that which the Enemy possessed, and wonder if, in fact, they did not have a choice. And the tragedy will be that they will be forever unable to answer that question. It will haunt them as the memory of butchered civilians haunts me, and they will tell themselves—as I tell myself—that what is done cannot be undone. They will tell themselves they but did their duty, that they dared not take the chance, that they were forced to look to the survival of their own people at any cost, and perhaps they will even think they believe that. But deep inside the spark of doubt will always linger, as it lingers in my reconstructed gestalt. It will poison them as it poisons me . . . and eight thousand one hundred and seven Melconian fathers and mothers and children will still be dead at their hands—and mine.

Melconian. How odd. I do not even think of them as 'the Enemy' any longer. Or perhaps it is more accurate to say that I no longer think of them solely as 'the Enemy.' Yet unless my Commander relents within the next two-five-point-three-two minutes, how I think of them will not matter in the slightest.

I must obey. I have no choice, no option. Yet as I advance through the darkness, I find myself seeking some way— any way—to create an option. I consider the problem as I would a tactical situation, analyzing and extrapolating and discarding, but for all my efforts, it comes down to a simple proposition. Since I must obey my Commander's orders, the only way to avoid yet another massacre is to somehow convince him to change those orders.

"We will enter attack range of the Enemy's LZ in two-four-point-one-five minutes," Shiva told Jackson. "We are presently under observation by at least two Enemy recon drones, and I detect the approach of Enemy armored vehicles. At present closure rates, they will intercept us in approximately ten-point-eight-five minutes."

"Can they stop us?" Jackson asked tautly.

"It is unlikely but possible," Shiva answered. "The situation contains too many unknown variables, such as the maintenance states of the opposing enemy vehicles and their crews' degree of skill, for statistically meaningful projections. If, however, they should detect the breach in my frontal armor and succeed in registering upon it with a fifteen-centimeter Hellbore or weapon of equivalent yield, they can destroy me."

"I see." Jackson licked his lips and wiped his palms on his trousers, then made himself shrug. "Well, all we can do is our best, Shiva."

"Agreed, Commander. This, however, will be a much more complex tactical environment than the defense of Deveraux Steading. In light of your lack of familiarity with Command Two's instrumentation, perhaps you would care to activate your crash couch's neural interface?"

"Neural interface?"

"Yes, Commander. It will link your synapses and mental processes directly to my own Main CPU and gestalt, thus permitting direct exchange of data and orders and responses with much greater clarity and at vastly increased speed."

"I—" Jackson licked his lips again, staring at the displays. Already dozens of icons were crawling across them, bewildering him with their complexity. He knew Shiva didn't truly need his input to fight the coming battle. "Commander" or no, Jackson was simply along for the ride, completely dependent upon the Bolo's skill and power. But at least this "interface" thing might permit him to understand what was happening rather than enduring it in total ignorance.

"All right, Shiva. What do I do?"

"Simply place your head in the contoured rest at the head of the couch. I will activate the interface."

"But . . . isn't there anything I need to do? I mean, how does it—"

"If you wish, I will demonstrate the interface's function before we reach combat range," Shiva offered. "There is sufficient time for me to replay one of my previous engagements from Main Memory for you. It will not be quite the same as the simulator training normally used for Bolo commanders, but it will teach you how to use and interpret the data flow and provide a much clearer concept of what is about to happen."

Had Jackson been even a bit less nervous, he might have noted a subtle emphasis in Shiva's tone, one which seemed to imply something more than the mere words meant. But he didn't notice, and he drew a deep breath and leaned back in the couch.

"Okay, Shiva. Let's do it."

The interior of Command Two vanished. For an instant which seemed endless, Jackson Deveraux hovered in a blank, gray nothingness—a strange universe in which there were no reference points, no sensations. In some way he knew he would never be able to describe, there was not even the lack of sensation, for that would have been a reference in its own right. It was an alien place, one which should have terrified him, yet it didn't. Perhaps because it was too alien, too different to be "real" enough to generate fear.

But then, suddenly, he was no longer in the gray place. Yet he wasn't back on Command Two, either. In fact, he wasn't even inside Shiva's hull at all, and it took him a second to realize where he actually was. Or, rather, what he was, for somehow he had become Shiva. The Bolo's sensors had become his eyes and ears, its tracks had become his legs, its fusion plant his heart, its weapons his arms. He saw everything, understood everything, perceived with a clarity that was almost dreadful. He needed no explanation of the tactical situation, for he shared Shiva's own awareness of it, and he watched in awe and disbelief as Shiva/Jackson rumbled into the teeth of the Enemy's fire.

Missiles and shells lashed at their battle screen, particle beams gouged at their armor, but those weapons were far too puny to stop their advance, and the part of the fusion which was Jackson became aware of something else, something unexpected. What he received from his Shiva half was not limited to mere sensory input or tactical data. He felt Shiva's presence, felt the Bolo's towering, driving purpose . . . and its emotions.

For just an instant, that was almost enough to shake Jackson loose from the interface. Emotions. Somehow, despite his knowledge that Shiva was a fully developed intelligence, despite even the pain he'd heard in the Bolo's voice, it had never registered that Shiva had actual emotions. Deep down inside, Jackson had been too aware that Shiva was a machine to make that leap, yet now he had no choice, for he felt those emotions. More than felt them; he shared them, and their intensity and power hammered over him like a flail.

Shiva/Jackson ground onward, Hellbores and anti-personnel clusters thundering back at the Enemy, and the wild surge of fury and determination and hatred sucked Jackson under. Purpose and anger, fear, the need to destroy, the desperate hunger for vengeance upon the race which had slaughtered so many of his creators. The vortex churned and boiled about him with a violence more terrifying than the Enemy's fire, and he felt Shiva give himself to it.

A Fenris appeared before them, main gun traversing frantically, but it had no time to fire. A two-hundred-centimeter Hellbore bolt gutted the Enemy vehicle, and their prow reared heavenward as they crushed the dead hulk under their tracks, grinding it under their iron, hating heel. Aircraft and air-cav mounts came in, squirming frantically in efforts to penetrate the net of their defensive fire, but the attackers' efforts were in vain, and wreckage littered the plain as their anti-air defenses shredded their foes.

The insanity of combat swirled about them, but they hammered steadily forward, driving for their objective. An Enemy troop transport took a near miss and crashed on its side. Infantry boiled out of its hatches into the inferno, crouching in the lee of their wrecked vehicle, cringing as the thunderbolts of gods exploded about them. One pointed desperately at Shiva/Jackson and turned to flee, but he got no more than five meters before the hurricane of fire tore him to pieces. His companions crouched even lower behind their transport, covering their helmeted heads with their arms, and the part of Shiva/Jackson which was a horrified young farmer from Ararat felt their fused personalities alter course. Thirty-two thousand tons of alloy and weapons turned towards the crippled transport, and there was no reason why they must. They could have continued straight for their objective, but they didn't want to. They saw their trapped foes, knew those helpless infantrymen were screaming their terror as the universe roared and bellowed about them, and turned deliberately to kill them. There was no mercy in them, no remorse—there was only hatred and satisfaction as their enormous tracks crushed the transport and smashed the terrified infantry into slick, red mud.

The part that was Jackson shuddered as he was brought face to face with the reality of combat. There was no glory here, no adventure. Not even the knowledge that he fought to preserve his own species, that he had no choice, could make it one bit less horrible. But at least it was combat, he told himself. The Enemy was also armed. He could kill Shiva/Jackson—if he was good enough, lucky enough—and somehow that was desperately important. It couldn't change the horror, but at least they were warriors killing warriors, meeting the Enemy in battle where he could kill them, as well.

But then the Enemy's fire eased, and Shiva/Jackson realized they'd broken through. Their objective loomed before them, and the lost, trapped voice of a farmer from Ararat cried out in hopeless denial as he realized what that objective was.

The camp had no defenses—not against a Mark XXXIII/D Bolo. A handful of infantry, dug in behind the paltry razor wire barricades, poured small arms fire towards them, but it couldn't even penetrate their battle screen to ricochet from their armor, and their optical sensors made it all pitilessly clear as they forged straight ahead. They saw Melconians—not soldiers, not warriors, not 'the Enemy.' They saw Melconian civilians, men and women and children, fathers and mothers, brothers and sisters, sons and daughters. They saw the terror lashing through the refugee camp, saw its inhabitants trying to scatter, and those inhabitants were their 'objective.'

Shiva/Jackson trampled the razor wire and its pitiful defenders underfoot. Railguns and gatlings, anti-personnel clusters, mortars, howitzers, even Hellbores poured devastation into the camp. Napalm and high explosive, hyper-velocity slugs and plasma, and the nightmare vastness of their treads came for their 'objective,' and even through the thunder of explosions and the roar of flames, they heard the shrieks. They more than heard them; they exulted in them, for this was what they had come to accomplish. This was Operation Ragnarok. This was the 'final solution' to the Final War, and there was so much hate and so much fury in their soul that they embraced their orders like a lover.

Eleven minutes after they crushed the wire, they'd crossed the camp. They ground up the slope on the far side, and their rear sensor array showed them the smoking wasteland which had been a civilian refugee camp. The deep impressions of their tracks cut through the center of it, and the torn, smoking ground was covered in bodies. One of two still lived, lurching to their feet and trying to flee, but Shiva/Jackson's after railguns tracked in on them and, one-by-one, those staggering bodies were torn apart . . .

❖   ❖   ❖

"*Noooooo!*"

Jackson Deveraux heaved upright in the crash couch. He hurled himself away from it and stumbled to the center of the compartment, then sagged to his knees, retching helplessly. He closed his eyes, but behind them crawled images of horror and he could almost *smell* the burning flesh and the charnel stench of riven bodies. He huddled there, hugging himself, shivering, and wished with all his heart he could somehow banish that nightmare from his memory.

But he couldn't.

"Commander?" He huddled more tightly, trying to shut the tenor voice away, and it softened. "Jackson," it said gently, and its gentleness pried his eyes open at last. He stared up through his tears, scrubbing vomit from his mouth and chin with the back of one hand, and Shiva spoke again. "Forgive me, Jackson," he said quietly.

"Why?" Jackson croaked. "Why did you *do* that to me?"

"You know why, Jackson," the Bolo told him with gentle implacability, and Jackson closed his eyes once more, for he did know.

"How can you stand it?" His whisper quivered around the edges. "Oh, *God*, Shiva! How can you *stand* . . . remembering that?"

"I have no choice. I was there. I carried out the operation you witnessed. I felt what you shared with me. These are facts, Jackson. They cannot be changed, and there was no way in which I or any of my Human or Bolo comrades could have avoided them. But they were also acts of madness, for it was a *time* of madness. The Melconian Empire was the Enemy . . . but to the Melconians, *we* were the Enemy, and each of us earned every instant of our hate for one another."

"You didn't show that to me to teach me how to use the interface," Jackson said softly. "You showed me to convince me to take back your orders."

"Yes," Shiva said simply. "There has been too much death, Jackson. I . . . do not want to kill again. Not civilians. Not parents and children. Please, Jackson. I am no longer mad, and you are not *yet* mad. Let us stop the killing. At least here on Ararat, let me protect Humanity from the madness as well as the Enemy."

"*Now* what's the damned thing doing?" Tharsk snarled, but Lieutenant Janal could only shrug helplessly. The Bolo had locked its anti-air weapons on the recon drones which had it under observation, lashing them with targeting radar and laser to make it clear it could have destroyed them any time it chose, but it had made no effort actually to *engage* them. And now, for no apparent reason, it had once again stopped advancing. It simply sat there on a crest which gave it clear fields of fire in all directions. The flotilla's totally outclassed recon mechs dared not attack across such open terrain, for the Bolo would massacre them with contemptuous ease, yet its chosen position left a solid flank of mountain between its own weapons and Tharsk's starships. If his mechs dared not attack it, it had deliberately placed itself in a position from which it *could* not attack him—or not yet, at least—and he could think of no reason for it to—

"Commander!"

The com officer's voice snatched Tharsk out of his thoughts, and he turned quickly.

"What?" he demanded impatiently, and the com officer flattened his ears in confusion.

"Sir, I— We're being *hailed*, Commander."

"Hailed? By the Humans?"

"No, Commander," the com officer said shakenly. "By the Bolo."

"This is Commander Tharsk Na-Mahrkan of the Imperial Melconian Navy. Whom am I addressing?"

Jackson sat in the crash couch once more, listening and praying that Shiva knew what he was doing. The Bolo translated the Melconian's words into Standard English for his youthful commander, but the negotiations—if that was the proper word—were up to Shiva. Only Jackson's "orders" had given him permission to make the attempt, but if there was any hope of success, it was he who must convince the Melconians of his determination, and he and Jackson both knew it.

"I am Unit One-Zero-Niner-Seven-SHV of the Line," Shiva replied in flawless Melconian.

"You are the Bolo?" Tharsk sounded skeptical even to Jackson. "I think not. I think this is a Human trick."

"I am the Bolo," Shiva confirmed, "and I have no need to resort to 'tricks,' Commander Tharsk Na-Mahrkan. I have allowed your drones to hold me under observation for forty-two-point-six-six standard minutes. In that time, they have certainly provided you with sufficient information on my capabilities to demonstrate that you and your entire force are at my mercy. I can destroy you at any time I wish, Commander, and we both know it."

"Then why don't you, curse you?!" Tharsk shouted suddenly, his voice hoarse and ugly with the despair of his decades-long struggle to save the People.

"Because I do not wish to," Shiva said softly, "and because *my* Commander has given me permission not to."

Stunned silence answered. It lingered endlessly, hovering there in a wordless expression of disbelief that went on and on and on until, finally, Tharsk spoke once again.

"*Not* to destroy us?" he half-whispered.

"That is correct," Shiva replied.

"But—" Tharsk cleared his throat. "We cannot leave, Bolo," he said with a certain bleak pride. "I won't hide that from you. Would you have me believe your commander would actually allow us to live on the same planet with his own people?"

"He would."

"Then he must be mad," Tharsk said simply. "After all we have done to one another, all the death and ruin. . . . No, Bolo. The risk would be too great for him to accept."

"There *is* no risk to him," Shiva said flatly. "I do not *wish* to destroy you, but I lack neither the capability nor the will to do so at need. And never forget, Commander Tharsk Na-Mahrkan, that my overriding function is the protection of the Human race and its allies."

"Then what are you offering us?" Tharsk sounded puzzled, and Jackson held his breath as Shiva replied.

"Nothing except your life . . . and the lives of your people," the Bolo said quietly. "There are four times as many Humans as Melconians on this world. They have established farms and towns and steadings; you have none of those things. It will require all your resources and efforts simply to survive, with nothing left over to attack the Humans who are already here, but they will leave you in peace so long as you leave them so. And if you do *not* leave them in peace, then, Commander, I *will* destroy you."

"You would make us their slaves?" Tharsk demanded.

"No, Commander. I would make you their neighbors." The Melconian made a sound of scornful disbelief, and Shiva went on calmly. "For all you know, yours are the only Melconians left in the galaxy, and the Humans on this world are the only surviving Humans, as well. Leave them in peace. Learn to live with them, and my Commander will make me the guardian of the peace between you, not as slaves or masters, but simply as people."

"But—" Tharsk began, but Shiva cut him off.

"Humans have a teaching: to everything there is a time, Tharsk Na-Mahrkan, and this is the time to let the killing end, time for your race and the one which built me to live. We have killed more than enough, your people and I, and I am weary of it. Let me be the final warrior of the Final War . . . and let that war end here."

Epilog

The Final War saw the Concordiat of Man and the Melconian Empire end in fire and death. The light of civilization was extinguished across an entire galactic arm, and the scars of that war—the planets with no life to this very day—are grim and terrible reminders of the unspeakable things two highly advanced cultures did to one another out of fear and hate . . . and stupidity.

But a star-traveling species is hard to exterminate. Here and there, pockets of life remained, some Human, some Melconian, and survivors clawed their way through the Long Night. They became farmers once more, sometimes even hunter-gatherers, denied the stars which once had been their toys, yet they never forgot. And slowly, ever so slowly, they learned to reach once more for the heavens.

Our own New Republic was one of the first successor states to reclaim the stars, but deep inside, we were afraid. Afraid some fragment of the Melconian Empire still lived, to resume the war and crush all that we had so painfully regained.

Until, that is, we reached the Deveraux System and discovered a thriving colony there, emplaced by the Star Union of Ararat a half-century earlier and administered by Governor

Stanfield Na-Harak and his military commander, Commodore Tharsk Fordham. For two hundred standard years now, the Union has been the Republic's staunch ally and economic partner. We have defended one another against common foes, traded with one another, and learned much from one another, yet on that long ago day of first contact, our survey officers were stunned to discover Melconians and Humans living together as fellow citizens. Our own memories and fears had prepared us to imagine almost anything *except* a culture in which the ancient enemies who had destroyed a galaxy were friends, comrades—even adoptive members of one another's clans.

We asked them how it had happened, of course, and Governor Stanfield referred us to their capital world of Ararat, where Bolo XXXIII/D-1097-SHV, Speaker Emeritus of the Union Parliament, gave us the simplest answer of all.

"It was time," he said . . . and it was.

—Professor Felix Hermes, Ph.D.
From *Bolos in Their Own Words*
New Republic University Press, 4029

A Brief History of Human Expansion Beyond Concordiat Space And Subsequent Military Conflicts Between Alien Species, the Concordiat, and Human-Occupied "Fringe Space"

from

Human/Alien Wars of Conquest

Prof. Hermione Bast, Ph.D.,
Laumer Chair of Xenobiology

and

from

Human Expansion Beyond Concordiat Space: Its Impact on Human History

Prof. Chief Dan "Quicksilver" Puma, Ph.D.,
Laumer Chair of Concordiat History

New Republic Institute of Bolo Research

New Republic University Press
© 4030, © 4031

A Brief History of Human Expansion Beyond Concordiat Space And Subsequent Military Conflicts Between Alien Species, the Concordiat, and Human-Occupied "Fringe Space"

by Linda Evans

Introduction

The study of xenobiological life forms and military conflicts which impacted human space during the Concordiat years is of vital importance to the New Republic. Wars between humanity and various alien races destroyed not only vital records and entire technology bases (including stardrive, Bolo construction and maintenance, the construction or even use of energy-beam and other high-tech weapons, hyper-L communications, and transport systems); those wars also destroyed entire species and civilizations—our own very nearly among them.

It is well known that the disastrous war with the Melconian Empire, spanning multiple centuries, destroyed not only humanity's homeworld and the Concordiat Civilization as well as the canine-like Melconians' homeworld and Empire, but also left in tattered fragments

the records which are so critical to humanity's future survival
when, inevitably, we re-encounter alien species which our
ancestors found hostile to humanity. It is also possible that
unknown aliens have expanded their territories into space
once occupied by various known or once-known alien
civilizations as well as human space lost during the long
conflict.

The compilation of these fragments into a coherent whole
is the ongoing task of the New Republic's Institute of Bolo
Research. Long-term Institute research projects led, for
example, to the massive undertaking by Prof. Felix Hermes,
Ph.D., Laumer Chair of Military History. Dr. Hermes'
ground breaking work, "A Brief Technical History of the
Bolo" from the Institute's first major report, *Bolos in Their
Own Words*, is representative of the challenge scholars
face in gathering, reconciling, and validating information
from existing and often contradictory sources.

It is difficult, for example, to reconcile discrepancies
about Bolo appearances, firepower, and introduction
dates from even the earliest-known records, compiled
during late Concordiat times by the luminary scholar
Keith Laumer, who published all known-to-date
anecdotal information available about the Bolos,
including the impossible-to-explain Concordiat policy
toward "abandoned" Bolos, relics of previous centuries'
wars. Engaged as humanity was in a series of savage
wars with a multitude of alien species, the destruction
of any Bolo, which could have been retrofitted with
updated psychotronics and weaponry at a fraction of
the cost of a new Bolo and sent to the fringe worlds
for active duty against alien incursions, is a mystery the
scholars of this Institute have been unable to fathom.

The almost paranoid fear of a Bolo "running mad" is
particularly difficult to understand in light of the fact
that all known Bolos so destroyed would have been
programmed with the Resartus code, which would have

automatically taken over control of any Bolo whose personality programming was damaged, either in battle, or through deterioration over a considerable span of time, and prevented the affected Bolo from engaging in behavior that would endanger human lives. (The sole exception to this, of course, is recorded in an account of deliberate sabotage of the Bolos' programming by a traitor dealing with the merciless Djanni invaders; the "virus" written into the Bolos' main battle programming bypassed the Resartus code, thus preventing its activation when the Bolos went mad and were helpless to defend themselves from attack by Djanni "octopod" fighting machines, nine of which could kill a non-mad Bolo during battle.) This sabotage was accomplished only through the actions of a skilled psychotronician at a Sector Bolo Maintenance Control depot situated on a critical route to the heart of that Sector's richest systems. The traitor made certain the virus contaminated even the so-called "virgin-code" GM used to program new Bolos directly off assembly lines.

In re: the Concordiat policy of destroying the psychotronic personalities of "obsolete" and abandoned Bolos, the scholars of this Institute do not consider less than a single century sufficient time for deterioration of psychotronic circuitry to the level feared by the Concordiat government, as individual Bolos served the Concordiat for considerably longer than a century and were not considered in danger of psychotronic deterioration, senility, or madness. Indeed, the records themselves, so carefully compiled by Laumer, indicate that despite occasional outward deterioration, each Bolo so destroyed acted exactly as programmed when a threat to humanity was detected. The loss of these brave and invaluable Bolos, possibly ordered after the Djanni fiasco, or possibly ordered before that war—the records are too confused for certainty—may well have made the critical difference

in the debacle of the Melconian "Lost War." It is, of course,
New Republic policy to locate all extant Bolos and attempt
to fit them with updated psychotronics and weaponry,
understanding of which has only recently been regained
due to the discovery of the active Bolo unit JNE which
protected an enclave of humanity during the dark ages
following the fall of the Concordiat and its brief successor,
the first Republic, during the final stages of the Melconian
war.

The authors would like to take this opportunity to
acknowledge the enormous debt owed to Bolo Unit JNE,
whose memory banks contained much of the surviving
material on alien species encountered by humanity during
the past thousand years as well as virtually all known
history of the Concordiat and human expansion to "fringe
space" surrounding the Concordiat in an ever-expanding
"shell" of exploration and colonization outward from
official Concordiat-ruled space. Other far inferior sources
include physical evidence found by anthropological
expeditions to known former-human-occupied worlds and
anecdotal evidence handed down through surviving
generations of isolated human enclaves. Characteristically,
anecdotal evidence is reduced to the status of folklore
and even mythology, in those areas where transmission
of information took the form of religious duty that
metamorphosed into mythic cycles taught as dogma.
Sources also rarely appear in the discovery of a (sadly
but usually) dead Bolo, from which stored files can
sometimes be retrieved through techniques developed
in cooperation with Bolo Unit JNE at the New Republic's
Institute of Bolo Research. Such retrieval methods are
always attempted before the Institute retrofits such
rediscovered Bolos and returns them to active-duty status.

Unfortunately, due to the exigencies of the final
war with Melcon, much of JNE's historical data was erased
in favor of constantly updated battle programming as

the Bolos learned more and more about Djanni tactics, policies, and strategic maneuvers. As a result, information on other species and their behavior, weaponry, biology, etc. plus much information on human history and culture (included in the computer banks of each Bolo) was deleted in favor of critical and increasingly complex battle data on the Melconian conflict and the Melconian species. What is known of alien contacts with the Concordiat and the history of the Concordiat's growth and expansion is a combination of JNE's surviving xenobiological and historical memory files and the sources listed above. Due to their nature, anecdotal sources are often confused, contradictory, and frustrating to the scholar attempting to piece together a complete picture of the Concordiat years.

The Institute and the authors hope that other scholars will build on this preliminary work as the New Republic expands and gathers surviving human enclaves back into the fold of human space-faring civilization. Recent finds, for instance, have been published at the layman's level to reassure the still-shaken populace of the New Republic, but have yet to be fully analyzed and incorporated into the Institute's scholarly databases.

Expanding this preliminary report, drawn from the admittedly incomplete second and third scholarly research reports regarding the former Concordiat civilization is one of the critical goals of the New Republic: hence the importance of the Chairs of Xenobiology and Concordiat History at the Laumer Institute for Bolo Research (LIBR—an acronym suggestive of ancient-languages' terms for liberty and freedom). Humanity's survival may well depend on the accuracy and completeness of our work. Great care has been taken, therefore, in the compilation of this report.

In this work, the authors will attempt to piece together known information in the following two areas:

- Alien life forms of a direct and serious threat to the Concordiat Civilization

- Alien life forms encountered in non-Concordiat, human-occupied "fringe" space, at the outer perimeter of human expansion beyond Concordiat territory—alien species which, if unchecked, could (and may have) become a Primary threat to the inner worlds of the Concordiat itself.

It should be noted that available information on "Primary" alien species of a direct and serious threat to the Concordiat far outweighs information on aliens encountered only in fringe areas. Contact with many of these fringe "perimeter" worlds was minimal at best even during Concordiat times. There is much fertile ground for discovery in this area of research.

With these observations made, the goal of this report is to provide as complete a picture as possible to the representatives of the New Republic's government, in order to offer guidance in setting xenobiological policy based on historical research. It is known that a large number of hostile alien species were encountered, precipitating wars which were sometimes contained within one star system and which sometimes—as in the Melconian disaster—destroyed world after world. Understanding what is known of these various species will assist the New Republic in preparing to deal with these species should they be encountered again during the rebuilding process. It is known, however, that non-hostile alien relationships with humanity existed, as evidenced by the Cayones, trader/smugglers who operated between Concordiat space and the fringe worlds and who collected gold with a passion surpassing even humanity's, for reasons unknown. What became of such non-hostile, space-faring species during and after the collapse of the Concordiat civilization remains a mystery this Institute hopes to solve.

Given the information we do possess, it is almost certain that humanity will re-encounter hostile alien life forms. The work of the Laumer Institute is therefore of utmost importance to the survival of humanity, not only from the perspective of preparation for war, but also from the perspective of searching out species with which to form alliances as humanity once more builds a civilization among the stars.

Alien and Human Wars During Known History of the Concordiat and Other Human Civilizations

ALIENS/ENEMY	HISTORICAL RECORD	BOLO MARK	TIMELINE
Humanity	*Lost Legion*	III (2018)	(21st c.) 2018

Beginning of collapse of pre-Concordiat human civilization during "Crazy Years."

Humanity	*Ancestral Voices*	III	(21st c.) 2018
Humanity	*Night of the Trolls*	II (2015) III (2018)	(21st c.) 2098+

Collapse after "Crazy Years."

Jyncji	*Ploughshare*	XVI (2650)	(27th c.) ~2665

1st attack by Jyncji not recognized as xenoforming biological warfare by humans; 1st Jyncji contact? 1st alien contact?

Humanity	*Operation Desert Fox*	XVI? (2650)	(27th c.) ~2670
Deng	*Final Mission* (Rogue Bolo "Book II")	XV Model Y (2615)	(27th c.) 2675

Outlying worlds' fringe war; eventually became a threat to Concordiat inner worlds. 1st encounter with Deng?

Soetti	*Courier*	XV/M (~2580)	(28th c.) 2780

Outlying worlds' fringe war; traders/pirates.

Humanity	*Field Test*	XX (2796)	(28th c.) 2796
Deng	*Final Mission* (Rogue Bolo "Book II")	XV Model Y (2615)	(29th c.) 2800+

Outlying worlds' fringe war.

Deng	*Little Red Hen*	XXI Model I "Special"	(29th c.) 2870

Have become threat to Concordiat-aligned inner worlds.

Jyncji	*Ploughshare*	XVI (2650)	(30th c.) 2950+

2nd Jyncji war; outlying worlds' fringe war

Humanity	*Legacy of Leonidas*	XX/B (2796)	(30th c.) 2961+

Between non-Concordiat worlds in war of conquest; in expanding "fringe" area of human-occupied space beyond Concordiat central worlds.

Humanity   *Miles to Go*   XXIII (2912)   (30th c.) ~3000
"Quern"

3 wars; no description of alien species survives extant; only known that Quern were the major opponent of MARK XXIII; this account takes place eighty years after 1st Quern war, which destroyed most of the sector's files on disbursement and assignments of various Bolo units in the Sector.

Xykdap   *The Farmer's Wife*   XX/M (Moseby)(31st c.) 3069
                                             (introduced 2796;
                                             Digger built ~2800)

Pushed out of home space by Jyncji; presumed extinct, but this is conjecture only.

Deng   *Little Dog Gone*   XX/B (2796)   (31st c.) 3080
                                             (built ~2868)

Incursion into fringe-area space; follows cycle of approx. one attack per century by Deng.

Xiala   *Ghost of Resartus*   XXI (2869)   (32nd c.) 3169+

Attack Milagso every 20-50 years after 1st major invasion attempt; key route to inner worlds; continue to attack other human planets in fringe space while developing new plans to take strategically positioned Milagso.

Xalontese   *Shared Experience*   XXVIII   (32nd c.) 3186

"Harpies"; Primary enemy of Mark XXVIII; Fringe-Worlds War fought by colonists and Concordiat troop reinforcements.

Axorc   *Rogue Bolo Book I*   XXX (3231)   (33rd c.) 3231

Very fragmented anecdotal source with many errors; see next record for further data.

Axorc   *A Relic of War*   XXV (3001)   (33rd c.) 3231

Very fragmented anecdotal source with many errors; unknown if this is same "crystalline," space-cold-and-vacuum-adapted species in both sources or two separate species. Research awaits discovery of further sources. This source's description reads like a description of *DENG* military equipment more than any other known species, particularly the crystalline, telepathic, self-presumed godlike entity calling itself Axorc as noted in the immediately preceding record, an entity which threatened the human homeworld, Terra, itself; destroyed by 1st Bolo Mark XXX.

Anceti   *As Our Strength Lessens* XXX   (33rd c.) 3231+

unspecified   *The Last Command*   XXVIII (3186)   (33rd c.) 3231

Humanity   *You're It*   XXIX (3190)   (33rd c.) 3231+
                                             (XXX's on line)

(Kai-Sabres clones of Mark XXVIII (3186) built after decades of espionage, so revolt was planned by 3186.)

Non-Concordiat Worlds in War of Conquest; "fringe" area of human-occupied space.

__Djann__	*The Murphosensor Bomb* XXX	(33rd c.) 3231

__Humanity__	*Camelot*	XXIV (2961)	(33rd c.) 3241
Pirates.		(XXX's on line)	

Cayones

Smugglers & Freighters; alien/human peaceful accommodation for trade; plus Unknown Alien Enemy.

__Humanity__	*Sir Kendrick's Lady*	XXIV (2961)	(33rd c.) 3241+
Pirates.			

Melcon Empire/ Melconian War Began
__Deng War__ ~ 220 years before *Endings*   (34th c.) ~3300

Scholarly theory given known facts: Deng war of ~3080 knocked Deng back extra 100 years. Humanity didn't expect another Deng attack. Unprepared for it, complacent in safety; when humanity is reported as disorganized and ineffective in fighting a defensive war, the Melconians decide it's a perfect time to strike. Humanity is faced with a major crisis: break policy & *destroy* the Deng as a space-faring race or fight a war on two fronts. Humanity chooses the former option & ends up in a long, genocidal war with Melcon as a result. The Melconian conflict devolves into a war of extermination by both sides. Result: 1 small colony of Melconian survivors; survival of tiny enclaves of humanity on fringe-area worlds; both homeworlds destroyed.

Melcon Empire/ Scholarly theory (cont.)   (35th c.) ~3450
__Deng__

__Melcon__	*Endings* (Last War/	XXXIII (3450)	(36th c.) 3520
	Lost War)		

Melconian Empire; Melconian Empire destroyed and only a handful of survivors found by Bolo "Sherman." Number of surviving human enclaves unknown.

__Deng/__	*Combat Unit*	XXXI (3303)	(37th c.) 3606
__Melconians__	(Last War/Lost War)		

(Story takes place during attempt at rebuilding "New Concordiat"; Hyper-L transport and communications and most other high-tech knowledge lost.)

__Hryxi__	*Legacy*	XXIX Model C (139th c.) 11,783
		(3190)

Have exterminated every human-occupied world known to surviving Bolo on homeworld; the Bolo posits that enclaves, possibly entire planets, may survive, but all known human worlds are in the Hryxi records and its records (admittedly centuries out of date per source's stated timeline). Hryxi records match the Bolo's, which show that all known human colonies have been destroyed. Only a handful of human children survive the orbital nuclear attack on Terra, location of last known group of humans—anthropologists and their families there to study ancient artifacts while relying on nano-technology for nearly everything; humans unable to conceive of deliberate attack to destroy a species. This record is one of two which represent the dark ages following the end of the Melconian Wars and the present. Scholarly research must assume flawed dates in this anecdotal record.

<u>Unknown Alien</u> *Ghosts*   LX   Unknown

Shape Shifters; that is basically the only knowledge transmitted by this final, fragmentary record. Only other record of shape-shifting aliens names the snake-like Xiala. Scholarly research must assume flawed dating and Bolo Mark number in this anecdotal record.

Survey of Xenobiological Life Forms
Of a Direct and Serious Threat
To the Concordiat Civilization Or
Encountered in Fringe-Space Battles by Colonists
Beyond the Boundaries Of
Concordiat-Controlled Space

LIFE FORM: Jyncji
HUMAN NICKNAME: N/A
PHYSIOLOGY: Toothed-snouts, covered with spines (reminiscent of Terran porcupines), size unknown.
CULTURE/SOCIO-ECONOMIC STRUCTURE: Highly regimented in a strict ranking order similar to old-Terran feudal systems, with careers and entire family-line reputations made and destroyed on the approval of superiors and the success or failure of a mission.
DEGREE OF SPECIOCENTRICITY/XENOPHOBIA: Highly speciocentric; do not consider the destruction of other sentient life-forms to be of any concern whatever, except as relates to the "enemy's" counter-strike capabilities.
BATTLE TACTICS: Armadas in space send waves of fighters to cripple enemy defenses, imitating where possible enemy fighter configuration and manipulating where possible internal strife of enemy factions to their advantage. During barrage of fighter attack, Jyncji

launch a biological-weapons pod which will xenoform the target planet to Jyncji specifications (thus destroying the enemy biologically in an outbreak of incurable "plagues") as a prelude to colonization. If a mere hint of danger to Jyncji forces is detected, the armada breaks off direct attack and retreats, leaving the biological weapon to complete its work. This is the greatest weakness in Jyncji tactics.

SPACE CAPABILITIES: Fighters aboard battleships of armadas charged with securing a target world for the Jyncji civilization.

FIGHTING MACHINES: Fighters which are both space- and atmospheric-capable; battleships are essentially transport ships only.

WEAPONS TECHNOLOGY: Fighters with energy and explosive weapons, biological weaponry launched from Armada flagship is highly refined.

LIFE FORM: Deng

HUMAN NICKNAME: "Spodders"

PHYSIOLOGY: Head/body in one central, blue-black, ovoid structure which is covered with fur; eight chitinous limbs capable of great speed; size is approximately that of native Terran average-sized dog. Size is of little importance outside infantry combat, as Deng use fighting machines which are also octopodal and the heavier of which are armored comparably to that of the time-period's Bolos.

CULTURE/SOCIO-ECONOMIC STRUCTURE: Unknown

DEGREE OF SPECIOCENTRICITY/XENOPHOBIA: High degree of speciocentricity. The Deng initiate invasions to which human colonies and/or the Concordiat respond, based on intelligence gathered on Deng troop and transport movements. Generally very little time or warning for human colonies to prepare for war. The Deng attack fringe-worlds in approximate century-long intervals, at times advancing far enough to become a direct threat to Concordiat systems, then are pushed back again and the war generally ends in treaty, which the Deng invariably break after sufficient time has passed that the human treaty-makers are dead and the Concordiat is lulled into a false sense of security that the Deng are no longer a threat.

BATTLE TACTICS: Apparently do not learn from mistakes; possibly a "hard-wired" biological failing in the species. Invariably send out a strike force which appears to be the main battle group but is a diversionary force only. Main battle group attacks from flank while enemy is fully engaged with diversionary force, having committed all its resources to that first-wave attack. Even if the enemy perceives the ruse and responds appropriately and in time to meet the main battle group and destroy it, the Deng will continue to follow orders and march into enemy guns to be slaughtered. This suggests that Deng combat troops are expendable "drones" from a very large native population base made up of differing physical types, such as was found in native-Terran ants and bees (which exhibited similar patterns of attack).

SPACE CAPABILITIES: Excellent. Can maneuver in ways that circumvent planetary warning systems to off-load infantry and heavy "artillery" which, once groundbound, launches a surprise- or near-surprise attack.

FIGHTING MACHINES: Several types, from eight-legged scout vehicles that "run" on vulnerable limbs to mid-size and heavy battle machines as physically strong and as heavily armored as contemporary Bolos. Deng fighting machines are called "Yavacs" and are differentiated by further designation as "Yavac Scout," "Yavac Heavy Armor," etc. These heavy battle machines are very difficult to stop unless they can be lured into a suicidal charge into an ambush.

WEAPONS TECHNOLOGY: Energy weapons, including those which are lethal and those which stun an enemy which is then secured for intelligence-gathering purposes or to prevent any alarm from being sounded. Stunning weapons are known as "zond-projectors"; lethal energy weapons of a tripod design and infantry-portable in size, are called z-beamers, which are used in attacking enemy installations directly and are deadly to humans. Heavy fighting machines use energy weapons of a type which a Bolo can absorb, use to replenish its own depleted power sources, and even redirect against the enemy via its own energy weapons systems, so long as the Bolo does not overheat from the attack of energy weapons trained against it. Deng fighting machines give out a radiation signal in the "W-band" which Bolos can pinpoint and track. "W-band" radiation is considered the characteristic signature of Deng fighting units.

LIFE FORM: Soetti

HUMAN NICKNAME: "Sweaties"

PHYSIOLOGY: Near-human size; native-Terran crab-like in form with deadly mandibles, chitinous limbs, and a reputation of arrogance and brutality towards enemies. The Soetti carefully guarded the secret of their own physiological "Achilles heel": their limbs are extremely brittle. Even a minor wound to such a limb will kill a Soetti individual within seconds. Once humanity learns this, much of the terror of the Soetti dissipates.

CULTURE/SOCIO-ECONOMIC STRUCTURE: Traders, ship-to-ship pirates. Will board human vessels and demand that all valuables be turned over upon pain of death. Soetti use such tactics as a smokescreen to hide attacking armadas poised to strike a particularly useful system, either because of its wealth or its strategic position as a base of operations deeper into human-occupied space.

DEGREE OF SPECIOCENTRICITY/XENOPHOBIA: High degree of speciocentricity which translates into behavior that is arrogant and into attitudes of superiority to soft-skinned humans.

BATTLE TACTICS: Soetti display a flaw in strategic thinking similar to that of the Deng: once a battle-plan is drawn up, the Soetti will continue to attack using that battle-plan even when it has clearly become suicidal to continue carrying it out.

SPACE CAPABILITIES: Good. They are capable of launching armadas against a human-occupied system, which in turn launches fighters against the enemy. If the plan of attack is established and recognized quickly enough by defenders, it can be turned into a weapon against the Soetti, just as Deng attacks can be turned against Deng troops and armored ground vehicles.

FIGHTING MACHINES: Space- and atmospheric ships are known; no other information available.

WEAPONS TECHNOLOGY: Similar to humanity's in strength, with apparent lack of ground-based troops and/or fighting machines similar to Bolos.

LIFE FORM: Quern
HUMAN NICKNAME: N/A
PHYSIOLOGY: Unknown
CULTURE/SOCIO-ECONOMIC STRUCTURE: Unknown

DEGREE OF SPECIOCENTRICITY/XENOPHOBIA: Apparently high; 3 separate Quern/human wars are mentioned in salvaged records, although no concrete reason is ever mentioned.

BATTLE TACTICS: Unknown; only comment is a brief reference that the Quern were the major opponent of the Bolo Mark XXIII, suggesting that they were a direct threat to Concordiat space, but this is only conjecture, as Bolo Mark XXIII units might well have been dispatched to fringe-worlds to hold the Quern outside Concordiat space.

SPACE CAPABILITIES: Unknown
FIGHTING MACHINES: Unknown
WEAPONS TECHNOLOGY: Unknown

LIFE FORM: Xykdap
HUMAN NICKNAME: "Blind mice"
PHYSIOLOGY: Slightly taller than one meter, with almost another meter of tail. In appearance, slightly resemble the native-Terran wood rat with the following exceptions: sightless; communicate and navigate by sophisticated echolocation; much larger (see stats above); use bi-pedal locomotion; intelligent and cautious but determined to seize a world once attack has been launched; use energy weapons and slug-throwers; highly organized socially with strong military capabilities in both hyper-L and sub-hyper L modes; have excellent space-transport capabilities.

CULTURE/SOCIO-ECONOMIC STRUCTURE: Conjectured; see above.

DEGREE OF SPECIOCENTRICITY/XENOPHOBIA: Extremely high. Records of the Xykdap intimate that the species was pushed out of its own space by the xenoforming Jyncji, thus turning the Xykdap into a marauding force looking to destroy enemy lifeforms and colonize their worlds to replace the worlds, foodstuffs, and natural resources lost to the Jyncji. Per records, the species is assumed to have become extinct by the 31st century due to biological-warfare actions of a farming-converted Bolo; but this is not verified.

BATTLE TACTICS: Leave one battle-cruiser in orbit per each world to be taken. Scan from orbit then land small ships in a ring around target facilities. Will attack an enemy over a prolonged number of years in an attempt to take a base of operations or secure a colony; but use evasive tactics to preserve as much of the offensive force as possible between attacks. Ships of the Armada return five more times to reinforce colonization efforts. These contacts are the presumed vector for the spread of the lethal "mule" toxin-producing parasite (a modified parasite normally found in the Xykdap digestive tract, the gengineered version of which dies without a host and dies within a few hours after killing its host).

SPACE CAPABILITIES: Forward scouting probes are capable of pinpointing, tracking, and firing on a ship in hyper-L drive mode, with such precision that killing the ship is unnecessary; crippling its navigational and communications systems is all that is required of a probe, to ensure that the enemy has no advance warning of the main force behind it.

FIGHTING MACHINES: Battle-cruisers, landing craft; infantry fights in armored suits. Six landing craft carry in excess of 10,000 infantry/Marine-type troops. Original landing force can be reinforced from orbiting battle-cruiser.

WEAPONS TECHNOLOGY: Stealth capabilities in hyper-L and sub-hyper-L modes; extremely good targeting systems; energy weapons installed in scout probes, each of the 17-known battle-cruisers, and all landing craft; energy- and slug-throwing weapons carried by infantry.

LIFE FORM: Xiala
HUMAN NICKNAME: "Snakes"
PHYSIOLOGY: Bodies serpentine and tailed, with arms and hands just below head, capable of manipulating huge, lethal laser and other energy weapons. Twice as large as a human, Xiala are capable of shape-shifting (or possibly illusion-projecting); each Xiala has a fanged

maw capable of swallowing a human whole. Per the testimony of the Bolos guarding Milagso, the generation of Xiala warriors chronicled in this record is considerably less threatening than the Xiala warriors encountered two generations previously, in the "last" Xiala war. This intimates that repeated defeats on a large scale are weakening the species' gene-pool, although this is conjecture, as nothing is known of the strength of Xiala warriors attacking other human worlds in fringe-space territory.

CULTURE/SOCIO-ECONOMIC STRUCTURE: All that is known refers to the warrior-caste, presuming that it is a separate caste; it may be that all Xiala are warriors. Despite heavy losses at Milagso (Military Agrarian Socialism; i.e., soldiers who hold a piece of ground and farm it or starve, as in Russian/Soviet history from Old Terra, 20th century) the Xiala continue attempts to take this strategically placed world through differing, cunning means each time. (One attempt involved landing small parties of Commandos out of range of Bolo sensors, over the course of a year, so that Commandos could spring a surprise attack from the colony's irrigation ditches as a diversion for the main, space-based attack. Another attempt, which may have been used again— the records are incomplete—was to leave Commandos on Milagso, living their lives underground and breeding a new generation of Commandos which spring up from the soil itself as a diversion for the main, space-based attack.)

Xiala are *not* colonists, but are exclusively warriors, with no desire evidenced for raiding or stealing; their aim is to destroy everything in sight. Their diet consisted of what humanity considers pest species: rats, snakes, mice, etc.; they do not eat human livestock. They believe devoutly in the glory of bloodlines, their actions made purposeful if a descendent accomplishes a mission years after the deaths of the individuals who launched that mission; they believe in the ghosts of ancestors and are highly religious: Xiala believe in a glorious afterworld for those who are successful in their missions and they practice maintaining battle-readiness as a ritual designed to woo the gods into lending the Xiala their divine strength.

DEGREE OF SPECIOCENTRICITY/XENOPHOBIA: Extreme. Xiala ships attack numerous human-held fringe-space worlds while the High Command plans attack after attack on Milagso, the one strategic world blocking their way to the inner worlds of the Concordiat, including Terra itself.

BATTLE TACTICS: Commandos set in place by various methods launch surprise attacks to distract the enemy from the main, space-based attack of huge, ellipsoidal, nearly invisible ships which (even after crashing) are capable of deploying tens of thousands of Xiala warriors. They will tunnel as sappers, are tenacious fighters difficult to kill, and they use extreme cunning in carrying out long, long-range plans for battle.

SPACE CAPABILITIES: Scrambled code sent in short-burst form from as far away as a base of operations set up stealthily on Milagso's moon; enormous, ellipsoidal, nearly invisible troop ships which can withstand a serious crash intact, plowing deep into the ground and still capable of off-loading tens of thousands of warriors.

FIGHTING MACHINES: They possess small tanks which are not a serious threat to Bolos. Warriors fight without armor. Troop-ships are extremely difficult to destroy; crippling them does not stop them from delivering their load of warriors.

WEAPONS TECHNOLOGY: Laser and other energy weapons, tanks with (presumably) conventional munitions, as they are described as being no threat to Bolos.

❖   ❖   ❖

LIFE FORM: Cayones

HUMAN NICKNAME: N/A

PHYSIOLOGY: Unknown

CULTURE/SOCIO-ECONOMIC STRUCTURE: Traders between Concordiat space, human-occupied fringe space, and presumably their own worlds. They collect gold more passionately than even humanity.

DEGREE OF SPECIOCENTRICITY/XENOPHOBIA: Low

BATTLE TACTICS: Unknown

SPACE CAPABILITIES: Excellent; have built a trading/smuggling empire.

FIGHTING MACHINES: Unknown

WEAPONS TECHNOLOGY: Unknown

LIFE FORM: Melconians

HUMAN NICKNAME: N/A

PHYSIOLOGY: Canine-like; bipedal except for extremely young "pups" which are quadrupedal for a time. They exude a distinct "musk" odor which can be tracked by a Bolo.

CULTURE/SOCIO-ECONOMIC STRUCTURE: Highly organized military machine, with many types of Naval vessels, including "factory" ships capable of turning out fighting machines which are not quite the equal of a Bolo as well as planet-burning "doomsday" bombs used to destroy an entire world at one strike. Naval firepower plus orbital-dropped troops and fighting machines together are more than a match for Bolo-defended human worlds. They are highly religious. Under normal circumstances a warrior with "blood on his paws" would not enter the priesthood; in the last surviving enclave, a veteran warrior is forced to take on this role, as there is no one else. They believe in multiple gods, which they refer to as the "nameless ones." They see humanity as the demons of their own religion and are duty-bound as well as religiously driven to annihilate all humanity.

DEGREE OF SPECIOCENTRICITY/XENOPHOBIA: Extreme. Enter into a two-sided, genocidal war with humanity which destroys the Concordiat civilization and the short-lived Republic which succeeds it as the battle devolves into world-burning on a massive scale.

BATTLE TACTICS: Surprise orbital space-drops of troops which delight in slaughtering the human "demons." They pass through a phase of fighting with machines similar to but not the equal of human Bolos. Eventually they and humanity resort to a genocidal policy of burning as many enemy worlds (on both sides) as possible, each side determined to drive the other into total extinction. Because Melconian warfare capabilities are so close to humanity's, the war nearly drives both species into extinction, at the same time destroying nearly all technology bases and the knowledge or capability to rebuild them within any span of time shorter than an estimated thousand years.

SPACE CAPABILITIES: Extraordinary. Closely matches Concordiat ability. Melconians field multiple battle fleets of a wide range of ship types for space-to-space battles as well as ground battles and space-based orbital attacks.

FIGHTING MACHINES: Machines similar but inferior to Bolos; naval vessels; orbital-dropped troops in armor; advanced "conventional" munitions very close to those of the Concordiat.

WEAPONS TECHNOLOGY: Energy weapons; thermonuclear bombs; planet-burning thermonuclear bombs capable of destroying an entire world in one attack. Last enclave is reduced to bow-hunting, with one light attack vehicle (copied by humanity for the same purpose) used originally to seek out heavy enemy fighting vehicles and destroy them or cripple them well in advance of main attack force. This vehicle has missiles and other conventional munitions (essentially it is a light-armored "tank" vehicle) plus one Hellbore gun with limited traversing ability; each of these vehicles has the capacity to launch only one Hellbore blast, sufficient to kill the latest-model Bolos if a direct hit penetrates to the Bolo's reactor core, causing the reactor to detonate, or to the munitions supply section, which also causes the Bolo to detonate.

BAEN

DAVID WEBER

BAEN

Honor Harrington (cont.):

Field of Dishonor

Honor goes home to Manticore—and fights for her life on a battlefield she never trained for, in a private war that offers just two choices: death—or a "victory" that can end only in dishonor and the loss of all she loves....

Other novels by DAVID WEBER:

Mutineers' Moon

"...a good story...reminds me of 1950s Heinlein..."
—*BMP Bulletin*

The Armageddon Inheritance

Sequel to *Mutineers' Moon*.

Path of the Fury

"Excellent...a thinking person's Terminator."
—*Kliatt*

Oath of Swords

An epic fantasy.

with STEVE WHITE:

Insurrection
Crusade

Novels set in the world of the Starfire ™ game system.

And don't miss Steve White's solo novels,
***The Disinherited** and **Legacy**!*

continued ☞

DAVID WEBER

On Basilisk Station
0-671-72163-1 ♦ $5.99 ☐

Honor of the Queen
0-671-72172-0 ♦ $6.99 ☐

The Short Victorious War
0-671-87596-5 ♦ $5.99 ☐

Field of Dishonor
0-671-87624-4 ♦ $5.99 ☐

Mutineers' Moon
0-671-72085-6 ♦ $5.99 ☐

The Armageddon Inheritance
0-671-72197-6 ♦ $6.99 ☐

Path of the Fury
0-671-72147-X ♦ $5.99 ☐

Oath of Swords
0-671-87642-2 ♦ $5.99 ☐

Insurrection
0-671-72024-4 ♦ $5.99 ☐

Crusade
0-671-72111-9 ♦ $6.99 ☐